PRAISE FOR

Break of Dawn

"A kick-butt ride from start to finish with plenty of twists, turns, and surprises." —*Monsters and Critics*

"The darkness and danger mount as Ms. Green exposes her characters' well-kept secrets and resolves many of the mysteries surrounding them. *Break of Dawn* ends with a well-planned twist that will leave readers eagerly anticipating the beginning of the next trilogy." —*Darque Reviews*

"[A] dark thriller . . . The characters are a good mix, strong yet flawed, and the plot takes some interesting twists and turns." —*Romantic Times*

PRAISE FOR

Midnight Reign

"A dark, dramatic, and erotic tone . . . Fans of Charlaine Harris and Jim Butcher may enjoy." —*Library Journal*

"An exciting, high-tension horror thriller with enough unresolved trust and family issues to make it credible, a hint of romance for spice, and a bit of black humor to lighten up the often dark tone, this is a nicely conceived modern vampire tale that will keep readers guessing." —*Monsters and Critics*

"Green writes a complex story featuring well-defined characters and more than enough noir mystery to keep readers enthralled." —*School Library Journal*

continued . . .

"An intriguing world that becomes more complex with every turn of the page . . . Kick-butt action."
— *Huntress Book Reviews*

"Green has given her fans an inside look at the Underground culture and social class system from the powerful Elite, bitten by the Master, to the lowly Guards, bitten by the Groupies . . . [a] fun urban fantasy mystery."
— *Alternative Worlds*

"A fast-moving urban fantasy filled with murder, mystery, and a large dose of the supernatural. The vivid characterization and danger at every turn will keep readers engaged."
— *Darque Reviews*

"A dark, edgy, and complex series."
— *Romantic Times*

"A dark and thrilling paranormal tale . . . a gritty and suspenseful ride."
— *Romance Reviews Today*

PRAISE FOR

Night Rising

"A book to die for! Dark, mysterious, and edged with humor, this book rocks on every level!"
— Gena Showalter, author of *The Darkest Secret*

"If you like your fantasy with an edge, then you've struck gold. There is a ring of truth to the biting—no pun intended—allegory. This is a fantastic start to a new series."
— *The Eternal Night*

Ace Books by Chris Marie Green

NIGHT RISING
MIDNIGHT REIGN
BREAK OF DAWN
A DROP OF RED
THE PATH OF RAZORS
DEEP IN THE WOODS

Anthologies

FIRST BLOOD
(with Susan Sizemore, Erin McCarthy, and Meljean Brook)

DEEP
IN THE
WOODS

VAMPIRE BABYLON

BOOK SIX

Chris Marie Green

ACE BOOKS, NEW YORK

THE BERKLEY PUBLISHING GROUP
Published by the Penguin Group
Penguin Group (USA) Inc.
375 Hudson Street, New York, New York 10014, USA
Penguin Group (Canada), 90 Eglinton Avenue East, Suite 700, Toronto, Ontario M4P 2Y3, Canada
(a division of Pearson Penguin Canada Inc.)
Penguin Books Ltd., 80 Strand, London WC2R 0RL, England
Penguin Group Ireland, 25 St. Stephen's Green, Dublin 2, Ireland (a division of Penguin Books Ltd.)
Penguin Group (Australia), 250 Camberwell Road, Camberwell, Victoria 3124, Australia
(a division of Pearson Australia Group Pty. Ltd.)
Penguin Books India Pvt. Ltd., 11 Community Centre, Panchsheel Park, New Delhi—110 017, India
Penguin Group (NZ), 67 Apollo Drive, Rosedale, Auckland 0632, New Zealand
(a division of Pearson New Zealand Ltd.)
Penguin Books (South Africa) (Pty.) Ltd., 24 Sturdee Avenue, Rosebank, Johannesburg 2196, South Africa

Penguin Books Ltd., Registered Offices: 80 Strand, London WC2R 0RL, England

This is a work of fiction. Names, characters, places, and incidents either are the product of the author's imagination or are used fictitiously, and any resemblance to actual persons, living or dead, business establishments, events, or locales is entirely coincidental. The publisher does not have any control over and does not assume any responsibility for author or third-party websites or their content.

DEEP IN THE WOODS

An Ace Book / published by arrangement with the author

PRINTING HISTORY
Ace trade paperback edition / March 2010
Ace mass-market edition / July 2011

Copyright © 2010 by Chris Marie Green.
Cover art by Larry Rostant.
Cover design by Judith Lagerman.

ISBN: 978-0-441-02052-2

ACE
Ace Books are published by The Berkley Publishing Group,
a division of Penguin Group (USA) Inc.,
375 Hudson Street, New York, New York 10014.
ACE and the "A" design are trademarks of Penguin Group (USA) Inc.

PRINTED IN THE UNITED STATES OF AMERICA

10   9   8   7   6   5   4   3   2   1

Here's to Elvira,
who haunted my Sunday evenings with *Movie Macabre*
and made me into the horror-loving fan that I am

Much appreciation goes to the hardworking staff at Ace. Thank you also to the Knight Agency, plus Sheree White-feather and Judy Duarte for the sweat and blood that have gone into this series. For inspiration, thanks are owed to the works of Marie-Louise von Franz and the books *Female Rage: Unlocking Its Secrets, Claiming Its Power*, by Mary Valentis, PhD, and Anne Devane, PhD, and *Queen Bees & Wannabes*, by Rosalind Wiseman.

Once again, I acknowledge all errors as my own. Any skewing of locations or historical details has been done for the benefit of increasing the drama in this story.

Have fun during this part of the hunt, guys. I've had a blast on my end. As Angela Carter wrote in "The Erl-King": "It is easy to lose yourself in these woods."

ONE

Already in Deep

ONCE there was a body sprawled under a set of night-darkened, raised train tracks in south London.

The body, a nearly lifeless shell, had eyes sunken into a withered mask of a face, his mouth shaped into a pruned O, as if his lips were on the edge of a cry that would have only been drowned out by a train, should one clack by overhead.

Morbid, indeed. But the curious thing was that his mouth was not preparing for a useless scream at all. The body was trying to smile while his breath wheezed in, wheezed out, his thoughts a blissful blank as the night wore down to the emergence of a chilly November dawn.

Buried amidst a fall of paper and refuse, he slumped against a support pole, just as if it were a leaf-spilling tree to nap against. He was trembling, numb, and so outrageously happy that his mind didn't grasp the fact that he was dying. Yet, he didn't care that he was fading away, unnoticed and left behind. Didn't care that he was so weak he would never even be able to crawl the few centimeters it might take for him to get out from under the debris so his fellow tourist friends—or anyone else—could eventually find him.

All he knew was that a final farewell should be just like this: satiated and complete.

Another breath whistled out of him. His chest, covered by a UCLA sweatshirt, had caved in, suctioned to a collapse. His form resembled a wiry experiment of arms and legs that had been sucked to thinness. His jeans were soaked through with ejaculate from the orgasm that had so recently torn through him.

As a train did approach, rumbling above, casting revolving shadows over the peek of moonlight through the bridge, he tried to remember how he'd gotten here. But all he could grasp were fragments: An almost ethereal whisper that had called for him as he'd come out of a nearby pub, stumbling drunk. A flash of the white dress that had lured him away from his friends toward the dark, mysterious expanse underneath the tracks. The hungry touch of lips over his mouth and the light pressure of fingertips over his zipper.

There was a stirring to his right, and as the train abandoned the space above him, once again allowing full slats of illumination, he used the remainder of his strength to glance over.

He saw the white dress, the slim body of *her*.

An angel, he thought. A figment of death, or at least of the best sex he'd ever had, even though he couldn't remember actually doing her.

He tried to say something, to thank her in a way that almost struck the part of his mind that was still working as perverse. But he couldn't manage any words.

Meanwhile, his skin puckered to his bones, bringing him closer to his end. The suddenly unbearable weight of his head was too much for his neck, and his chin dropped forward, his skull pulling at his spine.

He heard her move toward him, and through the descending mire of his consciousness, he realized that whatever she was, she couldn't just leave him here like this. Still, he didn't care what happened from hereon out. He only wanted her to touch him again.

And she did, though he barely even felt it when she easily picked him up and cradled him in her arms. The contact of her body against his brought one last convulsion, one last spurt from his cock before his vision and mind went black.

Time must have passed, because the next thing he knew, he was lying on his back, the hint-of-dawn sky rolled out above him while the harsh sounds of a shovel sliced into dirt. He instinctively knew that she was preparing his grave.

That was when it hit him. He was *dying*.

He tried to move, to ask her to stop this from happening, to touch him and make him feel another anesthetic, blissful rush. But he couldn't even open his mouth. He didn't have the strength.

She stopped digging and came to him, just as he'd wanted. She stood above him, the flow of her light hair and darkened face covering his view of the sky. Then, as he tried to take in one last breath, she bent to press a tender kiss on his forehead. She lingered, her hair brushing his face, and he spasmed one last time, his hips lifting, wet warmth coating him.

As life seeped out of the rest of the body, he felt the white lady's lips curling into a smile against his skin.

TWO

The Masterful Interrogation

Morning

DEEP within the lab of the vampire hunting team's headquarters, Dawn Madison stood over one of the two London Underground masters as he sat propped in a chair.

At first glance, her stance in front of the staring, captivated vampire would've seemed casual to any observer—her hip cocked, one arm hanging loose at her side as she faced Claudius. But then came the most telling detail.

Her other hand was hidden behind her back, where her fingertips lightly rested on the weapon in her jeans pocket: a crucifix that she was ready to draw at a split second's notice.

However, this master didn't seem to be aware that she was even in the room. His eyes were fixed straight ahead, his gaze stupefied. Dawn didn't know if he was resting, open-eyed, during the daylight, which only weakened the powers of these vampires, or if he was just acting like he was too out of it to respond to her entering the lab only moments ago.

Since he wasn't giving her much of a clue as to where his head was at right now, she took an extra sec to assess him: a tattered, brain-fried former warrior, with his long brown hair falling over a face boasting strong, refined features; his pale, otherwise naked body bundled in a blanket. He hadn't changed into the female or catlike forms that he could shift back and forth from at will. The glaze in his eyes was thanks to Dawn's regrettably rough handling last night, after she'd tried to extract the Underground's location from him. More recently, he'd also been subjected to a round of much gentler questioning from Costin, who'd eventually decided to rest before confronting Claudius again. It'd been after sunrise when the boss had retired to bed, leaving the master vampire alone, finally giving Dawn the opportunity to sneak out of their room while avoiding any of the other team members. She'd come here, not caring that she and the rest of the hunters had been banned from the lab.

Yup—screw it. She was tired of these games, waiting for Claudius to shuffle out the information that would lead to exterminating this newest Underground. There were so many other vampire communities to take care of besides just this one.

She waved her hand in front of him, but nothing changed. *Was* he faking her out by pretending to be hazy?

Willing him to move, she tugged at his blanket, which wasn't the only thing binding him. Dawn's coworkers, the invisible, deceased former-hunter spirits called "Friends," were also wrapped around Claudius with their jasmine essences, making sure he wouldn't be able to strike out physically if he was awake. The blanket was some sort of humane treatment that Costin had insisted on, something to show the master that, if he started spilling the beans about the Underground, there'd be other nice things in store for him.

If he talked.

"Hello, in there," Dawn said, giving one last wave in front of Claudius's face.

Blank-o.

She didn't let down her guard, because this vampire had some major charming abilities. If he was playing possum right now, hoping to lull Dawn and surprise her by lashing out with his controlling voice, he had another think coming.

She was hardly comforted by the fact that she'd kicked his ass last night, after he'd almost enchanted her. Actually, while she'd been going to town on him, doing what she thought a hunter should do to overcome a vampire who'd just as soon kill her as look at her, she'd broken something in Claudius.

Had she turned his brains to mush?

Just the thought of it got to her—a shaded, bladed delight, a sense of victory screwing through her. But, God, it was wrong. She shouldn't feel any kind of triumph after what she'd done, so she shut it out. Costin would be appalled if he knew that she'd even entertained an instant of gratification.

She felt the dull pounding of the dark mark that had shown up on her face last night. A black crescent, the world's ugliest beauty spot, on her left cheek. She'd noted a tender patch on her skin at the end of her encounter with Claudius—and it hadn't been any kind of bruise or injury, either. Why or how it'd gotten on her, she didn't know. It could've had something to do with what she'd become over a year ago when she'd saved Costin during the Underground siege in L.A., when she'd needed to succumb to the bite of another master vamp in order to become a vampire herself, exchanging blood with it and, in turn, preserving a dying Costin so he could exist to fight more Undergrounds— the only way he could gain back his soul.

For a short, incredible time, she'd been one of them. But she'd had to kill that master vamp to destroy the Holly-wood Underground, turning herself human again in the process, although something had remained behind on her soul. A heaviness. A stain that she didn't have to see to know it was there.

Was it coming out on her now, in a very real way?

Had she somehow earned this mark by whaling on Claudius last night?

She walked around the master vamp, still scanning him while the lab's fridge/freezer hummed, sawing over her nerves as she touched that crucifix in her back pocket. Holy items didn't get to all the vampires she'd ever confronted—the dragon's line seemed to have different talents and weaknesses, based on the personality traits they'd brought with them into the afterlife. But she knew this piece would work on Claudius since he'd been a religious man before going vamp all those centuries ago.

"Claudius," she whispered.

His head canted forward, and she could tell he was about to wake up, that he'd only been resting and that the sound of his name was finally nudging him back to consciousness.

"Morning, sunshine," she said, coming to stand in front of him.

His muddled gaze struggled to lock onto her. When it did, he winced so violently that the blanket fell away from his neck, exposing the still-healing wounds there. Based on the intel that Costin had gotten from Claudius since they'd brought the master back here, Dawn knew this creature had earned his injuries from a fight with the lesser vampires in his Underground. But she only knew this because, after things had calmed down around headquarters and Costin had sequestered Claudius for a private questioning session, the boss had scribbled notes so the team would be in the loop. Then he'd settled down to rest without even talking to Dawn face-to-face.

That's right—notes had been the extent of their communication. He was that angry at her.

It'd been at sunrise, after she'd found the papers taped to the inside of their bedroom door, that Dawn had snuck down here to the lab, thinking she could take her interrogation skills down a notch and maybe get even more answers out of this master vampire, who had the ability to move about during the day, although his powers were at an ebb now, just like Costin's.

As Claudius regally tried to compose himself in front of her, she saw the fear in him. Saw herself in the pitch-black of his pupils, which looked like hellholes she would have to claw her way out of.

"I'm not here to hurt you," she said.

It took a minute for the master vamp to process this—she could practically see his thoughts clicking together in his eyes like he was a slow-moving machine that was recovering from a malfunction.

Dawn dug the nails of her free hand into her palm. She hadn't *intended* to mess up Claudius so badly. In her desperation to help Costin, she'd just lost patience.

But she'd keep control from now on, she thought. Control would get her the answers to the biggest questions of all: Did this particular Underground house the dragon, who they suspected might be the most revered and feared monster of all? Was this the community that Vlad Tepes had chosen to keep himself hidden throughout the years? He'd turned Costin into a vampire centuries ago, along with Costin's fellow blood brothers, including Claudius. But then Costin had made a mysterious deal with an ethereal, and nearly anonymous, entity to slay the dragon and his direct progeny in order to win back his soul. The vow had made the boss a Soul Traveler who borrowed bodies from willing hosts so that he could slay one Underground at a time with the aid of handpicked teams.

But during the final attack on the last Underground, much to Dawn's horror, she'd been the one to turn him *back* into a vampire, trapping him in the undead body of his host, Jonah, who constantly fought Costin for dominance.

Now, as Dawn took a step toward Claudius, the master

vamp stiffened beneath his blanket. One of the Friends pushed the flannel back up and over his shoulder, as if the spirit wanted to play good to Dawn's bad.

"Claudius," Dawn said. "It's over. All you can do at this point is make the rest of it easy."

The vamp was grimacing. He was trying to shift, thin cat hair bristling out of his skin. But that was as far as Claudius got with changing into his more lethal vamp form.

Beaten, his body relaxed into his common disguise— that of a woman named Mrs. Jones. It was the identity he'd assumed aboveground to fool everyone.

The fruitlessness of Claudius's maneuvers was a little sad. Costin had told them that this master was a physically weaker one, and Dawn almost felt sorry that she was responsible for making him even more of a basket case. Then again, he would've slayed any one of them in a heartbeat. So why be so sympathetic about a master vampire?

As his more delicate female features warped back into stronger male ones—the more prominent nose, chin, mouth—Dawn took her hand off the crucifix in her back pocket, pretty sure she wasn't going to need it for now.

But she wouldn't forget it was there.

She dragged over a stool from a work counter strewn with nuts and bolts from several projects in progress. Hunting weapons. Then, sitting, she said, "You were with Costin for hours before he retired upstairs. I can see you're tired."

Finally, the vampire spoke, his voice hoarse from the still-healing damage to his throat. "Release me."

The command was slightly imperious, the tone of a monarch whose words were threaded through with attempted charm. It was easy to block out right now, not only because of Claudius's weakened state but because Dawn was prepared to use some fairly decent mind powers of her own; what she'd done to this master vamp last night, banging him back and forth with a psychokinetic verve that had only grown over this past year, testified to what she could do when she was at her best. Or worst.

The urge to do it again, the impatience to get answers, brutally flexed in her. She calmed herself.

After taking in a long breath, she felt a sting on her skin, near the jaw, and she scratched at it, almost as if the action gave her hands something to do.

In the meantime, Claudius seemed to realize that the charm held no sway. His eyes went wide.

"Come on now," Dawn said, avoiding any escalation in tension. "Work with me. That's all I'm asking, here. And that also means you won't call any animals to your aid so they can try to barge into this building and rescue you." He'd tried to do that last night, but she doubted his strength was up to it now.

"If I don't cooperate," he asked, "will you slice my gut open again?"

She withstood the attack. Hell, she took full responsibility for what she'd done. And Claudius's words were nothing compared to the terrified looks the rest of the team had given her after they'd taken the master vamp into custody. His barbs were zero next to the way they'd talked around her afterward, as if they didn't know what to say to her anymore.

"Does it need to come down to slicing?" Dawn asked. "According to Costin, you shared more information with him. You gave him a few details about being pushed out of the Underground by those vamp girls, among other little details about the community itself."

"I suppose you'd like me to convey the location then."

Dawn knew she had a snowball's chance of sweet-talking that out of him, but what the heck. "It'd save us all a lot of grief, wouldn't it?"

The vampire gritted out a laugh. "I had little choice in sharing with Costin. He used our blood brother Awareness to chip his way into my head. Unless you can finesse your troglodyte mind tricks to match his much more civilized ones, I don't believe you'll get as far."

So Costin had been breaking Claudius down bit by bit. The news was heartening, mostly because Dawn had been doubting Costin's strength recently. Most of his raw powers had been dulled after he'd been trapped in Jonah's coarse monster body, and the notion that he had mentally overcome Claudius was good news. If Claudius were a more powerful master, it would've been even better news, but she'd take this for what it was worth.

"So then," Dawn continued calmly, "why don't you save your own skin by sharing even more? You don't really think you're going to be rescued by your little vamp girls anytime soon. They tossed you out like three-day-old fish, remember?"

"They will follow Mihas's orders. I've put in calls to him. He'll respond once he checks his messages."

Mihas—the beloved co-master of this Underground. "Hate to break it to you, Claudius, but unless Mihas has the guts to lead an attack in public—and I don't think he's dumb enough to expose what he is and risk discovery—you're up merde creek. Those girls are glad you're gone."

For a second, Claudius's high-and-mighty expression had Dawn thinking he'd never reveal anything. Costin, with his hypnotic talents as well as the Awareness that blood brothers could have between each other—a thought link that either one could shut down under normal circumstances—might be able to dig real deep into Claudius's psyche if he had all the time in the world. But in spite of what Dawn had just said to the master about his Underground not riding to his rescue, she did fear that she was wrong.

What if they came battering down headquarter doors tonight, if they were careless enough to chance the public exposure? They'd already done some pretty stupid things that had led Costin to them in the first place.

For some reason, Claudius was putting all the strength he had left into guarding his Underground when it had betrayed him. Dawn thought it might have something to do with the other master, Mihas, also known as "Wolfie." He loved Claudius, but only when he was "Claudia," in womanly form.

Was Claudius clinging to that, even though he actually wasn't "Claudia" at all?

The very idea disturbed Dawn, but she wasn't sure why it should.

"They're not coming," Dawn gently repeated. She was relieved that she had that kind of tone in her. "At least, not for you."

The vampire's face lost all arrogance. Dawn almost hurt for the creature, but she knew it'd be a mistake.

"I know this," she said, "because your Awareness revealed a lot to Costin. Since he was already acquainted with you from back in the day, he's been able to make an educated guess or two about your place in this Underground. You're a second master, a lower one. Mihas is your superior. The main Underground is his, not yours. And those girls who fill the community—the ones you both created together? The ones who kicked you out? They adore *him*. Nothing really belongs to you down there."

The vampire opened his mouth as if to retaliate, then shut it, probably knowing nothing he could say would change the truth.

Dawn continued, realizing that she was using a different kind of attack, and it was working even better than getting physical.

See, she *did* have a better part of her that worked just fine.

Just fine.

"Costin says Mihas was always a flake," she said, "and this dates back to centuries ago, when you all fought together for the dragon. But you were always there for Mihas, even after the brothers went off on their own to test their vampire powers on the world. Even after the master commanded you all to form Undergrounds and build armies for the time he'd need them, after awakening from his long sleep. You were *always* taking care of business down below while Mihas would flit around above, enjoying what his vampiness allowed him to do. You were the constant one, helping him to build an Underground with girl vampire soldiers who would fight for the dragon's takeover. I guess Mihas was there for you, but only when it suited him."

Claudius pressed his lips together, his gaze on the ground. One of the Friends who was binding him shifted, pushing the blanket farther up, as if to cover his vulnerabilities.

"He thrives on his girls more than he does on you," Dawn added. "And he's got his girls right now, without you there to interfere."

She was getting to him. She recognized the posture of hopelessness bringing down his shoulders.

After she waited him out, he spoke.

"So what am I to do?" he asked. "Turn on him?"

"If you plan on . . ." She was about to say "surviving," but she couldn't. If Costin wanted his soul back, Claudius would *have* to be terminated. All the blood brothers would. That was the vow Costin had made to that cryptic force that had offered the deal. The Whisper.

Dawn started again. "There'll be a whole lot less awful complexity involved if you cooperate," she said instead.

"Don't you mean to say there'll be a lot less pain?"

"I told you—I'm not here to hurt you."

"But there's always pain." The vampire smiled vaguely. "And the thought holds no fear for me. Perhaps I exist for it."

Another flare of impatience—and maybe even discomfort—got to Dawn, but she pushed it down before it went anywhere. There was just that sting on her jaw again.

Before she could think too much about that, Claudius added, "I have taken centuries of pain, and I've come to think that I might have even enjoyed it."

A masochistic streak, she thought. She'd also seen it last night when Claudius had practically welcomed the cut of a machete against his neck. She'd sensed it in this relationship he had with Mihas.

And maybe she even recognized it in her own life with Costin and Jonah, as well her attempts to reconcile with Eva, the mom who'd deserted her for a vampire life of her own before she'd been turned back human with the death of the L.A. master.

Dawn leaned forward, resting her forearms on her thighs. "Don't you think it's time for *Mihas* to feel *your* pain?"

Claudius looked her up and down, and Dawn wondered if she was really being as successful with this mode of questioning as she'd thought. Vampires, for all their supposed coldness and lack of emotion, could be the opposite: the condition brought out what was already in them, whether it was love, sorrow, rage, or remoteness. It was an extreme of the mind and of the body. It substituted excess for the absence of a soul.

"All my existence," he said, "I've been what Mihas has needed. I loved him so completely that I obliterated myself, and it wasn't worth it. Now, in what I realize might be my last hours, do you believe that I'll become what *you* need?"

Dawn couldn't find anything to say for a moment. Then she offered all she could.

"No, I don't believe that."

Then again, that'd been the story of her life. That was why she hadn't needed anything from anyone, ever.

The vampire seemed taken aback by Dawn's honesty. Maybe he even sensed the remorse in her for so many things, including how far she'd gone in striking at him earlier.

He reclined in his chair, observing her. "Well, now. You're quite pitiful, aren't you?"

She almost laughed. *Him* thinking *she* was a sorry thing?

He continued. "A hunter reduced to hanging her head in front of a victim who won't give in."

"Are you trying to goad me into attacking you again since you have such a yen for agony?"

"No, no. I could hardly stand another bout of torture."

Dawn wanted to say it hadn't been torture, but she wasn't sure about that. Wasn't sure about anything that'd happened last night. All she knew was that she had a mark against her, and it was there on her face for everyone to see. A non-scarlet letter that was bound to spell out what she'd become lately.

Claudius tilted his head, a vampire trait she'd seen in all of them. "What did it feel like . . . stringing me up and slicing into me with that mental power of yours? I must say, from a purely impartial point of view, it was an impressive show. You would have been quite a soldier in the Underground I helped to cultivate."

Great. Complimented on her methods by a master vampire. Dawn was officially awesome.

"My actions were what I felt was necessary at the time," she said. "And it helped you to get captured. I can't say that the end didn't justify the means."

"If you mean to get every last answer from me, I would suspect you haven't come to *any* end."

Cute. "Then *Costin's* going to get what he wants from you."

"Maybe so. In time. But perhaps the time will be costly, and it will allow my Underground to mobilize against you. Perhaps my community *will* come for me, and they will track me here, where they can crush you during the witching hour, when most humans are too asleep to notice."

"Eloquent," Dawn said. "But, again, I suspect you don't believe in that scenario one bit."

The Friends—some of whom could be slightly less ruthless than Dawn, even though their spiritual state of grace didn't allow them to kill—were getting restless. Dawn could see their invisible pressure pushing against the vampire, as if to impede his breathing. Even though Claudius was undead, the maneuver was working. The dragon's line of vampires had bodies that functioned like humans in many ways, but during the exchange of blood and loss of a soul, something had happened to change their composition, their matter, spinning them into beyond human instead of just the norm. She knew this because she was familiar with Costin's shared body.

She slid off her stool, her boots hitting the floor with a soft thud. A good cop would ease down with Claudius, begin again. Reset.

"You could ingratiate yourself with me by giving up a freebie," she said. "What do you say? You start off small, telling me something like . . . Well, say, why London seems to attract Undergrounds more than the average place. With an answer to that, I'll be in a much better mood. Maybe I'll even ask the Friends who're binding you to let up a bit."

Claudius shrugged, like this one answer was some kind of olive branch he didn't mind shedding. "I wish I had an explanation, but vampires aren't sages. When we exchange blood and lose our souls, we aren't given a secret handshake and the guide to solving all the world's puzzles."

Unfortunately, that made sense. Not even Costin was all knowing. In the beginning, Dawn had thought that just because these creatures were older than the hills, they'd have more of a clue than the rest of the general population. But no. Besides, if any of the blood brothers *had* formulated theories over the years about global warming or the end of days, they probably wouldn't have shared, seeing as all the dragon's progeny had drifted apart, growing greedy and paranoid about takeovers, and cutting themselves off from interacting with each other when possible. Mihas and Claudius seemed to be the exception.

Dawn said, "You can't even tell me why you and Mihas settled here?"

Claudius shook his head, and it almost seemed like he wanted to add a feisty little tsking sound, too.

"I suppose," Dawn added, "that would veer disturbingly close to talking about the dragon, wouldn't it. Maybe your big master just wanted to settle here in London, along with you and Mihas. Maybe he had the same plans and whims as the so-called fictional count in *Dracula* did. He has a real thing for this area, and you guys inherited that from him."

"You assume the dragon is with our Underground, and you know what they say about people who assume."

"It makes an 'ass' out of 'u' and 'me.' " Obviously, he was so old he didn't have any new jokes.

"Besides, if you're depending upon a work of fiction—one that's been said to not be based on Vlad Tepes at all, in spite of all the speculation—you're even more pitiful than I suspected." Claudius sucked in a breath as a random Friend took exception to that and pushed the blanket around his neck against the healing wounds.

Dawn watched her fellow hunters, even though she couldn't see them. Did any of them *want* her to whip out her mental persuasion tools right about now?

But she wouldn't do it. She could be just like the other members of the team, who'd been recruited because of a true-blue streak of justice that Dawn had always doubted she possessed, too. Yet, she did have it, didn't she? She wanted more than anything to get Costin's soul back for him.

Wasn't that kind of a noble cause?

The thought weighed on her, because sometimes she wondered if she did it all *for* him or because it was the only way she'd ever feel redeemed for turning him into a vampire.

"Okay then," Dawn said. "Looks like we're done here. I'll just wait for Costin to roll out of bed again. He'll know how to get the dragon factoids out of you."

Claudius just smiled enigmatically, reminding Dawn of a sphinx.

But Dawn didn't leave just yet. She moseyed toward the vampire. "Too bad you can't call anyone else to your aid. Costin's only going to get more and more persuasive."

The creature swallowed beneath the blanket, not knowing that Dawn was only being optimistic about the extent of Costin's remaining powers.

"Those shadow things?" she said. "Guards? Whatever they are? Why aren't *they* here to help you?"

"I don't know what you're talking about."

Hah. Dawn gestured toward the fridge/freezer, where the team had stored the corpse of a young man. A little over a week ago, they'd encountered him lurking around a vampire remains burial site, and he'd fallen from a building to his death before they'd even been able to question him. They hadn't known who or what he was until the other night when Dawn had encountered a female dressed in all black techno ninja-type gear, just as he'd been.

Shadow things, Dawn had been calling them. And the team didn't know whether the things were tracking vampires or if they were barring intruders from finding the Underground . . . or anything the vampires might be hiding down there.

Like the dragon.

Just as Dawn was about to pursue the subject, Claudius sat up straight in his chair, then bolted backward, as if mentally attacked. But Dawn hadn't done anything—hadn't thrown any mind punches or pushes.

His gaze had frozen on something behind her, and before she even turned around, she knew who'd entered.

THREE

THE BOSS

SHE pivoted to find Costin standing at the foot of the stairs that led to the main rooms, and her pulse caught in her throat, in her veins. She was his master, and they were connected in so many ways when they were open to each other: mentally, physically through the blood he thrived on when he sipped from her.

But, again, that was only when they were open to each other, which hadn't really been the case lately.

Her heart twisted in her chest as he glanced at her, but when she discerned the blue in his eyes—not the topaz color that denoted Costin's dominance in the body he shared with Jonah—she knew that the other entity was in charge right now.

Jonah grinned at her in his cocky, American-guy way, confirming her guess. But then again, maybe she should've known from the way his dark hair was ruffled carelessly. Costin's style would've been neater. And their lean body

would've been postured like a soldier's rather than a cowboy's if Costin had been here instead of Jonah.

He was wearing a long-sleeved black shirt untucked
from dark trousers, heavy black boots that nicked the floor
with every fluid vampire step as he came forward, close
enough so she could see the injuries on his face that had
almost healed from last night's showdown with Claudius.

Dawn never knew quite how to act around Jonah, especially nowadays. Where Costin could scorn her for a lack
of control in fighting, Jonah seemed to understand that she
was only human.

Or at least as human as she could be with these weird
psychokinetic powers that'd woken up during the Hollywood Underground hunt.

"Where's Costin?" she asked. "He was in charge the last
time I knew."

"And I'm in charge now."

Jonah halted near Dawn's side, his clothes smelling
wash clean. A ridiculous flutter painted the lining of her
belly, but that shouldn't be happening around Jonah. Just
Costin, her lover. The only one she allowed to take her
blood.

"He didn't have a problem with me assuming control,"
Jonah added. "I wanted to get things moving, and I kept
jarring him out of our rest. But Costin needed a mental nap
after all the Awareness digging he was doing with Claudius.
Still, he'll be back soon enough, even if daylight hours
won't see us at our best."

It occurred to Dawn that Costin and Jonah had started
to work together as much as they could. But what else
could Costin do when Dawn had pretty much made her
own deal with Jonah to facilitate his occasional emergence? Jonah had gotten so strong that he was able to push
Costin down into their body for as long as he wanted, and
Dawn had seen no other choice if she wanted to keep their
ultimate attack weapon against the Undergrounds func-

tioning. Of course, since Costin was bound to Jonah's vampire body now, he didn't have a fraction of the powers he'd possessed when he'd been a free Soul Traveler, so none of them even knew how effective he'd be when it did come time to infiltrate this Underground and destroy the master vamps.

Even so, they had to keep faith that Jonah and Costin combined would be enough to vanquish all the Undergrounds they had left . . . as well as the dragon.

God, she thought. How was Costin going to deal with the dragon if he was so limited?

Cocking his head, Jonah was considering Claudius, and Dawn stared at her partner in return, finally comprehending the reason the master vamp had been thrown back in his chair when Jonah had entered the lab.

He'd connected with Claudius's gaze, even from across the room, and he'd used his vampire powers to enter the weakened master's unprotected mind, reading his thoughts while Dawn had been asking about the shadow things. Claudius had been either too off guard since he wasn't worried about Dawn breaking into his thoughts, or too lacking in strength to resist.

"What did you get from his head?" Dawn asked Jonah.

Jonah continued watching Claudius as the other vampire squirmed in his seat. Dawn wondered if, when Costin had been questioning the master earlier, Jonah had emerged and raised some hell. Jonah was just as bad as Dawn in the control department, if not worse.

"*Custode,*" Jonah said, his grin widening with this success. "While you were talking about the shadow things, Claudius, here, thought of a *custode*, which means 'keeper,' if I'm not wrong. But a keeper of what?"

Dawn could hardly contain herself. The dragon. They had to be "keeping" the dragon, right? Or were the shadow things only guards of the community itself?

"And," Jonah added, "Mr. Claudius is really regretting

that he didn't summon a *custode* before we got ahold of him last night."

The team had found Claudius in an abandoned building, threatening to take the blood of a female victim, probably so he could speed along his healing. He'd been a bit too busy when they'd arrived to make a phone call. Too bad.

In his chair, Claudius was shutting his eyes, keeping Jonah out. If Costin had been dominant, his blood brother Awareness and hypnotic skills would be even more powerful than Jonah's vampire abilities.

She felt a vibration in her second back pocket, where she'd tucked her cell phone. She ignored it. No way was she going to take a call now, even if it was from Kiko and Natalia, team members who'd told Dawn last night that one of them had gotten a vision about the shadow things—*custode*s, as she'd just learned—and the psychics intended to go over to Eva's flat first thing in the morning to investigate the site where Dawn had tangled with one of the keepers. Kik and Nat had the idea that, maybe, he could use his psychometric powers to conjure more visions and, thus, produce leads to the Underground. If Claudius had been more cooperative, further detective work wouldn't have been so necessary.

Casually, Jonah folded his arms over his chest. "It was easy to read him," he said about Claudius. "His will is weaker because of the damage you did last night, and I think he's even more tired now, after having to fend you off this morning." He loosened his collar. "It's time for Costin to wake up out of his snooze. A catnap should've bucked him right up."

"You're letting him out?"

"I'm a team player. I do what I have to do." He used his grin again. "Just like you've always done."

There it was again—Jonah's odd support of her. And the fact that it made her feel like she wasn't such a monster after last night lent her some solace. Jonah truly wanted to do his part in saving the world; he just tried to do it in his own warped way. He loved using his vampiric powers and did it when Costin, who detested the monsters he'd always hunted before Dawn had turned him into one, refused to resort to it.

Dawn could only watch as Jonah winked at her. Then he reared back his head, and after a few seconds, righted it, revealing burning topaz eyes while he slowly dropped his hands to his sides and straightened his posture.

Dawn's skin buzzed, the sensation drilling through flesh to bone, heating her.

He was back—Costin.

He didn't look at her, and she knew she'd earned that.

"Dawn," he said, and his tone held that exotic, world-weary drag of vibration that only made her want him all the more. "Please gently encourage our guest to open his eyes."

Huh?

Was he asking her to assist? He *trusted* her?

When he didn't say anything else, she moved toward Claudius. But just as she was thinking about how to be gentle about forcing someone's eyelids open, the vamp did the favor for her.

"I can intuit," Claudius said through clenched teeth, "that I shall be wide-eyed no matter the situation. I'd prefer to handle this myself, thank you."

"Have at it," Dawn said. "But if you don't keep your peepers peeping, it's *A Clockwork Orange* time for you."

She shouldn't have said that, even if she needed to sound like she meant business. Nonetheless, one of the Friends broke her silence and tittered with that wind-tunnel laugh they had.

Costin frowned, cutting off the Friend's giggle.

Dawn cleared her throat and waited to see what she needed to do next to help out.

Claudius said, "Just so you know, Costin, I'll be doing my best to block you."

"I would expect nothing less from a warrior brother," Costin said.

"I—"

Claudius jerked, falling back in his chair and smacking the ground as Costin pounced toward him, keeping eye contact by poising himself above his blood brother—the fellow creature who'd also taken the oath to follow the dragon through the centuries in exchange for the glories of vampirism.

The master vamp's legs were frozen in midkick, his eyes saucered, and Dawn stood there, feeling an electric vibration eating at her skin.

Costin was putting his all into this—more than even last night when he'd tried to get into Claudius's mind via their Awareness. He was shaking so badly that she really thought he was going to implode, but she knew that if she interrupted him, he'd be angrier than ever, so she backed off, waiting.

Waiting.

Claudius was quaking, too, his mouth twisting, his head straining to the side, as if trying to break eye contact and unable to do it. A low moan whined from him, growing louder, louder, until it became a shriek.

Costin's spine arched as his blood brother's cry burst apart, echoing in Dawn's chest as if she'd made the sound herself.

She pressed a hand to her heart because it felt like it'd been punctured. Then Costin backed away from Claudius, whose mouth stayed fixed in a silent cry.

She went to Costin, catching him before he slumped to the ground. "Are you all right?"

He couldn't talk, only grapple for steady breaths. But she could also feel him resisting her embrace, so she let him go, stunned that he wanted to get away from her. Wounded at his reaction.

He seemed to realize what he'd done, but she couldn't

be sure, because his hair was covering most of his topaz gaze. Meanwhile, more Friends had entered the lab, swishing by with their jasmine scent, relieving the other contingent and smoothly taking the spirits' places to bind Claudius, who was still shivering on the floor.

"What did you do?" Dawn asked. "How . . . ?"

"He was primed to fail," Costin said, his usually dark and heavy voice thin. "He has been whittled down, hour by hour. I made sure to lay the foundation before you even got in here this morning. Fear of you drained him further, and I used all of what I had in me to exploit that now."

"You knew I'd come in here after you went to rest."

"You are as predictable as the sunrise." He sucked in a few breaths, then gritted his jaw, slowly rising to his feet.

She wanted to chide him for not telling her what he'd had in mind, but that wouldn't do any good. It wasn't in Costin's nature to share. He was secretive, even with her—the master he resented in his heart of hearts.

She wondered how long she could take that. If there would ever be a time he would actually allow her in all the way . . . or a time she would do the same with him.

While Costin pieced himself together, pushing back his hair into his preferred neater style, Dawn thought that, in spite of his trouble in entering Claudius's mind, he might not have gotten much.

Just as she was about to ask him, he turned away. Mortified, she finally took out her phone to check it, just to show herself that she did have things to do, people who wanted to talk to her.

The old Friends, who were relieved of duty and would go to their painted portraits lining the hallways to take their rest, breezed out of the room while Dawn listened to a message from Kiko.

"Dawn! We're getting something here! Tell Costin that we'll be back in headquarters by dusk so he doesn't have to worry so much about our security."

They were getting something. Visions of Shadow Girl?

Costin headed for the stairs, Dawn just behind him.

"Kiko and Natalia are tuning in to some shadow-thing vibes over at Eva's flat," she said. "They might have some clues we could use to find out what those things are and how they fit into the Underground."

"Those two need to be inside headquarters as soon as possible. Please relay that information to them."

He sounded as if he'd witnessed something in Claudius's mind—something to put him on alert.

"Why so soon?" she asked. "Did you see any kind of planned attack from the vampires in Claudius's head?"

"No."

As they ascended the stairs, traveling under the steel plating that lined the way, she looked back to see Claudius still chair-bound on the floor, the Friends captivating him as he continued staring at the ceiling, back to the near-comatose state he'd been in after Dawn had gotten through with him last night.

They reached the door, and Costin paused with his hand on the knob. "But I saw enough to warrant our own attack."

Before she could suck in a shocked breath, he opened the door, leaving Dawn standing there.

Their *own* attack?

The final step in vanquishing this Underground?

Already?

"Did you get a location?" she asked, dogging him as they entered the main floor, with its stifling dark wood, bas-reliefs of friars, and angel heads, looming around like mean curly haired kids who kept constant watch.

"I gleaned enough of a location from Claudius to justify action."

"Wait." She pulled at the sleeve of his shirt, making him stop. "*Enough* of one?"

"Yes, enough."

He made as if to continue walking, but she cut him off by standing in front of him, palms over his chest. His heart beat placidly beneath one of her hands.

"Costin, as far as I recall, the last time you 'got a location' in L.A., you meditated forever before you went on the attack."

"There was rather a lot to deal with before that particular siege, Dawn." He was talking about having to come clean with her back then, about using her as bait. About telling her what he really was—a former vampire turned savior of the world in a race against the dragon's rising.

Then she remembered the rest of it.

"Right," she said, lowering her hands. "You didn't know the location until you kicked my ass out of the L.A. headquarters, driving me to the Underground after you'd planted a locator on me without me knowing it. That's how you got the location."

She could've sworn he looked guilty about that, but when it was weighed against all her own sins, it all balanced out.

She stepped out of his way. "So you're off."

"After some preparation, yes. I will have Friends with me, just as last time."

"It's all set then."

"Almost." He tilted his head, then seemed to catch himself, righting it.

He'd been falling into the vampire habit lately.

"With good on our side," he said, straightening his spine, as if to get back to the righteous soldier within, "I hope to find the Underground while most of the schoolgirl vampires are emerging to track down our headquarters, provided they decide that Claudius is worth the cost of hunting."

"They might be coming with those shadow things," she said. "You're prepared to have us and the remaining Friends defend against all of that while you're gone?"

"Yes." Costin paused, as if just now doubting his plan. But then he recovered. "Breisi has studied the boy's body in our lab, and although the anatomy differs, she believes the *custode*s to be humanlike. You and Frank, with the great aid of Friends, should have no problem taking them down, especially with the arsenal we have here." He paused. "You will be able to defend yourselves."

He went to the ornate stairway.

"Costin," Dawn said. "This isn't like last time with an Underground. Or the time before. *You're* not the same."

He slowed his steps. He didn't like being reminded that Jonah's vampire body had locked in Costin's essence, which had always been able to emerge, full force, to knock out previous Underground masters. "Haven't you wanted me to test what I can do outside these walls?" He hadn't turned to look at her. "Haven't you questioned whether I have what it takes to continue my quest?"

She nodded, unable to speak. Her voice seemed too laden to get out of her body. She'd doubted his courage ever since they'd tracked this Underground to London. So why was she trying to hold him back from proving himself now?

He was a warrior entrusted with a duty so significant that she was nothing next to it, and she suspected not only that he was going to emphasize that to her—and maybe to himself—but that he had no other choice. This was why he'd been saved by The Whisper, who'd offered him redemption if Costin would conquer the dragon and his ilk.

She couldn't and wouldn't stop him. Besides, she remembered all too clearly what disobeying Costin had brought back in L.A., when she'd screwed things up so badly that she'd turned him into what he hated the most.

Out of anyone, Costin would know what he was doing. Who the hell was she to know better?

"Blood," she said softly. "You'll need my blood before you go. You'll be stronger with it."

"Yes." She thought she heard a hint of regret, anger at his weakness, and thankfulness in his voice, all at the same time. "I will be stronger with you in me."

As he left, she trailed up the stairs after him, hearing the vague ticking of every clock in the house counting down to when she'd have to let him go again.

FOUR

London Babylon, *Custode* Monitor Room

FAR under the earth, where the walls seemed to close in and rip at the skin with their darkness, a *custode* named Lilly was sitting at the monitors that allowed the keepers who were linked to this Underground to watch over London. She'd been here for hours, mainly to search the bank of tellys for Claudia—or "Claudius" or "Mrs. Jones" or whichever identity the old cow had assumed tonight. The vampire had simply gone off the Underground's radar after escaping the clutches of the younger creatures, who had attacked their elder, ousting her from the community.

The ruckus had all been due to Lilly, and she didn't regret orchestrating Claudia's banishment for even an instant. She would have loved to have done it herself, but for the vow she had taken upon activation into this holiest of holy positions.

She had promised no harm to the Underground.

Yet Lilly hadn't harmed the community in the least by encouraging *others* to go after Claudia. It had been more a "beneficial maintenance maneuver," and all Lilly had needed to do was utilize her tuner on one of the girls: Della, a budding, feral girl in her midteens who would make the finest of soldiers for the dragon.

The tuner had implanted vivid stories—paranoia-inducing true nightmares of the vampires' pasts—that had urged Della to share the tales with the rest of the higher vampire schoolgirls. Based on those visions, plus a suspicion that Claudia had been up to no good with their school chums who had gone missing over the years, the group had decided to attack the vampire who Lilly believed was the primary reason this Underground had gone to such crap. Claudia had a cancerous influence on the main master vampire, Mihas, who had once been quite the soldier himself, serving the dragon and their country with a blood-hungry ferocity that seemed to have disappeared with all Claudia's soft indulgences.

She had never been a good co-master, and Lilly was somewhat relieved that the vampire had disappeared into the London night without even a summons for *custode* aid.

Even so, Lilly had turned to these monitor screens, which were mainly connected to the CCTV surveillance cameras round London, to track Claudia. Not that the vampire would have the stones to return and exact revenge on the Underground—she would never betray Mihas like that, Lilly suspected—but the *custode* wished to keep tabs on the community's security, and Claudia bore watching.

Concurrently, Lilly had been surveying the Underground itself, with the recruited lower-class girls lounging about their common areas and Mihas still engaged in one of his fantasy rooms with the group of upper-crust Queenshill schoolgirls who had decided to seduce him, no doubt intent on taking his attention off the missing Claudia. They were the same girls who had so fiercely thrown the co-master out of the Underground, and they had been at Mihas since last night.

On a screen reflecting the goings-on in the "pirate suite," with its timber and silks and mock ship cabin details, Lilly saw how the girls kept Mihas willingly captive, kissing and biting, using their tongues and giggles. In spite of youthful appearances, most of the vampires were actually far beyond a tender age, having been turned decades ago, and their experience showed. Lilly couldn't help but notice that the newest class of schoolgirl vampires—the truly teen-aged Della, Noreen, and Polly—had not entered the sexual, bloody fray, although Mihas kept gesturing to them.

Smart birds, Lilly thought. They were withholding. She knew that, since Claudia had been the one to raise them in her own sub-Underground, Mihas had not yet tasted of this freshest crop. Their blood would be a treat for him, unlike the older, already used schoolgirls, or even the other young vampire recruits from the streets who didn't have Queens-hill breeding.

As if these other viewings weren't enough to keep Lilly occupied, she turned her attention to a third: a monitor showing recorded images from Highgate Cemetery, which was terribly near the main Underground. Recently, she had been constantly checking the footage to see if there had been any suspicious activity, if there had been any trouble-makers like the ones who had engaged the schoolgirls in a conflict on the Queenshill campus only a few nights ago.

She especially kept her gaze peeled for the woman with the long, dark brown braid whom Lilly had encountered in Southwark, in a flat above a pub. Lilly had intended to detain and question her, but unfortunately the interview had never come to pass, since the woman had managed to stave off Lilly, impressing her with mind powers in the form of mental punches, plus trained fighting skills. But this didn't mean Lilly wasn't going to find the woman again.

She smiled, recalling when she'd impulsively kissed her opponent. Lilly was definitely going to find her, and she would bet heavily that it would be in Southwark.

But, at the moment, the *custode* was primarily playing a hunch about the cemetery, and she directed most of her attention toward it. She suspected that if the mind-powered woman's group did equate to trouble, they would be skulking about near the main Underground, just as they had on the Queenshill campus, which had housed Claudia's sub-Underground before the vampires had needed to desert it.

As she worked, a groan sounded from a corner of the cavelike room.

"Up and about?" she said to her older brother, Nigel. Last night, he had attempted to interfere with Claudia's ouster, and he had even almost put a stop to Lilly's best-laid plans to clean out the Underground, starting with that particular vampire. But Lilly had knocked Nigel out with the judicious use of pressure points. Afterward, she'd used her tuner to persuade him into an uninterrupted rest for the night. Poor dear had needed it after what he'd been through.

She could hear her brother standing, then gaining his bearings, yet she kept on with her labors. Due to the tuner, he wouldn't recall a lick of what had transpired since his mind had been wiped of any superficial memories regarding their confrontation. Hopefully, he would remember what had occurred with Claudia, but nothing beyond that. In fact, she had tuned him to believe upon awakening that he had been sleeping in his quarters and had only just sauntered into this monitor room.

And, indeed, he muttered, "Claudia?"

"She's off and away, remember?" Then Lilly smoothly added a lie. "I went after her whilst you stayed behind and minded the monitors. Both of us couldn't go running off. One of us always remains here to protect."

"Yes, that's right."

Good. He wasn't questioning. The mind-tune had worked.

Lilly paused the Highgate recording and spun around in her chair. Nigel was in the shadows and, for a moment, with his face muted, she imagined that he was her other brother, Charles, who had been mysteriously killed on the job, causing her to be activated, though she was merely a female. Yet, she had been the only available Meratoliage within this generation who had been of age to serve and protect these vampires.

At the thought of Charles, whose body had never been discovered, an ache stretched through the right side of Lilly's chest, where her heart beat. The unusual positioning was an anomaly that every member of the family endured owing to the Meratoliages having been selectively bred for over a century to fit this honorable job. Black-art hearts were their blessing and curse, killing quite a few valuable males at a young age. Her own father had been cast aside from active duty because of coronary weakness, and he had resented it, especially when Lilly had been called to duty.

When Nigel stepped away from the shadows, her heart stopped aching, her chest actually chilling at the sight of him: the sandy hair, combed back from a face with light green eyes, a tilted patrician nose, a slight overbite. He was a male mirror of her.

The air quivered, digging into Lilly, just as it always did so far down in this Underground.

Nigel's gaze rested on the monitor showcasing Mihas and his girls, and the tips of his mouth turned down.

"He still has no idea why his darlings turned on Claudia," he said.

"I accessed earlier audio from when the girls first approached him last night, when they told him that Claudia suddenly attacked Noreen and they responded in kind. He didn't entirely buy their explanation, I gather, but if I know Mihas, I would say that he believes he's got plenty of time to care later, after he's had his fill."

"Did you discover the reason the girls *did* attack Claudia?"

"I assume they somehow fit the pieces together and discovered that she was selectively feeding on and killing their classmates. I'm not certain that they suspect Mihas knows about this, but I'd like to tune the girls so they never realize he was involved. If they already do suspect, they haven't told him, and it needs to stay that way. It would come to no good if they knew that Mihas had been a party to Claudia's hobbies."

"They need to stay subservient, just as all proper soldiers do."

"Yes. But even if they suspect, Mihas seems to have them in his thrall right now." Lilly paused, just now realizing that the main master's greatest talent might rest in his charisma. It had certainly swayed Claudia, along with the rest of the girls. It occurred to Lilly that, perhaps, even *she* might have been slightly fascinated by the main master's charms, as well. Not appreciating the thought of that, she added, "We can begin our tuning after Mihas has finished amusing himself. The girls haven't allowed him a moment away since Claudia left."

Nigel nodded. "We can't be too careful. We've tuned the girls before when they've shown too much adolescent overexcitement. I see no problem in doing it again."

With every passing second, Lilly relaxed all the more, delighted that she'd already become so proficient at tuning, even if she had only recently been activated to take Charles's place.

"As long as Mihas doesn't know we're tuning them, we'll be fine," she said. Up until recently, as the masters had increasingly shown a reliance on the *custodes*, the keepers had worked independently. They had been created to serve a higher purpose than merely guarding the homes of an individual blood brother, who hailed from a group that, in general, had grown complacent and lazy over the years. When the dragon had commanded his progeny to go forth and populate, he had never guessed that his best men would fail him by pursuing their own base desires and straying from his directive.

Lilly didn't add to Nigel that she planned to correct this course and make Mihas into the perfect soldier again. He had once been quite a destructive terror, and now that Claudia was out, true rehabilitation could begin. Every male *custode* up until Nigel hadn't seen how the dragon's mandates had been degraded, and it had taken her, a mere woman by Meratoliage standards, to bring about some much required change.

"I've never seen anyone assert his manhood the way Mihas does," Nigel said, leaning closer to the pirate room monitor.

"If your mistress was such a scold, you, too, would be quite taken with the younger ones."

He switched his focus to the Highgate recording while she continued talking, catching him up on her present purposes: minding Mihas, and searching throughout London for Claudia and those troublemakers from Queenshill.

"So, as you see, I've got my work ahead of me," she finished, leaning back in the chair, propping her ankle just above her knee. "There's much to do besides sitting here and watching these screens."

"For instance . . . ?"

"I'd like to take up where my patrol in Southwark left off the other night. After I encountered that woman in the flat . . ."

Nigel keenly observed her.

She met his curiosity with her own head-on gaze.

"This woman," he said. "If I didn't know better, I would think she's taken precedence over all else, Lilly."

"Rubbish." As she faced the screens again, she felt a flush come over her skin. But the monitors' glare would hide it. "That woman was in the flat for a reason. I'd like to investigate who lives there, discover a link. Perhaps it would lead us to where we might find the entire group."

"Haven't we been over this before?" He sounded more confused than argumentative.

Clearly, the tuner mind wipe hadn't erased his stance on the troublemakers, who had aroused enough suspicion with their appearance on the Queenshill campus to keep Lilly very interested. Nigel hadn't believed them to be such a problem, whereas she felt they could very well be.

"I had a thought," she said. "What if Charles was killed while he was on the path of this group? What if he went to Billiter Street after realizing the burial ground had drawn their attention? Then, what if he tried to lure one of them for questioning?"

"He *was* headed for Billiter during his patrol . . ."

Plus, she mentally added, the cameras *were* clouded in that area on that night. It was a stunning detail, one that Lilly thought to be a signature of the attackers.

Neither of them said anything more until a bit later, when something on the recorded Highgate Cemetery footage indeed caught Lilly's attention.

One of the panels . . . clouding.

Just as so many other views had been clouded, from Billiter Street, where Charles may have died, to the Queenshill campus, where that group had confronted the girl vampires, to Southwark, where Lilly had tangled with the mind-powered woman. . . .

"They were at the cemetery," Lilly said, rising from the chair. Her heart was pounding now. Hours and hours of observing old tape, and it had finally paid off. "Look. They've been to Highgate, and that's too near the Underground for my comfort."

Nigel punched a command into the keyboard, bringing up a larger view of the clouded panel. Then he pushed away from the console.

She didn't know if he was angry because she had been correct in her assumptions about the group and he had been wrong, or if he was adrenalized because these interlopers had wandered too close to where the main Underground waited, accessible through tunnels branching out from the village of Highgate.

Then Nigel sat down in the seat she had vacated, tacitly conveying that he was giving her control.

Bless that mind wipe.

"Go to Southwark," he said. "I'll keep watch here."

"Try to access information about whoever lets that flat above the Bull and Cock Pub, as well, Nigel. Contact me when you have something."

Without even taking the time to gloat, she snatched her mask and goggles from their hanging spot near the door, then accessed the button to open it. As it swooshed aside, Lilly walked, then ran, toward one of the Underground's exits, her wrong-sided heart pounding.

She was going to find them.

What she didn't acknowledge, however, was that she was even more excited about finding that woman again.

FIVE

LONDON BABYLON,
"THE PIRATE SUITE"

DELLA stood by the wall, half hiding behind a sheer lilac curtain draped from the rock ceiling. Next to her, Noreen and Polly hung back, as well, all of them dressed in a uniform that signified their circle of friendship: white shirts, slim red ties, long skirts with boots.

And all of them were keeping their distance from Wolfie and the other Queenshill schoolgirls on the bed.

The three were the only classmates remaining from what had started as a group of seven handpicked vampires who composed the newest Underground class. Little had they known that Mrs. Jones—or Claudia or "the cat" as they had called her—had chosen the lot of them for her own benefit, picking them off one by one every six months to stock her youth-infusing blood rituals.

And Claudia had been feeding off her charges for years. She hated the girls because of how her vampire lover felt about his darlings, and her rituals must have been all the sweeter for that reason alone. As far as the survivors knew, Wolfie hadn't even known about the atrocities.

At least, that was what they were hoping, though Della often wondered. . . .

Polly, with her strawberry blond bob and athletic, loose-limbed stance, tapped in to a mind-link so she might communicate with her two classmates. *How far away do you think the cat is now?* She had been asking the same question ever since the girls had attacked Claudia last night.

Noreen was slyly peeking through the fluffy red hair that covered part of her sprite-featured face, watching Wolfie on the bed, too, but not as obviously as Polly. *Certainly Mrs. Jones is gone for good,* she mind-said. *Far and away from here. We chased her out properly.*

True enough. The Queenshill girls had grouped together after Della had endured dreams about vampires that had come upon her like living nightmares. She had no idea of their origin—perhaps her subconscious had woven together subtle clues about Mrs. Jones and the way she constantly, intensely watched them—but the dreams had led Della to the truth about the cat. And after Della had told the other Queenshill girls about those warped tales, they had ambushed their housematron, forcing themselves into Mrs. Jones's head to see if Della's strange visions held any validity.

They had. And, worse, the girls had seen proof that the old vampire had been murdering their classmates.

Accordingly, Mrs. Jones had suffered at the hands of the betrayed crowd. Out of control, they had clawed at her skin, chased her down the tunnels, driven her out. Afterward, they had been at loose ends, realizing their folly as well as what Wolfie was sure to do to them now. They also wondered what Mrs. Jones would visit upon them if she should ever return.

Like Noreen, Della hid behind her own hair, as well as the lilac curtain. The mousy veil of frizz had allowed her to fade into the background so many times, and she needed that security now, as Wolfie occasionally lifted his head to call to them from the bed. Calls that they were hesitating to obey.

She didn't wish to look at the vampire girls worshipping every inch of Wolfie's skin, but she kept doing it. They had exhausted him to sleep at dawn, cuddling with him until dusk had returned to awaken them. There were girls holding his hands, kissing his palms. Girls at his feet, stroking his legs. Girls combing their fingers through his brown rock-star hair. Girls running their tongues over his thighs, stomach, and chest.

Stacy, the eldest, who had decades over Della, even as she remained an eternal platinum blond sixteen-year-old, had taken charge of the rest of Wolfie, nestling between his legs to love him there.

Blood rushed through Della, spearing her deep in the belly. Fortunately, the love play would keep him from accessing their thoughts with a master-progeny mind-link; they couldn't afford for him to see what they had truly done to Mrs. Jones.

But she feared that, soon, she, Noreen, and Polly would have to give in to his desires. They were the newest of the Queenshill vampires, freshly brought over from the cat's yearly crop; those who survived her graduated to Wolfie's main Underground, joining the girls whom the Queenshill darlings had recruited on the streets—girls who would not be missed in society and had found a genuine home down here. Della, Polly, and Noreen were the only ones from whom he had not enjoyed the gush of virgin blood.

Through a set of alarming circumstances, they had been brought to the main Underground early. A motley group had wandered onto the Queenshill campus several nights ago, a vampire having been among their number. "Frank" was seeking some of his own kind as company and had found the schoolgirls. Yet, Della had been suspicious of the group's story, and the meeting had got out of order, ending in a melee. When a far more dangerous and mean vampire had shown up to help the intruders—and when one of the intruders had proven to possess strong mental powers that had almost captivated Della—the schoolgirls had fled back to their dorm house. As a precaution, they had been taken off campus, then transferred early to the main Underground.

Even now, Della didn't know how their absence from their "normal lives" at school was being explained. Mrs. Jones, who had masqueraded as a school employee, had been working on explanations that were surely holding. It might be days before the administration thought something amiss and contacted their parents. Not that their mums and dads had ever cared about much when it came to girls like Della, Noreen, and Polly, who had been all but dumped at school and forgotten.

Memory tweaked at Della—the pull of life as it had been before those intruders had shown themselves on campus. School days spent walking under the sun, as their line of vampires could do in modest doses. The mentorship of Mademoiselle, the French teacher. The pull of Melinda, a classmate whom Della had admired beyond any other.

Then Della remembered how, one night, Violet, their former group leader, had coerced Della into feeding from Melinda. Della's stomach tied into knots of guilt.

Just as she crossed her arms over her stomach to press against the tight feeling, to obliterate the remorse and the confusing stimulation, she recalled, also, what she had eventually done to Violet, the bully.

A black cloud formed over Della's vision. Ravens, summoned and spurred on by Della's rage.

Polly and Noreen seemed to sense Della's disquiet, and they glanced at her, their gazes cautious, as if seeing firsthand the carnage Della had wrought on Violet.

Wolfie called to them. "So far away in that corner. You've saved yourselves long enough. Come here, my dears."

Noreen's and Polly's gazes changed from wariness of Della to something else altogether. Though Wolfie had often stopped in Mrs. Jones's sub-Underground to visit and play innocently with them, Mrs. Jones had made certain they had remained untouched—all the tastier for her blood rituals, Della imagined.

Wolfie had propped himself up on his elbows, the other girls continuing to lavish him with their experienced hands.

Noreen accessed Polly and Della with the classmate mind-link. *He wants something new.* She had been his most recent favorite before all the trouble had come upon the Underground, and she knew he would probably rip into her first.

They had all looked forward to the night when it would happen, but now that it was here . . .

Della pushed aside the sheer curtain. Every time Wolfie was near, she knew how much he wanted to have at them. There had been a power in withholding, too. She had intuitively realized this last night, when the older girls had taken the lead.

Polly inched closer to Della. *What now?*

Della stepped away from the fringes, smiling at Wolfie, though she wasn't feeling the same on the inside. *You two know that we are the ultimate distraction for him,* she mind-said to her classmates. *The longer he doesn't know about what really happened with Mrs. Jones, the better.*

But . . . Noreen started.

Hush, Noreen, Polly thought. Back in the sub-Underground, she had acted so knowledgeable, yet her pounding vital signs showed that she was just as afraid as Della and Noreen. Just as excited, as well, because as Della was learning, power was a rush.

Polly continued. *Are you still such a little girl that you can't handle this?*

Noreen shook her head, raising her chin a notch, her red hair falling away from her face. She was shaking, but she stepped away from the curtain, coming just behind Della and Polly.

"There," Wolfie said, his smile growing, his fangs lengthening. Rivulets of blood ran down his pale chest, girls licking at the red. "Come, now."

Stacy, her platinum hair cascading over Wolfie's skin, looked up at Della from where she was rubbing her cheek against his stomach. Della didn't glance lower though. Aside from what she had glimpsed of the boys kept captive in the Underground, she had never seen a grown male's parts in real life. Only in movies and magazines.

The older female vampire grinned at Della, her fangs glinting just past her lips. Their connected gazes allowed them to share thoughts since they weren't immediate classmates.

You're what we need to keep him going, the other girl thought. *He won't be thinking about Mrs. Jones for a while with you three to take our place in bed.*

Still, Della and her classmates hadn't come any nearer. Wolfie must have taken this for coy virtue. All of them had been chosen for the Underground due to their purity, among other reasons, though Violet and Polly had experimented the most before being turned. Yet they had *all* waited for the right one, and Wolfie had been it: The protector who had rescued them from boring, despairing human life. The one who understood them completely.

This was one reason that deciding to become a vampire had been so easy.

He shifted halfway into his wolf form, snout and ears lengthening, his grin growing even more. It was the form he had always used during playtime with them—their lovable, constant Wolfie.

"Come here," he whispered in a growl that was, for the first time, losing its carefree lightness.

Della's body responded, starting its own shift into the wolf-feline form she had inherited from the exchange with both Wolfie and Mrs. Jones, the cat. Children vampires such as Della didn't possess all the abilities and strengths their creators held since blood power weakened from generation to generation, but they were still dangerous with their teeth, their hunger, which had only grown and grown with each hunt.

As the emergence of hair tickled Della's skin, she felt Noreen's fingernails pinch into the back of her arm, and her shift came to an immediate halt.

Noreen was right, Della thought. They still had power over Wolfie. She should hold to that.

The three of them approached the bed while their master shifted back into his humanlike form, his dark hair hanging over his shoulders while he leaned forward, anticipating them. A few Queenshill girls moved aside to make room for the newcomers while Della, Polly, and Noreen arrived at the edge of the mattress.

But, as Della looked into his famished, golden gaze, she saw that this wasn't the Wolfie she had always loved. He was . . . devilish.

That was the term. He was *different*, and the nakedness of his need made her believe that he indeed knew what Mrs. Jones had been doing to their missing classmates.

When he reached out a hand to her, she stepped back, her heart sore. She had been trying so diligently not to believe it.

He seemed raddled. "What is it, Della?"

She could feel Polly and Noreen stiffen beside her. They must be careful, keep him occupied. . . .

But Della had hesitated in answering too long, and now, Wolfie grasped her wrist. She had never seen him like this—so frustrated by his cravings. He had been primed by the other girls, and he was clearly expecting to be brought to greater heights with new blood.

"Wolfie . . ." Della said, uncertainty making her voice shake.

He was beyond chatter, and before she knew it, he

plunged into her mind, as if he had been waiting to go there after the sexual haze from the other girls had worn off.

Out of pure impulse, Della took control, just as she had learned these last several nights: she mentally pushed false images to the front of her mind, lying to him.

She showed him how Mrs. Jones had supposedly attacked Noreen out of jealousy for Wolfie's affections. How the rest of the Queenshill girls had protected one of their own and chased Mrs. Jones out.

When Della was done, Wolfie tilted his head, and she could tell that he had taken this sharing to be a moment of guilt tumbling out of her. In the past, she often became so anxious around him that she made embarrassing errors in judgment, just as he apparently thought she was doing now.

He interpreted what she had shown him to be the truth. She could see it.

What he didn't know was that Della had depended upon this: that a girl who doesn't lie much would be taken at face value when she *did* choose to do so, for when a girl was good, she could get away with quite a bit when she decided to be bad.

He loosened his grip on her, and Della could feel him slipping away, for seeing Mrs. Jones in her mind had reminded him of his companion.

All the other girls glared at her, encouraging her to give Wolfie everything else he wanted. Yet he had already lain back on his pillows, his hair spread, a look of great sadness consuming him.

"Claudia," he said on a sigh.

And that was, as they say, the last straw.

She imagined Wolfie kissing Mrs. Jones so passionately that it made Della feel like nothing in comparison. Then she imagined killing Mrs. Jones, although terminating one half of Della's creators would make her lose half her powers. A termination wouldn't even cause Della to regain her humanity, since Wolfie and Mrs. Jones had both contributed their blood to the exchange and he would have to die, as well.

But it would be worth losing Mrs. Jones's powers—even the ability to drink through skin—just to have Wolfie to themselves.

A sorrowful heaviness rested on Wolfie's mouth as he continued staring at the rock ceiling. "I'm not certain *what* to do with you girls anymore."

Della could feel Stacy still glaring at her.

"Wolfie," Polly said, her voice higher than usual. She was more afraid than any of them, and that surprised Della, especially when the other girl took a deep breath and then coasted a finger over their master's bare forearm. She was obviously game to be the first to sacrifice her blood.

He placed a hand over Polly's fingers, and the very air in the room stilled.

He was not appeased by Polly's willingness. It was too late.

"I realize," he said, growling, "that you lot merely over-reacted when you chased Claudia out, but it was still a sin."

Noreen's mind-link came to Della like a whisper. *Of course he would want her back. We were foolish to think we could take her place. . . .*

His eyes narrowed, almost as if he'd overheard Noreen. "I ought to send all of you above to find her."

Although none of the girls showed a change of expression, Della could sense the waver of trepidation in the room.

"Wolfie," Stacy said, placing a hand on his thigh. "I hardly think—"

"None of you were thinking," he said, finally sounding like a master vampire and not the smitten rogue they'd been wrapping around their fingers. "You had no business banishing her."

"But should she return," Stacy said, "she would punish us, even over a misunderstanding."

"Let me handle her." Wolfie sat up, pressing an ireful look on each one of them. He had passed the point of toying with the idea of getting Mrs. Jones back Underground, clearly having embraced it. "You will track her, since she no doubt spilled enough blood to leave a trail. You will bring her back down here, and then we will talk about misunderstandings."

When he looked at Della, she clutched the silken sheets, more angry than afraid of Mrs. Jones's return. But there was no argument against him—they were in deep trouble. They would have to obey his wishes and endure the consequences.

Unless there was some way out of this.

As Wolfie carried on with looking at the other girls, Della glanced up and made eye contact with Stacy. In the older female's eyes, Della could see a reflection of her own wild jealousy, the hatred of Mrs. Jones as well as Wolfie's abiding affection for the murderer.

If we find the cat . . . Della thought to Stacy.

Without Della even having to finish, the other schoolgirl smiled in understanding. Despising Mrs. Jones trumped even the frustration the other girls were feeling for Della at the moment.

If we find the cat, Stacy thought back, *we* find *the cat.*

Now Della smiled, too, knowing that none of the girls would allow Mrs. Jones back down here. They would undertake this task of Wolfie's because he had commanded it, yet they would make this task their own, too.

Polly had been watching Della and Stacy communicate, and without having to be told, she slid closer to Wolfie while nailing open a slice of skin on her neck.

The scent of her previously forbidden blood made him shiver. His eyes went hazy once again as he sank to the pillows, taking Polly with him as Della and Stacy arose from the bed to prepare the other schoolgirls to go aboveground, where they were not only going to track the cat.

They were going to kill it.

SIX

The Therapy Candidate

Dawn was tangled in Costin's arms, his lips working at her neck, his fangs piercing her. She was dizzy from the small amount of blood Costin had already sucked out of her, and he was taking even more. Not enough to disable her though. Just enough to pump him up, to give him the power that the supplemental bags that he quietly procured from a blood bank didn't.

Since she was his mainstay—the "key" to his quest—her blood had this effect on him. At least, that was what Kiko kept telling her, based on a vision he'd had, the one that'd caused Costin to lure her, an out-of-work stunt-woman, to L.A. in the first place so she could join the team. Kiko even thought she'd be the hunter who was going to destroy the dragon in the end.

But how was she going to do that while Costin waged his *own* attack on this Underground?

With a semipainful slide, he withdrew his fangs from

her vein, then pressed his fingers to the small wound to heal it.

She was high, her knees almost giving out like she didn't have any steel to keep her standing. But Costin's strong hold helped, one of his arms supporting her, bringing her close to his body, making her heart feel like it was being dunked underwater and held there, thudding, thudding, expanding all through her. She could feel his cock, hard against the center of her legs, and she arched against him, giving in to the stirrings of a wildness that marked their feedings.

Then he said something that ruined it all.

"What is this?" The fingertips of his other hand brushed her jaw, near her ear. Her skin burned at the contact, even though his skin was cool.

She'd detected some concern in the question, even while Costin kept his tone steady and low, and it made her remember that she'd felt a sting on her skin in this same exact place earlier.

She reached up to push his hand away, but Costin ignored her, gently tilting her head so he had an even better look. His breath smoothed over her neck, and it didn't do anything to ease the sharp cravings that were tearing her from belly to clit.

"Dawn?" he said.

She moved away from him. His tone scared her.

After trying to read his face—no dice there, because it was as *un*readable as ever—she tried for his mind. She was his master, after all. But he was closed off, even though he'd just been feeding off her blood and they were usually connected during the flow of the act.

Then she thought she saw something like worry pass through his eyes, which were just turning from the silver of his vampire excitement back to his calmer topaz, pacing the retraction of his fangs.

Even more afraid now, Dawn all but stumbled from the

main bedroom and into the marbled bathroom, where she flicked on the light and peered into the mirror.

As she saw the second beauty mark stamped on her jaw, her pulse crept up to choke her. It wound itself into the fresh bite on her neck, pounding like a creature caught and unable to escape.

A second mark—a jagged little circle without much of a shape. A small sign on her skin that was just beginning to form into something new and unpredictable.

It took a few seconds for her to really get it—that this was *her* she was looking at in the mirror. That this was her skin, her face, not some stranger's. But then the fear and panic caught up to her, and she headed for the toilet, her stomach roiling.

As she got to her knees, Costin put his palm on her back. His touch singed into her, even through her shirt. The braid she wore flopped down to smack her bite wound, and Costin pulled the hair back again, pressing his fingers to the injury, seeing to the last of the healing.

Minutes passed and she didn't get sick, so she kneeled back from the porcelain god. Costin took a washcloth out of a drawer, wet it, then offered it to her. When she wiped it over her face, it was cold.

Why wasn't he saying anything? Didn't he know that some comment, any comment, would do wonders right about now?

"No feedback?" Dawn sounded like she was gagging on her words. "Haven't you ever seen a hunter mutate before your eyes?"

They'd had discussions about why he'd always switched out his teams with every new Underground hunt. He said it was basically because a few "employees" had learned too much information and used it to pursue their own agendas with the vampires, thus, ignoring his orders, so he'd taken great caution to see that this would never happen again. But Dawn had also found out that he was trying to prevent his

hunters from going insane, as the humans he recruited had
the habit of doing after too much mind-boggling stress.

He'd only kept Dawn's team intact because of what *he'd*
become: something other than a Soul Traveler. A weaker
creature next to what he used to be. A desperate leader in
need of all the trusted backup he could get so he could hit
the ground running with this new Underground.

He'd probably been right to dismantle his previous
teams before they became walking disasters like Dawn.
Maybe he was always right about the precautions he took,
the moves he made, the secrets he kept.

"I have never seen the likes of this before," he finally
said. "These marks, coming out on the skin."

"During all your years of fighting Undergrounds, you
never noticed any of the other vampires-turned-humans react like this after their maker was terminated?"

"No."

So she was something brand spankin' new. A real
trailblazer.

"However," he added, "until now, I have never kept in
contact with reformed vampires. After being freed from
their master and receiving their souls again, they have always tended to react just as the Hollywood crowd did,
committing suicide or running away, never to be heard
from again. When some are turned human, they even die an
accelerated death because of returning to their true age."

When Dawn had gotten her soul back after becoming
one of "them" for a few minutes, she'd felt something different, just like her mom had. But as far as Dawn could see,
Eva hadn't exhibited any outer changes.

Dawn got to her feet, her legs still shaking, then met her
own gaze in the mirror. She had her mom's eyes.

But the thought died right there as she angled her head,
looking at the new beauty mark again. It was barely there,
but screamingly obvious just the same.

"I don't understand," she said. "When I got the first one,

it was when I was raging at Claudius. But I thought I felt *this* spot pop out when . . ." She swallowed, reaching for the spigot, twisting it on, and running some more cold water over her hands, then her face. As she shut the faucet off, the droplets plunked into the sink. "I thought the first one was a mark against me, like a scarlet letter or whatever. But today, I held back with Claudius. I didn't Hulk out. So how did this new one get here?"

"I am not certain. However, there are those who believe that our cells react to our thoughts and emotions. Our bodies change when the mind affects them, and perhaps the marks are a more intense result of what is happening inside of you."

"Like hives?"

"Perhaps. It could be a release of even more poisonous energy."

While the water kept dripping, Costin walked out of the bathroom and her mind raced.

She'd held back today. She'd repressed the ugliness, but it'd come out anyway—a situation that echoed the one from over a year ago, when she'd mentally boxed away the memory of seeing Eva's supposedly dead body in a crime scene photo. Yet, back then, Dawn hadn't been marked on her face when she'd forced back the hideous emotions. It'd been her mind powers that'd emerged full force instead.

Was she just operating differently now because of her tarnished soul? Had the darkness inside just been waiting for her to cross over some previously taboo lines to start up with this new fun?

Costin returned within a minute, urging a bottle of supplement juice on her, along with a bagel. She took a swig of the juice and it slid down her throat to her stomach, which was still churning.

"I have no solid answers about what is occurring with you," he said, "but I do have a theory."

Great, one of those.

He gave it to her. "We are seeing that, no matter if you keep your anger back or give freedom to it, it will materialize."

The juice lined her mouth with a bitter aftertaste.

"And," he added, "perhaps these marks have something to do with how you . . ." He trailed off.

"Just say it, Costin."

He lowered his tone, but it didn't sting any less. "Perhaps you have come to enjoy your anger, Dawn, and your body is punishing you for it."

"Wait, I see where this is going. You're going to tell me that there's a difference between fighting against the enemy, doing the job I have to do, and actually liking it. And I've started liking it too much." Costin was an example of a hunter who didn't cotton to his calling, whereas night by night, it was becoming apparent that she was the opposite.

Maybe that should've frightened her more, but it didn't.

Forcing down the bagel and the rest of the juice, she left the bathroom on still-wobbly legs, going to the closet, where there was a weapons locker in back of all the hanging dark clothing that both she and Costin—and Jonah—preferred to wear. She unlocked the cache door behind a rack of coats as he followed her.

"Or," he said, "we could look at your changes in this way: sometimes, I think you despise yourself more than you do the enemy. The marks could be a sign of that, as well."

"Like self-mutilation? I'm no cutter." Grabbing a hip holster from the locker, she wrapped it around herself, buckling it. She didn't add that she thought Costin probably resented her even more than she did herself, what with this whole human master/vampire progeny relationship that he'd never wanted.

"When I return from the Underground," he said, "we need to talk about this at greater length."

He was so damned sure he *was* going to return.

She should be, too. "So we'll talk then."

"I mean we should *talk*. And we should include . . . others."

The way he said it made her bristle. "Why do I have the feeling you're suggesting a shrink?"

"I would not rule out professional guidance."

Jay-sus. "I don't do therapy. Never have, never will."

"It might have been appropriate, given your relationship with Eva, for one matter. I am sure it led to where you are now."

As she grasped a machete to shove into her holster, she tossed a miffed look at him. Had he really just brought up her whole "I love my gorgeous, former-superstar mom/I hate my gorgeous, former-superstar mom" thing? Sure, an Eva complex had shaped her life and wigged her out plenty, but she'd learned to cope in her own way. Dawn had competed with Eva for over two decades before her mom had come back from the dead, compliments of the Hollywood Underground.

"Yes, Costin. I'll get right on doing an Internet search for a therapist who specializes in addressing the pansy side of vamp hunters. I'm sure I'll get a million hits."

"Why can't you understand that I am delicately trying to suggest some anger management?"

Anger?

She'd grown up with it. It'd raised her better than Frank ever had, protected her, kept her going.

She reached into the locker again, this time for a UV grenade. "Are there any other instructions you need to give me before you leave?"

Costin knew that when she was done with a topic, she was done, so he cleared his throat as she went for a second UV grenade and tucked that one into her holster belt, too. In her back pocket, her cell phone vibrated with what was probably another voice mail from Kiko. Before she'd fed Costin, she'd called the psychic and left her own message for him and Natalia to get back to headquarters. Hopefully, he was telling her they were here.

Costin said, "I do have a few important items to discuss with you." But, first, he scanned her weapons and addressed that instead. "Dawn, you know that the Friends have been on high alert since Claudius arrived."

"And you know I like to be prepared, even if I'm surrounded by fortified walls. Or are you just thinking that I'm going to be sneaking outside with this stuff and following you Underground, like I did in L.A.?"

"No, Dawn, I don't think you will do that, mostly because you are aware of the ammunition I bring with me to an Underground. I have complete faith in the Friends. They have never before let me down and they will not now. They have their own ways of fighting, as with the silver flakes they used in the Hollywood Underground."

"You should believe in them, Costin. And I know you've faced the dragon before and come out of it in one piece. Thing is, that's when you could get out of body."

He was brooking no argument. "Dawn, you are to wait until sunrise to inform the rest of the team that I am gone. The information detracts from what you will all need to focus on—guarding Claudius throughout the night. Chances are high that the vampire schoolgirls will come for their second master under the cover of darkness. There is no reason for the team to worry about me during this time. I am only telling you because, out of everyone, you would most notice my absence."

Sure, Dawn thought, closing the locker door. It had nothing at all to do with him distrusting the team because most of them had interfered with Costin's ultimate attack in Hollywood.

"Can you tell me why we don't just kill Claudius?" she asked. "If we did, it'd cut those schoolgirls' vamp powers in two—they would only have the ones they inherited from Mihas."

"There is more than one reason, but above all, Claudius is our insurance."

Insurance? She glanced over her shoulder at Costin, who seemed so damned self-assured, even though he'd just revealed that he might not be. Her heart hurt at the thought of him suffering in any way. Stupid heart.

"Are you telling me," she said, "that you suspect Claudius isn't being entirely truthful with you about the Underground's location, even though you read it through your Awareness?"

"Although my misreading him is unlikely, keeping him alive is a wise policy . . . just in case. If he has lied to me and covered it up, it will be on you to extract the true Underground location from him, then carry on from there."

He was so nonchalant about his possible death that it took a second for the impact to hit her.

This might be the night he left her.

As she wrestled with this, she said, "If it came down to that, I'd want to get *your* location from Claudius, along with the details of any trap that caught you. That way we'd be prepared to avoid what you couldn't if we had to make a rescue."

"I forbid you to come for me before you take care of the Underground. Is that clear, Dawn?"

She didn't argue, even though she knew she'd never leave Costin to any vamp trap.

He went back to being matter-of-fact. "As I said, we should expect that Claudius will lure the lower vampires here and leave the Underground that much less populated. And if they do come aboveground for him, this means you are aiding me in the fight, Dawn. You would make my job that much easier. This is also the reason you and the team must stay."

He might be gone by morning. . . .

She stood, still a bit dizzy, but not really because of the blood he'd taken. "All right."

She had to believe that he knew what he was doing. He was Costin, and he'd survived this long. Besides, there was the tiny fact that she'd learned the hard way in Hollywood that following directions was a good idea.

"So you've chosen the Friends who'll be with you?" she asked, trying to let him go gracefully.

He almost seemed relieved, not that his ramrod posture assured her or anything.

"I have chosen those who work best with me," he said. "We have pulled most of the Friends off patrol from around the city. A group will remain here, of course, but Breisi will be leading the contingent that goes Underground with me. Although the Friends' lulling didn't seem to have any effect on Claudius when they first tried it, while I was conducting an earlier interview with him, they discovered that modulating their voices to a higher frequency was working. We hope to use the element of surprise by retuning the lulling to control the lower vampires while I question Mihas about the dragon and then terminate him. After Mihas is taken care of, I shall send word back to you, and I expect you to do what needs to be done in order to turn the vampire girls fully human."

Dawn had no problem with killing Claudius when required. That was what needed to happen if Costin was going to get his soul back. Short of killing herself, she didn't know what else to do to free him from Jonah's body. As she was Jonah's creator, her death would make him human again and hopefully release Costin's essence, restoring him to the Soul Traveler he'd been before. On occasion, Frank had accused her of having a death wish that would fulfill this option, but she'd rather release Costin from Jonah the long way—through completing Costin's mission.

"You can count on me to take care of Claudius," Dawn said. "Are you going to tell me where you're going? Just in case?"

"I will give the location to the Friends who remain here."

Dawn tried not to give way to a cutting laugh. But how could she blame him for these precautions—never giving out too much information to a hunter who had a history as a loose cannon—when this was exactly the sort of safeguard that had kept his teams running smoothly in the past?

She'd just thought she was his "key."

"The Friends know all the backup plans," he said.

"But what if this Underground has learned how to captivate them, just like in Hollywood, and we corporeal team members find ourselves without spiritual aid?"

"Without the Friends, I am as good as gone this time."

In denial of that, her anger rose, and it placated her with its familiarity. "I still want to come with you. I wouldn't get out of line—not like the first time."

"Dawn." Apologetic. But he wasn't going to give an inch. Not the warrior, no matter how special he said she was to him. "Each member has her or his own function on the team, and you very well know why *you* are important."

Functions. She thought about how Breisi, back before she'd died and become a Friend, had known more of Costin's hidden strategies than any of the team. Then Dawn wondered who had taken Breisi's place on this hunt.

"Is one of us going to know where you're headed, too, Costin? I'm guessing you'll be wearing a locator, so you can be monitored."

He remained silent, showing his commitment to keeping this a secret, even though she had her suspicions about who that team member was.

But he didn't need this right now, so she backed off. His plans *would* work.

"I just hope Claudius isn't sending you into some kind of trap," she said. "That's why I'm being such a bitch about this."

"Dawn."

She walked right past him, out of the closet and into the bedroom.

"*I* only hope," he said from behind her, "that this is the Underground that is holding the dragon. What I would give for the end to be near."

She glanced over her shoulder to see him smiling—a smile from an exhausted soldier who sensed possible deliverance within his reach.

Dawn tried not to think about what that meant: what life would be like without him as a purpose, as a companion. If she'd be better or worse off without him.

Girding herself, she went for the door, opened it, and a burst of jasmine gushed in, as if it'd been eavesdropping outside.

Costin didn't react as he moved into the hall, just behind Dawn. "Kalin," he said, greeting the most annoying Friend in the bunch. She was an older hunter, active around the time of Henry VIII. As a human, she'd had witchlike powers that included summoning fire—a trait she couldn't carry over into the Friend world.

Dawn heard the spirit's voice airily chattering away at Costin while they headed for the stairs.

"She doesn't want you to go," Dawn said, stating the obvious.

"True," Costin said. "Like you, Kalin wishes to accompany me and Jonah, but she will be staying here, guarding headquarters."

Aw, crap. "I thought you were going to give this idgit some real guff for the trouble she's been causing." Dawn gestured at the air. "Her little crush on Jonah has been nothing but a headache for everyone because she takes up his side instead of yours. Is her big punishment to stay here instead of going with you?"

Kalin bumped into Dawn, but Dawn was used to the scrapping.

"Kalin," Costin said, and it was the first time she'd heard his tone even approach a bark.

The spirit let out a high-pitched scream of frustration that rang in Dawn's ears until she had to put her hands over them. Costin withstood it, as unruffled as always.

When Kalin was done, Dawn said, "Don't tell me— she's trying to get Jonah to come out so *he* can take her Underground with him."

Costin nodded.

"Yeesh." Dawn looked where he was looking, thinking it'd be Kalin she was addressing. "Would you get with it? You should know that Jonah's going to be dominant when the body gets outside. He'll shelter Costin until it's time for some heavy-duty hypnosis, then it's Costin's game. They'll keep each other safe."

Big words from a woman who doubted them.

Kalin screeched again.

"Silence," Costin said, raising his voice enough so that Dawn could've sworn the walls shook a little. "Kalin, you are in charge of defense here. I have trusted you over the years and you have always been one of my strongest. This is no time to disappoint me."

Kalin shut right up at that. She was exasperating, but Dawn knew the spirit was loyal to the cause itself. Otherwise, Costin would've destroyed her home portrait, if that was how to send a Friend into the afterlife before their vow of service was complete. Costin hadn't validated Dawn's theory when she'd asked him about it once, maybe because he thought she would go straight for Kalin's picture and slash it to bits.

As the Friend lingered, Costin continued down the hall, his brow furrowed.

Why? Had Kalin's attempt to bring out Jonah discomfited Costin? Could it be that he was expecting his host to assert himself at any time now?

Maybe he shouldn't trust Jonah, even though the host was behaving right now. He tended to get excited, and if he thought Costin wasn't handling things properly, he wouldn't hesitate to take over; he'd grown so strong in his own body that he often assumed control of it.

Costin seemed to anticipate her pointing all this out, and he turned around just as he stopped in front of a door that led to his own strategy room—a place where he sometimes retreated without her.

"Soon," he said, "this *will* be over."

She wanted to remind him that they'd only be going after another Underground—one they'd have to hunt down and learn all over again since all of the communities had specific skill sets and modes of operation.

Unless Costin vanquished the dragon tonight. If previous master deaths were any indication, the ultimate master's demise would turn its direct progeny human again, and all Costin would have to do is fulfill his vow to The Whisper by terminating the rest of the much easier to kill humanized brothers.

"Just one more thing," she said, hanging on to every second. "What about Kiko's 'key' vision, where I—"

"Vanquish a key vampire." Now he looked more troubled. But then he was back to being Costin. "Who is to say that you will not be encountering an important vampire on your own, Dawn?"

So maybe this wasn't about trust. Maybe he'd put more of it in her than she'd realized.

At his vote of confidence, she went to him, grabbed ahold of the front of his shirt. He'd be changing into something more battle-worthy. Something more comfortable to fight in.

"Then this is it," she said. "You're preparing the last details before you leave."

"Yes. And, Dawn? If I do not return by tomorrow's sunset, you must follow my wishes. Find the real Underground without me. Even if I am gone, the world will still need you and the team to help it. But do not make a move outside before dusk tomorrow, no matter what you think you should do. Understood? I might need the time to infiltrate this Underground, and for the team to come rushing in would destroy any progress I might have gained."

She shook her head, but he rested a palm against her cheek, peering into her eyes and allowing her in for one precious moment.

She saw golden days stretching into the future. Hope. Confidence.

As he pulled out, leaving her with a sizzling ache, she tightened her grasp on him. Her throat closed around her next words.

"If that's the way you want it, Godspeed, Costin."

She'd said it, even though she didn't believe in much of anything. At least, that was what she'd always told herself. Then she angled forward, closing her eyes as she rested her forehead against his, putting her mouth to his lips.

Costin wrapped his arms around her as she kissed him, pulling her closer, harder, like this would be the final time.

Then he slowly eased back, opened the door behind him, and retreated with one last long gaze.

Good-bye, she thought. It might've been their final time together, and there was still so much to say. To admit.

But, as the door shut, Dawn didn't move.

He *would* be back.

She forced herself to head down the stairs to make sure every inch of headquarters was fortified, playing her own role in this nightmare, too.

SEVEN

The Shadows Know

Dawn spent the rest of the day and much of the night keeping busy by going over security precautions, overseeing similar assignments for the rest of the team, and meeting with the Friends to make sure they were all on the same page.

She was busy enough to almost forget that Costin had no doubt already left and was probably Underground.

But she never *did* quite forget.

After she'd submerged herself in checking to see that the outside UV lights were functioning properly, she went to one of the lower-level rear entrances in a rarely used area that everyone only paid cursory attention to. Luckily, she spent a little more time than that, because she noticed one of the safeguards—a laser tracker—had been tripped within the past twenty-four hours.

At first, she pulled a machete out of her holster as she inspected the cemented, empty area for an intruder. Then, when nothing jumped her, she thought, *Why didn't the alarm alert a Friend?*

Nerves at level "oh my God," Dawn went down the spartan hall to access a security camera feed to see what the problem might've been. All the while, she went over logistics: There was a Friend entrance near the rear door, but the spirits had never tripped the alarm before. And the team was usually real good about resetting anything and everything.

Maybe Natalia, the new girl on the team, had gone through this entrance and forgotten . . . ?

Dawn could only hope.

Nearly at the security camera room, Dawn summoned a Friend and let her know they all should be on even better lookout. Then she entered the room, where feeds from all over the house were gathered. But when she took a look at the footage, there was nothing to show that this back door had been used lately, much less breached.

Was it an alarm malfunction? *Had* a Friend, with the spirits' invisible ins and outs, tripped it without knowing?

Or had something else without form come into headquarters and hidden itself, and was now waiting to materialize?

Even though Costin's interrogation of Claudius hadn't indicated that these vamps had invisibility powers, Dawn's stomach clenched. She called for a Friend again, identifying this one as Evangeline, her French accent making it pretty obvious.

She was just as stymied by the glitch as Dawn was, and she took off to network with her spiritual buddies to see if she could get to the bottom of this.

Meanwhile, Dawn dialed up Kiko on her cell to see where he and Natalia were. Headquarters was too big to shout to each other in, like the Waltons' house or something.

Kiko told her they were in the computer room, a place decorated with the hand of technological necessity, with big plasma computer screens, televisions, virtual reality stations that could play training scenarios, and a bevy of readouts and maps marked up with locations they'd investigated as well as possible spots where the Underground might be located.

Dawn stumbled over the word on the way to the room. *Underground.*

Costin.

She hadn't told the others he'd gone, but that was how he wanted it. This time, she was going to do what was right and let him do his job.

Taking in a long, achy breath, then expelling it, she walked into the computer room. Kiko and Natalia glanced up from their project du jour. They'd put red tape on the carpet, and even though Dawn didn't have the first idea what the hell they were doing, she suspected it'd make sense after Kiko motor-mouthed an explanation.

When he nodded in greeting, she noticed a spaciness to him, and she knew that he'd been lulled by a Friend since he'd gotten back from Eva's flat. Back in the States, he'd gotten addicted to painkillers after breaking his back during a vamp fight. He'd traded one addiction for another, and Dawn didn't know what else to do about him.

But it wasn't like a Friend could de-lull him now, so Dawn rolled with it, thinking he'd probably still do okay in a vamp attack if there was one. Lulling from a Friend wasn't half as destructive on the brain and body as pills—he was just more relaxed than usual.

"We finished our security checklist," he said, getting to his feet. He wore a grin, along with little-person-sized canvas pants—the multitude of pockets bulging with various weapons—and a long-sleeved T-shirt with a surf logo on the pocket. He didn't do the sport, but his California blond hair marked him as an eternal Los Angeleno who might drive around with a board on top of his rig, just to pretend he could ride. Hell, he'd spent a lot of years *acting!* in the Hollywood biz, so why stop in London?

Next to him, Natalia Petri, who also had psychic powers, took notes on a pad. As an average-sized gal, she towered over Kiko, her curly dark hair pulled back in a barrette, revealing the slight bump on her forehead she'd gotten when she'd passed out during a Ouija board interviewing session. Her healthy figure was decked out in a beige pantsuit and flats she'd brought over with her from the mother country in Romania. What pockets she had were also full of what Dawn guessed were smaller, basic-level weapons like crucifixes, silver knives, and small stakes, since she was still a newbie.

"Visual aid," Natalia said, motioning at the red tape. Being the one team member who'd been appalled at Dawn's technique with Claudius last night, she was obviously still trying hard not to make eye contact. "We have laid out the scene, based on the Shadow Girl visions we had at Eva's flat. Since we've been so successful with visions in the past"—they'd basically guided the team step-by-step toward the Underground—"we're paying close attention to anything we get."

"I'm telling ya," Kiko said, "when we've had enough of this vamp hunting, I'm looking into freelance psychic work. The Pentagon would be asshats not to use me and you, Nat."

As Natalia smiled at him, Dawn looked right past the new closeness between the two psychics, who'd started out at each other's throats when Costin had first hired Natalia.

Instead, Dawn perused the scene again, putting her questions about the tripped laser alarm on the back burner for a curious second. There were black-marker numbers scribbled over taped arrows and lines.

"So, let me get this straight," she said to Natalia. "After you had your vision last night of Shadow Girl attacking me in Eva's flat, you two tramped over there to see if Kiko could use his psychometric skills to get anything more. This is the bewildering result."

Kiko elaborated. "I got a fragmented bunch of images from touching everything around Eva's place. We're trying to make sense of it, and having you here to help us is just what the doctor ordered. We've got a thousand things to ask you."

While Kiko spoke, Natalia glanced at the door, as if she sensed someone entering.

Dawn turned around, but no one was there—not until her father showed up, walking on those vampire-stealthy feet. Natalia had sensed him early because she had a psychic gift that allowed her to know a vamp was nearby—a sort of auditory perception, almost like she was tuned in to a frequency nobody else could access.

Frank—an ex–bar bouncer who'd retained his muscles in the afterlife—was garbed in basic black shirt, pants, combat boots, and a knit cap that tended to stifle his heightened hearing, which drove him crazy sometimes. He half sat on the corner of a table, gesturing for them to ignore him and keep talking. Then Frank glanced at Dawn, and she anxiously waited to see if he'd changed his mind about being all good with her after the incident with Claudius.

Frank had comforted her afterward, but the pathetic part of her who still wanted to please Daddy hung in the balance, even after years of his neglect and the start of this newfound, tentative relationship they had now.

Did he really think his daughter was okay? Or had he just been *acting!* like everything was all right?

Dawn continued the conversation with Kiko. "Before we start with show-and-tell, I need to know this: when you guys went out this morning, did you use the lowest rear entrance?"

Both Kiko and Natalia shook their heads.

"Why?" he asked.

"Because something tripped the laser tracker back there," she said. "I need to find out what it was."

Natalia scribbled down notes while Kiko asked, "Don't we have a camera trained on that area?"

"We do, but nothing seemed out of the ordinary on the recording. The timer count wasn't disturbed, either. Evangeline's checking into it with the other Friends."

"Maybe it's something harmless," Frank said. "A malfunction that's only bound to make us paranoid."

"Or not," Kiko said.

Natalia had lowered her notebook. "Aren't Friends guarding the property? Watching out for strange occurrences?"

"Yup." Dawn almost added that Friends were watching over all of them while Costin was Underground on his own, but she knew she should give him a little more time before she made that dramatic announcement. It wasn't sunrise yet, when the team was allowed to know and the chances of a schoolgirl attack lowered considerably since no sane vamp would be so obvious in the daylight, especially when their powers were weaker.

She just wished the sun would come. That Costin would hurry up, too.

Kiko grinned at Natalia. "I'd bank on any Friend to keep an eye on my back. You shouldn't be nervous about a breach."

"It's only that the timing is . . . nerve-wracking," Natalia said. "We bring Claudius here and then there's a security concern."

"Costin didn't mention any concern about it," Dawn said. And she was sure he would've if it had been a problem.

But what if the alarm had failed to notify *anyone* during the flurry of activity before he'd left?

Frank grumbled. "Costin doesn't mention much. We all know that."

The only time Dawn had seen her dad question the boss was in L.A., when he'd gone on the Underground siege. But Frank had mellowed since then.

"Anyhow," she said, "the time stamp on the tracker indicates it was tripped just before sunrise. If someone or something wiggled into headquarters and intended to get to Claudius, I imagine it would've already rescued him by now. Or that the Friends would've already noticed a presence."

"Whatever the sitch, I'm walking around fully armed," Kiko said, nodding toward a weapons cache near a map on the wall. Then he patted one of the bulging pockets of his pants. "I've been packin' because of Claudius, anyway."

Natalia just looked like a deer in the headlights, and when Dawn tried to send her a reassuring glance, she wasn't sure it worked so well.

"Has anyone checked on Eva recently?" the new girl asked. "Maybe she tripped the tracker."

"She's been in her room nonstop," Kiko said.

"And that camera would've caught her sneaking out," Dawn said, glancing at Frank. He was staring at the ground, his jaw tight. Eva, his former wife, had tried to win him back with her blood before the Claudius situation even happened, and Breisi, his Friend lover, had gotten on his case because he'd almost given in to the temptation of a live feeding. He'd been taking sustenance from Eva's bagged blood since it did something for him that other blood didn't, but a live feeding was manna to a vampire.

"Aw, let's just say what's too awkward to say," Frank muttered. "Eva's holed up because she's avoiding me. She's embarrassed about our own little soap opera."

Dawn felt herself blushing. Who wanted to think of their parents acting all hormonal? "I just can't shake this feeling I've had that there's something up with Eva, and her staying in that bedroom is just the half of it."

Frank leaned forward. "And the other half would be . . . ?"

Jeez. Her dad should've picked up on everything else. They'd been married, in love, for God's sake.

But maybe that was what love amounted to: a great big nothing. Destructive, bubble-brained antics that ended with a grown woman holed up in her bedroom for nights on end.

"You haven't noticed any depression?" Dawn asked her dad.

"Well . . ."

"Well? Shit, Frank, I guess I'll have to get the two of you together for a convo after the Underground is taken care of." Maybe they could all use the same shrink. "You really haven't seen Eva dragging around, trying to look happy when it's obvious that she hasn't been since L.A.?"

"Dawn, if this is another tirade because you feel guilty about turning her back human—"

"It's not." Fuck it. And screw it all, because she *wanted* Frank to be with Breisi, who fulfilled him in ways Eva had never done. Breisi was good for him. But Dawn also wanted to piece together the family she'd never had while growing up.

Hell, who knew what she wanted.

While Kiko and Natalia stood by, looking like they were wishing the computers would suck them into their screens, Dawn wrapped up family dirty laundry hour. It all seemed so idiotic when an attack could come at any time and when there'd been a tripped alarm.

"Kik, could you do me a favor with Eva when things calm down?"

"Name it."

"Could you visit her? Try to get some kind of reading to see if there's anything I can do to help?"

Kiko agreed, yet Dawn could see his puzzlement. But none of them had been with her on the night she'd brought Eva back from running away, after her mom had attempted to seduce Frank with her blood. They hadn't seen how weird her mother was acting, all giddy and girlish, a one-eighty from sorrowful, wistful Eva.

What had happened in that wine bar she'd run to? What had caused her to turn around her attitude like that?

Dawn gestured toward the tape markings on the floor, knowing there was nothing much else she could do about anything until Friend Evangeline got back with news about the alarm. Or until they heard something from Costin. For all Dawn knew, he was on his way back from the Underground and there'd be a big party in store.

But just in case, she'd keep detecting.

"Want to tell us what you found out about Shadow Girl?" she asked Kiko.

He rubbed his hands together. He loved Sherlock Holmes–ing. "I think we reconstructed Shadow Girl's attack on you. How's that for a start?"

"Truthfully? It's not that helpful. I already know how we fought." Shadow Chick, looking like an evil Spider-Girl and sounding like a tangle-voiced assassin, had almost kicked all kinds of ass until Dawn had used her mind powers to level the playing field. Breisi had charged into Eva's flat to chase Shadow Girl out, yet they hadn't caught her.

"But," Kiko said, raising a finger, "do you know *why* she fought you?"

Okay. Interested now. "Do *you* know?"

Kiko went from looking hugely superior to deflating a bit. "Kind of." But then he puffed up again. "See, while I went around Eva's flat touching things and receiving images and vibes, Natalia opened herself up for impressions, too."

The other psychic held up her notebook. There were numbers as well as what looked to be a running commentary. "Every numeral that's written on the tape matches an impression we received while concentrating on that particular location."

Kiko moved to the left, where the number one was written on some tape that was strung from the top of one computer screen to another. "Let's start right here. This is the window where Shadow Girl first looked in to get a peek at you."

"I caught what was in her mind," Natalia said.

Dawn waited, but the new girl hesitated.

Kiko rolled his eyes. "Nat's too much of a lady to say it, but when the shadow thing saw you, she thought, 'Well, fuck me!' But it was a happy, excited 'Well, fuck me!' like what a hunter thinks when it spots its prey. Pure elation and anticipation."

"Never thought of myself as prey," Dawn said. Watched. Tracked. Shit.

"She'd been observing you way before you got into Eva's flat," Kiko said.

As Dawn held back a shiver, he moved to number two written on some tape on the floor.

"And here," he said, pointing, "is where Shadow Girl landed after she crashed through the window. Now we find out that you were in for a real battle, Dawn."

Natalia spoke up. "She wanted you to fight her with all you had. We felt that this shadow thing takes great satisfaction in stalking, in trapping. She was going to capture you, Dawn. Question you."

Dawn had already known about the questioning part since Shadow Girl had taunted her with that bit, but she tried not to let the reminder creep her out, too.

"Let's get to the nitty-gritty," she said, thinking they could be here all night if she allowed Kiko free rein to show off everything he and Natalia had sensed. "Is this Shadow Girl on the side of the vamps or is she a rival hunter?"

"No confirmation either way," Kiko said.

Natalia was shaking her head.

"What?" Dawn asked. "You disagree?"

"Somewhat. I felt a vague defensive instinct in her. *I* would interpret it as her wishing to protect the vampires."

"Not the answer I was hoping for."

Somewhere in the house, she thought she heard a door slam, and she spun toward the room's entrance.

Costin? Had he already come back?

Then her blood turned cold. Costin wasn't a slammer.

Frank had heard it, too, and he was already on his feet, his knit cap tossed to the ground as he headed toward the room's exit. Dawn followed, a stake already drawn from its holster.

"Stay in here," she said to Kiko, who already had a revolver loaded with silver bullets in hand. He was in front of Natalia like a bodyguard.

Dawn gave Frank the lead, since his vampire senses could pick out scents and sounds way beyond her reaches.

The tripped alarm, she thought. Had an intruder decided that now was a good time to come out of hiding?

Or did the team have company of a different sort?

When Frank and she got to the foyer, they found the source of the sound.

"Dawn!"

It was a Friend, and from the inflection, Dawn could tell it was Evangeline.

"Do you know who might've tripped that laser alarm?" Dawn asked. Maybe the slamming door had been caused by Evangeline's windy speed after she'd reentered the house through one of their activated entrances.

"It was due to none of the Friends," the spirit said, her voice spinning, ethereal. *"Dawn, we must—"*

She was drowned out by the forceful trills of other Friends as they entered the room, their jasmine swirling around Dawn and Frank. One even knocked down a pewter vase balanced on a shelf.

"Lock down!" she said as she passed Dawn.

"They're coming!" said another. *"And they're not alone!"*

"Who? Vamps?" Even though Dawn had half expected

them, she still couldn't believe that this relatively flagrant Underground would be moronic enough to attack in public, whether it was the dead of night or not.

"*Charmed humans,*" Evangeline said. "*The vampires seem to be rounding them up!*"

Charmed humans?

Dawn should've known. If the vampires were coming, smart ones wouldn't be doing it so obviously at first—not until headquarters was broken down enough for them to easily enter, under quieter cover. The humans were probably going to do the dirty work for them.

So. How did a person fight other humans who were on the side of vamps? How did a hunter avoid killing innocent bystanders caught in the crap?

Frank strode to the weapons cache near the door, opened the safe, then extracted two machetes and a couple of earpieces, one of which he handed to Dawn.

"Those vamps're here to get Claudius," he said calmly. "And they're gonna be spanked for it."

Some of the Friends shot off to different areas, no doubt to guard Kiko and Natalia while the rest of them zoomed toward the walls, positioning themselves on high ground.

"Is my mom going to be covered in her room?" Dawn asked.

One of the Friends answered; Mary-Margaret, with her Georgia accent. "*We've been leaving Eva alone since she's been bed-bound, but one of us has gone to her now, Dawn.*"

"Good." She knew what she had to do next, where to position herself.

Dawn fitted the earpiece into her ear, then headed toward the lab and the vampire Claudius.

EIGHT

ABOVEGROUND, I

A LINEUP of Queenshill schoolgirls loitered in a dark alleyway, thirty meters from where they thought their target to be in a brick building across from the gated concrete slab known as the Cross Bones Graveyard.

Back in the Underground, the vampires had taken merely five minutes to come up with a plan that was sure to alleviate their problems. First, they would indeed utilize their animalistic vampire senses to track Mrs. Jones, thus obeying Wolfie. But when they found their former housematron, they would finish off what they hadn't been able to accomplish last night: her death.

Wolfie would never know, for he and Mrs. Jones would have too much distance and earth between them to communicate with each other, mind-to-mind. And the schoolgirls would always keep her fate amongst themselves. They had vowed it to each other.

Since Mrs. Jones had been bleeding when she had been disgorged from the community, the hunt had been rather simple, the schoolgirls' noses leading them from Highgate to an abandoned building in Dalston, to the edge of the building here in Southwark where the scents disappeared. Much to Della's excitement, there was a bonus in this hunt, for what else did she and Noreen discern but the smell of those attackers who had trespassed on the Queenshill campus nights ago.

For some reason, they were with Mrs. Jones in the building.

Though Della was excited, she was also afraid. The mean vampire—the lean one with the dark hair who had killed the dogs at Queenshill, exhibiting such bloodlust—would surely be inside, too. But the girls numbered twenty-five, whereas there were far fewer of the others.

Yet, how would the girls go inside without being invited? This was the quandary. Their head girl, Stacy, had also noted the presence of well-camouflaged light sources near the door, and Della frightfully recalled the UV grenades that the attackers had used on them during the melee.

So the schoolgirls had stayed hidden at first, heeding Della's warnings about these attackers and their possible motivations. Della had believed the group might even be from a rival Underground intent upon taking over Wolfie's community. In any case, if they were entertaining Mrs. Jones, or keeping the old vampire against her will, they were to be treated as the enemy.

Stacy—smarter, wiser, savvier Stacy—had suspected that the girls probably wouldn't be able to sashay into this building without a care. It was only a shame that they couldn't shift into any other human shape, as Mrs. Jones clearly could; their blood was weaker and they had inherited merely the ability to take animal form.

But the head girl had come upon an idea certain to maintain their safety, as well as their identities, while gaining access.

Charmed humans, she had said. Though the older girls
weren't at the level of Mrs. Jones's charm, they had honed
this power far beyond the ability to keep prey quiet. Plus, in
the dark of night, outside the closing pubs, at a time when
most wiser men and women had already taken to their
homes, it hadn't required much effort to approach several
plastered subjects who still hadn't abandoned the streets.

Easily persuadable. Easily charmed to do a vampire's
bidding so the girls could take care of Mrs. Jones, once and
for all. They must use charm sparingly, though, as it could
require the task of erasing the thrall from the human. And
if that wasn't done thoroughly, it could result in trouble for
their kind. In spite of occasional missteps, the girls had
been taught to avoid producing any suspicion of strange,
paranormal activity that would put the public on alert,
though Wolfie had always promised that, one day, they
could be more open about their abilities.

One day.

At the moment, Della watched from the very rear of the
pack in the alleyway as Stacy extended her hand, inspecting her nails from beneath a large, hooded coat, the better
to hide her skin from any ultraviolet attacks. She was listening for their humans, who had already been charmed to
enter until commanded to retreat. One of them was to attempt a peaceful entrance at first—a lone person knocking
and crying at the door for the help of a Good Samaritan.
All the girls required was for one sympathetic, unaware
occupant to open that door so a vampire could persuade
him or her into permitting them admission. If that did not
work, the other humans were to try to find an alternate way
in, as *they* would be able to enter windows or other doors
with the crazed strength the girls had lent them. Then they
would isolate a resident and bring them to where a vampire could work their charm on a member of the attacker
group.

With this human aid, the girls would find Mrs. Jones . . .

and perhaps then finish the fight with those Queenshill attackers.

Many of the older vampires, clothed in gaping, head-covering coats, too, were staring up at the sky between the buildings, impervious to the post-midnight cold, night-dreaming to pass the time away. A distance away from Della, a similarly covered Noreen fidgeted, no doubt missing Polly, who had stayed with a few of the other school-girls to keep Wolfie occupied.

Della wandered farther away from the group, where she could compose herself without anyone noticing. She was hungrier than usual, and her body growled with it. She hadn't hunted, ripping into flesh and gnawing to the bone, for nights now. She longed for just a bite. Two.

More.

As she pressed her arms over her tummy, she listened to the slow, measured footfalls of the charmed humans in the near distance. They were certainly taking their time in get-ting to the building, and she sighed, leaning her head back.

Then she heard it: a movement beside her, round a corner.

She began to stand away from the wall, but she was pulled behind the corner so subtly that she doubted her mates had even noticed.

In a flash, her hood was pushed back from her head, and something touched her temples—a brace of sorts—clamping and then sending her into a numb zone of compli-ance. There, she existed only in the black cove of her mind, where the snaky, warped sound of a voice echoed.

Was it coming through whatever had been attached to her head . . . ?

"Della," it said.

Fear waved over her flesh, and she couldn't even turn round to focus on the entity that had put this captivating instrument on her.

Yet she already had a good idea of what the creature

might be. She thought of the red eyes she'd seen one night when she'd found herself too far off the main paths of the Underground—the murky fright, the quivering and oppressive air, the terror.

But now . . . Now she didn't feel the same slippery push against her skin and bones that she had back then.

Out of the corner of her eye, she dared a glance. And she found just what she'd been dreading—red eyes coming from the blackness.

A scream lodged in her throat.

Make a sound and I'll make you sorry, the *custode* said in the thickets of Della's mind. The caretakers were known to keep guard for the Underground, though Della didn't feel safe round them in the least, so obedience came easily. The other vampire girls would not even know the caretaker was here, as the *custodes* carried no scent and took such care to remain nothing more than a shadow.

As Della sank further into the depths of her captivated mind, she answered, but only in her head.

I won't tell anyone you're here.

Good, it said. *I didn't expect to find the group of you aboveground until my partner communicated that Mihas had requested you retrieve Claudia. You tracked her here, didn't you?*

Yes.

The *custode* didn't comment, and in that pause, Della could have sworn there was menace.

Why? Was the caretaker angry with them for being here? Angry with all of them for getting so far into a compromising situation?

Della panicked, thinking she should do all she could to help the *custode* and land on its positive side. *We believe Mrs. Jones is in a building with those attackers from Queenshill. They're shielding her or holding her, I'm not certain which it is.*

It mind-spoke again. *Hear me well, Della. You tell your*

chums not to kill those attackers. Then the caretaker seemed to reconsider. *Well, perhaps you can do away with their vampire. Frank was his name, yes? The same goes for that more lethal one who hurt the dogs.*

Della could only hope she would be able to face up to the mean vampire. *I understand.*

I want the remainder of the group for questioning. And be quiet going about this. I know what you girls are doing with those charmed humans, using them to get you into that building to Claudia. That was clever in this case. Your efforts could take any fight or exposure indoors, where the public won't bear witness. But if your humans should attract any attention outside, call them off, Della.

We will. It'll be as if we were never here. We intend to erase all evidence of our presence—

Della stopped herself. She'd been about to tell this creature that the girls intended to kill Mrs. Jones. In fact, she feared that the *custode* might have already gleaned the information.

She held her breath, hoping, hoping . . .

Yet, from the way the *custode* didn't comment, Della wondered if the caretaker even cared that Mrs. Jones would die.

But that was ridiculous. Of course it would care, and Della shut down her mind, lest the caretaker access any further plans for Mrs. Jones.

I'll be near to see that this remains a private affair, the *custode* mind-said. *Do you understand me? Secrecy in this is imperative to the continued survival of your community.*

We stay quiet. We withdraw if the trouble spills into the streets.

Yes, the caretaker thought, tweaking Della's cheek. *Precisely.*

The *custode* released the contraption from Della's temples, pulled the hood back over Della's head, then seemed to fade into the dark of Della's mind.

The rest of the night world rushed back: The *swick* of what sounded like outside lights turning on in the distance. The shuffled steps of the charmed humans as they halted. The knock one of them pounded upon the front door as the other ones hopefully hid themselves from view, as instructed.

Della crept back round the corner to her mates, just in time to smell jasmine and to see that Stacy was missing, having already hidden near the building's front door now that the humans were stationed.

The rest of her pack crouched, their backs arched in readiness for what was to come, and Della joined them.

As Dawn walked down the stairs to the lab, saving her energy, she heard Kiko and Frank over the earpiece, checking who had what weapon, communicating with the Friends as another knock pounded on the front door.

A charmed human. The vamps had no idea that the scouting Friends had seen what they were up to outside.

Frank's voice came over loud and clear. "Dawn, we've got a count of twenty-four vamps in an alley close by, plus one right outside next to a human who's whining for help. He's saying he got in some accident and he's putting the pity squeeze on us."

"Amateur plan."

"Yeah. Some Friends are surrounding the other vamps to try and keep them back if they do come closer."

This was one of those times Dawn wished the Friends could kill, but she knew that their souls would be forfeit to the same place Costin was trying to avoid. That'd been the deal with Costin when they'd agreed to come on board to help him after their human deaths.

"The UV lights outside will also keep vamps at bay," she said.

"Did I mention they have thick coats with hoods on?"

"Okay, we've got outside silver darts aimed and ready, too, and maybe those'll pierce the coats."

"Vamps are fast, remember? They can avoid those."

"Then they'll have to deal with us, no matter how many of them there are." Besides, headquarters was fortified to the nth degree, with booby traps and everything. "Hey, Natalia, you're in the communications room now, right?"

The new girl came on, her voice frazzled. "Just as the boss said I should be in this situation, Dawn."

"Tap into the anonymous, nontraceable computer call program." Breisi had installed it ages ago. "Report a drunken riot a few blocks over—but don't give our own location. We can't afford to have the law snooping around too close." Costin was as eager to avoid the public limelight as any vamp. His operations depended on secrecy and ease of movement. "If the vamps are smart, they'll hear the sirens a long way off and call away their charmed people. Vamps won't want to be discovered, either, I'll bet."

"Copy," Natalia said.

Dawn heard Kiko on the earpiece. His voice still carried that cosmic-ranger floatiness she'd noted earlier from being lulled by a Friend, but he was in ass-kicking mode.

"I'm in Dawn's room," he said, updating his position.

There was actually a window up there, unlike the blocked ones downstairs. Thanks to Breisi, it was shatterproof, so Dawn wasn't worried about anything busting it open. But Costin did use it occasionally to receive any psychic vibes from the Underground, and there was a chance other vibrations might come through. If the lower vamps' charming techniques were anything like Claudius's, Dawn didn't want to take a chance.

"I can see some activity down below," Kiko added. "Not sure what it is though."

"Maybe you shouldn't stand so close to that window, Kik."

"Backing away, right now."

"Okay. Are any Friends with you?"

"Nope. They're all in more important places. That's why I came up here—so I could keep watch from this position. I'll scoot downstairs, if needed. But I think I see something . . ."

"Keep us posted."

"Will do."

Things seemed ready to go, and the most important element was that Costin wasn't in-house. That meant the vamps wouldn't get to him.

At least not here . . .

Don't think about him in that Underground, she thought. *You've got a job to do yourself.*

But as Dawn reached the bottom of the stairs and saw Claudius waiting there in his chair, a smug smile on his mouth, she wondered if maybe Costin wasn't as safe as she'd hoped.

The vampire spoke, calmly, surely, while a Friend bound him. Dawn knew it was only one spirit, because the rest of the headquarters' guard had been called to defend the building.

"I told you they would come," he said in that damaged voice. His throat had stalled in its healing.

Was it a sign of his continued weakness?

"They're not gonna get closer than they are now," Dawn said.

"Are you here to kill me, before they arrive down here to take me back?"

She wouldn't reveal that Costin had ordered her to keep Claudius alive, just in case.

God, where *was* he? In the midst of an Underground fight? Couldn't he have spared a Friend or even a damned phone call to let them know how it was going? It'd be nice if she had permission to get rid of Claudius, if Costin didn't need him alive anymore.

Dawn held her stake in front of her, but the vamp seemed to know it was an empty threat.

"You're too afraid that I've misled your sweetie with bad directions to the Underground, aren't you?" Claudius made a pseudo-sad face. "Not a wonderful position to be in."

Over Dawn's earpiece, she heard some shouting, and her gut told her to stay here, no matter what was happening up top.

When would the bobbies respond to Natalia's call? Even a hint of sirens should be enough for the vamps to wave off their humans—*if* they were interested in not getting caught out there.

"*Did* you mislead Costin?" Dawn asked.

Claudius laughed, and it reminded Dawn of a witch who was presenting a riddle. She had the horrific feeling that Claudius hadn't been so mentally weak after all, that he *had* been playing Costin.

Her temper rumbled, and she got closer to the vampire, face-to-face, holding up a finger. "You're not gonna win this."

In a show of astounding bravery, Claudius bared his teeth, his fangs emerging as pinpoints. White needles.

Before Dawn could draw back, Claudius struck at her, catching the pad of her index finger.

As the Friend on duty pushed Claudius back, Dawn jerked away, then glanced at her finger, where blood beaded to the surface, stinging.

But, strangely, it didn't make her angrier. It sent her into a place beyond rage—white-hot and calm instead of red and explosive.

Dawn sucked on her finger, erasing the blood. Everything—Claudius, the noise from the earpiece, the anguish of worrying about Costin—it all stopped existing.

She took her finger out of her mouth and, inspecting it, spoke so quietly that it surprised her. "Did you stop to think that Costin *wanted* to see if your vampires would come for you? Based on how your girl Violet paid us a visit before she was torn to shreds by some ravens that swooped down from the sky the other morning, he suspected your underlings would have enough brass to come aboveground and take that kind of risk. We've been waiting for another chance at more girls."

Claudius didn't look as smug now.

There. "I've never known an Underground to flash around their powers like you guys do. Sometimes you're careful, but when you've got little girls going rogue and making offers to people they think might be hunters, that's trouble."

Now Claudius's expression was very not-smug.

"Ah," Dawn said. "You're hearing me now? You're catching on that Violet came to us so she could offer some revenge on one of your other vamps? You don't have as much control over them as you think. Undergrounds never do, and that's why you fall with just the slightest push."

"We won't do any such thing." Claudius was back to smug. "I guarantee that."

"Why?"

As Claudius shrugged, Dawn heard Frank—definitely Frank—yelling over the earpiece. The floor above shook, probably from force being put on the front door, which was so solid she doubted it would fall.

If it *was* the door making that noise. . . .

The anger was inching back up inside Dawn now, because it was never far away. The heat melded with the cool of her composure, just like the two masters who had joined to form this one London Underground.

The need to attack more forcefully boiled in her. "Why do you guarantee that your Underground won't fall, Claudius?"

The vampire laughed, and that was all it took to topple *her.*

Vision muddled, Dawn exploded, her mind force banging outward, zipping to the master vampire and shoving itself into the creature's mouth, then down its throat.

Claudius gagged, his eyes bulging with shock. The Friend binding him didn't castigate Dawn, who wanted to stop *herself*, but couldn't. It seemed beyond her control. It felt too . . .

Necessary.

"Don't make me drag it out of you," Dawn said, and it was almost a plea. "Just tell me what you showed Costin in your mind. Show me what he's headed for, whether it's the real Underground or a trap."

Claudius hissed around Dawn's mind-conjured choke.

All Dawn could imagine now was Costin, heading under the earth, so sure he was going to find Mihas and maybe the dragon, that he was going to beat them with the help of the Friends, just as he'd done so many times in the past. Then she pictured him torn apart by Mihas's teeth, by any remaining famished girls, as he died because he didn't have all of his powers.

Claudius moaned, and Dawn took satisfaction in it. Another spot on her neck pounded, right near Costin's earlier bite on her left side.

A new mark?

She retreated out of Claudius, her limbs shaking now. The vampire dry heaved as Dawn got to a crouch. She couldn't stand anymore, and the stake fell out of her hand, to the floor, but she didn't reach for it. She didn't want Claudius to see her falling apart.

The Friend pushed at Claudius's blankets around his skin-mangled neck. She was showing her unification with Dawn, relaying that she was ready to make Claudius distinctly uncomfortable in any way she could. Dawn didn't know which way she should go—pursuing more of what was in Claudius or retreating from herself.

The vampire moved his mouth, and Dawn thought he'd

come to his senses and was cooperating. But then he started to laugh again, just as screams sounded from the earpiece.

"Dawn! Get up here!" It was Frank.

She looked at Claudius, then at the stairs.

The binding Friend spoke, and Dawn recognized her rough tone.

"Go up and gather those vamp girls," Kalin said. *"I'll be ready down 'ere with the safeguard when you get 'em to come to me. Meantime, I'll keep* talkin' *to our guest. You can 've at 'im again in a bit."*

Dawn didn't have time to do a double take at the spirit who'd always disliked her so much. She didn't have time to argue that Kalin's plan was so risky that it scared the shit out of her. But did she have another choice if the vamps had broken in somehow?

She sprinted up the stairs, Claudius's laughter growing louder as he said, "Safeguards, you say? Traps? Every good lair has them for intruders, you know. . . ."

Maybe Kalin would get something out of Claudius before Dawn came back—

Over the earpiece, Natalia babbled to her.

"Dawn! Kiko invited one in! I've been doing damage control up here, but a Friend told me that, earlier, she thinks he was looking out the window when a girl appeared, catching his gaze through it. She had climbed the wall outside, and the Friend thinks the vampire popped up to look through it and Kiko was too slow to glance away. He was caught by it and he could have possibly heard her if they were both close enough to the window. The vibration of her tone might've even traveled through it to get to him. He went to a rear entrance and opened the door without anyone else knowing."

Goddamn it, she'd told him to get away from that window. Had the vamp gotten him before he complied with Dawn's suggestion? Kiko's Friend-lulled mind hadn't been where it usually was.

How had he lost so much of his edge?

Dawn should've known better because, last night, both Kiko and she had been suckers for Claudius's charm until Natalia had broken the spell. For some reason, the new girl was immune to the vamp ability, and it could've had to do with how she heard a vampire's presence, how her senses worked differently than the rest of theirs.

"Okay," Dawn said as she kept running up those stairs. "We've got a lot of surprises left for these girls. Natalia, you're still in the comm room?"

"Yes—I'm at the controls."

Was Natalia the one Costin had trusted with all the deeper information that he wouldn't share with the others? The new girl, whom he'd seemed to take under his wing, training and keeping apart from the rest of them.

It ate at her. "Did the cops come yet?"

"The scanner says yes, and based on cameras and Friend intelligence, the vampires seem to have let the charmed humans go already."

Would the humans know what'd hit them?

Hell, now wasn't the time to wonder.

Dawn got to the door and yanked it open to the chaos.

Girls. Screeches.

Just below Kalin's empty home portrait, where the spirit usually rested in the guise of a woman wrapped in a cloak of fire, Frank was wrangling down two female vamps who were in full-on hairless cat-and-wolf mode, with long ears, nose, teeth, and claws. The UV lights outside hadn't gotten to them because of their thick coats and hoods, but now those hoods had fallen off most of them as the battalion of Friends attacked, pushing the girls toward the exit or toward Frank, who was wielding two machetes in a blur of vampire motion, already decapitating one of the vamp intruders.

She screamed and withered to nothing, her coat shriveling to air just as quickly, like every part of her had been eaten right up by some acid. Frank got the other girl vamp, too, then turned to another one that the Friends pushed at him. He was a whirring cutting machine.

Meanwhile, Kiko was by a wall, far under one of the wooden angels that hovered overhead. His eyes were glassy as he beat off some Friends.

Dawn made her way over to him, mentally punching a redheaded vampire out of the way and into the essence of a Friend. She did it to the next three vamps, too. At the same time, she took out the crucifix from her back pocket.

Stepping in front of Kiko, she brandished the holy item. The crucifix had stunned Claudius before, and she hoped there'd be a connection.

As Kiko shied away from it, Dawn lifted her other wrist, squeezing the small bag at her palm and firing a burst of holy water into his face.

He yelled, convulsed, then spit out the water, glaring at her.

Kiko?

She got ready to give him another dose in case he wasn't back yet.

Then he blinked, looked around the room, his expression horrified as he realized what was going on . . . as well as his part in making it happen.

He'd have to deal later.

"Now's the time to get them back for what they did to you," Dawn said, lowering the crucifix and starting to leave. She hoped Frank was listening to what she was about to say over the earpiece. "Just round these girls up near the lab door for a takedown."

"But—" he said, because the idea was too crazy to not say "but."

"Friends have got us covered."

He nodded, going back to business, grabbing a silver knife out of one of his pockets and heaving it across the room. Dawn didn't know if it found a target because she was already mentally kicking and punching her way back to the door that guarded Claudius.

But a vamp was already there, sniffing at the edges. By now, she was the only one whose hood was still over her head.

Dawn took a slight detour to a secret panel in a wall—an additional weapons cache. She pressed on it while shoving the crucifix back in her pocket. The door spilled open, and she reached inside, taking out a saw-bow, with its blade cocked and ready to fly.

As she was turning around and lifting it, the vampire girl at the door stopped sniffing, then turned around, too, while Dawn avoided focusing on the eyes.

They recognized each other right away, and it wasn't just because the girl hadn't changed into full vamp form yet or because they'd met when the team had gone to Queens-hill.

Dawn saw a reflection of her own rage in Della's shadowed face, and for a second, she couldn't move.

Just like looking into a fractured mirror . . .

Then Dawn blocked her thoughts from invasion. *Della could be more insurance for us,* she thought. *Capture her or one of the other vamp girls. They'll know the real Underground location if you can't get it out of Claudius.*

Intending to stun Della, Dawn began to draw the crucifix out of her pocket, but there was a yank on her braid as something wrapped a hand around it and jerked her upward, toward the stairs.

Yelling at the pain in her scalp, Dawn dropped the crucifix and grasped the root of her braid with one hand as she was hauled over the stair banister. But she kept ahold of her saw-bow with the other, swinging it.

As her assailant slammed her toward the stairs, Dawn brought down the saw-bow butt first, but the dark figure dodged out of the way. Then, flash fast, it got Dawn in a headlock, its fingers at the tender Vulcan hold spot near her neck.

The enemy applied just enough pressure so Dawn dropped the saw-bow. She could see through the banister slats below them to where the Friends and Kiko fought the vamps; by now, Kiko had gotten ahold of machetes, racking up kill numbers, and Frank was closing in on Della by the door with his own furious blades.

A slithering electronically altered voice spoke in Dawn's ear. "Miss me?"

Shadow Girl.

As Dawn tensed, preparing to attack, the *custode* applied pressure to her hold, and Dawn went weak, brought back against what felt like body armor beneath the keeper's chest.

"Don't," Shadow Girl said. "Why don't we just let Della do her work? I'll do mine quite happily up here, as well. But I anticipate having to accomplish matters rather quickly."

Last time, this thing had wanted to question her, and Dawn suspected the same was in store for her now—and in her own territory, too, right above her own team.

She thought of accessing her earpiece, telling Natalia where she was, but the new girl wasn't proficient with weapons yet. She'd be walking into sure trouble. Frank and Kiko were pretty occupied themselves.

"Fancy place," the *custode* said, as if she were looking around, admiring the antique touches. "You and the others run quite an operation. What exactly are you about?"

Dawn kept her mouth closed, and Shadow Girl used her other hand to cup Dawn's chin, bringing her head over to one side. Dawn recognized the position: the *custode* was threatening to break her neck if she didn't offer anything.

She gathered her rage, knowing it was her only way out of this.

Shadow Girl caressed her cheek with a gloved finger.

Dawn shivered, taken off guard, remembering the black widow kiss this thing had put on her at Eva's flat.

"Don't even think about battering at me with whatever powers you might have," the *custode* whispered. "I'm ready for them this time."

Thing was, Dawn hadn't shown her full hand to Shadow Girl before; she had a lot more to play—and she wasn't talking about taunting her enemy with information about the other, deader *custode* the team was keeping in the freezer downstairs. She wasn't dumb enough to fire this one up with that news.

"Then ask away," Dawn said as best as she could with her neck about to be snapped off.

Meanwhile, the anger simmered higher, faster.

The *custode* kept hold of Dawn, like she was loving every second of this. The girl's touch was almost even . . . sexual.

Stimulated by the hunt.

It spoke to Dawn—the infliction of pain that Costin had said she enjoyed too much.

Shadow Girl took harder hold of Dawn's jaw. "I believe I asked what sort of operation this was."

But then there was a fritzing sound that came from near the keeper's head, and Dawn heard the murmur of a voice as the *custode* seemed to listen in.

An earpiece? Was she getting a message from another of her kind?

The shadow thing made an electronic, thwarted sound, then muttered, "Bloody hell." She leaned in closer to Dawn's ear, her mask brushing skin. "You didn't happen to send one of your number to *us*, did you? Perhaps that 'mean vampire' the girls talk about who killed the dogs at Queenshill? I haven't seen him about."

Fuck.

Dawn's imagination ran rampant: They'd caught Costin. Trap. Sure death.

Or was the *custode* talking about something else?

"Come along then," the girl said as she removed one of her hands from Dawn to reach for what were probably cuffs.

Dawn thrust out with her mind, grasping the *custode*'s arms, puppeting them away and flipping Shadow Girl to the stairs. Simultaneously, she dove away, leaping to a higher level, getting a better view of the keeper's red eyes and shadow body as it righted itself.

Not letting up, Dawn mentally flipped her assailant again, and the girl landed on her back with a crash. Dawn used her mind to push the keeper down the stairs as she grabbed the saw-bow, getting to her feet and giving chase.

Had the shadow thing been talking about Costin? Had they gotten him?

She wouldn't let this bitch anywhere near him.

Feverishly, Dawn pursued her quarry, finding the *custode* at the bottom, having regained her standing balance.

Swick, went the saw-bow as Dawn triggered it from only feet away.

The *custode* leaped out of the way of the blade as it spun toward her in a shower of sparks. She screamed as it caught her in the shoulder, and Dawn ducked out of the arc of the blood spray.

The blade ricocheted off the keeper, to the right, into a vamp who was wrestling with a Friend, and buried itself into the schoolgirl's chest. She screech-howled as Dawn dropped the emptied saw-bow and went for a machete in her holster.

The *custode* clutched at her shoulder, then in a moment of surreal cheekiness, seemed to look with great disappointment at Dawn before taking out a gun from her belt and aiming it at a high-flying angel.

She shot the device and a cable spat out to attach to the angel platform. With a whiz, she flew up, out of Dawn's reach, and crouched on the platform, disappearing behind the angel's head.

Gone—just like last time.

Dawn itched to chase it, but instead she went to Frank, who was grappling with Della.

There was a plan to carry out. Kalin's plan.

And time was really ticking now if the *custode* had been called to the Underground because of Costin.

NINE

ABOVEGROUND, II

DELLA *knew* Mrs. Jones was just beyond the door. She could smell the vampire's hair—the thick tresses that held a hint of the shampoo the housematron had always used in her masquerade aboveground. She could smell Mrs. Jones's old blood, too, and it was driving her mad as she swiped at the vampire Frank—the one who had deceived them and attacked them at Queenshill.

Once again, he had been attempting to peer into her eyes, but she wouldn't let him. She was sure he was attempting to snatch the location of the Underground from her, and Wolfie was still down there.

He couldn't get to Wolfie.

She'd changed into wolf-cat form and was just grabbing Frank's neck, her mouth watering, salivating for a bite, even of vampire's blood, when the woman with the braid came to stand in front of Della, murder in her gaze.

Della fell back against the stalwart door that blocked her

from Mrs. Jones. She scream-hiss-howled, drawing the attention of her classmates.

Or, at least, what was left of their number.

They were down to nine, with Noreen and Stacy still fighting with those invisible entities—the jasmine the girls had been smelling round them for a while now. Her mates cocked their heads, broke away, then came running toward Della en masse, making the same terrible sounds as Della had.

"They're all together!" an odd, windy voice yelled as a force seemed to shove Frank away from Della while more jasmine corralled the girls.

Frenzied, their minds on only Mrs. Jones, they all barreled toward the door, crashing against it.

Then the jasmine swooshed away, the hunters retreating as, out of the blue, the door fell.

Della didn't stop to think that the entry had been all too easy. She didn't think about how the attackers weren't nearby any longer. She and the others rushed down the stairs in their haste to get to Mrs. Jones, their fangs bared in their hunger for vengeance.

Too late, Della saw that the walls surrounding them were steel. Too late, fire burst down from the ceiling, crisping at the girls' coats and exposed skin.

They flew like lightning out of the flames, back up the stairs, their flesh crisped to near black. When they reached the upper room, they rolled on the floor, dousing the fire from their ruined coats and pained skin.

After their screams had abated, Della lay there. Little by little, she realized the room was empty. All the hunters had disappeared, and, of course, the girls had uncharmed the humans outside, hoping they would serve as a distraction for the bobbies who had been approaching.

It was just them now.

"What do we do?" asked Noreen in her cat-wolf voice.

Like all of them, her flesh was blackened, the whites of her eyes standing out of a singed, hairless skull. "How will we get to Mrs. Jones?"

"There must be another way down there," Stacy said. She'd been the one who'd tricked the little man into opening the door, and the group looked to her for leadership once more.

"Fire," Della said, shell-shocked. "Only a wall of fire keeping us from having everything we ever wanted."

The others stared at her as if she'd gone completely off her trolley. And perhaps she had.

Whimpering, Della moved stiffly to the top of the stairs, her skin and what was left of her clothes smoking. She stood there for the longest time.

Then she took another step down.

"Della!" cried Noreen.

She paid no mind. Della was going to find Mrs. Jones. She would run through the fire, using all the speed she could, and if she were attacked by flame again, so be it.

Yes, Della thought, she was going to die trying, because if Mrs. Jones ever made it back to Wolfie, there would be no life, anyway.

When she arrived just before the area where the steel covered the walls, she doffed what was left of one long boot and tossed it ahead, to see if the mechanism was motion activated.

No response.

Della inhaled deeply, went up a few stairs, then used all the speed she had to bolt through the steel section.

When she reached the bottom, tumbling to a halt because she'd been moving so quickly and she couldn't slow down, she realized there hadn't been any fire this time.

She gained her feet, sniffing the air, crazily trying to locate Mrs. Jones. But the room was rife with jasmine, masking all other smells, including that of her own burned skin.

Then she saw the empty chair in the empty room, and

she sank to her knees, knowing the attackers were much smarter than any one of the schoolgirls, including Stacy.

And that Mrs. Jones was still alive to tell the tale of what the girls had done to her.

THE Friends had completely taken over and, now, Dawn, Kiko, and a bound Claudius were being zoomed along in wheeled carts by the spirits as they all traveled a tunnel to a secondary headquarters location. Frank zoomed along on his own, running just ahead of them.

Their injuries were minor, and none of them had fallen. This time.

However, Claudius hadn't revealed anything to Kalin while she'd guarded him, so Dawn had a lot of work to do—especially after what Shadow Girl had told her.

"Eva's already at wherever we're going?" Dawn asked Kalin, who was pushing her conveyance. She'd grabbed her saw-bow before evacuating headquarters, because she didn't know just how well stocked this temporary place was. Jonah's impressive fortune bought a lot, but she didn't know how much Costin would've invested in backup.

Behind them, a part of the tunnel sealed shut as a hidden doorway rolled down. The Friends were blocking everything off as fast as they could. The doors would blend with the rest of the tunnel, disguising where everyone had gone.

"Eva was transferred earlier," said Kalin. She wasn't on Claudius-binding duty anymore, having been spelled by a different spirit.

"And Natalia?" Dawn asked.

"She's bein' led by Evangeline, and they'll both meet us there."

The Friends had been the ones to cue Natalia in on setting off the lab stairway booby trap from the comm room, although the vamps had escaped the fire faster than they'd hoped. But at least it'd allowed the team to flee to this backup.

A spirit contingent had remained behind to keep guarding the old headquarters, but that hadn't stopped Frank from almost fighting the Friends so he could remain behind to grab Breisi's portrait.

"Don't tell me Breisi's gonna have to come home to nothin'," he'd said as the Friends had settled Kiko and Dawn in their carts.

"The vamps 've no idea what those pictures 're for," Kalin said. *"Don't get yer panties in a bunch, Frank. They'll be fine."*

"You'll all be living at old headquarters, even though it's been compromised?"

"It's secured, 'ey? Friends 're remaining behind to keep watch over our 'omes."

From the way Frank grunted, Dawn knew he'd be making a return visit to tear Breisi's bolted portrait off the wall, and maybe rescue a few others while he was at it.

Then they'd taken off, only to slow down now, as they reached a temporary headquarters that Dawn was just now finding out about. But it was the Friends' job to always be prepared.

It was Kiko's turn to ask questions as they disembarked. "Where was the boss during all that mess, huh? Usually he's dealing out instructions."

Even though it wasn't time yet, Dawn knew she needed to share. It was close enough to sunrise, shit was in motion, and she'd need help if she was going to handle Claudius to prepare for their own Underground attack, should Costin have already failed.

And based on how the girls had been a combination of wolf and cat until the very end, she had the feeling Costin hadn't gotten anywhere. Mihas still had to be alive.

She felt stabbed by pessimism, and she tried to staunch the wounds by being practical. If Costin never made it Underground, she'd need more help than ever to wrangle Claudius into telling them if Costin had been set up for a trap and what the team would need to know to avoid it if they went after him.

Sure, she'd promised him she'd pursue a real Underground location first if he didn't destroy it by dusk, but it didn't seem right. In any case, he hadn't even gotten his allotted amount of time to complete his attack yet, so why was she freaking out now?

When the next sunset came, then she'd decide what they should do. . . .

She faced Frank and Kiko, her voice cracking. "The boss is already Underground, guys."

The look of betrayal on their faces was so vivid in the blinking strung-up lights of the tunnel that she could've probably even seen them without the illumination.

ACROSS the Thames, just north of the main city and below the earth, Costin was indeed under the ground.

But it was not where he had planned to be at the beginning of the night.

He sat in the middle of a silver cage that had sliced down from the ceiling and around him hours ago in this tunnel, when Jonah—who had been sheltering him—had tripped a clever sensor neither he, nor the Friends, had seen. Costin had emerged to take over from there, believing he could find a way out.

However, in this vampire's body, he could not touch the squared bars, because the silver would seep through the skin to poison him and Jonah. Covering his hands with Jonah's long coat had not ensured progress, either, as it was like fumbling about with mittens on, and the bars were so sound even a vampire's strength could not bend them. And when he had dug at the dirt, thinking to burrow under the cage, he had met silver plating.

Even the Friends had not been able to dismantle the structure due to having no actual hands, merely essences. They were also trapped here, below, unable to escape, as the entrance had been automatically shut behind them when they had entered.

A trap. And a good one.

If only the cell phone or the earpiece worked. Yet they were too far below the surface for either to be of any use.

Breisi, his best and brightest Friend, sailed around the cage, inspecting it for faults. Although she and the others would be growing weak soon if they could not return to their portraits for recharging, she still had not quit.

But she would not be Breisi if she had done so.

Deep within their body, Costin heard Jonah speaking.

"Getting any Indiana Jones vibes here? He'd know how to outsmart a booby like this."

"I am glad you see fit to joke, Jonah. That will surely keep me in a pleasant mood."

"Old man, you know that the team's going to realize what's going on when they don't hear from us or the Friends soon."

Costin wished he had not listened to Claudius, no matter how certain he had been that his blood brother was telling the truth. He had assumed the other to be so weak that he would offer up any and all valid information, but he had thought wrong. Claudius had been a strategist in his day, and he had never lost the talent.

But the main reason Costin had fallen into entrapment was because he had been too eager to prove that he was still the powerful Soul Traveler when he knew all too well that he was not. Once he would have been able to slip out of Jonah's body and out of this cage. But perhaps his blood brother had sensed his diminishment.

Unwilling to accept this position, Costin wrapped the coat over his hands again and attempted to pull apart the bars. No use.

Despair came upon him. Once more, he would require aid from another. Not in all his centuries of fighting Undergrounds had he run into such a spell of misfortune.

Not until he had summoned Dawn into his life.

Jonah was communicating from his submissive resting spot again. "The team will use the locator to find us after sunset, just like you told them. We'll wait this out, Costin. We'll be okay."

"They will not come straight here. They are to hunt us only *after* they find a true Underground. I was adamant about that."

It was the way of the quest. Undergrounds first, personal concerns second. If he should fall here, he would need a seasoned team to carry on; he couldn't risk the death of them all, especially since Dawn was the key.

Sometimes, Costin wondered if she would be more important in winning back his soul—in securing the safety of them *all*—than even he was.

Jonah vibrated up the inside of their body, closer to taking over. "You think *Dawn* would leave you here to die? Right. Now, who do you think she is, Costin?"

He saw her as she was last night, rage transforming her into someone he hardly recognized. Saw the marks on her skin that were slowly taking her over.

As an answer eluded Costin, his gaze landed on the silver bars surrounding him and Jonah, and he felt more trapped than ever.

TEN

LONDON BABYLON, THE LION AND THE LAMB PUB

To look at them, one would think this was a celebration.

Della watched her fellow vampires—the recruited girls who hadn't been in Southwark—frolicking about the Lion and the Lamb as the windows showcased a bruised sky readied for the sun's climb. The pub's country simplicity held court to the vampires masquerading as girls, some of whom had tucked flowers from the pots decorating the tables into their hair. The recruits provided stark contrast to the nine Queenshill schoolgirls who had only now trudged into the pub, their healing skin still burned in places that even the ragged strips of their coats and hoods couldn't hide.

The owner of this establishment, who had clearly left the pub to them at this hour, had once struck a deal with Wolfie to ask no questions about the female patrons who attracted a young, male tourist clientele. And the vampires had clearly encouraged a great many to stay here earlier in the night; though the pub was technically closed, young human men still played table games such as snooker in one room with the stealth vampire girls while, in dark corners, they snogged with others.

Or, more to the point, the girls were discreetly feeding upon the prey, here above the ground. In a half attempt at modesty, instead of drinking in the usual way, they were taking blood through their skin, which mewed open into little mouths, just like the cat from whom they had inherited this ability.

The sight of the girls' boldness startled Della, as they had always been instructed to take better care than to indulge in casual feeds without the benefit of running in a pack during their nightcrawls, where they would quietly hunt victims, feed in the dark, then bury the remains.

Then again, Wolfie had always looked forward to the day when vampires would have the freedom to show themselves in public. With the way the Western world was moving—one debauchery becoming commonplace this year, another more shocking one the next—he estimated that their kind would be at home among humans within the decade.

Clearly, his time spent here in the pub, more and more recently, was a part of his agenda.

Della and the other survivors found more girls gathered round him in a back room. With his hair brambled over his shoulders, his leather pants and poet's shirt, he was sitting in a chair, a leg propped on a bench, one recruited girl under each arm. He spared a glance at the new arrivals and cocked his head, assessing their burns. He didn't even care to touch-heal them as he used to.

They stared back at him. Della was hollowed out by the loss of her classmates. Shouldn't he have felt the deaths of his half-offspring, too?

Out of the survivors, Stacy spoke, the older vampire's once-long platinum locks in crisped clumps on her skull as she pushed back her hood. By now, they had healed enough for skin and hair to begin growing back. Otherwise, they hadn't bothered to tidy themselves yet. It hadn't seemed important.

"Sixteen of us, gone," Stacy said, her voice flat, sounding for the first time as if she was truly far older than the teenager she seemed to be.

Wolfie blinked, his eyebrows knitting as if he didn't quite comprehend what Stacy was telling him. It was at this instant that Della thought that perhaps he did feel the loss of his darlings.

But then his eyes seemed to glaze over. "Claudia—she's still alive, yes? The cat's abilities are still active in you. . . ."

He turned to one of the girls in his grasp, cupping her under the chin, angling her face this way and that, lovingly assessing her, obviously searching for signs of the cat in her.

The girl, with her short, curly black hair, dressed in knee-high socks and a miniskirt with a blouse, was reduced to a fizzy smile at his attentions. Being new to the main Underground, Della hadn't met this recruited dear yet.

But as Wolfie started raining kisses on her face, a jolt traveled through Della. And from the manner in which Noreen, Stacy, and the other survivors stiffened, she knew they had experienced the same shocking epiphany.

Were they all little mirrors of Mrs. Jones to Wolfie? Didn't he love any of them for who they were and not what they carried over from his mistress?

And where *was* the sadness from Wolfie about his fallen vampire daughters as he continued kissing Mrs. Jones's proxy?

Della heard herself speaking, her tone just as dead as Stacy's had been. "Mrs. Jones was with a group of hunters, the same crowd who attacked us at Queenshill."

"Hunters?" he asked, running a finger along the recruited girl's cheek now.

Surely he cared about hunters more than he did about Mrs. Jones, especially since hunters could represent a rival blood brother.

"They must be that," Stacy said, "based on their weaponry and expertise. And they've taken Mrs. Jones captive, unless she surrendered to them."

When Wolfie finally turned aside from the recruited girl, his eyes were a livid gold under his thick eyebrows. "Claudia would never surrender."

Della and the rest of them shrank under his statement, not daring to contradict him.

He dismissed his two fawning admirers by lifting his arms off them, and they sulked away, easily cast aside.

As any of them could be.

"Why didn't you bring me back the heads of those hunters?" he asked with the same condescension they'd often heard from Mrs. Jones.

Noreen volunteered her only statement thus far. "It seemed they were ready for us, and they fought well. But they're gone now."

"Where did they go?" Wolfie snapped.

They all flinched, the other survivors cowering behind Della, Noreen, and Stacy, just as they had been doing since they'd entered the pub.

Della knew the only way to get through this was to get through this. "We don't know where they went, but their building is deserted now."

"Wonderful good that'll do us," Wolfie said. His fangs had emerged slightly to jut past his lips. "They still have Claudia."

"Yes," all the girls said.

"Then we shall continue tracking her."

"But Mrs. Jones's trail has disappeared," Della said softly. "We have very little to guide us now unless we can find the route the group used to escape. They took care to mask their scents, and the jasmine stink from ghosts who help them confused our senses since many of them remained behind."

Wolfie's claws emerged, but then he seemed to come

upon an idea that retracted them a bit. "My mobile and answering service. Perhaps Claudia left a clue to her whereabouts there. . . ."

Oh, no, Della thought. Mrs. Jones had fled the Underground without her mobile; she had possessed nothing. Would she have stolen one? If so, who knew what Mrs. Jones might have said during a message?

As Wolfie wiped his palm down his face, laughing at such an obvious option, Stacy glanced at Della, connecting minds.

We must make certain he has no time to check messages.

Her face purposely blank, Della gave no indication that she and Stacy had linked.

Meanwhile, Wolfie said, "Taking a master, right out from under our noses. I wonder if they even know what they have."

A . . . master?

Della wanted to ask Wolfie how Mrs. Jones could be a master if she was a female. All the Underground blood brothers were . . . brothers.

But she didn't enquire.

"Who are these hunters?" he asked, almost to himself. "Were there any powerful vampires with them?"

He was asking about a blood brother, and only now did he seem to recall how Della had mentioned that mean, dog-killing vampire after the Queenshill attack.

When they didn't answer right off, he hit the table, shaking the flowerpot that served as decoration. It jarred the girls, causing them to stand all the straighter, but not enough to make them lose all the composure that Queenshill, good breeding, and the lessons of vampire life had instilled in them.

As Della waited for him to speak, she realized that they were more or less at attention, acting like the soldiers he and Mrs. Jones had raised them to be.

But she had never wished to be a soldier. Just Wolfie's girl, forever and always.

He rose from his seat, hardly looking at them, his gaze focused inwardly, as if that was where he kept hope for the return of Mrs. Jones.

Della glared at him—a prince on the outside, a prat underneath. He had promised them such happiness, but he had lied, hadn't he?

Lied.

Shame covered her inside and out. Shame at having been fooled so easily.

As a tremble began to shift under her skin, Wolfie addressed them as if they were a team of assassins. The finely trained, elite Queenshill girls. The dirty less-than-a-dozen, now that their numbers had been so chiseled down.

"Sunrise is near and you're weary. So before you go back out there for Mrs. Jones . . ." A small smile took over his mouth. ". . . Claudia . . ." The correction seemed to make him feel better. ". . . you will need sustenance and rest. Tomorrow night, when our powers are high again, you *will* succeed in tracking her and bringing her back to where she belongs. With us."

With you, Della corrected him in her mind. The tremble was turning into a quiver.

Wolfie gestured to the remaining human males round the pub—boys who would be mind-wiped, no matter the risk, and taken care of so they would think they had only massive hangovers and a developing further illness come morning.

"Drink up," he told his girls, "then it's to rest."

"Yes, Wolfie," all of them said.

From the way the survivors voiced it, Della knew that they *all* had realized they were his soldiers, not his darlings. Not any longer.

And she knew that they, too, felt just as much shame as she did for being taken in by Wolfie.

ELEVEN

†HE ΠEW DIGS

Dawn stood in the center of their new headquarters, her hands on her holstered hips.

"What a *dump*," she said, and it wasn't for the first time. They'd been here a few minutes now, and she still couldn't believe this.

Their temporary HQ looked like one of those deep level underground shelters used during World War II. Dawn had heard most of them were being utilized as bureaucratic storage chambers now, but this one seemed to have been forgotten by society altogether. It stretched for what looked like a half mile, and an iron spiral staircase led up to another level, where there was probably a shaft. Along the concrete walls, there were lines of bunks, only a few of which had mattresses, pillows, and blankets. But the ventilation was good, and it'd been outfitted with a kitchen, foodstuffs, computers, and weapons lockers.

Still, it was bare bones. And, since the heater had just been activated, it was colder than a witch's tit.

Dawn had cozied her way into a down jacket and gloves while getting used to the degraded conditions. Not that she was high maintenance, but . . .

Jeez, maybe she'd gotten used to the luxury of Costin's homes. Maybe she *had* become a frakkin' princess lately. And this, coming from a stuntwoman who used to crash at buddies' houses instead of getting a place of her own.

A jacketed Kiko stood right next to her with an equally bundled Natalia, who was plugged into a portable scanner radio and earbuds. He wasn't complaining about their new HQ, probably because he blamed himself for putting them here since he'd been the one to let in the first vampire. Plus, he was still dragging around because he wasn't so happy about Costin just taking off for the Underground without a word to most of the team.

"It's good enough for temporary," he said.

The blanket-wrapped Claudius spoke from one of the bunks, where Friends were binding him, pushing him against the wall. "What I enjoy most about it is the knowledge that the vampires put you below the ground while they were last seen above. It begs the question of just who the hunters really are."

Kiko pointed at the vamp. "Shut it, Fangoria."

Frank, who'd been inspecting some private offices that contained single beds and doors, came out of one. Dawn supposed he'd claimed that particular room as his, since it'd be darker and better for vampire resting. Eva had settled in another of those closed-off rooms, and Dawn had yet to check in with her since her mom had arrived before the team. It was even possible that, by now, with all the bed rest, her mom should be taken to a doctor to see if there was something wrong.

Just another thing on the to-do list.

"Yeah, how about you shut your mouth up, Claudius?" Frank said, sauntering toward the group. He was dressed in layer upon layer of clothing, although Dawn doubted it was because of the cold. That amount of protection could only mean he wanted to block his skin from the sun.

"My, my," Claudius muttered in that hoarse voice before closing his eyes and leaning his head back against the concrete. It was about thirty minutes away from sunrise, but if he was thinking of falling into some rest, Dawn had news. She wasn't letting up on him.

Since the Friends had already sealed the tunnel entrance that'd led to this area, Frank was heading toward the stair exit, pulling a sun-proofed ski mask over his face to cover it from daylight. Even during these hours, he would be able to run fast enough outside so that no one would see much of him.

"Hold on," Dawn said. "I know you want to go after Breisi's portrait, but don't you think barging up top could attract attention, especially right now, when things are still level orange?"

"True enough," Kiko added. "We can't take the chance of going out until we need to. We know the vamps have access to cameras around the city, and if one's trained near our exit . . ."

Not to mention that Ms. Shadow Girl was still out there, Dawn thought. Shouldn't Frank be more cautious since Dawn had already mentioned the *custode*'s appearance— then disappearance—to the team?

Frank kept going up the stairs. "There's no cameras around here. A Friend already said so when I asked her."

The only thing that stopped him from reaching the upper level was another Friend who was winding her way down the stairs since there must've been an entrance for them near an exit shaft. She pushed him back toward the group.

Natalia took out one of her earbuds as the Friend spoke.

"There's talk among the authorities," the spirit rushed to tell the team. She was one of the Friends who'd been stationed with the police. Tammy, Dawn thought, recognizing the businesslike Midwestern accent. She'd been some kind

of feminist CEO before dying. *"The cops don't know what to make of those charmed humans. Evidently, the vampires adjusted their victims' memories before sending them away from our old headquarters. Maybe the girls barely mind-wiped them, because the humans are talking nonsense."*

"Elaborate?" Dawn said.

"They're saying terrorists got to them and brainwashed them, but I suspect this is only their confusion talking."

"Shit," Dawn said. "That's high profile, and it might lead to the authorities canvassing the area."

"Or," Kiko said, "the law could chalk it up to a bunch of loony chatter. Let's pray the media doesn't get ahold of this."

Dawn pulled her jacket closer around her. "Let's also hope that we'll already be through with this Underground and out of London before any full investigations can get underway."

Tammy the Friend flew off, and Natalia said, "Should we contact Detective Inspector Norton?" The team had never met him, but he was one of Costin's sources. "Do you think he could help?"

"We might be beyond the police now," Dawn said, glancing at Claudius, who was clearly listening with his eyes closed and that maddening grin on his face.

"But . . ." Natalia began, and Dawn knew exactly what the new girl was going to go off on.

"Natalia," she said, "this isn't the time to be doing follow-up work on what you consider to be the most important part of this hunt. The Friends have already told us that Norton's come up empty with the Kate Lansing case."

The psychic stared at the ground. She'd become attached to the first victim they'd "encountered." Since Natalia could hear the dead, she'd latched onto Kate Lansing's voice at the Billiter Street burial grounds, and she'd never let go. Dawn wouldn't even be surprised if Natalia sneaked out to go to Kate's upcoming inquest.

In a lot of ways, Natalia—the most naïve one of them all, but also the most intuitive—was the team's grounding force. But sometimes grounding wasn't what a hunter needed.

Dawn moved on. "Kalin? Where are you?"

The Friend breezed over; she seemed energized by all the action.

"Could you plug up Sleeping Beauty's ears over there?" Dawn asked, jerking her chin toward Claudius. "We've got some sensitive issues to go over before I spend quality time with him. But it shouldn't be more than a few minutes."

Kalin shot over to the master vamp, who started to protest as the spirit pushed him to the bed, then nudged her essence over a pillow to the ear that wasn't against the mattress. Her force, plus the pillow, should do the trick.

Back to the team. "Even though Costin hasn't run out of time to complete his attack yet, I want to know which one of you has the information about where he is. And don't BS me. He told me someone on this crew would be privy to his destination and would be able to access his locator, if needed. I want to be as prepped as possible if dusk comes around and he's still MIA."

She wouldn't think about his other order. To go for the Underground instead of a rescue.

Kiko was looking around at the team, and Dawn didn't know if it was because he was the secret holder or if his pride was just as wounded as it'd been back when he'd found out that only Breisi had known a lot of Costin's secrets in Hollywood, when she'd been a human hunter, too.

"Well?" Dawn asked when no one came forward.

Kiko said, "I can start touch-reading. At least with Natalia. That'd tell me if she's the one. I wouldn't be much good with Frank though."

Dawn didn't ask if Kiko's mind was in decent order for any readings; he could've still been fuzzy from the lulling.

He seemed to get that, and his posture slumped. Soon,

he'd be promising her that he would wean himself off the lulling, but she'd heard it all before with the medication.

Yet she couldn't blame him, really. Not with all the visions and vibes that were always assaulting him, especially in this intense job.

Natalia and Frank were still mum, so Dawn fixed her attention on the new girl, willing her to blurt out the truth—that Costin had entrusted her with this piece of the puzzle.

But then Frank talked.

"He didn't want anyone to know until he got back."

You could've knocked Dawn over with mist. Even Kiko gaped at her dad.

"You?" she asked him. "Costin gave the location to you?"

Frank nodded. "I learned my lesson but good last time in Hollywood, when we shot off to help him. Breisi gave me what for, too, and I promised her and him that I'd keep everyone from joining in an attack this time. I guess Costin took that for worthiness. And the icing on the cake? Kiko can't touch-read me for the information. I'm a vault."

"Where is Costin, Frank?" Dawn asked.

He folded his arms in front of his barrel chest.

She stepped up to her dad. "The last thing I want to do is go after him, but I'll be honest. I'm getting nervous, here. He hasn't even sent a Friend back with news. Not even a phone call, either, saying he's on his way."

"You shouldn't have expected any of that. He's probably busy."

True, and maybe she was just overreacting. But there was something picking away at her, and she only wanted to be ready to go to him at the first opportunity, if required to.

"I got it, Frank—you're a vault." She glanced sidelong at Claudius. "But, if I wanted to go to him now because I have the bad feeling he's in trouble, there're other ways for me to find out where he is."

"You're only supposed to use Claudius to get at a true

Underground location if you need to, Dawn. That's what Costin told me."

She tapped her foot on the ground.

When her dad didn't take her baiting, she blew up. "What if Claudius *did* set Costin up? Wouldn't you regret not saying anything?"

"I doubt Costin would want us to stumble into the same trap, so, no. I wouldn't regret it." He shook his head. "I just wish I'd grabbed Della and brought her down here. She would've been an easier interview than Claudius."

The Friends had barred the team from the girl vamps during the evacuation and, besides, the Queenshill chicks had been real fast in getting down those stairs and to that fire.

Dawn huffed out a sigh as she glared at Frank. Damn it. It wasn't like she was going to work him for information like she had with Claudius, so the only source available to her was in this room, on a bunk, acting like an asshole. And to make matters worse, Costin had told her not to go after the info, anyway, unless there was definitely a worst-case scenario—and she couldn't prove there was.

He *so* didn't trust her to stay put and allow him to do his job. But she probably wouldn't have trusted her, either.

Hell, it was only because she wanted him safe.

Her gaze swung toward the master vamp, a pillow still over the side of his head.

Surely I'd feel if Costin was gone, Dawn thought, wondering just how far she'd take this paranoia that was chipping away at her. Costin was probably kicking ass in the Underground and the team just hadn't been around the schoolgirl vamps long enough to see them change, reflecting the termination of Mihas.

Kiko moved toward Claudius's bunk, and the vamp's nose twitched from the space between pillow and blanket, as if he'd scented someone coming near.

"How about this for a compromise?" Kiko said. "I say we

go ahead and parlay with Claudius, here, for peace of mind. If he could tell us the real Underground location, Frank can verify if it matches what Costin told *him*. That way we'd know if we should be worried about the boss or not."

"And if Claudius gives us a random location just because he knows it'll make us worry?" Frank asked.

Natalia spoke. "That's a possibility."

Dawn didn't care.

Her voice was thick as she said, "Maybe we could just get Claudius to reveal what would be waiting for us if Costin *is* trapped and we had to go after him . . . after we dealt with the Underground, of course."

Before she could truly see if emotion would overwhelm her or not, she reached for Claudius's pillow. Kalin allowed her to tug it away from him.

Kiko was right by Dawn's side. "Hey, Mr. Bloodsucky."

Frank backed up Dawn, too, and Natalia did the same to Kiko.

"Before you drift off," Dawn said to Claudius, "we'd like to pose some questions."

The master vamp yawned, showing his disdain, and Dawn whipped out, mentally smacking him.

She almost did it twice, too, until she felt a burn near her neck, attaching itself to the latest mark, which she hadn't even bothered to look at yet.

She gritted her teeth and held back.

ABOUT an hour and a half later, Claudius was in a deep, probably self-inflicted rest, his eyes open, hearkening back to his near-coma state.

They'd gotten nothing out of him, and Dawn had been sweating with the effort to contain her temper.

"Stubborn dick," Kiko said.

He and Natalia sat on one of the lower bunks, holding the shirt and jeans Dawn had shed in favor of a shower and another set of black clothes, including a turtleneck that covered the smack of darkness she'd known would be on her neck, attached to the one before, just like some kind of growing tribal tattoo.

But she'd gone beyond fighting it and into accepting that this was her life now. There was no consistency, even when it came to this mutation or devolution.

As Kiko and Natalia looked over Dawn's clothing, she remembered the saw-bow, the injury to the keeper.

The flying blood.

"Check my shirt for Shadow's blood stains," she said to them. Black material wouldn't make the blood obvious, but they'd find the traces.

Dawn let them go for it and headed toward Eva's room. In Claudius's present coma state, he had a reprieve since it was just about impossible to get him out of it right now. But she'd try again soon to put the full-court press on him. Meanwhile, the Friends would guard and bind the master vamp since the spirits were refreshed, relieving each other after some of them took root in their portraits back at old headquarters.

Since the Friends weren't complaining about the inconvenience, Dawn had persuaded Frank to take some rest, too. Then they could talk about him going back to regular HQ to rescue portraits before any vampires might return. It wasn't as if they'd realize the paintings were special, and God knew Frank needed to recharge his own powers during the daylight. Besides, there was the whole "low profile" thing they needed to keep.

Grumbling, he'd agreed, then gone to his own small room, which was next to Eva's.

Dawn halted on her way to her mother's, a thought popping into her mind.

"What if we split into two teams?" she asked Kiko and Natalia.

"Huh?" he asked.

"If I was able to force Claudius into cracking and he told us what we'd need to be prepared for with any traps Costin might be caught in . . . What if, then, Frank and I, plus some Friends, went to the Underground while you two went to Costin? *You* didn't promise him you'd stay away from a rescue."

Natalia glared at Kiko. He frowned. She was keeping Kiko in line, and he was a prime candidate for it after letting in that vamp earlier.

"Okay," Dawn said. "Just thought I'd put it out there."

"It's just not a good idea to split any attacks up," Kiko said. "Maybe that's what Claudius is trying to get us to do, anyway."

Point to Kiko.

Dawn left them to go about their investigation, cruising by Claudius's bunk. His staring eyes made her think of those holographic images in Disneyland's Haunted Mansion—eyes that followed you as you passed.

She just wished this *were* an amusement park ride.

Reaching the room where the Friends had tucked Eva, Dawn rapped lightly with her knuckles, then eased open the door. A slat of light fell onto a metal bed in a corner, where a shape filled the blankets.

Sleeping, Dawn thought. When was the last time her mom had woken up?

She entered, leaving the door open for some scant illumination. Eva's long, salon-blond hair silked over her pillow, her face turned toward the wall, one hand peeking out of the covers.

It was her healthy hand—the one she hadn't drawn blood from the other night—so there wasn't a bandage on it. Then again, Dawn hadn't really spent quality time with her mom in days, so it'd probably be scarring up by now, especially with the aid of healing gel.

Her mother's breathing changed rhythm, and Dawn waited for her to wake up. But what would she say?

"Mom?"

Eva's breathing evened out. Pretending to still be asleep. *Acting!*

Not a surprise since her mother had been the best actress ever, setting up her supposed human murder to cover her vampiness and her existence in the L.A. Underground.

Dawn's hands hung at her sides. She said something anyway, even if she was only talking to the air. "I just wanted to see if you were okay after all the excitement. And I'm . . . Well, you've been in a bed for a long time. I don't think that's a good thing."

And . . . silence.

But she had the feeling that Eva was hearing every word.

"Mom, I know what's going on. After the debacle with Frank, you feel like there's no hope. Nothing for you. But I want you to know that there is . . . something. I'm here." She'd always been here, wishing for Eva.

She thought she heard her mom's breathing stop for a second, but then it started up again.

"All right." Dawn started to leave. "I also wanted you to know that Frank's not as angry as you think he is about 'the incident.' I'm not angry, either. I even . . ." Dawn pulled at the side of her jeans. "I just want you to come back, Mom."

Now, even if her mother had said anything, Dawn didn't want to hear it. She was too used to not having Eva around, and she was sure her mom was just going to tell her to bug off, anyway.

So she shut the door behind her, going back into the main room, choosing a random bunk distant from where Kiko and Natalia were working.

She couldn't sleep, so she kept one ear tuned for Claudius to stir and one tuned for the hopeful return of Costin.

Time seemed to thunk by as neither one happened.

TWELVE

DEEPER

EVA had turned onto her back, and long after Dawn departed, she stared at the ceiling, her blanket tucked around her neck. It was quiet—almost too quiet—and she was waiting to get out of bed until she knew what the team was doing.

So she listened. Listened closely.

With a clarity she was still getting used to, she heard Frank moving around in the room next to hers and, even though he didn't have his light on, she was able to see the outline of the adjoining door through the darkness, as if Frank was emanating preternatural energy. Strange to be able to sense that. She also caught Kiko and Natalia talking in low tones just above the grind of the temporary headquarters generator—something normal hearing wouldn't have sorted out from all the other sounds.

But Eva wasn't very "normal" anymore. She wasn't . . . the same. She wasn't even aware now of the heavy sensation she'd carried in her soul ever since she'd turned from a vampire back into a human—an inner weight that constantly reminded her of how she'd been *inhuman*, how she'd sinned against nature by trading herself in for the promise of long-lasting fame and glory. Dawn had confessed that she'd felt the same soul stain inside of her, too, and Eva had heard through the doors when no one thought she was listening that her daughter had started changing, maybe because of what they'd carried over with them during the transition.

Eva had always wondered if every vampire-turned-human was cursed to change, and it seemed that, like Dawn, she was finally doing it . . . but only after Frank's last rejection.

And after meeting the man at the wine bar.

She smiled, enjoying the sharpness of the sounds and sight. She'd missed these sensations from her time in the Hollywood Underground. Recently, as "Mia Scott," a private citizen who'd been remade under the care of plastic surgery and relocation, she'd been so bored. Deadened to life.

But not now.

Pushing down her blanket, she sat up. She'd been bedridden, her hair matted and tossed, but her body felt clean. Everyone thought she'd been sick, and they'd left her alone as she'd gotten better . . . and better. But she wasn't physically ill. Maybe stoned was a better word. In fact, when those little girls had attacked headquarters earlier, Eva had hardly even needed a Friend to protect her while she'd been ushered to these temporary quarters, because she felt strong.

Stronger than ever.

She hadn't told anyone that, though. She'd just come here to her new room, waiting until everyone went to sleep.

Waiting until the time was right to feed herself again.

She closed her eyes, hungry. She knew what would fill her though, and she was ready to get up and do what she'd wanted to do so badly for a long time now—longer than she'd been in London, mooning around Frank and wishing he would realize how much she still loved him and how good they could be together. Longer than she and Dawn had tried to mend their relationship since settling here when Costin had gotten a strong bead on this Underground.

She had the means to get what she wanted now.

Taking off the bandage she'd put on her hand to hide the marks where she'd drawn blood for Frank, she thought of how she'd run far away that night, humiliated, out of headquarters. She'd run and run until she'd ended up at a wine bar, where she'd met a man who hadn't told her his name. A man who'd offered her a finely made handkerchief to dry her tears. And when she had looked up at him, she'd seen understanding in his slightly tilted light brown eyes.

Handsome, with black hair slicked back and coming just to the line of his jaw, an alluring smile. Much too tempting for a lonely woman who'd just been rejected.

Now, she looked over her healed hand, and she wasn't surprised that there were no scars. Not after what the man from the wine bar had given to her.

Memory surged: The man taking her downstairs to a silent cove under the wine bar, where bottles were stored. The man whispering to her, making her an offer. Her accepting it.

It had all happened so fast, before Dawn had gotten there. A prick of Eva's skin, a bit of her blood, a pact she had gladly entered into . . .

Carefully smoothing out her nightgown, she paused at a faint smudge of dirt that had been hidden by the draping of material.

Thinking that she would need to change soon—but not now, not yet—Eva walked to the adjoining door, as drawn to Frank as she'd ever been. And maybe even more now, as her appetite for him pulsed.

Last time she had gone to him, she'd failed, but this

time, he wouldn't be able to resist, and unlike before, Eva didn't second-guess what she was doing.

She opened the door, not knocking this time, and she saw another door besides, on his side. Her hunger pierced her. Then she noticed an alarm system rigged to sense movement.

Please. With Frank's vampire abilities, he'd know she was coming, anyway.

Or would he . . . ?

Eva touched a wire that led to a box on the alarm. She wasn't well versed in the team's systems, but she knew that she could fool this one into ignoring her, just as she'd done to the Friends as well as the laser tracker and security camera back at primary headquarters when she'd sneaked outside the night before last. Manipulating them had come as a surprise to her, but she'd done it naturally, as if there was a voice whispering instructions in her head. She'd only followed its direction, just as she was following her hunger now.

She opened the second door, finding Frank, a glowing figure in her eyes, in the darkness. He wasn't resting, like he should've been. Instead, he held a mini flamethrower, inspecting it.

He was already cocking his head at her entrance, his sensitive vampire hearing having picked up her approach.

"I guess we need to check these alarms," he said, already dismissing her. She'd caused him a lot of grief because Breisi hadn't blamed him for giving in to the lure of her blood as much as she had for him taking pity on Eva afterward.

"Hello, Frank," she said, making her voice different—a call over the waves of normal sound.

He stopped fussing with the weapon and ran a gaze over her.

She was glad she was wearing the nightgown—an intimate garment, long and white. Maybe it reminded him of their honeymoon, before she'd tried to secure a future for her family by going Underground, deserting him and Dawn, who'd been just a baby. But Eva had thought she'd been doing the right thing until she'd learned otherwise.

When Frank's voice came out choked, she knew that she had more power than ever—even over him, a vampire.

"If Breisi comes back from patrolling outside to find you in here," he said, clearly fighting what he'd heard in her voice, "there'll be trouble."

"You have no idea what sort of trouble." Eva wasn't sure why she'd said it, but she was certain she could live up to the threat. She felt that good. That . . . renewed.

Her comment made him wary, and he resisted some more. "I've got to go back to headquarters, get Breisi's portrait, maybe even a few others. The Friends won't have any place to refuel without those paintings, and they can't risk rooting to them in a place that's been compromised by those vamps."

Just being near him, her body was humming, wanting, needing. And it needed more than it had gotten earlier, before she'd returned to the old headquarters, creeping back into her bed after feeding outside.

But it wasn't blood that sustained her.

"Baby," she said, urging him, using the endearment from long ago. "Just come to me."

He tilted his head again, then rose, dropping the flame-thrower to the bed and walking toward her.

Joy shot through her. She had him.

She lifted her hand, her fingertips brushing his cheek. A raw, electric current seemed to zap through her, nourishing her, taking from *him*, and he jolted, his eyes widening.

His skin was cold, inhuman, but he still had a heart that beat. He was still a male, with male memories and urges that hadn't been stolen by vampirism, and *that* was what she yearned for.

The adoration.

Even a hint of it made her go hot, her pulse digging into

her. Her own memories rose to the surface—her and Frank kissing, them loving each other so fiercely that she had almost given up stardom and worship from millions just to live happily ever after with him.

Until the Underground recruited her.

She touched his cheek again, her fingertips lingering on his jaw as his skin—even a vampire's—shriveled a bit.

"Relax, Frank," she said. "Then you can go get that portrait. And I can see to it that you don't remember what happened here, between us. Not until you're ready to accept it." She had altered the memory patterns of that boy in the college sweatshirt, and she was going to give it a try with Frank, too.

When she trailed down his throat, whisking over the center of it, she knew that she'd stolen his power to move. But she wouldn't have to take as much from him as she'd taken from her earlier victim. The college boy had been her first, and she'd been unable to stop herself from pulling out too much sustenance. Frank's vampire power was stronger—what he gave her would be a hundred times more potent and wonderful.

It was only up to her to make sure he wouldn't remember afterward, when he was healing, as a vampire surely would heal, because unlike the human college boy, Frank wouldn't die from this feeding. Besides, she would give him her blood in exchange, nursing him, bringing them together again.

Eva's throat closed with emotion. Her husband. The man she'd never stopped being married to in her heart. And she'd been given this ability to join with him again.

Silently, she thanked the man from the wine bar who'd chosen her, then slid her other hand beneath Frank's shirt, touching his cool skin and hearing him moan with the beginning of what she knew would be unbearable ecstasy for both of them.

THIRTEEN
†HE ΠEW LEAD

MERATOLIAGE."

When Dawn first heard the word, she was in a daze—not really asleep, but not so much awake, either.

She sat up in her bed as Kiko said it again.

"Meratoliage!"

He scrambled off his bunk and toward Dawn's while still holding her clothing. Natalia followed.

"I got it," Kiko said, banging into Dawn's mattress and shoving her shirt at her. "I hit some blood from that *custode*, and BINGO—trance time! 'Meratoliage.'"

"What does that even mean?" Dawn's heart was working double time; Kiko's excitement was contagious.

"I don't know!" he said optimistically.

He kneeled on the floor, closed his eyes, touched Dawn's black shirt again. She didn't want to think that he was desperately trying to overcome his screw-up status, but Kiko had tried to compensate for the effect his pills had pushed on him before. Now it was about the lulling, not meds, but the mea culpa was the same.

Natalia kneeled by Kiko. As he concentrated, she put her hand on his shoulder, closing her eyes, too, as if to ride his mind.

Dawn looked away, almost like they were kissing or something, and her gaze landed on Claudius, who still reclined on his bunk, staring straight ahead. He was in "pause" mode, too seemingly weakened or permanently damaged by being worn down after Dawn's initial treatment of him.

But why did his eyes look a little wider? Did he seem . . . scared?

Trying not to disturb the psychics, Dawn rolled off of her bunk, sauntering over to him, her blood pounding now, mostly in her temples.

"You see that?" she said. "We're going to find what we need to with or without you."

No blinking. Just staring.

Dawn bent lower, the scent of the Friend who was binding Claudius especially strong. In the background, the sound of the air turning on was like a dragon breathing, and it made her feel like they were all in the concrete belly of a beast.

"I know what you're up to," she said. "You're taking your revenge out on everyone before you die. You don't want to go down alone, so you're getting great pleasure in working over Costin, your blood brother. Or maybe you really did send him to the Underground to destroy Mihas, who betrayed you."

Claudius's eyes flicked to Dawn's, pistoning her heart as she looked away just in time. His facial features seemed to melt from male to female, but he didn't shift all the way.

As a half-and-half creature, he softly said, "You're so very young, aren't you? Young enough to avoid what you're headed for."

There wasn't any charm in his voice. Was Claudius being . . . sincere?

Hah. Right. He was just trying to get out of more questioning.

Claudius went on. "Why do you strive for him when he never hesitates to leave you behind?"

"He did that for a purpose."

"They'll always leave us behind, don't you realize that?"

Claudius was setting a trap for *her*, right here, right now. But she wouldn't fall into it.

She hardened herself as he continued.

"Once the separation happens, it's a shock to the system. You crave him more than anything. You think you would move mountains to get him back. But then the miracle occurs. You realize that you're still functioning, standing on your own, finding strength in staying true to your own beliefs, even if you never realized you had any."

Maybe it *was* a sign of insanity, but Dawn could almost imagine Claudius/Claudia as an older advisor, one who spoke the truth until it hurt.

"And what's your belief?" Dawn needed to twist this back to the Underground and away from her.

Claudius tilted his head, his voice going even softer. "I believe that, when you kill me, Ms. Madison, you will do it quickly and cleanly. You still have that much compassion in you, and I would request it."

That hadn't been what Dawn meant at all.

As the master vampire's seemingly honest statement hit home, Dawn thought she should say something off the cuff and quippy. Something to show she'd kill him however she wanted to for Costin's sake.

But her new marks tingled on her face, her neck, and she wondered if she would enjoy the actual kill as much as she'd reveled in the buildup to it.

Stomach knotted, Dawn watched Claudius's gaze float

over to where Kiko and Natalia were communing. The half-man, half-woman vampire seemed to be deep in thought.

Was Claudius mulling over what waited for him in true death?

Or was he thinking about Mihas?

When the vampire shifted into a full male again, Dawn thought it was some sort of big statement. Final independence from Mihas, who'd accepted the "Claudia" version of him more than the "Claudius" one.

She whispered, "What do you *really* believe in, Claudius?"

The vampire's strong features went resolute just as, in the background, Kiko and Natalia mumbled something at the same time, both of them still in their trance states.

"Dragon."

What?

Then they screamed it. "Dragon!"

Claudius gaped, and Dawn wondered if Natalia had somehow picked up on the power of the vampire's answer to the question "What do you really believe in?" Had the master vamp inadvertently added psychic power to Natalia's, and then from her to Kiko? Had Claudius's mind wandered and joined with the vibes they were getting off of that *custode* blood?

Dawn didn't take her gaze off of the vampire as she talked to her team. "Keep going, you two. See if you can get any more."

Then she turned her attention on Claudius, her head swimming. This was a new method of questioning, and she hoped to God it'd finally work.

"Meratoliage. Is that word connected to the dragon and the *custode*s, too, since that's the blood of one of them on my shirt?"

"No."

"Are we getting closer to them, Claudius?"

He bared his teeth. "No, you're getting farther away . . . from him."

"From the dragon?"

"Not the dragon."

Dawn didn't have to ask who he meant. Claudius was back to psychological warfare, attacking Dawn through Costin. Preying on every doubt she'd had when she suspected that maybe she was in the relationship because she believed it was only going to end badly. It was a form of self-sabotage, but Dawn had already known that, because if you were with someone who was bound to abandon you, you could fulfill your own prophecies when he did leave. Right?

Claudius was smiling again, and it was because he was positioning her right where he wanted her.

Hardly.

"Here's the thing," Dawn said. "I've been through all lanes of this mystery maze with you vamps. False leads, like the Highgate Vampire, then Thomas Gatenby, who turned out just to be your stooge." Costin had confirmed this information during his own interrogation. "But I can see you're frightened now, because this is the real thing, isn't it? Your community is going down, whether you're trying to protect it or not."

A slight hiss came from between the vampire's lips. A warning.

This went beyond Mihas, Dawn thought. Maybe Claudius did respect the vow he'd made to the dragon, and now that he'd lost everything else, he'd desperately returned to it, like a fallen believer coming back to his true faith in a time of crisis.

"No . . . dragon," the vampire said from between growing, needled cat teeth.

The Friend on duty pushed Claudius back, and Dawn minded her distance, remembering that nip she'd gotten the last time she'd been too close.

Claudius chafed under the confinement. "No . . . dragon in our house!"

Both Kiko and Natalia gave little shouts, but Dawn kept guard on the vampire as the psychics rushed over with Dawn's clothing in hand.

Adrenaline seemed to bind them together, and Dawn's heartbeat surged.

Claudius was shaking his head, as if the harder he did it, the more they'd disbelieve their theories.

"Know what I saw?" Kiko said. "An estate. It had sweeping lawns and a fancy study where ledgers of birthrights and history books fill the shelves. And guess what? Them books also contain procedures, spells, information about alchemy."

Dawn jumped in. "An Underground location?"

Natalia stared at the vampire, avoiding his unfiltered gaze. "No, the estate is not the Underground. Not directly. But it has resources that *could* lead there, and the information is housed only in the ground-level study." The new girl narrowed her eyes. "This vision you helped us with could put an end to the murders of the young, recruited girls your group pulls from the streets. Girls like Kate."

Kate Lansing, their initial lead, again. But if it lit a fire under Natalia, all the better. The psychic had grown up hearing voices from the dead, and being unable to help them until now had tortured her.

Cocky Kiko sounded off. "You must've really been thinking over here, Claudius, because we felt your vibes and saw some real good shit."

Natalia didn't even mind the cussing. "Meratoliage. It's an old family name that they don't use publicly anymore, and these people live in a big country house with gardens and pastures in . . ."

"Kent," Kiko said. "Near the River Darent."

Claudius blinked. The reflex gave him away.

Unless he was lying again.

Dawn grabbed on to both Kiko's and Natalia's shoulders, so proud of them she wanted to bust right open. Then she pulled them away from Claudius and went for a weapons locker, calling for some Friends who'd just returned from resting at the old headquarters.

She asked Kiko and Natalia to give the spirits a full description of the house and other details they'd gotten in their visions, then the Friends took off to the Kent area, where they'd concentrate their search near the River Darent. After isolating the house, they would enter it, then track down where exactly one could find these books and documents.

After they returned to brief the team, it'd be time for a field trip. They only had until dusk to get this done.

Kiko said, "We've got some prepping to do before we go there."

"Not we," Dawn said. "Me."

"What—?"

"Listen, Kik." Dawn bent to rest a hand on his shoulder. "I've *got* to go. I'm not sitting around here banging my head against the wall with Claudius when there's a lead outside. Claudius is impossible, so we're going to have to take another route. In the meantime, though, someone's got to stay here to keep working on him, just in case he's pulling our legs and we need to take another run at him. He needs to stay worn down. Besides, maybe someone else besides me would be more effective in their questioning techniques."

"Kiko," Natalia said in that practical way of hers. "You're in no shape for a field trip, anyway. Dawn should go."

Then she glanced hopefully at Dawn, as if expecting an invitation to accompany her.

"No," Dawn said.

Kiko already knew that arguing with two determined women was fruitless. "What if the place is guarded by vampires or . . . something else?"

"More *custodes*?" Dawn asked. "I'll be ready."

A Friend whizzed up to her.

"*I'll be ready, too,*" Kalin said. "*Bein' round 'ere's punchin' a 'ole in my 'ead.*"

"You don't have a head for any hole to punch into," Dawn said, then went right back to Kiko and Natalia. "Looks like my back's going to be covered. While we're gone, just keep on Claudius."

"But—" Kiko said, offering one last try.

"We're so close," Dawn said. "Can't you feel it?"

Without waiting for an answer, she went to a weapons and costume locker to see what was on hand for her field trip. She'd wear a disguise outside, in case they were being watched. Also, until she got to the estate, she'd don a pulser, which would throw off her body rhythms should vamps be around to listen to them. Hopefully, Kalin's jasmine would confuse any scent tracking, *if* the vamps were near or if Shadow Girl had any way of using smells to find them.

Then again, Dawn thought, the saw-bow did get a piece of the shadow thing. Maybe she was out of commission for the time being.

Dawn grabbed a crucifix necklace out of the locker, intending to wear that, too.

A tug on her shirt got her attention. It was Natalia, who was looking up at her with those serious, dark eyes.

"Dawn," the new girl said, "don't take unnecessary chances while you're out there."

"Who me?" she asked, trying to laugh it off.

But Natalia was a bulldog under all that girly stuff. "What I'm trying to say is that you shouldn't try to save everyone except yourself. Use caution."

Dawn thought about what Claudius had told her about Costin always leaving her behind.

God, maybe she *was* always trying to catch up by doing dumb things. . . .

"Saving everyone's all a part of insanity, Nat," Dawn said, wondering if she was joking.

And also wondering if she wasn't.

UNDER the ground, Jonah had taken over for Costin and was now at the bars, his hands wrapped in the long black coat he'd dressed in before they'd started on their Underground journey. With the help of the Friends, he was again attempting to pry open the cage with his vampire strength.

Costin had submerged himself in the body, resting in case Jonah did set them free. If that happened, and if Jonah found the Underground, the boss would need all the strength he could get.

All the same, Costin was still awake down there. Jonah could feel it.

He pulled at the bars again, shaking with the effort, but they wouldn't give, even with the push of the Friends.

With sighs, the spirit girls backed off. They were getting tired and needed to go back to their portraits to rest.

As they all sank to the ground, Jonah realized an invisible cloud of jasmine still haunted the air.

Breisi.

He imagined her as she'd been as a human—a Louise Brooks Latina, with her dark hair bobbed. A petite, rosy skinned hellcat mad scientist with a lady's manners and a bunch of weird shirts boasting everything from Disney characters to teddy bears.

"Not giving up?" Jonah asked her.

"Not yet."

She swirled around the cage, probably looking once again for any way to trip the trap. He didn't ask why she was so anxious because he already knew—and it wasn't because she longed to get back to her portrait. It was because of Frank. She hated being separated from her boyfriend, and it didn't help that Eva, the former wife, was back at headquarters with him.

And then there was also the matter of bringing havoc to the Underground. She loved her job.

"There's got to be a release lever," she said in that whirly voice while she combed her essence over the walls.

Jonah felt like an ass for being the one who'd stumbled on the catch in the first place. It'd been buried in the floor, and he'd been too excited about fighting alongside Costin— not against him for once—to take his time and notice it. Earlier he'd mentioned Indiana Jones to his body mate, but Jonah hadn't added that *he* felt a lot like Short Round, tripping traps and putting them between a rock and silverbarred hard place.

What a hero.

"Well," Jonah said to Breisi. "We've tried everything on this contraption." Blades, a revolver he'd packed, but none of them had been of any use.

As Breisi continued exploring the walls, Jonah sat down again, checking his watch. Hours away from dusk, when the team had Costin's permission to let loose. It'd been a desperate option, because if Costin failed in his bid to decimate the Underground, the vampires would be on higher alert. They'd probably be ready for more attacks, and that put the team in double the danger.

But who else was there to slay the masters and then the dragon?

From deep inside, Costin rolled, as if giving up on his rest.

"You are just as invested as any of them, aren't you, Jonah?" he said, as if surprised by that. But he couldn't be.

Both of them shared almost everything: a body, thoughts, knowledge. It was just that when it came to things like feeling physical sensations—touching a woman's skin or drinking blood—the submerged entity couldn't enjoy it.

And that was the real problem between him and Costin.

"Investment is why you chose me, though, right?" Jonah asked. "Because I had ideals and what you used to call a pure heart at the beginning."

"Before you became overzealous about taking over? Yes, I did believe you would be a perfect host."

Jonah shrugged, a loaded gesture. "I tried to be. I really did."

Costin weighed heavily in Jonah, too. "I know this. You did it in your own way. But then . . . matters grew complicated."

He was thinking of Dawn. It used to be that Jonah had wanted her only because Costin had her. But lately . . .

Well, Dawn had come to mean more. Maybe it was because she'd seen Jonah as his own man or whatever you called what he was.

"When this is over," Jonah said to Costin, "what do you think'll happen?"

Costin knew that he was talking about more than just the further pursuit of Undergrounds.

"I will not share her," Costin said.

"And you shouldn't." Jonah didn't have a chance with her. He'd always known it. Dawn would always love Costin, even if the two of them had a dysfunctional way of relating. Costin's pride kept him from admitting that she was his master, even if she tried hard not to act like it. Dawn's . . . well, her *everything* didn't allow her to commit to any man.

But Costin was far beyond a man, and maybe that was what she needed.

Jonah was more, too, though.

"How," he added, "can you be with a woman you feel

mortified by because she can rescue you? And don't tell me I'm wrong."

"I only wish I could."

Jonah knew Costin was still coming to terms with the last time Dawn had saved him. Even so, he said, "Let her rescue you, man. Rescue *us*. That's who she is, so don't hate her for it."

But the he-man soldier in Costin—the way he'd been for centuries—was too ingrained.

Jonah had one last comment. "You've got to learn to let it go."

The words echoed between them, and he heard every syllable, taking it to heart, too. Costin wasn't the only one who had a lot of work to do on himself. Jonah had enough baggage, too: the bitterness of a life that hadn't turned out the way he'd wanted it to when he was human, the false relief of being something new.

Costin sensed Jonah's realization, then the determination to improve. And, for the first time, the Traveler truly admired him.

They didn't come to any kind of agreement, because who knew if he and Costin would ever get out of here? Jonah just wished there was some way to communicate with the team, to let them know that they were still "alive" and kicking.

He closed out his discussion with Costin. "No matter how this ends, it's been a privilege. I mean that."

Costin hesitated, then sighed, as if in appreciation. "Yes, Jonah. You have carried me through some trying times, and I will be ever in awe of how you succeeded."

As their thoughts joined in something like an inner handshake, Breisi's essence came screaming back through the tunnel.

"Shadow!" she said, posting herself in front of the cage while the other Friends joined her, even as weak as they were.

But Jonah and Costin weren't that broken down yet. They'd had plenty of blood before coming here, including Dawn's.

The sustenance wouldn't last for much longer, but it would work for now.

When the red eyes appeared in the darkness down the hallway, Jonah rose to his feet, bolstered by the handshake he and Costin were still engaged in deep within their body.

FOURTEEN

ΠΕΑR ΤΗΕ LOΠDOΠ BABYLOΠ, AΠSWERIΠG ΤΗΕ *CVSTODE* ALERΤ

So one of the old custode *traps has snagged fresh meat,* Lilly had thought minutes earlier as a door slid shut behind her and she traveled the tunnel, which was located a kilometer from the main Underground.

She and Nigel had been observing this tunnel's camera, watching while their prey attempted to escape its cage. The idea was a prudent one, allowing the *custode*s to inventory the creature's habits, strengths . . . weaknesses. And they had seen how it was put off by the silver of the cage, unable to conjure the strength to pry apart the bars.

Initially, the captive's intrusion had set off a priority alarm that called Lilly away from regular patrol duty in Southwark. Since the trap was so close to the Underground, it was imperative that both *custode*s investigate what precisely had been caught; they were here to protect what was below the ground, not frolic about in an attack above. Just because the schoolgirls had launched their own rescue attempt up top, this didn't mean a keeper had any business remaining there instead of doing her primary work down here.

That was why Lilly had been compelled to leave the action with "Dawn" and rush straight over on her motorcycle. She'd barely even found time to bind her shoulder wound with a shirt she had filched from a drunk who was wandering home on the north side of the Thames. Fortunately, the blade that "Dawn" shot at her had resulted only in a superficial injury, so tending to it had been simple once she had returned here.

Lilly walked round a tunnel corner, rolling her compromised shoulder, feeling the bite of the cut.

Dawn. Now she knew who the mind-powered woman was, because Lilly had heard the rest of the hunter group calling to her after Lilly had sneaked into their house along with the vampires themselves. Now she could give a name to the humiliation of being bested and having to desert a confrontation with this female hunter yet again.

The first time Lilly had run off, it'd been out of prudence. The second time, she'd been called away.

Next time, Lilly wasn't going to leave for *anything.*

After she turned another corner, the cage with the trespasser came into view. One intruder, its eyes flaring in the dimness beyond the glaring squares of the trap cage. In her goggles, the creature's gaze burned blue, the color marking it as a vampire, since their eyes retained their true hue in a *custode*'s night-vision equipment, unlike a human's.

Lilly had already made an educated guess as to its identity. Was this the "mean vampire," as the Underground girls called him? He hadn't been with his group back in Southwark. . . .

Then she smelled the jasmine, and her heart beat faster.

Ghosts? Whatever one called them, the entities were accomplished. Lilly had seen them in action earlier as the spirits had tossed the vampire girls about in Southwark, but she hadn't witnessed the spirits kill.

A weakness? she wondered. *Or a choice?*

She moved down the tunnel toward the blue eyes, absorbing the vampire's features with her night-vision, now that she was closer. The camera hadn't been so detailed with its higher view.

The creature was a male, with dark, slightly curled, tossed about hair. High cheekbones. Nice, full lips. Very fit under a dashing black shirt, pants, and boots. His long coat bunched on the ground next to him whilst he faced her as if he were in a standoff.

Ah, yes. He did match the description the girls had provided for the mean vampire, didn't he?

When Lilly spoke, her tone was altered by her voice box. "Catch of the day."

"Who's the catch—me or you?" he asked, and she was delighted to note that he didn't sound afraid.

This would be much more fun that way.

Then a blast of jasmine took Lilly off her feet, away from the cage, but she controlled her body, using the force of the attack to roll over the ground and spring back up. When the scent came at her again, it was noticeably weaker, and Lilly sparred with the invisible cloud of it, tumbling with the punches until the entity retreated.

As she crouched, hands up in anticipation of another attack, her shoulder throbbing, Lilly wasn't certain of how to fight these creatures. Her training hadn't covered interacting with ghosts, only solid enemies. Perhaps the copies of old *custode* files culled from Menlo Hall—a place that seemed a remote memory—and then stored in the computers would hold answers. She would learn the information quickly enough.

The entities jammed Lilly farther away from the cage, as if they were defending the vampire.

Afterward, she got to her feet, hardly beaten. The jasmine provided a definite connection between this vampire and the hunters. Not a bad night's work so far. "Body-guards, I assume?"

"Just some good friends," the trespasser said.

"They're not as hardy as I noticed them to be in the building where the rest of your group was fending off the schoolgirls earlier. Pity I had to leave before I witnessed the outcome."

She'd meant to draw a reaction out of the vampire, to see how this suspenseful news regarding his comrades would fare with him. But he remained cool.

Lilly admired that, but she also enjoyed trifling with her prey, so she added, "You don't seem to care how they might be faring in a conflict. Are you communicating with them, even from under the ground?"

His sarcastic side-smile told her he wouldn't be answering any specifics. "Oh, I care about them." His tone was tight.

So he had been affected.

She added, "There was an alarm that called me away, you see, and I had to come here to inspect what got tangled in this trap. You've been a bad boy, sneaking into places you shouldn't be."

"I've been worse."

In spite of his studied coolness, Lilly could tell he was on tenterhooks because she'd dangled the bait of his mates' confrontation with the vampire girls in front of him, then yanked it away.

And she would keep it away for now.

"So," she said, "it seems we find ourselves in a situation. Your chums have one of ours and now we have you. What a game of chess this is, eh?"

"Let's stop beating around the bush," the vampire said. "Either you're going to kill me now, wiping your hands of any trouble I might be, or you're going to question me about why I'm here, among other things."

"Just as I'm sure you're questioning our vampire. But based on your being here, in a cage, I would say Claudia gave you some false information." Lilly motioned toward the trap. "This cage was built using silver just in case other vampires did wander here. Most creatures like you are vulnerable to the poison."

The vampire remained silent.

"Claudia, Claudia," Lilly said. "She's a brilliant one, setting you up like this."

"Claudius does have his attributes," he said, using the male name of the master, probably just to show how far his friends had got in drawing information out of the master vampire.

But Lilly was certain Claudia/Claudius would never crumble under interrogation. When push came to shove, the vampire owed her allegiance to the dragon, even above Mihas, for she knew that the dragon would reward her beyond everything else some day. *None* of them were idiot enough to ever cross the dragon.

"Just out of curiosity," Lilly said, "why are you after them?"

"Them? The vampires?" He cocked an eyebrow. "That includes *you*, too, doesn't it?"

She would have to watch her phrasing. There was no need for him to know that she worked independently of the Underground.

"Semantics." Lilly took a step forward but a wall of jasmine blocked her. She could feel its force, but there was also a sense of melting, as if the entities were losing verve.

Interesting.

"You like to avoid questions," Lilly continued. "But may I point out to you that you're in a cage and I'm not?"

"The better for you not to get to me."

"If you're also referring to this jasmine"—Lilly waved her hand in front of her face, as if to chase away a stink—"I wouldn't depend on it ultimately keeping me away. And as for the cage? I know the only way out of it, and it certainly isn't through digging or pulling at the bars."

"Why does it sound like you're about to make some kind of offer?"

Smiling in acknowledgment, Lilly attempted another step, but the jasmine wouldn't allow it. "You talk, I listen. Then we shall discuss your release."

"Release. That's a good one."

Though he'd resigned himself to termination—he couldn't stay alive, not with all the trouble his group was causing—he didn't seem defeated.

She took out the curved knife she used during each night's mandatory Relaquory ritual. Normally, the blade drew blood during an offering to the heart of the Underground, but the instrument often came in handy in other matters.

Lilly slashed out at the jasmine, and the essence seemed to part, darting out of the way. Encouraged by this display, she unsheathed a more conventional dagger from her belt, then cut the air with both of them in a swift crisscross.

But she only found her arms pushed above her head, much as they'd been when she'd fought with Dawn earlier. But this movement lit pain to her shoulder injury, and she allowed herself to fall to the ground in order to relieve the anguish.

Yet her mind kept working: Was this jasmine prone to wounding? Or had the entity only been beating back an attack?

Her stronger-than-human body allowed her to get over the pain, and she gained her feet, whirling the blades in her hands just before she sheathed the weapons.

"Good to know what you're made of," she said to the jasmine.

It seemed to ignore her, even while it rejoined with the others, rebuilding an invisible wall again.

Lilly's injury pounded in time with her heartbeat. The

wound needed further attention, but she would be back here soon enough afterward. Yet, first she would research the computer files for methods of ghost fighting, then, when she returned, she would get close enough to the vampire to use her tuner on him, persuading him to answer any and all questions.

Meanwhile, it wouldn't come amiss to consult with Nigel since this situation had gone beyond all others in the history of this Underground; they had never been attacked. Perhaps she and her brother would agree to bring their own girl vampires here to distract the jasmine so Lilly could make her way through to the cage.

Or they could even request that Mihas question their visitor from a distance with his greater powers.

But doing this before the *custodes* attempted to pull information from him themselves would be daft, for what if this vampire did represent a blood brother and, via proxy, he was able to engage Mihas in an Awareness battle, debilitating the only functional master remaining in the Underground? Lilly had heard of stranger things. Or what if this particular vampire's master was attempting a slow takeover of the community, as they had been known to do while the ages wore by and greed got the better of them?

What if this was even another brother in disguise and he was here because of what this Underground had to offer besides girl vampires?

Lilly didn't often overreact, but this disturbed her. Without a word to the captive, she turned on her heel and left him to stew about what might happen to him next. He wouldn't be going anywhere.

The jasmine followed her.

How to dodge it?

Meandering along, Lilly headed for one of the unobtrusive catches in the floor—the type that had tripped the silver cage in which the captive now resided.

She stepped on the slight indentation in the ground, and

a trapdoor opened beneath her. Quickly, she curled into a ball lest the slice of the closing door cut the top of her head as it shut above her, and she landed on a cushion, rolling to her feet again while holding a hand over her swaddled wound.

Then she waited, trying to detect jasmine.

Satisfied that none had leaked in with her—the trap had surprised it, opening and closing before the entity could react—she continued on her way to the Underground, staying mindful of the smells around her. But there was only the dank, deadened stench of the tunnel as she followed it past a ramp that led to the Underground rooms, then to the level where the *custode* area was located.

She shut more doors behind her, sealing off entries. Gradually, the air grew thicker with vibration because she was close to the core of the community, the center that held the heart of any and all Undergrounds.

She went to that particular room, unmasked herself as she entered and shut the fortified door behind her. Then, although it wasn't yet time for Relaquory—the nightly exchange of energies—she approached the altar, her head down.

It was the second time she'd been here tonight, and she again welcomed the electricity buzzing through her as she kneeled by the coffinlike box. She raised her face only enough to catch a glimpse of the native soil, the nose and mouth peering from the dirt.

Lilly used her curved blade to cut herself, as she did during a ritual, drawing two drops of blood so it landed on the soil then sucked into it with what seemed to be a yanking heartbeat.

She laid a hand on the dirt, the vibrations sawing into her as she inhaled, blissful, then scooped up the soil and stood.

"Thank you," she whispered while backing out of the room, making certain the door was secured.

In her quarters, she redressed her wound, removing the old soil and packing the new over the injury, then wrapping it. She tidied up before going to Nigel in the monitor room.

He was at the console, watching more of the recorded Highgate Cemetery footage, which showed Dawn and her comrades as they wandered among the graves. The other screens were alive with real-time, red-highlighted vampire activity, most of it aboveground in the Lion and the Lamb Pub, where Mihas was accompanied by a crowd of crisped schoolgirls.

Della? Lilly thought.

"Mihas has been in fine form," Nigel said in greeting. He was rewinding footage, so these were recordings pulled up from the vampire alert system. They hadn't reviewed anything beyond what it had isolated. "Look here."

He played a snippet of Mihas speaking to the nine burned Queenshill survivors. There was a new fire in the master as his charges reported to him about how the attack in Southwark had concluded—with the escape of the hunters.

But since the hunters' leader might just be a captive of the Underground now, Lilly wasn't so agitated. Not with the soil healing her wound, with the pulse of the greatest master of all lending strength to her own heartbeat.

Lilly trained her gaze back on the screen, where the schoolgirls looked the worse for wear as they faced Mihas. She held back a smile. Unbeknownst to Nigel, she had been responsible for this new, feistier Mihas. Hadn't she known that Claudia's absence would remind him of who he was and his purpose?

Now the schoolgirl soldiers only needed to kill Claudia for him to reach the next step toward becoming the blood brother they needed him to be; Lilly had heard in Della's mind earlier that this was what they planned.

Then, and only then, would the girls be tuned in to compliance for Mihas's sake.

When the recording finished, Nigel said, "That was the good news. Unfortunately, as you heard from the girls, they lost several of their number while attempting to extract Claudia from her captors."

"Aren't soldiers always expendable?" Lilly asked, knowing a *custode* could be just as disposable, even if they were chosen by a higher source, activated by genetic imprint and the vision/tales that called to them. But she had taken her vows and was comfortable with her life's work. Actually, she would wager that she was the most devoted Meratoliage to come along in eons.

"True enough—the girls can be replaced and trained." Nigel pushed back the wheeled chair, stretching his arms above his head. "And they did their duty tonight, exposing those hunters and sending them running. The vampirelets will catch up, no doubt, after they've had enough rest to heal from the fire trap that toasted them."

"I'd like to join them in tracking."

"Don't *you* get all the fun."

There was a tweak in his tone. After being tuned, he'd been so agreeable that she'd all but forgotten how contrary he could be.

Keeping to business, she relayed details of the intruder in the tunnel, whom he still had been monitoring from this room via cameras. When she revealed her plans for tuning the captive, when or if his invisible bodyguards did wear down, Nigel said, "I'd prefer to go to him now. I'd like to take a read on him and these ghosts for myself."

Lilly began to protest, but he added, "So blasted territorial about everything, aren't you?"

"I'm only doing my job."

He relaxed in his chair, his arms resting on his head. "You may stop proving yourself now. It's getting wearisome, Lilly."

She raised her chin. Proving herself? As the only female *custode*—an "aberration," as Nigel had once called her—

she had to do more to keep pace. But then, she always had, even while growing up with an older brother who constantly degraded her.

As if he hadn't insulted her, Nigel continued with their strategy session, revealing that he'd been partaking in computer research about the flat in Southwark where Lilly had encountered Dawn the first time. A "Mia Scott" was renting it and, so far, she proved to have no ties to Dawn.

"I'm not certain we need this information right now," Lilly said. There was still a drilling tension in the room, and it wasn't due to the oppression in this area of the Underground. It was between her and Nigel. "We can already confirm the Southwark group as hunters. And there's no doubt we'll know more once we fully entertain our caged guest."

Nigel was staring at her, and his sprawling, intimate posture unsettled Lilly.

She jerked a thumb, indicating he should leave the chair to her. "My turn for monitoring. You take your shots at the visitor, as you wanted."

"Is there such a hurry?"

Fuck him. "Go, Nigel. You'd do well to remember that I'm a *custode*, and not anything less. If you desecrate that, there'll be retirement for you."

He lowered his arms, knowing this to be true. Treating her as anything other than a keeper would carry severe consequences.

As he donned his mask and left, Lilly breathed easier, but her pulse was still like a tiny, trapped thing in her veins.

For the first time since she'd arrived, he'd acted as if she was still what she'd been designated to be. A female Meratoliage. A breeder.

Then the anger came. Nigel should know better. Not that she had known her fate before she'd been activated, but it was clear to her now that she'd been fortunate to have been born the way she was. Sterile. Altogether useless in the eyes of the Meratoliage line until she had been called to service because no other male relatives had been of age.

Unlike *custodes*, who had the capacity for heightened physical abilities once activated, breeders normally developed a talent for witchery, and they facilitated the family's needs. However, their black-art talents obviously weren't divine enough to have discovered Lilly's recent activities. This was no doubt because she'd asked during Relaquory for the dragon to shield her orchestrations, and she believed he had heard her. Even in his resting state, he must have known that she was doing it all for him.

Perhaps he had always known that she would come to his rescue one day, and he had willed her destiny. Lilly's null breeding status had been discovered after a trip to a doctor, whom Lilly now knew to have been a cousin versed in the black arts. Nigel had left the estate afterward, then Charles. At that point, the family elders had turned to secondary resources for childbearing, such as cousins whose composition would require much more interference than a breeding couple in the strongest bloodline—her immediate family's—would have required.

Yes, her inability to breed had once marked her as a failure, even before she'd needed to prove herself here. But, as the monitors flickered with action in front of Lilly now, she threw herself into *this* blessed calling, grateful she was able to give her life to the Underground, as a keeper.

Never again would she be anything less.

FIFTEEN

The Great Estate

Sometimes vamp hunting could be a bitch.

Then again, sometimes you got a break, and at Menlo Hall, everything was going like such clockwork that Dawn thought there *had* to be a catch.

But so far, so great, as Dawn smoothed down her newly procured maid uniform that she was about to use to bust into a manor house.

She and a couple of Friends, including Kalin, were in a spacious closet in the newish servant's quarters on the grounds, where an unfortunate dishwater blond girl who actually owned this uniform was curled on the floor in her slip, lulled to sleep by the spirits.

It hadn't taken all that long for the assigned Friends to speed down to Kent and comb the area along the River Darent for an estate that matched the description from Kiko and Natalia's vision. Ninety acres of lawn, gardens, and pastures surrounded the Elizabethan manor, which looked

to Dawn like a brick structure out of Barbara Cartland territory or whatever. Not that she'd ever read much.

Anyway, after the Friends had inspected the house, observing employees who were using security codes to get in
and out as well as pinpointing this one maid in particular
who'd been cleaning the library/study, they'd come back to
temporary HQ, ready to roll while one spirit stayed at the
Hall to keep investigating.

When Dawn had arrived there with the Friends, she'd
been in a disguise that involved padding and a whole lot
of bulky skirt and sweater, plus the long, dirty blond wig
she had on now. Then, it'd just been a matter of the spirits facilitating the snatch-and-grab of the designated
maid.

After taking off the first costume, including the pulser,
then getting into this one, Dawn adjusted the sassy little
cap on her head. The rest of the gray uniform, including a
plain white full apron, was unremarkable—perfect for fading into the woodwork. However, Dawn wouldn't get too
cocky about fitting in.

"I just hope someone doesn't stop me in the halls," she
whispered to the Friends while still in the closet, hoping
her voice wouldn't carry. "My face won't be familiar to
anyone and that might raise a stink."

Greta, who'd been on duty at Queenshill before being
reassigned here, floated around her. *"We told you—we'll
scout in advance, keep others away, clear your path. You
worry about using your hands to do the jobs we can't do."*

Dawn further readied herself, taking care to make sure
her crucifix pendant was in plain sight. Before leaving
temp headquarters, she'd armed herself with smaller weapons like throwing blades and knives so that she'd be able to
move quickly, but there wasn't much room in the dress
pockets under the apron for many of them. In fact, she was
going to have to leave behind her silver-bullet-loaded ille-

gal revolver in this closet with her own clothing and the
real maid.

"Now," Dawn said, "before I go . . . You guys are sure
this is the place we need to be?" Damn, she sounded like a
worrywart. But they couldn't afford to blow this.

"Yeah." Kalin's words were as rushed as a clock pushing the seconds. *"All descriptions match—even the black-
art books in the study. Let's speed away."*

"Just making sure, because Kik and Nat said 'Meratoliage,' and this is 'Menlo' Hall. We don't have time to be
putzing around the wrong location."

Trudy, a third Friend, was already hovering near the
door, waiting for Dawn to open it. *"Sweetie,"* she said in
her truck-stop waitress tone, *"we can only guess that 'Meratoliage' is an old family name from way back. Like, you
know how Maria Shriver doesn't really run around with
'Kennedy' attached to her? 'Menlo' isn't even their last
name. It belongs to this Hall."*

"Gotcha."

With one last glance at the sleeping maid, Dawn went
for the door. If this field trip didn't produce anything, she
was going to hit the bottom of desperation. Claudius
needed to worry if she came back empty-handed.

Dawn opened the door to a slit, allowing Trudy out first.
The spirit was back in a lick, summoning her and Kalin.
Greta was going to stay behind with the maid, and there'd
be yet another Friend somewhere around the Hall itself,
coordinating the bigger picture.

They slipped unnoticed by anyone out of the detached
quarters, which seemed to have been converted from what
had at one time been stables. Earlier, Greta had mentioned
that a lot of servants lived downstairs in the main house itself, but the spirits thought it'd be easier to smuggle Dawn
into and out of the outside structure, so they'd waited until
this particular maid had taken a break there.

The noon sun disguised itself in a clouded haze as Dawn

followed the jasmine down a short path to the main house, its grandeur still imposing, especially under such a dreary sky. She kept her hands under her apron to protect them from the cold.

When they got to a back entrance, Kalin bumped Dawn to the side, where a panel waited.

"Open it," the Friend said.

Dawn followed instructions, finding a keypad behind the panel. Since the Friends had seen other servants using the sequence, Trudy gave her a code to punch in with her stiff fingers.

A lock clicked at the door, and Kalin urged Dawn forward.

"I can walk," Dawn said.

The ghosty backed off. *"Just chuffed to be 'ere, is all."*

Dawn related. Kalin only wanted Jonah and Costin back, and Dawn knew that she would also barge into any-place that would help them get that much closer to the missing guys.

She cut the chatter as they entered a stark hallway, Trudy zooming ahead, Kalin remaining behind as a silent escort. They moved quickly, Dawn keeping her head down, because the spirits had said there were security cameras around. Hence, the stolen uniform and the inclusion of two Friends right now; the spirits would be subtly manipulating cameras—especially the one they'd found in the study.

After going through the main hall, which was dominated by a grand curved staircase and a sprawling chandelier, they entered a long hallway, papered in a striped mahogany pattern so tasteful that Dawn even felt posh. It had that old house smell, too—closed-in air and must that hadn't been quite polished off with all the housecleaning.

Then Trudy sped back to them.

"Hostile approaching," she said.

Kalin pushed Dawn to the wall, and Dawn knew that she

needed to keep her head down, her hands folded in front of her. She was a servant.

As she assumed the position, she heard heavy footsteps on the carpeting. Someone passed, and she saw a pair of thick, stubby legs, perfectly creased trousers, and polished shoes.

Whoever it was sniffed as he went by. *The jasmine,* Dawn thought.

He paused, and her heart practically gouged its way out of her chest.

Hellfire. The shadow thing and the schoolgirl vamps had to have connected the jasmine with the team. Would they have communicated the information to the people here or did the Underground operate on its own to ensure as much secrecy as possible?

When the man spoke, he didn't address Dawn as much as ruminate out loud.

"New polish?"

In a low, barely audible voice, Dawn said, "Yessir."

The Friends had already told her that this family didn't have titles—only a fortune they'd gained through smart land investments nearly a hundred years ago. This guy wasn't a lord or duke or one of the million titles these English people carried around.

He didn't even break his stride. Dawn peeked up from beneath the strands of her wig to see the retreat of a stiff-backed, balding man tight-assing his way down the hall. Dude was even wearing a fine jacket, like he was all dressed up for a day strolling around the country house.

"Keep better watch," Kalin said to Trudy after the man had turned a corner. *"That one was the father."*

"He popped out of a door," the other Friend said. *"I can't be everywhere, sweetie."*

As Trudy took off again, Kalin pushed Dawn ahead.

A zing of belated adrenaline flooded her. Thank God the guy had barely noticed her. Luckily, to the rich, the house staff was meant to be invisible—like gremlins who magically kept their home functioning.

They reached the study without further incident, the massive doors like oaken gates in front of a fortress. Dawn accessed the keypad with the same code she'd used before.

"They'll be dependin' on the camera inside to see what kinda activity's goin' on 'ere," Kalin whispered by Dawn's ear. *"Go on—open the door, just a touch, though. Me 'n Trudy'll slip in for the camera and position it so that it shouldn't light on you—but if it does, you'll just look like that little maid yer imitatin'. Mind that you follow where we tell you to go though, so you basically stay out of its range, yeah? That way, our manipulatin' won't be as obvious. Also, there's another Friend patrollin' the 'ouse, and she'll be right outside to warn us of danger if it comes our way."*

Once again, Dawn did as Kalin asked, and the Friends eked in through the crack.

She waited a few moments, then came in herself, putting all her trust in Trudy and Kalin to have done their camera work.

Closing the door behind her, she surveyed the dim, windowless room, which was lit only by another chandelier in the center. The place looked Victorian, with burgundy and pinstripe-black wallpaper, not that Dawn knew what Victorian decorating actually was. But it sounded right.

The rest of it, though, was more "evil library extreme" in Dawn's terms. Floor-to-ceiling bookcases filled with leathered tomes that made the room smell like . . . well, old books. A frieze presented a sweep of dark, bodiless wings. And as if that wasn't creepy enough, there were grumpy-faced portraits on the far wall, lined up like the ranks of a small, nasty, in-sore-need-of-enemas army.

A shocking thought invaded her. What if these Meratoliages had living pictures, too, just like the Friends?

Nah, Dawn thought, getting a move on. Her spirits would've sensed that.

She heard Trudy's voice from where a camera blended into a high corner, where both she and Kalin had combined forces to manipulate its scanning.

"Left corner. Start there then back up ten feet so we don't have to keep on pressing this camera."

Dawn assumed the Friends were muting any sound devices on the mechanism.

Winding through the leather chairs and settees, she headed for an ornate wooden stand that held a ledger. Low shelves filled with similar books flanked it.

Trudy again. *"When I was in here before, I noticed that it looked like a register of some kind. Births, deaths. You know how families used to keep that stuff in their Bibles?"*

"What good is that going to do us?" Dawn asked.

Kalin talked now. *"The books round it might be of great importance. Friends've already scanned the titles on the shelves—mostly books 'bout black arts. Those in front of you 're untitled, and we couldn't read none of 'em on the inside. That's yer job."*

Dawn got right on it, not bothering to wear gloves this time. The team had already been made by the Underground, and fingerprints wouldn't matter now.

First, she fetched the ledger on the stand, backed out of range, then skimmed it. The pages contained a complex network of family trees, using symbols next to each name that she couldn't even begin to decipher. But she did notice that, with each grouping—about a century's worth of them—there were two names.

Couples? she thought, noticing that all the names were male, so it couldn't be about reproduction. Not unless black arts or a very modern technique was involved.

Then she remembered the dead boy in the lab freezer. Shadow Girl.

Had *they* been partners?

On the last filled page of the book, Dawn found the branched names and birthdates of what looked to be the most recent *custode*s: "Nigel," who was in his twenties. Next to him was "Charles," a late-age teen. But his stricken name was capped off by the date of his death.

And that date was just over a week ago.

Was Charles the boy in the team's lab freezer? When Kiko had done touch-readings on his clothing, they hadn't gotten anything to know for sure.

Next to his name was the only female one Dawn recognized throughout the pages.

"Lilly," who was near Charles's age.

Dawn tried to place the flowered name with the face she'd seen that one night in Eva's flat when she'd unmasked Shadow Girl during her attack. Light eye color, a wide smile accented by slightly bucky teeth, a heart-shaped face capped by light brown hair.

Even though she had a name now, Dawn still found it hard to think of Lilly as a person. She seemed to be more like a robot or . . .

A spine-rattling word came to Dawn.

A minion.

Driven by what she'd found so far, Dawn told the Friends she was going in, put the first book back, then squatted to a lower shelf and pulled out another resource, which seemed to be a very brief account of events. Dawn had never been a studier. She'd never even made it through college and had been pretty disinterested in everything but sports in school. But, now she retreated and settled on her ass to read for as long as she could.

She took out a penlight from a pocket on her uniform, scanning the first entry, which dated back to 1897.

Shit—she knew that date. The publication of *Dracula*, right?

Turning to the back of this book, she found the pages

blank. Then she backtracked to the middle, where the last entry had been labeled with the present year.

It read: "Lilly Elisabeta, activated. (The powers help us all.)"

Immediately above was: "Charles Edward, missing, deceased."

Hey, how would they know he was, in fact, dead?

Also, why was Lilly's name—again the only female—the only one to have that demeaning note next to it?

Dawn scanned backward now. The book was just a record of how the keepers had died, and it looked like some of them had bitten the dust while on duty. But a few entries had a word next to them that had a more sinister ring to it than it should've.

Retired.

What happened to those ninja-weird shadow things when they *retired*, for God's sake? Was there some sort of home for them where they could run around playing tag-the-spy? Was there a pension plan?

She read on, discovering entries that read: "excused from duty—heart defect." Actually, there were quite a few of those. And they accounted for deaths, too, with really young males.

But this research wasn't really getting Dawn anywhere. She needed proof that the dragon was in this Underground, and she needed to know where those keepers were stationed because, based on the psychics' visions, the *custodes* should lead to the big master. She supposed that this house in Kent, which was too far from London for the keepers to be on the scene as much as Lilly was, wasn't where the base would be located. Menlo Hall was obviously just a family estate—plus a cradle of records—and Dawn would put money down on the fact that there'd be no Underground or Costin here.

Her bet was still on Highgate, where the team had already found vampires gathered. It'd just been a question of what *sort* of vampires.

Find what you need, she thought, scooting into camera range and putting this book back, reaching for another. *Find the dragon. Hurry.*

Her next reading project looked like a regular Bible, but when she opened it to glance over the contents, she almost dropped it.

Once, when Dawn was in high school, she'd picked up a copy of *The Exorcist* from a used bookstore, of all places. It'd been summer, and Frank had barred her out of the house again in favor of communing with his bottle and memories of Eva's "murder," so she'd waited him out down the street at this new store, which also carried comic books. She'd been aimlessly wandering, pulling books, then losing interest and moving on to the next, when she'd opened the pages of the novel. And the pages had been . . . Damn, she could still smell them.

The pages had been unlike any other book Dawn had cracked. As she'd looked it over, she'd even gotten ill, and she'd ditched it, thinking that the evil in the book was coming off the paper.

Now, she detected the same page-stench with this item, but she couldn't shelve it.

The book was in narrative form, written as if a member of the family had sat down and done some casual journaling, but without providing the dates. Dawn rushed over the script, her blood thudding, cold fingers seeming to pluck at the back of her neck.

Meratoliage family . . . initially black-art bred from the best of military men and witches to be servants . . .

Dawn paused. Servants of what? Mihas and Claudius's Underground?

Or the dragon?

And "black-art bred"?

That would explain the strange body arrangement for the kid in the lab freezer. The heart, the not-quite-human blood . . .

Dawn sped on, trying not to let the smell of the pages get to her.

To keep bloodlines pure . . . interbreeding . . .

And she got sicker. Incest? Was this family like old royalty in Egypt? Brothers, sisters, together?

She continued, landing on an unfamiliar word.

Relaquory . . .

She could barely breathe. Vision blurring with excitement, she slowed down and concentrated on this passage, her heartbeat blipping in her throat.

Every night, there is Relaquory. We thank him for this gift, the ability to draw from the power he emanates.

Everything crashed together: the dragon. It had to be. And he had bodyguards.

*Custode*s.

Either there was a third wicked master—one unlike any blood brother Costin had ever encountered—or this was all the proof Dawn needed that the dragon was in this damned Underground.

Just as she was about to see if it told where the Underground was located, Kalin shouted.

"Leave!"

For a crazed second, Dawn considered staying right here. The location *had* to be in one of these books.

Trudy joined in. *"Someone's coming from the security room! I can hear Monica telling us from outside!"*

An alarm from a patrolling Friend. Had a security worker noticed something about the mobility of the study's camera, even though the Friends had been so careful? Was he or she coming to check it out?

Impulsively, Dawn ripped out a bunch of thin pages—not enough to be obvious—then shoved them under the top part of her apron just before putting the book back on the shelf. She crossed her arms over her prize, unwilling to give up the little she could take with her.

She thought she heard a murmur of approval from Kalin just before running for the door, opening it and following the speeding Friends as they guided her down the halls, which felt like they went on forever, then out of the main house, where the spirits led Dawn to a bank of tall bushes nearby.

They hid there for a while, Dawn's heart beating against the pages that could help end the quest for Costin's soul.

And maybe even save the world in the bargain.

SIXTEEN

THE JACKPOT

ABOUT forty-five minutes before dusk, Dawn sat herself in a chair in front of Claudius at temporary headquarters with the Meratoliage pages in her hands for the vampire to gawk at.

He must've recognized the scent of evil paper, but way worse than Dawn had, because he recoiled from those yellowed pages. Or maybe he was just shocked that she was holding them like a revealed full house in a poker game.

"You have no right to those," he said, recovering enough to act like he was royalty again, even though he'd been transferred to the throne of a plain wooden chair, his robe the same blanket he'd been wearing since his capture, his courtiers the same Friends who'd been binding him for most of the day.

Dawn realized she was holding her breath, and she let it go. She'd half expected Claudius to smack out with any remaining powers he might have, because this would be the time to lay all *his* cards on the table, with her, here, holding this all-important information.

But she really must've disabled him that first night when she'd mentally roughed him up. Costin's constant Awareness attacks had also done him further damage.

That would only help their cause now though. After returning from Menlo Hall—where she'd rushed to dress the maid back in her uniform so the girl would wake up thinking she'd just taken a nice nap—Dawn had scanned the evil pages, even while trying to drive back. Then she'd brought Kiko and Natalia far down in the shelter away from Claudius, where he shouldn't be able to hear them talking, especially with his hearing muffled by a Friend. The psychics had told her that they hadn't made any progress with the master vampire themselves, so after chatting about what Dawn now had in her possession, they'd formulated a new approach to questioning him.

They probably could've used Frank's help—he would've been some pretty intimidating muscle to back them up— but Dawn's dad was still resting in his private room, and she thought it best to let him snooze because he'd be that much fresher if they had to head out at dusk.

But to where? She didn't know yet.

She glanced at a digital clock on the wall. Still a little time left . . .

Folding one leg over the other, she rested the fragile pages on her thigh. Unfortunately, she'd managed to pull some pretty useless stuff from the book: history about the dragon, which Dawn was already pretty well acquainted with, thanks to Costin.

She just wished she knew more about the *custode*s than a vague idea of what Relaquory was or that a keeper's anatomy was screwed up because of all the black magic and genetic tampering that'd gone on with them.

"A treasure trove of information," she said to Claudius, nonetheless, acting like she had more than she really did.

Bluffing at its finest. "Surely you don't mind my borrowing pages from one of your *custode*'s library books? Sharing what you learn is a part of any great society."

Claudius remained regal. By Dawn's side, Kiko lightly knocked her with his knuckles, signaling her to go ahead with their strategy.

She would read to Claudius about the dragon, getting the vampire's mind on the subject while the psychics touched the pages, just as they'd touched the *custode* blood earlier. They were hoping that Claudius's thoughts would stray again and they would be able to pick up on something from him with their combined powers.

What else could they do besides beating the hell out of the closed-mouth vamp for information?

The smell of the paper kept at Dawn as Kiko made contact with it and Natalia leaned into him for a link.

"The dragon's background," Dawn said. "Oh, it already sounds like a most wonderful story."

"I know of it already," the vamp said.

"But to hear it again . . ." Dawn continued, adapting her best storyteller voice as she put the narrative into her own words. She hoped her antics would distract Claudius from their real purpose.

They'd see.

"Long, long ago," she said, "the dragon perished in his human incarnation, making everyone think he was truly dead and gone. But, really, the big bad master was lying very low instead of pursuing the political matters that had ruled his life before. His enemies moved on, giving dragon-face a chance to enjoy his vampiric lifestyle. And how he did enjoy it."

She smiled sarcastically, but Claudius wasn't so amused.

"Time slipped on by," she added, "all while he was making plans to regain his properties and then some . . ." Dawn turned a page over. ". . . and blah, blah, blah, until . . ." She turned to the next one. ". . . the late eighteen hundreds, when his legend was brought to major attention by an author who made certain the dragon's name would never be forgotten."

She glanced up at Claudius. "Wow. How about that? Thanks to Stoker, the dragon got so well known that he couldn't go outside without sunglasses and a baseball cap. Fame crapped on his plans to secretly go back to being a nasty prince and all."

Claudius's jaw clenched. "You really are trying so hard, aren't you?"

Dawn kept looking down at the pages; she wasn't going to let him play with her.

Reading directly from the narrative, she said, "'Knowing he would never again be able to maneuver in secrecy, the dragon enlisted his blood-vow vampire progeny to allow him an opportunity to rise, to become stronger and more powerful than ever so secrecy wouldn't be required in his efforts to regain his old political position. He was then buried for two hundred years. During this time of rest in a coffin that contained his native soil, he would gather inner power. He commanded his men to quietly invade society while multiplying their numbers. When he arose again, he would have more than just an army to command and more than his former holdings—he would go after the world itself, as well.'"

Dawn waited to see if Kiko and Natalia had divined anything, but they were still trancing. Damn.

"So," she said, flowing straight into question time for Claudius, "are we to take it that you were part of the lucky community who guarded the dragon all this time?"

No answer, of course.

"Why you?" Dawn added. "Why not some other poor schmucks?"

Natalia began to whisper. "Claudius . . . volunteered when the dragon privately approached him. Always with a plan . . . dragon always depended on Claudius's brains, not might . . . He took care of the dragon while Mihas was away, even when there was no Underground to support his efforts, only *custode*s standing by . . ."

Then, as suddenly as the new girl had spoken, she stood straight up. Dawn and Kiko did, too, reaching out to steady Natalia.

"What?" Dawn asked her.

"That smarts." Natalia pressed her hands against her head. "Claudius shut himself off and I went . . ."

She gestured with one hand and Dawn understood that to mean that she had slammed into a mental barrier.

Kiko seemed to have forgotten about whatever was distracting him, and he held Natalia's hand. He obviously didn't like to see her in discomfort, but with Claudius's diminished abilities, it wasn't a fraction as bad as it would've been if the vamp was healthy.

"Use me to get your mojo back," he said to her. "Just like we did earlier, together."

Natalia squeezed his hand and they sat down, assuming trance position, eyes closed, their breathing deep and synchronized. Jasmine gathered above them, as if trying to lend strength, too.

Dawn surrendered the book pages to the psychics, and she thought she felt a rub of energy near their skin as they both grasped the paper.

That could've been Dawn's imagination though.

"The dragon," she said to Claudius to get him back to where they needed him.

The vampire started to quiver like a tuning fork.

"Dragon," both Kiko and Natalia said.

Claudius made the same noise he had yesterday when Costin had used his Awareness to dig into his blood brother's head. It was a frightening groan pitching up to a shriek.

"Dragon!" repeated the psychics.

Dawn's temples felt like they were vising inward, a result of the pressure in the room. Even the Friends were getting hoppy, darting here and there. They were saying the name, too, but in their whispery, ghostly voices.

"Dragon . . . Dragon . . ."

As Claudius grated out a moan, the psychics hunched together, shutting Dawn out as she wrapped her arms over her head so she wouldn't have to hear the vampire. Still, his rising screech hollowed into her.

Kiko came up for air from his and Natalia's huddle, just as if he'd broken the surface of a lake.

"New Gilby," he said, gasping. "Hotel, one kilometer northwest of the Lion and the Lamb."

Dawn's victory cry was muffled as she fisted her hands at her side. She wouldn't put it past Claudius to be giving them a false location, tooling around with them, but at least they had something to compare with what Costin had given to Frank.

As Kiko and Natalia slumped against each other in an exhausted hug, Dawn sprinted to her resting father's room.

Almost dusk . . . Almost time to make a move if they had to. . . .

She busted into the dark room to find him in his bed, covered from head to toe in blankets.

"Dad," she whispered, not wanting to spook him. "Get up. We need you."

She didn't want to be too close when a vamp awoke suddenly, so she kept a couple feet between her and the bed. But when Frank didn't move, she inched closer.

"Dad?"

Kiko had stumbled into the room, too. Dawn suspected Natalia was still with Claudius and the Friends who were surrounding him.

"Frank?" he said. "Claudius got a little loose with his lips. . . ."

"He's out like a burnt bulb, Kik."

"But he always wakes up when you need him, even before dusk, which is close enough." Kiko opened the door a little wider so that light from the hallway shone over their vampire. "Frank?"

A groan sounded from beneath the blankets.

"Dad, Claudius gave us a location."

"The New Gilby Hotel," Kiko added.

"Frank, is that where Costin told you he was going?"

She and Kiko waited. Waited.

Then Frank spoke in a struggling whisper. "Dawn . . ."

After trading a frown with Kiko, she pulled down the blankets.

What she saw flashed a stark whiteness over her vision—a shock that sliced down her body until it became a thin pulse in her chest.

Her dad—paler than ever, skin wrinkled, eyes a weak green in the dimness.

"Not . . . feeling . . . good," he managed to say.

So this was what it was like to be soaked in ether, Dawn thought, floating in a state of bafflement.

Kiko gathered enough words to echo what she was trying to understand. "How can a vampire get sick?"

Frank tried to climb out of bed, but Dawn didn't let him. She pushed him back down to the mattress, and it was real easy, too. Usually, he would only have to flick his finger to send her flying across a room. Not that he'd ever tried it, but . . .

"Got . . . work . . . to do . . ." he said, once again trying to rise.

But he couldn't.

Kiko was already out of the room, saying over his shoulder, "There's stored blood in the fridge, but I don't know how old it is. I'll get a bag or two for him if it's good."

"Kiko's got you covered," Dawn said, sitting beside Frank, even though she wondered if she could catch what he'd contracted. But maybe this was a vampire flu or something, so unless it attacked former vamps, too, she'd be immune.

"Already had blood . . ." Then he seemed overwhelmed by puzzlement. "Or . . . I think I did . . . Wasn't enough . . ."

What the hell was he talking about? He'd been in here resting.

She hated to do this, but they were hunters. There was a situation that needed full attention, even with her father looking ready to puke.

"Dad, can you just tell me Costin's location? We need to see if it's a match." She felt like shit for playing boss girl instead of Florence Nightingale. "I know a match won't verify whether Claudius sent Costin into a trap or not, but at least we'll have somewhere to target if he doesn't come back soon."

"Near the New Gilby . . ." he said.

Dawn put her hand on his arm as his words faded. It was enough of a match for her.

She itched to start loading up on weapons, but her dad kept her planted on the bed. He hadn't even fought her on giving up the information Costin had entrusted to him, and that worried her more than his lethargy or complexion.

Kiko had gotten back in time to hear Frank, too, and he was already opening a blood bag for her dad. Dawn took it, then lifted Frank's head to help him drink.

"What're we gonna do?" Kiko asked her.

Her father's head felt like a hundred pounds of undead weight in her palm as she eased Frank back to the pillow, his lips ringed by red from the emptied bag.

"We've got to go, Kik, with or without Frank."

Her dad did a mild version of his usual grunt.

At least he sounded stronger after the blood. But not by much.

"Oh, yeah?" Dawn said. "I hate to say this, but you'd do more harm than good out there right now."

"Wait for the blood . . . to work on me," he said.

Kiko opened another bag, which Dawn also helped Frank to drink.

"And how long do you think it'll be until you're in fighting shape?" Kiko asked. "An hour? Two?"

"We can't afford either one," Dawn said. "Dusk is just about at our doorstep."

Frank finished the rest of the bag, then attempted to get to his elbows, but crumpled backward. He didn't do it as quickly or bonelessly this time though.

"Goddamn it," he said, immediately cringing at his cursing.

"More blood?" Kiko asked.

"No, this needs . . . to settle." Frank shut his eyes. "Start getting everything . . . ready though. I'll be out . . . soon." He ended on a spent breath.

"Dad . . ." Dawn said.

"Get your ass . . . out there."

She knew he was right, so she tore herself away. Kiko took her hand and pulled her the rest of the way out, shutting the door behind them.

"Not good," he whispered, probably knowing that Frank might hear them, even with the state he was in. "Are we really gonna take off without him?"

"What other choice do we have?" Dawn's thoughts veered around in her head as if they were on a racetrack, skidding and sliding into walls, crashing and burning.

"Maybe we should stick around and try to have Claudius reveal what we should be prepared for in a trap . . ."

"And how much time should we invest in that?"

"I think we should go as soon as we can, too, but I'm just thinking of every angle here. Costin's obviously in trouble, and I'm not about to desert him, either."

Either they were going to this location to save Costin—*God, please have him still be alive to* be *rescued*—or entering an Underground. But, even if she was "key," could she really take down a master vamp who'd no doubt be more powerful than Claudius?

And how would she do against the dragon?

Then the worst scenario knifed her: what would she do if Costin was . . .

No. He couldn't be terminated. She would feel it.

She *had* to.

Even Claudius remained quiet as silence pierced the shelter. Dawn, Kiko, and Natalia weaponed up; the new girl had just assumed she was going, too, and Dawn hadn't corrected her. They could use her vamp-dar to anticipate an imminent attack, and Natalia could withstand these vampires' charm.

She knew exactly what she was getting into.

Frank would have to stay back to facilitate communications, but it was clear that Costin might be too deep under the ground for the system to be working—that could be a reason they hadn't heard from him.

Dawn tucked an acid gun—one of Breisi's old inventions the team had previously used for break-ins—into her holster, then some throwing blades into her jacket pocket. She glanced at the wall clock again.

It'd be getting dark outside now.

Was she doing the right thing? Or *should* she give Costin even more time and try to gather more information from Claudius?

She held back a rush of heat that flared from her chest and through her throat in sharp agony. Costin had used plenty of time up already, and she knew in her gut that something *had* happened to him.

Kiko carefully packed his over-the-shoulder man-bag with small weapons, and Natalia was sorting through a variety of items representing different religions, but she was only plucking out crucifixes for these vamps.

Kiko said, "I just hope the Underground doesn't have animals in it or is close to critters who'd hear a vampire summon them. That'd be a bitch to deal with whacked out doggies like we did at Queenshill."

Brushing a hand over her holstered revolver, Natalia said, "I would hate to kill any animals."

Dawn couldn't take it. "Guys, if you think it's too dangerous to go, then don't."

Kiko laughed. "Yeah, like I'd ever let you into a situation like this alone, cowboy."

Natalia nodded her agreement. The new girl was in this to see if there were any more Kate Lansings down there. She wouldn't back off.

"I wouldn't think less of either one of you if you stayed here," Dawn said.

They didn't say anything else, just kept loading up.

When they had all their gear in place, Frank came out of his room. Even though his complexion wasn't as wrinkled or pale—it was almost like his skin had soaked up the blood from the inside out—his legs struggled to hold up the rest of his bulk. It looked like it was the last thing he wanted anyone to notice.

"You'll keep watch over Eva while I'm gone?" Dawn asked.

His forehead furrowed, as if the question perplexed him, or maybe it was like he was trying to grasp an idea that was on the cusp of his mind.

But then he just nodded and said, "I'll keep tabs on Costin's locator, too. It hasn't read any movement for a long time."

Again, that might be because this Underground was lower than even Hollywood's had been, and the locator wasn't registering anything.

"And you didn't tell me this before because you knew Costin wouldn't want you to," she said.

"That doesn't mean he's gone."

Frank cupped a hand at the back of her head and, for a flash, she saw what they could've been. A real parent and child, not the role reversal they'd practiced all their lives.

But then he seemed to lose strength, and he got to a crouch, like he couldn't stand anymore.

When Dawn started to bend down to him, he waved her off. She didn't let that needle her.

"When I get back," she said, "we'll find out what's making you sick, okay?"

"Just get out there."

It was only getting darker outside with every second that passed, but there was one thing left for Dawn to do before they went anywhere.

She took up her sharpest machete, then approached Claudius, who still sat in the middle of the room in that chair.

"And the clock strikes the dreaded hour," he said.

"We can't afford for your girls to have all their powers, Claudius. You know that. Besides, all the blood brothers have to die, not only for Costin's sake but—"

"For the greater good." He sighed. "We all have our causes."

Dawn wanted to get this over with. The prospect of killing him had gotten tougher for her to deal with, maybe because he'd said some things to her that showed he was a functioning, feeling thing.

But still a thing that would work them over if he could manage it.

It barely even occurred to her that there were no burning beauty mark sensations on her skin right now. Just . . . coolness. The hush of something inevitable.

"If I'd only been able to keep my mind from your psychics," the vampire said as everyone in the room watched, "I wouldn't be in this position."

Was he milking an act for all it was worth, hoping they would be so in doubt about where they were going that they'd hesitate to leave? Had he really been weak enough to give up information he hadn't meant to and he was buying time?

"You would've broken at some point," Dawn said. "Are you sure you don't have anything else to tell us?"

He got that sphinxlike grin again. "Wouldn't you like to spare me for more questioning so you would know for certain where you're off to and how to prepare for it?"

Don't beg, Dawn thought. Even though Claudius was the enemy, she didn't think she could take seeing him brought down so low.

"Well, then," the master vampire said, straightening in his chair like a nobleman before a firing squad. "Go at it."

But Dawn didn't. Not even when the Friends eased down his blanket to reveal his throat, which had healed only a little more since the last time she'd seen it. That spoke to the damage done to him—the prospect of him never mending at all.

"Come, Ms. Madison," he said. "After centuries of delusion and the spellbinding charm of Mihas, I've arrived at the point where reality is rather refreshing. Death by you is surely going to be less traumatic than what might've been at hand with my . . . girls." Bitterness etched his voice as he added, "When I think of all that I did for Mihas . . ."

Talk, Dawn thought. *Please keep talking.*

"I gave so much," Claudius said, inadvertently doing just what she wanted him to do. "And *this* is my end. But he'll have a harvest to reap, won't he?"

He started to shift into another form—it was an obvious habit—but this time, he didn't change into a woman as much as a combination of all his aspects: part male, part female, the shadow of a cat.

All of him meshing into one.

"Strangely," he added, "I think I might have gone on and on if the girls hadn't chased me out. I would have always been Mihas's 'it.'" His wrecked voice got emotional, but it also gathered strength. "But there's no more of that for me. No more 'it.' I'm Claudius. I'm—"

Dawn had quickly drawn back the machete with both hands and swung it, slicing off the vampire's head.

Before she even lowered the weapon, his body had eaten itself up, shriveling.

Quickly and cleanly, she thought. It's what he'd asked for.

Dawn waited for a new burning sensation to crisp her skin, but it never did. She hadn't enjoyed killing Claudius at all.

Kiko, Natalia, and Frank came to her, pulling her away from the empty chair, and she let them.

Then, with the psychics and a garrison of Friends, she took up her weapons and headed for the exit, ready to fight whatever waited for them now.

Costin knew his Friends were fading quickly. All of them save Breisi were slumped on the ground, their movements lethargic, even while they attempted to make him believe the opposite. Breisi's essence was thin, but she was still inspecting the tunnel.

He rose through Jonah's body, requesting dominance from his host, and they traded places with no resistance, Costin slipping into a state of vivid sight and sound.

After the tunnel and cage blossomed in his vision, he breathed in the dank air, getting back into the rhythm of dominance.

"You did well," he told his spirits. Only a quarter of an hour ago, his Friends had secured him and Jonah from the second red-eyed being who'd come to harass them for what seemed like hours as it clearly attempted to learn how the spirits functioned. Costin knew this one was a different shadow than the first creature, even though it wore a mask. The figure was taller, broader.

But now it had left them alone, allowing the Friends to finally collapse.

Costin was growing hungry. This body had not rested much while the Friends had guarded him, and he hadn't fed since leaving headquarters. He would need blood soon, but he did not know where he would get it. And he had rarely gone without Dawn before, whether her blood was bagged or fresh.

Jonah's voice sounded through their body. "I suppose it's time now."

"Dusk has come," Costin said.

"It won't be long."

"Until what? We fade to a useless, crawling shell?"

"Until *something* happens."

And Costin knew that his host was talking about the team going Underground, if they had succeeded in isolating the correct location. At least, he hoped that was where they would be headed, and not to him.

As Breisi returned to the cage, he could sense that she was all but vanishing to the ground with the rest of the group.

His best, his strongest.

And as she melted, Costin tried not to feel just as finished.

SEVENTEEN

LONDON BABYLON,
COMMON AREA MAZE

YET another game?" Wolfie said as Della and the other survivors, plus Polly and the few girls who'd stayed behind, locked him to a pair of shackles dangling from the maze wall.

Even hours after deserting the Lion and the Lamb Pub aboveground, they were manufacturing methods to keep him from hearing any of Mrs. Jones's messages, for if he did, it would be the end of them.

First, upon their return, an enthusiastic Polly had waylaid Wolfie after Stacy had instructed her to do so while the older girl sneaked into his quarters to nick his mobile. Polly had kept him occupied for perhaps thirty minutes before he'd got restless and went in search of his phone. When he couldn't locate it, he had scoured the remainder of the Underground, never knowing that, by this time, the Queenshill girls had done away or tampered with every communication device in the area so he might not go back aboveground where he could access them, should he think to.

Next, Stacy had thought to ease his concerns by lying to Wolfie that she and Della had postponed their feeding and rest time to go above and use a phone to access his answering service. However, she added, Mrs. Jones had left no word of her whereabouts. But Stacy *had* sent recruits out to comb London for Wolfie's mistress, knowing odds were the girls wouldn't find her. This and the fact that Wolfie's ego was of such proportions that he didn't think Stacy would possibly fib to him, had consoled him somewhat. Still, the lack of communication from Mrs. Jones had clearly frustrated him.

And frustration normally caused Wolfie to revert, which indeed he did—back to a place where he wouldn't have to think about his missing companion for the moment.

They knew him all too well.

This made it simple for Polly and the Queenshill students who hadn't gone to Southwark—the unburned, still-lovely ones—to set about soothing him, lying with him for hours during a binge rest while the Southwark survivors had finally fed and rested themselves.

And this brought them here, hours later, to the maze where they'd lured Wolfie after he'd awakened in a bid to once again steer his thoughts from Mrs. Jones. They normally kept any shiftless, easily missed boy they stole from above for playtime in this maze, where chains, shackles, and an array of blade toys hung from the walls while the aroma of blood and sweat lined the darkness. Tonight, the room belonged to Wolfie.

As the schoolgirls finished shackling him, he seemed to go along with their game, though Della knew that, at any moment, he might begin missing Mrs. Jones again.

So fickle.

"Now that darkness is here," he said, "I should really go back up top to roam for her."

Stacy and Della exchanged glances as they donned gloves and went to another area to drag out a coil of silver chains they'd set there earlier. They and the other South-wark survivors were still healing and growing out their locks of hair, so they had left the enticing of Wolfie up to Polly and the few others who had remained unscathed.

Hence, the unburned girls pushed Wolfie against the maze wall, tearing at his clothes while Della and Stacy drew on their lightning-quick speed, then wrapped the links around his bared skin.

As they stepped back and stripped off their gloves, he asked, "What's this?"

He writhed under the silver. They had known he was sensitive to it, since they had inherited the trait from him and not Mrs. Jones.

A poison, Della thought. A comeuppance. Now they would see how well he ordered them about to find his mistress.

But, just as Wolfie seemed to realize what they had done to him, *it* happened.

A blast of agony, a clawing into the very core of Della.

All the Queenshill girls hit the floor as one, moaning, screaming, rolling round as if to keep in what was coming out.

Della had felt pain such as this only once in her experience—when she had exchanged blood with Wolfie and the cat. Her body had seized up then, too, her innards seemingly pulled and tied as her composition altered, her blood thrusting through her and breaking every inner barrier.

Hurt . . . as if half of her was being ripped out.

And then . . .

Then it finished.

Della lay still, peering round. The other girls were just now gaining their bearings, as well.

There was something . . . different. Was it the quality of her sight? The smells of the old blood and fear-sweat from the boys the recruits had brought down here for fun earlier?

Had it all changed in a way she couldn't begin to describe?

Della looked up to where Wolfie gazed at them, his mouth twisted in . . .

Disgust?

Putting a hand to her face as she sat up, Della ran her fingertips over her cheek.

The same, she thought. But . . . not the same.

Then, as Wolfie's head lowered, he let out a groan, straining against his chains.

"Gone," he said. "All gone."

That was when Della knew.

One of the other Queenshill girls said it aloud. "Mrs. Jones . . . dead?"

As if wishing to test the theory, Stacy, who was just to the left of Della, shifted into her vampire form, letting out whimpers of fright as she did so.

When she finished, Della tried not to cringe from her classmate, for Stacy was a smaller version of Wolfie as a vampire—hairy, with pointed ears, canine teeth with two longer fangs in a long snout, hunched and beastly in the skirt and blouse made ragged from her . . . change.

Then Stacy glanced about the room at her classmates while she touched her own face, horror shaping her mouth.

Wolfie was weeping now, on his knees. He was seeing reflections of an unadulterated him, and it didn't seem as if he could withstand the lack of Mrs. Jones in the girls.

Though their old forms had been hideous, this somehow seemed worse to Della.

She couldn't take her gaze off of Stacy. No trace of femininity. No cat.

"Look at her," Della found herself saying to Wolfie as he kept hiding his gaze. "*Can't* you look at her?"

He didn't raise his face, instead wallowing in his grief for Mrs. Jones. The murderer.

Della's body seemed to explode as she changed into her new vampire-wolf form and leaped just in front of him, reaching out her clawed hand to force him to look at her new bearing.

He reared back from her ugly snout and hairy body—the unfamiliar shape of a different vampire.

"Look!" Della said. "This is what you made us! You had to know there was a chance we would grow into something else one day, didn't you? No matter how much you wanted us to stay the same, we didn't."

Behind her, the other Queenshill girls crept closer. Della could hear them mutating into their vampire forms, as well. Even Polly, who had hated Della for what she had done to Violet, was here, backing her up.

In the glassy reflection of Wolfie's eyes, Della could have sworn that she saw the awful visages of her class-mates warped and looming as they bared their teeth.

She could withstand no more from him, so she asked the one question she had never wished to have answered.

"You knew," she said to him, her wolf voice mangled. "You knew everything about what Mrs. Jones was doing to us."

"No—" he began.

Della swiped at his chest, drawing blood. Then, terri-fied, she held up her paw.

The smell of his blood filtered into her, the wetness run-ning down her clawed nails and into her numbing finger-tips. Even though he was tinged with silver poison, her stomach growled.

She thought she heard the same keening sound of hun-ger from her schoolmates, too.

Wolfie finally looked at her, and he clearly realized that there was nowhere left to go but to the truth.

"Yes," he said. "I knew about Mrs. Jones."

Suddenly, all the girls were on Wolfie, ripping at him as he howled. Yet he didn't struggle. Not even as they began sucking at his wounds, drawing blood because he had taught them never to be appeased.

Della also drank of him as he groaned. She was too famished—always so starved—to turn the tainted blood aside, so she drank and drank and drank until . . .

She broke away, the blood like bile to her, and not only because of the silver.

But she seemed to be the only one who tasted the wrongness of it as she sought a corner, cowering there whilst the other girls continued to ravish Wolfie, who seemed to enjoy every suck and scratch.

The blood . . . It felt like the food Della used to shove down during her human days, when she would be so upset that cakes and biscuits and ice cream would be the only comforting fillers. And like that food, it felt as if it didn't belong.

Just as she used to do, she brought it back up.

When she was done, she panted on the floor, watching the other girls—soulless, monstrous beasts—feast on Wolfie.

Our souls, she thought. *He took everything, including those.*

And the only way to retrieve those souls would be through his death now that the cat was slain. But when she thought of the concept of humanity, she wasn't certain she understood it anymore.

Yet . . . couldn't she return to it?

As some recruits entered the room, wearing their new vampire-wolf forms as they whined and begged at Wolfie's feet to tell them what had happened, Della wiped his blood from her mouth. She felt sluggish, numbed, from the blood that still traced silver in her.

Her fingers stilled near her lips when she saw Wolfie grip one schoolgirl, then another, tossing them to the ground in ecstasy as they all began to tussle in rougher play than she'd ever seen.

Rips, scratches, blood . . .

But, the silver. *He* didn't seem so addled by it.

Della gaped. It hadn't been enough to put the element on his skin, had it? They should have stabbed him with it so that it was more a part of him. He was a master vampire, after all, and the only thing they had done was to poison themselves by drinking from his slightly affected blood.

With a mighty howl, he busted up and away from his girls, furiously breaking out of his chains, sending the silver links flying.

It was a birth of sorts, a release from his progeny now that they didn't appeal anymore, wasn't it?

He stood there, taking in great, hollow breaths, bathed in his own blood, his clothes in strips, his long hair covering most of his golden-eyed face as the girls scuttled away from the return of their commander.

Della held her place in her own corner, for she'd been reborn, too.

EIGHTEEN

BELOWGROUND, I

My soldier, Lilly thought as she watched a live feed of Mihas and the girls on a telly screen in the monitor room. The terror of the battlefield had returned, and it'd be brilliant if he stayed this time.

It seemed as if he just might, too, with him standing so resplendent in blood and ripped clothing, his arms outstretched while he let back his head and howled.

The girls had confronted him with the truth about Mrs. Jones, and he had handled it as a master vampire should, rising above the trouble, seizing final control now that he couldn't hide his sins any longer. Best of all, there would be no need for Lilly to use the tuner on the lower vampires now since he had them truly under control.

Unless . . .

She leaned closer to the screen, seeing if the girls would rebel against his show of aggression.

When none of the female soldiers made a move to do so, Lilly reclined, smiling.

She had done it—restructured the Underground as it needed to be. From this moment on, the dragon would have his army with a stronger commander, and this Underground would no doubt flourish. All it had taken in trade was Claudia's banishment and death, which was obvious since the girls were no longer catlike. Dawn and her group had clearly helped Lilly in their own way by terminating the co-master.

Behind her, Nigel entered the room. He and Lilly were running tardy for Relaquory. She had delayed the ritual to see to Mihas's latest complication, but there was no need for further surveillance now that matters had come to a satisfactory point.

She was just accessing stored computer messages before leaving when she came upon this:

Menlo Hall
    Possible malfunction with library camera. Minor concern regarding mobility. Inspected and fixed. No further disturbances.

She stared at the log entry from the Hall. The *custode*s intercepted relevant updates from the family properties aboveground, but there were rarely any significant messages until now.

Menlo Hall. She remembered the place well—an ominous house she had visited only on occasion because her family resided on a different, more welcoming estate outside Oxford. However, her father often retreated to the Hall, honing his resentment at not being "fit enough" to be a *custode*, as she'd discovered after her own activation. Perhaps wandering the estate enabled his vitriol.

But what she recalled best about the Hall was being told to keep away from the west wing during her younger days. After she'd been called to *custode* duty, she'd discovered the reason for the rule, when she'd been ushered to the li-

brary and given free rein to absorb all the knowledge
housed in it.

Menlo Hall. Camera problems.

Bloody hell.

From just over her shoulder, where Nigel had been reading, too, he muttered, "They were there."

Bloody, bloody hell. Had Claudia let the location slip
while the hunters questioned her? How else would they
have tracked it down?

Chances had been next to nil they ever would have. . . .

Turning their attention to the vampire *they* held captive,
Lilly and Nigel highlighted the monitor screen that surveyed the far tunnel with its silver cage. The "mean vampire's" ghostly guards had still been strong after Nigel had
left them, but Lilly had been studying spirit warding techniques on the computer, and they were ready to employ
those after they finished with Relaquory.

"Nigel," Lilly said, "perhaps you should inform Mihas
that we might be receiving company soon." The progress
these hunters were making was unsettling, to say the least.
If they had found Menlo Hall, they might have found more.

This group was good. Very, very good, and for the first
time in this Underground's history, Mihas would have to
earn his keep, to actively protect and serve right along with
the *custode*s in the name of the dragon. Lilly chafed under
the interference.

In any case, it was time to see if her faith in Mihas would
pay out.

She readied the spirit defense items that she had already
gathered—mint, iron swords, salt, and a printout of incantations to memorize. Lilly wasn't certain how she or Nigel
would fare with the last item since black arts weren't a *custode*'s forte; that talent was more for breeders whose abilities would be increased tenfold once the dragon had risen.
Nowadays, they were no more than fledgling witches
whose power had decreased era by era. *Custode*s were the

ones who had access to the benefits of Relaquory, and they were the ones with whom main responsibility rested.

Meanwhile, Nigel went to Mihas. On the monitor, Lilly watched how the master vampire seemed to feed off the news of oncoming attackers as Nigel whispered to him, then disappeared into the darkness again.

Mihas ordered his girl soldiers to their feet, and they obeyed, although Lilly noted that the Queenshill students— the vampires who had, for all intents and purposes, been schooled as officers—were unsteady in their balance. But that was because they had taken Mihas's slightly silver-poisoned blood, the fools. Lilly could have told them silver would have more effect on them than it would on the master vampire.

When Nigel returned, she finally went with him to the adjacent room, where she had healed herself earlier. They needed Relaquory perhaps now more than ever.

They shed their drops of blood into the soil, taking strength and energy from the power that shuddered from the long box, and Lilly stole an extra moment to gaze down upon their dirt-covered charge.

What sort of face was under there? She had seen portraits, of course—a long nose, green eyes, an arrogant heavy-lidded bearing—but no *custode* ever dared brush away the soil from the visible nose and mouth to see for themselves.

Even so, she longed to do just that, witnessing another patch of pale skin, paying more homage to the object of her devotion . . .

A piercing beep sounded, and the *custode*s bolted to their feet. A breach?

Had the hunters already come?

No words were even needed between her and Nigel as they bolted back to the monitor room, where they saw how the camera that covered their caged vampire had been altered to another position, the view featuring the rock of the opposite wall now.

Another "malfunction."

Breathing deeply in order to tame their pulses, just as if they were commandos, Lilly and Nigel took up their ghost warding materials along with weapons, then brought everything to the well-protected Relaquory room, which had been prepared over the years by other *custode*s. Its surprises should prove fatal to even the best of hunters.

But defending it was Lilly and Nigel's first priority. More to the point, it was the one and *only* job of a *custode* now.

DAWN knew that once they breached this entrance, there was a good chance the vamps would know the community was under attack, especially if this did lead to the Underground itself. She was only hoping that the creatures would be so thrown off guard that it would take longer for them to get organized than it would take for the team to infiltrate and destroy.

But would Dawn and her crew be attacking vampires or rescuing Costin?

They were about to find out.

Friends had discovered a grassy, doorlike shape etched into a slope nearly one kilometer northwest of the New Gilby Hotel in a darkened, isolated area of the heath. Instead of using explosives, the team had opted for a quieter break-in as Dawn used her acid gun to trace the door. Then she'd pulled her mental energy together, shaping it inside of her, making it boil, and she punched out, knocking the door away and opening a hole.

The spirits rushed through it, clearing the clouds of dirt as some went off to scout, some to find any and all cameras.

Outside, Dawn, Kiko, and Natalia waited for a report, and it came an instant later via Kalin, who'd insisted on accompanying them, even though she could've used more rest.

"Found the trap! Jonah, in a cage, no way out! Friends, on the ground, useless . . ." She zoomed ahead. *"Go, go, go!"*

Costin . . . He *had* been hoodwinked by Claudius's false information, but he was here, just seconds away.

But was he animated or . . . ?

A bang of dread and adrenaline pushed Dawn forward. Kiko and Natalia moved, too, their mini flamethrowers and silver-bullet-filled revolvers drawn. The lights they wore on their heads made crazed squiggle marks on the darkness in front of them as they slid down one decline, then another, deeper and deeper, farther below than anyplace Dawn had ever been, where the only sound seemed to be a pulse tearing through her ears.

Don't be hurt, she thought to Costin, even though she doubted he would hear her mind. *Don't you dare be deader than you already were. . . .*

Then her headlight caught the glint of silver.

A cage—

When she saw a flare of blue eyes behind the square bars, her heart jumped, hitting the walls of her body and trying to spin its way out. She didn't care if the blue gaze belonged to Jonah and not Costin himself. The flash of them meant they were both still around.

She ran to him, crashing into the cage and holding its bars, and Jonah rushed her, too. But he didn't move as fast as usual.

"Knew you'd show up," he said, his skin really pale in her headlight. "We're both safe, but time was running down."

ThankGodthankGodthankGod . . .

Dawn couldn't stop smiling. Alive. Safe.

She didn't tell Jonah to let Costin out, because she knew the host was only sheltering him. Plus, this wasn't the moment to be all emotional about a reunion. Having him here and in decent working order was good enough.

Fumbling, she took out a small cooler flask of blood from a bag she wore over her shoulder, handing it to Jonah by sticking her arm through the bars. She'd give him a bit of a live nip when she got inside, but it wouldn't be nearly as intense as their usual feedings. They didn't have time for anything major.

Greedily, he uncapped the flask and drank her stored blood while she looked and looked at him, unable to get enough.

She'd almost lost him. So close. But this was a second chance, right? As soon as they got out of here, she'd make all her shortcomings up to him. Each and every one.

She heard the murmurs of the Friends trading information, the old guard catching the new one up with the tunnel's layout and also how two different *custode*s had already approached the boss, failing to get to him. Then Jonah was done drinking, and he gave back the cooler, which still had some of her blood left in it. She reached through the bars again to get the object so he could avoid the silver.

"Friends have been guarding us," he said. "They're in bad shape without being able to recharge."

"Figured as much." Dawn secured the flask in her bag and got out the acid gun again. It would work through silver, too.

"Those *custode*s have been dying to get at us," Jonah said while she applied the acid to the cage, "but the Friends kept pushing them away. They never give up, our girls."

The bars began to dissolve enough so that she was confident her psychokinesis would allow her to bang the rest of the way through.

Meanwhile, she could hear the Friends murmuring and, using her prerogative to command them—they'd follow orders from the team unless it meant hurting Costin—Dawn said, "Old guard, you should get on out of here and go home. Who knows how long this battle's going to last."

They could recharge and then come back here if it came down to it, but Dawn prayed there wouldn't be a long-drawn-out battle that would require the spirits to return.

None of the Friends stirred.

"Get your asses gone!" Dawn yelled.

Unable to resist the more strongly worded command, the Friends' jasmine blew back the stray hairs from Dawn's braid as they wound toward the exit, their essences like a breeze instead of the usual stronger wind. But Dawn could feel one Friend hesitating, shivering in rebellion, her own essence all but dissipated.

Breisi. It had to be. No one was this damned stubborn.

"You, too," Dawn said, backing away from the cage and motioning for Jonah to take cover on his side.

"Where's Frank?" Breisi asked in a fragile voice.

"Under the weather." She only had time to be blunt. "He'll be okay but he's holding down temp headquarters. Now get, Breisi. I mean it."

Dawn almost expected Frank to pipe in from the ear-piece, but as she'd suspected, they were down too deep for her to get an outside feed.

Breisi began to inch away, as if compelled, but she managed to say, *"I saw a* custode *using a trapdoor to get out of this tunnel. I think it leads to the Underground. I can show you."*

Well, crap. Breisi had something good to trade on after all. "Okay," Dawn said, rescinding the command. "You can show one of the fresh Friends where it is while I hammer on this cage. Then you leave—no more ifs, ands, or buts about it."

"Dawn . . ."

It had to be killing Breisi to be so weakened during this big moment. As a hunter, she also wanted to thrash the Underground, and Dawn knew she'd do anything to be here for it.

Damn it, Dawn had to be the world's biggest soft sell.

"Then show us the trapdoor yourself, Breisi. But Frank's waiting for you back home, you know."

That seemed to work, but if a Friend could trudge, that was what Breisi would be doing as she slid through the cage to wait on the other side of it.

Dawn was so eager to get past the bars and closer to Costin that she had no problem conjuring enough power for a mind blast.

"Fire in the hole!" she yelled. Then she banged out a mental punch against the acid-eaten silver.

Bam!

That got her partway there. A yawning, ragged hole provided a half entrance, the bars gnarled inward, and Dawn slammed out again to create a wider opening. Then, without waiting, she ran toward it, kicking out with her foot, crashing the bars aside as she landed in the cage, then sprang toward Jonah, throwing her arms around him. She didn't care who was dominant right now as she held him close.

"They didn't get you," she said.

"No." Jonah held her tight.

"Costin," she said, ignoring Jonah's embrace and appealing to the man inside, hoping that Costin felt the strength of her arms, that he would forgive her for being the one who'd had to rescue him again.

At the other name, Jonah tensed, and Dawn pulled back in time to see his eyes change from blue to topaz.

Every part of her flamed up as Costin smiled that world-weary smile, but it was tempered by something even more profound when he rested his palms against her face, as if seeing it for the first time.

She didn't want to be without him. Couldn't imagine what her future would've been like without him in it.

But she'd have to get him out of here now to tell him all about it later.

Would she even be able to do that if they killed the

dragon and Costin's quest came to an end? How long would it be before he was taken from her to rest in a better place, as he'd been promised upon the completion of his journey?

"Hate to do this," she said, the sentence snagging in her throat, "but if Breisi thinks we're close to the Underground, we've got no time to hang out."

She took her machete partway out of its holster, pushing up one of her tight black sleeves and nicking the back of her arm. When she pressed it to his mouth, he sipped at the slight cut.

He only took enough to revitalize himself all the more from the live contact, but that was all they could do for now. As she took her arm away from him, frustrated at the surge of desire that she couldn't satiate, he used his thumb to stroke her face. He knew what was at stake, so he slipped back into Jonah's body, summoning his host to dominance again.

Dawn already missed him, and out of an awful, ridiculous feeling that she might never see him again, she almost yelled for him to come back.

Then Kiko and Natalia passed on their way to the other side of the cage, bringing Dawn back to reality.

"What's the holdup?" Kik said, in total demolition mode.

Dawn backed away from Jonah, reaching into her bag for healing gel and a bandage, both of which she used to dress her minor wound. Costin was gone for now, and there was no help for it until they were done here.

Jonah's hold had lingered until she pulled away altogether to follow her teammates. Kalin did a flyby, whisking over Dawn's shoulder. Based on how she hadn't tried to knock Dawn over, the Friend must've finally understood that Jonah wasn't the one Dawn was here for, and the spirit joined her cohorts—all the strong, refreshed spirits—who would be fighting by the team's side.

Dawn went about using the acid gun on the other wall of the cage since the silver spanned the hallway and they couldn't use the first opening to get out. She quietly asked for more updates from Jonah, lowering her voice even though the Friends were manipulating the sound on the cameras.

"Has he been out of body much?"

"He was out for a little bit," Jonah said.

"Was he able to track the dragon with his senses?"

Jonah shook his head. "We're probably still too distant from an Underground to detect the big guy."

Dawn put the gun away while the acid did its thing. "When the time's right, we'll use Awareness to track him. In the meantime, Jonah, you're still on sheltering duty, got it?"

"Yeah."

She lowered her voice even more. "The dragon *is* here. I'd bet my life on it, so if we run into Mihas first, there's no need to question him about the big master's location. That means Costin can go at Mihas without all the fancy hypnosis and just terminate him. From what I already know, Mihas will be depending on his physical skills, not so much brainpower, so he might not bring his Awareness into an attack—not if he doesn't know that Costin's a fellow blood brother. The vamps might've already guessed that he is, though, so be prepared."

"Noted," Jonah said, picking his long black coat up from the ground and putting it on. His sinuous, casual movements reminded Dawn that Jonah was still the one who was here, present, dominant.

She shook all of that off, instead thinking of what would happen if they *did* get the dragon tonight. Would Costin have to go after the remaining masters, even though they should be humanized by their creator's death, according to what the team knew about how the dragon's vampire line worked? That was how it'd been before with these Undergrounds: the direct descendants got their souls back with a bit of damage attached to them.

Or maybe Costin would have to tie up the loose ends with all the vampire children who were orphaned by their masters. . . .

Who knew? Although The Whisper had been forthcoming with most of his plans, he obviously couldn't tell Costin—who'd accepted the deal out of pure desperation—every single detail. The entity hadn't given out a manual or anything. It could be that Costin would receive an extra special message after the dragon was destroyed.

Dawn cleared everyone from the other side of the cage, then popped out with a few mental thrusts that sipped energy out of her. She should probably conserve it from now on until she really needed it.

Freed, the team moved double time out of the curled bars, Breisi assuming the lead and guiding them to where she'd seen the first *custode* disappear into the grounded trapdoor.

While they followed Breisi, Dawn checked in with Natalia, who was wearing a black ensemble much like Dawn's own, including a long-sleeved spylike shirt, a shoulder bag, and a jacket. But the new girl was outfitted with more basic weapons, like a mini flamethrower, UV grenades, and revolvers—things she'd been able to train in during her short time with the team.

"Any vamp-dar?" Dawn asked.

"Not so much yet."

"Keep me posted."

Natalia offered a short nod as they came to a wall of Friends around the corner of the tunnel.

"Here," Breisi said in her wavering voice.

One of the spirits pushed Dawn forward, guiding her hand to where Breisi must've been indicating a catch. And, yup, with the aid of her headlight, Dawn could see a button nearly buried in the ground.

Breisi said, *"The* custode *stepped on it, and a door opened."*

She came over, got behind Dawn's arm, and pushed it around to pantomime the circumference of the square door in the ground.

"It closed very quickly—so quickly I was too off guard to pursue the keeper myself," Breisi said. *"But maybe we can stop it and force it to stay open with an object."*

"Jonah," Dawn and Kiko said together.

"I'm an object?" His voice sounded stronger from drinking Dawn's blood, thank God.

Dawn didn't joke back. "The instant that door is tripped, Jonah, you can whiz over to pry it open all the way, then keep it gaped until we all get inside. Your vamp strength should be able to handle it."

He seemed good with the plan, so Dawn activated the safety on her mini flamethrower, which had a long butt so he could use it to block the door, if needed. She handed it over to him.

"Breisi," she said, "when we're clear, you *are* going home. Understood?"

Dawn thought she heard a Spanish-inflected grumble.

Then she signaled for Jonah to step on the grounded catch. When he did, the door sliced open.

In a blur, he dove down to intercept it before it zipped closed again, then pushed it back open, maneuvering his feet and hands so that he was basically a bridge holding open the door. He'd left a gape on one side—large enough for any of them to squeeze through.

A Friend shot down into the hole, then bopped back up. *"Cushion below. Safe. Go!"*

Jonah's body shook as he said, "You guys need to get down there before I break in half."

Dawn sucked in her stomach and slid past him, a machete in her hand as she caught air and landed on a mat. She launched to her knees, then aimed around the area with her blade, even though she could smell the jasmine from Friends as they guarded her.

In the second before she moved from the mat, she thought that it looked like a pit down here, and she couldn't help but think that she was in a low, shaded place where the lack of light repressed everything.

Then she called up. "Ready!"

After she left the mat, she reached out with her psycho-kinesis, helping Jonah to keep the door open and allowing him to make more room for the next person. Even though she'd told herself to conserve energy, Jonah was still not at full force, and helping him until he'd regained more strength from her blood wouldn't come amiss.

Reaching out to aid him, Dawn's energy bobbed as she pushed against the sliding door. Natalia came through it, her curly ponytail flying behind her until she hit the mat, where Dawn was waiting to help the new girl balance. Then Dawn guided her away so Kiko could land.

Afterward, the rest of the Friends whooshed down. Then came Jonah, who tucked into a ball before the door could cut into him. Above, the door chopped shut just as he spider-landed on the cushion, grabbed the fallen flame-thrower, and sprang right back up into a cool walk.

Show-off.

Drained by the mental energy she'd expended, Dawn took a second to regroup as everyone else moved ahead.

"Breisi?" she whispered, just to check if the Friend had obeyed.

No answer.

Good. She'd finally gone home, but that left something like a bump in Dawn's composure. She'd miss Breisi, yet she didn't mull over it as she caught up to the back of the crowd.

Natalia was in front, starting to pick up the pace. Was she feeling something?

By the time the team climbed a slope to a higher level,

Natalia seemed out of breath; she was holding a hand to her head.

Yeah, they were close to some vamps, all right. Natalia was sensing it.

Kiko whispered, "The Friends see a door up here, and there's an access panel."

"Pull Natalia away from the front," Dawn said.

Kiko complied, guiding his fellow psychic behind him then assuming her primary spot. In spite of Natalia's unease, she took out some small bags that contained the same silver flakes that had stunned the Hollywood Underground when the vampires had inhaled the matter. It would be her job to parcel out the bags to the Friends as they protected her, so that they could spread the poison around. From there, Natalia was supposed to hang back, just defending herself; she was probably going to be aching from the large number of vamps around and would be in no real shape to fight hard.

Jonah handed Dawn's flamethrower back to her, then removed some knives from his long coat.

As she holstered the weapon and took hold of both her machetes, she said, "We're gonna be using UV grenades, so you might want to stay behind until after our grand entrance. Also"—she took out gloves and a surgical mask from her bag—"you'll want to wear this for the silver flakes. Careful of getting them on your face, too, 'cause they'll slow you down with poison—not as bad as sucking them in though."

"Good," he said, his blue eyes aglow. He was excited, as usual. He could probably even taste blood.

As he put on the gloves and mask, Dawn exhaled. Time for getting this really started.

"Earplug in," she said to Kiko. They'd have to use the plugs on one side so they could shield from any vampire charm; earpieces would fill their other ears. Natalia would no doubt be fine without the extra precaution unless she wanted to avoid the new lulling yells the Friends intended to use on these vamps.

"Frank?" Dawn asked, trying to see if she could contact her father on the earpiece since the team had walked upslope to a higher level under the ground.

The communication attempt didn't work, so Dawn signaled Kiko, who hit a button that opened a sliding door so the Friends could go first, checking for more traps.

As Dawn's heartbeat sped up, the spirits surged ahead, and within a couple of seconds, one of them rounded back.

"*UV time!*" she yelled, clearing the way for the team.

Everyone but Jonah rushed into what looked like a cavern. Dawn didn't know for sure where they were because she only had time to see a gulping darkness cut by their headlights, then the furious eyes of an oversized, hairy wolf that had launched itself at them along with rows and rows of sharp teeth.

They'd been waiting. . . .

Kiko released the first grenade, and the room lit up with a decimating pale light as Dawn charged toward the howling vampire.

NINETEEN

BELOWGROUND, II

WOLFIE had told Della and the girls to be ready for hunters.

Earlier, she had seen a *custode* slip into the maze room to whisper in Wolfie's ear so quietly not even the girls had heard the red-eyed creature. After the keeper had left, her supposed master and commander had turned all his attention to ordering the girls about. This was the ultimate night-crawl, he had told them. Yet, instead of finding the prey, it would be coming to them, and they would have all the liberty in the world to feast on flesh, meat, bone.

If he thought that would pique their appetites . . . he'd been correct. But even as the Queenshill girls had been set in charge of a group of recruits, then hidden in the maze so they might ambush the hunters, Della was loath to defend anything of Wolfie's, though her veins did rumble with hunger. She had purged all that blood she'd taken from him, but it still left her a bit poisoned, slow.

As she waited in her own area with her charges, the

maze's walls so tall that they could see nothing but the rock ceiling, she heard a door opening, saw the flash of white light licking over the top of the barriers.

Ultraviolet . . . ?

Howls, screams, the roar of weapons and gunshots—

Della had been commanded to wait until Wolfie summoned her, and she had given every indication of obeying him. Nevertheless, she'd been thinking, *Why?*

Why defend the prick?

She'd been fairly certain that her Queenshill classmates were asking the same, but there'd been no opportunity to commune with them before they'd been separated and stationed in their strategic locations.

One of the recruits pawed at Della, and she slapped the irritant away.

"Shouldn't we attack, also?" the soldier said in her new girly wolf voice.

"Belt up," Della snapped, and all her charges cowered.

Saliva was dripping from her many wolf teeth to her chin. There'd be blood, much of it, and *that* was when she would emerge. When she could feed without hindrance.

More screams, more roaring sounds, the color of orange lighting the ceiling.

Were the hunters using . . . fire?

Della's skin burned with the memory of what flame had done to her during the Southwark attack, and she thought of her schoolmates.

They'd been poisoned by Wolfie's blood. Were her chums suffering out there because they were moving slower than usual?

Torn between going to them and punishing Wolfie, Della leaned forward, then back, until more orange flares and screams echoed down into her portion of the maze.

The screams . . . Had Briana and Sharon and Blanche sounded like this when Mrs. Jones had killed them?

Della gained her feet, hunching, unable to tolerate not

knowing how her mates were faring here and now. She couldn't save the girls Mrs. Jones had murdered, yet perhaps with the ones who were out there, fighting . . .

Just as she was ready to lead her charges out, the jasmine came.

The spirits swooped down, pounding the girls to the ground, banging the breath out of Della. The recruits had only been briefed about what these entities were, and they had no experience in fighting them, so they flailed as Della pushed against the jasmine, attempting to move forward, to go to her schoolmates.

Then high, screechy banshee yells from the jasmine brought the girls to their knees, and they all began to howl mournfully while the jasmine's cries screwed in Della's eardrums, even as an odd mellowness sang through her body.

This must *be the work of a blood brother,* Della thought as she dragged herself onward, her claws gouging the ground as her charges tried to follow.

They crawled out of the maze, the jasmine still hounding them, and the colors—orange, white, and silver, flashes of lethal brilliance—made her cringe.

In the open, she saw the hunters battling her wolf-snarling friends. Her mates were slow, yes, much too poisonously slow to respond to every attack, but they . . .

Were they indeed just as betrayed by Wolfie? Had they little reason to fight for him, too . . . ?

Then the attackers' scents took control of Della, and she wanted to rush them, bite into them, eat, and drink. She wrestled with the lure of springing at them, instead creeping onward to aid her mates.

She was losing strength by the moment under the jasmine-issued banshee yells. There were also silver flakes floating down from above as other spirits batted about small bags, and when Della saw her sister vampires—Polly, Stacy, Noreen—breathing the sparkles in and slowing down even more, she turned to her own group.

"Cover your faces!"

Without question, they ripped off their already torn shirts and pressed them over their noses and mouths, their wolf eyes wide and flaring in the explosive lights.

When the silver drifted toward them, they sought cover under rock shelving until the flakes stopped their descent. But Della saw that almost all of the wolf-vampire girls—including Stacy and Noreen—had become petrified, their skin burned by the UV under patches of canine hair, their bodies fully poisoned by the floating silver, just as if they were scarred statues posing in a gentle winter storm. Simultaneously, the little man whom Della knew to be one of the hunters was running round and binding her stiff-still mates with silver strings he was taking out of his shoulder bag. Another young woman whom Della didn't recognize was helping him as she held a hand to her head in obvious pain of some sort.

Then, just behind her sister vampires, Della saw the most frightening sight of all.

The woman. The one who'd used mental powers at Queenshill. The one who'd faced Della in Southwark.

With her braid trailing round as she engaged Polly, one of the last girl vampires standing, in blade to claw combat, the woman looked every inch a hunter. And with each slash of her machetes, Della saw a reflection of her own personal need to strike out with something just as sharp.

Her claws. Her teeth. Her grief.

When the woman took both blades, crossed her arms, then sliced through Polly's midsection both ways, following up with a backward cut to the neck that sent Polly's head flying off, Della felt . . .

Nothing.

For Polly had hated Della for killing Violet, and Della had never forgotten this.

She didn't even feel anything as Polly's body shriveled and disappeared. She didn't actually feel until the machete woman peered round for her next target, the light on her head sweeping the area, shining over the silver flakes coating the frozen vampires' skin and hair as they posed in midmotion round her.

When the woman's gaze found Della and her group hiding under the rock shelf, she hesitated, the blades at her sides.

It was almost as if . . .

No, she couldn't have recognized Della, not in wolf form.

But then the woman suddenly glanced to her left, where Wolfie was engaging with a—

Oh.

Even with a white mask covering most of his face, she could see it was the mean vampire from Queenshill, and he had his own dagger blades, which were clashing with and sparking against Wolfie's long claws and canine teeth. But the master had the mean one on the retreat. Even with the barrage of those jasmine ghosts assaulting Wolfie with their banshee cries and pounding him with their invisible essences, plus the silver flakes, her master was clearly stronger and faster than the mean vampire. The rips in the inferior creature's long coat also told Della that Wolfie had put in some licks.

The machete woman was staring at Wolfie, and it reminded Della all too much of how she had appeared on that night at Queenshill, when Della could have sworn the woman was using her mind to attack them.

When Wolfie flew backward, hitting a wall, Della thought she might just be right about the woman.

The mean vampire ran at him with his blades aimed at Wolfie's heart, but Della's master vampire swiped out an arm, swatting the mean one away.

Then it was Wolfie who assumed a strange, concentrating expression, and the mean vampire flew backward, as if hit by something Wolfie was thinking.

The confrontation raged on as the woman kept staring at the fighting males, as if she were gathering her own energy to strike out again. . . .

Behind Della, a recruit let loose with a frenzied howl, then before Della could stop her, she took a run at the woman, straight through the forest of petrified wolf-vampire girls.

Hardly even looking back, the huntress casually raised her machete, and the girl impaled herself through the heart. Then the woman extracted the blade and simply chopped off the girl's head without much effort at all.

There seemed to be no more lower vampires moving, save for Della and her own. But before the woman could set her sights on them, Wolfie cried out while he kept fending off the mean vampire with his mind powers.

"Della!"

He had summoned her—his final backup garrison. But with a salacious snap of glee, Della could hear that he was also wondering why she wasn't fighting.

Her recruits responded to his call, galloping to him on all fours with their temporary shirt masks flapping away from their hairy faces. But even as he still held back the mean vampire, Wolfie kept his gaze on Della, as if checking to see why she had not yet come to him.

She realized that the attackers were outwitting her master, whose only recent combat exercise had been hunting with the girls and playing with them.

Very slowly, very surely, she stayed where she was and smiled at Wolfie, flashing her big wolf teeth.

Everything played out on his expression as it fell: He knew she wouldn't come. He could see in her quivering smile that there were consequences for hurting her.

His brief loss of focus was all it took for the machete woman to fix her gaze on Wolfie again, and before Della could swallow the juices flooding her mouth, her master had zoomed back into a wall on a bolt of invisible energy from the woman, his head connecting with a splinter of rock thrusting out from it.

The recruits reached Wolfie just as that splinter jammed through the rear of his skull and out the front, but as they howl-screamed at the spray of Wolfie's blood, the jasmine spirits whirled round and round at the remaining recruits' feet, raising the silver flakes into a whirlpool. The wind lifted the girls' shirt masks, allowing the silver to puff up to their snouts, causing the final girls to choke until they froze, as all the others had.

From her spot so far away under the rock shelf, Della returned her gaze to Wolfie as he was slammed back again and again by the woman's mind powers, his eyes rolling in his head while the rock splinter kept ramming out his forehead.

Then, as if wanting to put an end to it, the mean vampire ran at Wolfie with his knives pulled, plunging them into Wolfie's chest and slashing them about so quickly that, in the next instant, he was able to reach into the master's body to yank out his heart just before everything about Wolfie shriveled to nothing.

Immediately, Della doubled over, flailing, pulling the shirt from her face in her panic to breathe, sucking in silver as she fell to the ground then froze like her mates. But, even statued, she could feel the last part of her own vampire being severed out, cell by wailing cell, as she became human again. It was as if Wolfie himself was snatching out each part of her, disassembling everything she had believed about him.

Minutes later, it was dark all round Della, who couldn't move, couldn't do anything.

But, most horrifically, it was dark inside, too, her returned soul like a seething stain of blackness.

MIHAS was dead, but the worst was yet to come.

In the aftermath of the initial attack, Dawn took out her

earplug and slumped to the ground, recovering from the purge of hatred, the whipping she'd given to the master vampire. The only way she and Jonah had even matched up to him was with the aid of the Friends and their silver, plus . . .

God. Plus her anger.

It'd been primed when she'd seen the one big male wolf vampire who had to be Mihas dueling with Jonah, and it'd only gotten worse from there. And she'd taken great satisfaction in making sure that the master vampire wasn't going to hurt the man contained inside of Jonah.

As skin burned on her neck in what was probably a new collection of beauty marks, she forced herself to stand and walk through the copse of posed, barely clothed vampire girls, who'd gone from semi-wolf form to their fully human ones upon the death of their master. Some had matured drastically, even though their motor skills were frozen, and the sight of old and middle-aged women in the rags of girly skirts and outfits seemed bizarre.

Then again, what wasn't bizarre?

"Kiko, Natalia," Dawn called, her voice sounding as if it'd just been put through a slashing machine, "Jonah and I are going on alone."

Kiko, who had several pawed scratches marring his skin, said, "Not likely, Dawn." He hated being left out, just like Breisi. "Those *custode*s are somewhere around, and I suspect they'll be with the dragon, guarding the tar out of it."

If they haven't already evacuated the dragon, Dawn thought.

Or maybe the *custode*s were so confident in themselves that they hadn't moved him anywhere. Besides, an evacuation might take too long.

Dawn could only hope. "If Jonah and I fail with the dragon," she said, "we'll need a second attack wave. You'd need to go to Frank, rebuild a team, and try again later."

It'd be too late for Costin though. He would've already forfeited his soul if the dragon got the best of him. Yet it wouldn't be too late for everyone else who'd have to suffer under the dragon's rule.

Natalia wandered away from her inspection of a frozen former vamp girl with aged features and platinum hair run through with gray, then came to Kiko's side. He glanced up at her, then sighed.

With just a gaze, Natalia had done Dawn's work for her by somehow persuading Psychic #1 to see reason. This meant that Dawn was free to go to Jonah and see how he'd fared.

He was resting on the ground, his eyes blue above the surgical mask. His coat was ripped, gleaming with silver flakes, and the clothes underneath had been slightly shredded, too, blood running from the pale skin underneath. Jonah was already healing, but he must've been spent from keeping the master vampire out of his head during Mihas's Awareness attack.

Thankful that they hadn't gotten to the point where they'd had to let Costin loose to wield his own Awareness against Mihas's, Dawn joined Jonah on the ground, brushing the silver off him, careful not to get any in his wounds.

"Did the flakes land in any of your scratches?" she asked.

"No." The mask muffled his voice. "I would feel it."

She reached into her bag, giving him the flask cooler containing the last of her blood.

After removing his mask, he drank, then put the mask back on so he wouldn't have to smell the blood. Dawn eased off his coat, using it to wipe him down the best she could. Then she placed her fingers under his chin, raising his face so she could read his gaze.

When he looked into her, opening himself up much more eagerly than Costin had ever done, she saw that he would be okay. She'd just give him a few minutes to heal before they went on.

He glanced at her neck, where the new marks had settled.

Yeah. She'd noticed it when she'd been whaling on Mihas, smacking his head against the wall, scared to death that he'd destroy Costin and Jonah. Yet, she'd taken some contentment in the fact that she could stop the vamp. A lot of contentment. Mihas had been a master, but he'd lost strength and focus over the centuries. He'd been beatable.

But she'd paid a price for winning.

"So I've got more on me," she said to Jonah. "I'm sure, after the dragon, I'll be covered with beauty marks."

When he didn't say anything, she got ready to go, then offered her hand to help him up.

He accepted it, his grip strong but not overwhelming as they both pulled him to a stand. At first, she wondered if a vampire like him—a weaker one by most standards— would last against the dragon. He'd just faced a master, and that had to have drained just about everything out of him.

Then his hold on her strengthened. Was Jonah the only one clasping her hand?

Was Costin also telling her they'd get this done?

He reared back his head, facing front, his eyes changing to topaz. He was here, and it wasn't just to reassure her. Costin would be using his master/progeny Awareness with his own creator to track down the dragon, then he would be giving his all to see this through.

He kept ahold of her hand as he led her out of the room and toward what very well might be their last stand together.

TWENTY

Lost†

At temporary headquarters, Eva had waited in her room until all of them but Frank had left.

His presence cut inside of her, pulling her apart and leaving a large, hungry tear down the middle. He hadn't seemed as happy as the college boy had been to have her attentions. Yes, Frank's body had responded to her, hardening, climaxing, but afterward she'd needed to clear his mind since there was nothing resembling joy in him.

What had she done wrong with Frank?

All she wanted from him was the love that used to be so easy for them to share.

And she was going to get as much of it out of him as she could.

She finished sponging herself with water from the basin in her restroom, then put on a new, plain flannel nightgown she'd found in the costume locker after Dawn had left and Frank had retreated to the communications room. She noticed that she felt a distant tweak of worry for her daughter, and this bothered Eva somewhat because it should've been more than just a twinge.

The pre-wine-bar Eva would have been pacing, entirely concentrating on the safety of Dawn and the others. But now . . . ?

She was worrying less and less about anyone else.

As she looked at herself in the mirror, she saw a bed-headed woman she didn't know. A flash came to her: the man in the bar, his tilted, light brown eyes filled with prom-ise while he held her hands in the wine cellar. His black hair, which came to his chin, had added to his exotic sexuality.

"You're so sad," he'd told her, his voice as mellow as the flow of the wine she'd already drunk. Too much wine, and that had made her bold enough to come down here with him when he'd given her that look.

The kind of look every woman needed to see when she was down and out about herself.

"A woman like you has no business being so unappreci-ated," he'd added, "so denied everything she deserves."

"How would you know?" She'd been wary of how much he seemed to see in her, but she was tempted by him, too. He had an allure that she hadn't seen in anyone since Hol-lywood, but he wasn't a vampire.

He was . . .

Just a man?

"Eva," he said, smiling. "You weren't hard to discover. You're just what I've been looking for—so beautiful. So elegant and perfect."

His confession should have made her run. Was he a stalker who knew she wasn't really "Mia Scott," even after her plastic surgery to hide her real identity as Eva Clare-mont?

As he stroked the backs of her hands with his thumbs, she thought she sensed a vague, seething buzz on his skin, but she'd told herself that it was just the wine, and he had the touch of someone who didn't think she was only a piece of baggage dragged along to a new place from a past life. That was all she was to Frank, and she was sure that, in spite of everything, Dawn felt the same way. The suspicion had isolated Eva, even in the middle of a city.

The man, with his soft words and caresses, had gone on. "What you'd give to be a part of something again. I know you, Eva. I know what you want and, because of that, I found you, like I find others."

"Others?"

"Yes. Your souls all call out in one way or another. As for you, there's a dark spot that only grew larger tonight, even after you tried so hard to contain it. I came before it overtook you."

Eva couldn't believe it. The soul stain, as Dawn called it. After Frank had refused her blood, had she sunk into the darkness of sorrow—the stain?

Whatever had happened, there she was, with the man.

He whispered. "I knew you would be ready now. Are you, Eva?"

Ready . . . for what?

His gaze had heated, and she'd understood. She didn't know what he was, but she knew that she needed what he had. She could see it all in his eyes—a completion she hadn't possessed since her vampire days, but . . .

Not a vampire, she kept thinking. Not in the way she thought of them, at least.

Then he'd changed. Or maybe it hadn't been so much his appearance as the allure she'd noticed. All she'd seen when he suddenly pricked her palm with a hooked thimble he'd slipped on at some point was a fire in his eyes. True fire. And when he wounded himself, drawing a drop of blood from his own palm, he'd asked her one last question.

"*Do* you want it all back?"

Did she want everything she'd lost?

He'd pulled her in with his gaze, setting her in the midst

of her glory days, when she'd received breathless letters from people who said that her movies had spoken to them, perfumed pages from young girls who confessed that they wanted to be just like her. When she'd been pursued by the silver screen's most desirable men and she'd rejected them because she'd been so in love with Frank.

When she'd owned the world and she hadn't even known it.

She looked at the globe of blood on his palm, and it held those everythings.

"You can really give it back to me?" she asked.

"Yes, I can make you feel loved, a thousand times over."

He hadn't said it outright, but she knew this meant he could get Frank to love her again, and her eyes went blurry with tears. She didn't ask what the cost would be. She was fairly sure she already knew.

So she held her bloodied hand out to him, just as she'd offered it to Frank earlier that night.

"Yes," she said.

This man had smiled, his mouth sensuous and tempting, with a glint of white teeth. Something flashed in his eyes again, red and irresistible as he touched his wounded skin to hers, melding the blood.

A spike of lust, happiness, orgasmic fulfillment drove through Eva, and she fought for breath, crumbling to the stone floor. It was like he'd reached into her and yanked her inside out, pain and pleasure fused and simmering as the soul she'd regained back in L.A. left her once again.

But this time its departure felt more like Eva was giving birth to a new life. A quiet, terrifyingly easy birth.

"You belong now," the man whispered as she reveled in the chaos of her high. "And you'll come to me soon."

And, minutes later, when she came down from it, he was gone.

Even now, she had no idea what the man in the wine bar had made her—she was only finding out hour by hour.

Feeding by feeding.

Called by that hunger, she left her room to wander the hall, and she found Frank in the office studded with computers and communication equipment. Earlier, she'd heard him muttering to himself, encouraging his body to get better and fast, because he wanted to go to the team—to Dawn and Breisi. Eva wouldn't be surprised if he was planning to join them after he could stand up without swaying.

He was holding an earpiece and what she knew was a locator unit as he sat in a chair, leaning his elbows on his thighs, as if still regaining strength from the encounter the two of them had enjoyed earlier.

She'd fed him some of her blood, and he'd healed, just not as quickly as she'd expected. She had taken too much from him, and it startled her to realize she was that powerful. With a touch, she had even made Frank forget that they'd been together and that he had taken her own blood to help him recover.

Next time, though, she'd have to give him more of herself, because obviously, it hadn't been enough.

But, as she'd thought, she hadn't needed to bury him like the college boy she'd put into a grave in a nearby construction lot.

Eva felt herself frowning, as if she were sad about the young man's death. But was she really?

Frank slowly looked over his shoulder at her, his forehead creased, almost as if he didn't recognize her. Or maybe his mind was trying to work around what they were to each other now.

He put down the locator and the earpiece. "You should get back to bed. A lot's going down and I need to be on standby."

But *she* needed *him*.

She walked closer, her nightgown brushing her legs, creating a waving friction against her—inside her—that she'd never experienced as a human or a vampire. She almost felt like she could float like a ghost, even though she was still solid. Yet, as she went to him, she also felt pulled away, as if something was reeling her in from outside headquarters.

She had a feeling it was the mysterious man, asking her to find him now that she had evolved. And she would go, just as soon as she consumed more. Just as soon as she felt satisfied.

"Frank," she whispered, reaching out to run her hand through his brown hair, which had started to recede when he was human.

"I'm busy."

He shrugged away, turning back to the locator, and she lifted her hand, stung. But then she rested her fingers on his neck, a tingle sending waves of bliss through her.

He gripped her wrist, removing her from him.

"I *need* you, Frank," she said, the hunger for his adoration—for taking it from him since he wouldn't give her any—rising and consuming her.

"What *are* you?" he asked, stopping her.

She shrank away from him. He didn't know? He'd loved her and he had no idea?

"I'm not sure there's a name," she said, holding a hand over her heart to still it. It was beating, just like any woman's.

Then Frank snapped his head toward the doorway and, at the same time, Eva scented the jasmine with her higher alertness.

She smiled. "Ah. Breisi."

"Breez," Frank said to his girlfriend as she blew into the room, "just get to your picture at old headquarters, okay? There's nothin' happening here."

"*Eva . . .*" Breisi said in her wispy voice. It sounded weak, but it grated in a drawn-out threat.

"You're about to collapse," Frank said as the girlfriend circled him, surrounding him with her essence.

Eva held up her arms, but not in surrender.

No more surrendering.

She caught a flash of herself in a mirror that had been positioned in a corner so the room occupant could see behind them. White and flowy . . . light hair that had matted into near coils from all the bed rest . . .

Eva thought about what she'd done to that laser tracker back at the old headquarters—how she'd manipulated it and the security camera with only a touch. Thought of how she could make anyone shrivel.

Try it on the spirit, said the instructive whisper in her head. But it was her own voice she heard.

She reached out to Breisi, pulling at the spirit's essence with a touch of her fingers.

There was a scream, and the jasmine retreated, as if Breisi had been shocked.

Eva went for her another time, connecting with the Friend's essence again, and an electric bolt traveled up her skin. It didn't go under it though—not like Frank's or the college boy's.

It wasn't the same at all, and Eva didn't like it.

Even so, when Breisi flew away, Eva attacked once more, enough to expel her enemy from the room as Frank grabbed Eva from behind. Without even turning around, she gripped him by the neck and lifted him off the ground as his energy zapped up through her arm and down into her core, making her want him all the more.

Then, using her foot to back-slam the door after Breisi flew into the hallway, Eva lifted her husband even higher, realizing only now just how strong she was.

Frightened by the level of it, she dropped him, and he slouched to the ground.

He peered up at her, one hand raised as if to ward her off.

She backed away, but it wasn't enough to get her out of

range of that mirror, where she saw all of her: a white-gowned Medusa bride with feral hair, her gaze famished.

The woman he left behind, she thought. *Me.*

Me . . . ?

But then the hunger overcame her, and she rushed Frank, sealing her mouth to his and drawing as much of him in as she could.

TWENTY-ONE

The Lair

Dawn and Costin had unlinked hands far back in the tunnels, when they'd needed to get a grip on their weapons. She was holding her mini flamethrower in her right hand, then one of two regular grenades she'd brought in her left. He had a silver dagger and a revolver handy, even though silver bullets might not work against a *custode* who wore the kind of body armor Dawn had detected back in Southwark, when she'd come against Lilly.

Most important of all, Dawn's best weapon—her psychokinesis—was on amped-up standby after the fight she had just recovered from.

As she illuminated the tunnel with her headlight, Costin kept his surgical mask on so any remainder of blood wouldn't distract him. He tracked the dragon with his Awareness, and the closer they got, the more he trembled. The Friends also sensed the discord in the air as they wove in and out, darting around while they scouted ahead and behind. Hell, even Dawn felt the swampiness of bad vibrations.

"He's somewhere nearby," Costin said in a near whisper under that mask. His usually low, composed voice was muddled and unsteady. "I think his power even permeates the rock nearest him."

"When we get to him, you should probably close yourself back into Jonah," she whispered. It was all so quiet except for the "mmming" of her body. "Just until you're ready to strike out."

"If my Awareness is even enough to affect him," he said. "Remember, I encountered him once, long, long ago, and I was no match."

"But you trained through the years. You said you even holed up for a while so your own powers would grow."

Neither of them mentioned that, because of being encased in Jonah's vamp body, those powers weren't exactly at a high. But, then again, they'd just conquered Mihas along with the Friends' help, and they had to believe that, united, the team would be able to throw down with the dragon, too.

Because if not them, then who?

The Whisper?

Right. Like the enigma who'd made Costin into a Soul Traveler would come out of hiding to beat the dragon himself. If he'd been able to take on this mission, he wouldn't have sworn in Costin to do it for him. It was definitely up to them to come up with the goods.

God, if Dawn survived this, she was going to find whoever or whatever The Whisper was.

One day.

They moved rapidly down the tunnel, curving here, there, led by Costin's intuition and the light on her head. But it was the smell that told them they'd arrived, even before Mary-Margaret zipped over with a hushed report.

"Mint!" she said in her wind-tunnel Southern drawl. *"Those* custodes *are trying to use mint to keep me and the girls away!"*

Dawn guessed Mary-Margaret sounded offended because mint was supposed to ward off evil spirits. But the Friends weren't evil. Not to Dawn, anyway.

Or did "evil" depend on a point of view?

Before she could ask Mary-Margaret if the smell was doing anything to the Friends, some of the invisible hunters sped ahead, prompting Dawn and Costin to pump up their pace, too.

Lian, another Friend, said, *"They're just around the corner!"*

The air got heavier, pressing in. They rounded the bend with their weapons up.

In the flash of Dawn's headlight stood two *custode*s. Black masked and red-eyed, the taller of the two shadow figures was spreading salt in the air, calmly aiming it at the Friends and chanting in some unintelligible language with that baleful, electronically altered voice. Both keepers were surrounded by a bunch of mint sprigs and a semicircle of salt on the ground in front of a wall.

Was it protecting the entrance that led to the dragon?

Surely there's more than this, Dawn thought, just before the smaller *custode*—Lilly?—sliced two swords that looked to be made of iron through the air at the prodding Friends.

Iron—another ghost repellent.

Dawn heard a squeal from a spirit and wondered if the element had warded her off or if she was just enjoying herself, being a daredevil hunter and all. But then Dawn noticed that *something* had to be keeping the Friends at bay, because aside from whizzing around the area, they weren't being very aggressive.

Was it the mint? The salt, the iron . . . or the chanting?

Black arts, Dawn thought, focusing on the taller *custode* who was uttering the mantra. She was pretty sure that malevolent incantations would ward off even the best intentioned of spirits.

She recalled what she'd read in that book at Menlo Hall. *Initially black-art bred from the best of military men and witches . . .*

Well, magic or not, she was pretty sure she could shut the keeper up.

Holstering her mini flamethrower, Dawn activated one of Breisi and Frank's modified, non-UV grenades, yelling a coded warning to her team, just in case the impact affected the structure of the tunnel itself.

"DANCE!" she cried as she hucked it at the *custode*s.

The force of the retreating Friends bolted against Dawn as Costin rammed against her, too, throwing them both away and back around the corner just before the explosive boomed.

As rock shifted then thudded to the ground, Dawn turned to Costin while they both lay there. In the glare of her headlight, she saw that his eyes had silvered and he'd pulled the mask away from his face, exposing fangs.

He was excited, probably because of the dragon vibrations, the prospect of finally coming to the end of his mission.

Looking at him, she felt as if he'd already left her behind.

But this was his soul they were fighting for. His eternal peace.

"Jonah," she whispered, the harshness of her tone betraying her hurt. "Come out to protect him while we get past these guardians."

She saw his body stiffen and guessed that Jonah had already taken over. Then she hopped back to her feet and darted around the corner, her flamethrower raised. She could feel her partner right behind her as they all rushed ahead, to where the *custode*s were still standing, the smoke clearing away from them.

The taller keeper—it had to be Nigel—began chanting again, and the Friends hung back, even though they were

trying to push forward against whatever those words were
doing to them. Dawn heard one moan, then another spirit
do the same.

It would've been enough to dishearten Dawn if she
hadn't caught the gape in the rock wall behind the
*custode*s.

But it seemed as if the keepers didn't give much of a
care about the hole as Lilly pointed at Dawn with one of
her iron swords, which Dawn could see was tipped to a
wicked sharpness.

In answer, Dawn let Lilly peer down the nozzle of her
mini flamethrower as she started to squeeze the trigger.

The only thing that stopped her was a slight metallic
clicking sound from above.

Being a vampire, Jonah had heard it before Dawn, and
he tackled her, pummeling her far out of the way as two
banks of long, gleaming blades swung down from opposite
sides in front of the *custode*s.

The Friends moved so fast that they sounded like
screams as they smashed into Dawn and Jonah, too, pushing them farther away from the blades that crashed into
each other like jagged teeth, sparks flying at the friction.

As an out-of-breath Dawn glanced up at the composed keepers behind the barrier, she thought, *The
dragon is* so *here*. Lilly and Nigel had lured them forward to a booby trap that not only could've killed the
hunters—it now provided a sharp wall to the bit of
grenade-blasted hole.

Swirling into Plan B, the Friends cried out with their
lulling voices to the keepers, but behind the blades, Dawn
could see Lilly and Nigel glancing at each other as if the
sound was hilarious.

Lulling worked on the majority of humans. Then again,
these guys weren't quite that.

But *something* had to bring them down.

As the Friends switched to the banshee yells, in case

that worked, Jonah whispered, "I can watch for more traps while you do your thing."

He was telling her to use her mind powers for all they were worth, but it felt like Dawn was just about near empty on the inside after all the energy she'd pulled on already. Yet she still had adrenaline kicking through her.

She still had Costin to save.

Making sure her anger was juiced, just in case she needed it, she grabbed her second and last grenade from her bag, activating it, yelling another code word.

"FEVER!"

She heaved the explosive at the bladed trap, and the *custodes* ducked into the hole behind them.

Dawn and Jonah had already scrambled behind the corner when the grenade *ka-bamm*ed, sending blades flying into the wall opposite them like it was under attack by a Roman legion.

After the metal finished clattering to the ground, Kalin zoomed over.

"Tunnel's still solid. Pursue?"

"Sic 'em," Dawn said, hoping Kalin would be bitchier than ever when she caught up to the keepers.

As Kalin and her Friends shot ahead, Dawn and Jonah came out from the corner again and made toward the blade trap, which looked like a giant fist had punched it in the teeth and left some shattered dental work.

To clear the rest of the way for Dawn and Jonah, the Friends slipped behind the top of the trap, then pushed the framework aside, using every ounce of their essences to open up just enough space for their more solid teammates to squeeze through.

"Ears open?" Dawn said to Jonah, hoping he'd sense any booby traps ahead of time.

"They're open."

They negotiated their way through the sharpened entrance, through the hole in the wall.

Luckily, Jonah had been listening, because within a second, he cried, "Down!" and clamped his hand on Dawn's head, pushing her to the ground, where her face hit dirt just as a cutting breeze swooped above her neck. Peeking up, she saw a large scythe passing to the other side.

Then Jonah picked her up, tossing her forward like a sack of feathers as a bank of knives came at their torsos. He dove over it as another scythe came down from the opposite side, and he grabbed her, flipping into the air with her pressed against him. Then spears barged out of the ground, one of them skimming the sole of Dawn's boot, but he twisted her out of the way before it impaled her. As soon as Jonah gracefully hit the ground, he pushed her forward into a run.

She raised her flamethrower, off balance, not knowing where to target yet, and impressions of the room came at her, all coalescing into one thought.

A . . . temple?

That was how it seemed in its reverent austereness. A rock altar lit by low lamps that were buried in the walls like sleepy eyes. A long, wooden box on that altar—

She couldn't see what was inside of the box, but the vibrating awfulness was a hundred times worse now, making the lining of her stomach shake, her limbs feel like weights were hanging from them.

It seemed like an hour since Jonah had manhandled her into this room, past those blades, but just like that, time snapped into fast motion as she spied the *custode*s stepping in front of that long box, both armed with swords now.

Even behind their masks, they were staring at Dawn and Jonah with those goggled red eyes, as if stunned that the attackers had gotten this far.

Dawn was a little stunned, too, as the taller keeper, Nigel, began chanting again. His words were rushed, as if maybe he was coming to the last tricks in his arsenal.

Jonah leveled his revolver, no doubt aiming for the neck

where there'd hopefully be no body armor; he intended to shut Nigel up so the Friends could come forward and help.

Leaving her partner to his own devices, Dawn targeted the flamethrower at Lilly, but the keeper was too damned quick, and she was out of the way with a casual tuck, roll, and stand. But Dawn reacted fast, too, skinning her revolver from its holster with her other hand and faking Lilly out by shooting at one of the swords the keeper had already raised.

As it clanged out of the *custode*'s grasp and to the floor, Lilly flipped her other sword in her hand, bringing it back, then throwing it at Dawn.

The blade spun, and just as Dawn's brain was registering its approach, she dodged, and it only struck her flamethrower away. The weapon clattered to the ground as Lilly jumped off the altar, crashing into Dawn and chopping at one of her arms, breaking it.

At the burst of pain, Dawn stumbled back, crying out; it'd happened so suddenly that she wasn't processing the injury beyond the initial shock. But the aftermath of the attack itself . . . ?

It raged. It flamed all on its own.

Now she had all the energy in creation, and she used her mental powers like a boulder pounding down on Lilly, sending the keeper flat to the floor.

Lilly got right back up and kicked, sweeping Dawn's legs out from under her with whip-fast speed.

Maneuvering her body so that she thudded onto the side with the healthy arm, Dawn flipped to her feet again, then crouched, her injury throbbing as vaguely as her mind and pulse.

In the background, she thought she heard Nigel's *custode* chants going mum, and she knew Jonah had done something to him.

More fuel for the fire.

When she mentally punched out this time, it was like

she was on the outside of her own body, watching Dawn
Madison go to work. She was remote—a person controlling a video game that wouldn't have any reset button.

She watched Dawn push out with cutting violence, just
like her mind power had become two machetes whipping
through the air on their way to slicing a victim to ribbons.
And when her power hit Lilly's mask, Dawn heard *whisk-
whisk-whisk-whisk-whisk*—

The *custode*'s facial covering flew off bit by bit as she
stumbled away from the attacking Dawn. The keeper was
clearly unprepared, even though she should've expected
something like this to happen with Dawn's history of using
her mental blasts before.

And Dawn kept cutting, unstoppable now, even though
her energy ebbed with every move. She left Lilly's mask in
strips that revealed a young girl's face Dawn remembered
from Eva's flat, during their very first encounter.

A panicked face that looked all too human with her
mouth agape, her eyes filled with what-the-fuck questions.

Out of control, Dawn kept going, cutting and cutting
down Lilly's body, leaving only slashes on the black uniform because the keeper had started to duck and dodge,
groping on the ground for one of her swords.

When she clasped a weapon, she swung the blade willy-
nilly, parrying Dawn's invisible attack, which didn't do
shit. On Lilly's body, blood trickled in stripes where her
uniform had fallen away.

Then she pulled back her sword like a battering ram and
lunged at Dawn, who was so caught up in her mental world
that, in the physical, she didn't react fast enough to move
out of the way.

Lilly's blade gouged her in the thigh, not enough to run
her through, but enough to rattle Dawn's consciousness
back into her own body, to make her yell in agony.

Right away, a Friend wrapped her essence around

Dawn's thigh, putting pressure on it so she wouldn't bleed out.

"*Got you*," said Kalin's voice.

That was when Dawn realized that Nigel hadn't gone back to chanting.

Time caught up to her. So did her surroundings. Kalin was here, and the Friends were flying around the room . . .

In fact, they'd taken it over, banging their essences against Lilly, keeping her away from Dawn as the *custode* fought to get free of them, her iron sword useless against one spirit who pinned the keeper's hands to her sides.

Dawn's arm and leg spiked with pain as more Friends arrived to contain Lilly.

But the keeper wasn't done. "You won't win!" she yelled at Dawn. "You can't!"

She sounded like she was in denial, and she should've been, because when Dawn glanced at Jonah to see how he was doing, he and the Friends had Nigel at their mercy. They'd pressed the other *custode* against a wall, and Jonah was hissing, baring his fangs at the keeper, his bloodlust raging, just like that night at Queenshill when he'd gone nuts.

This time, with the stakes this high, was Costin inside Jonah, lending urgency and strength during this final attack?

As the spirits who were controlling Lilly forced the keeper to turn toward her partner, a berserking Jonah took Nigel by the masked head and tore it clean off, tossing it to the side.

Lilly screamed as Nigel's arms flopped against his decapitated body, as if he were still trying to fight.

For a second, Jonah held his bloodied hands in the air, as if he couldn't believe what he'd done. Then, just as rapidly, he took out his daggers and extracted Nigel's heart, stilling the body for good, then stepping back, his shoulders rising and falling with his gasps.

*Custode*s weren't vampires, but you couldn't be sure, and when a Friend pushed Dawn's mini flamethrower over to Jonah on the ground, he used that to burn the rest of Nigel.

Lilly unsuccessfully tugged at the Friends' restraints. "You can't do this," she said, her voice still electronic, disassociated. Dawn hadn't gotten to her voice box. "We—"

"—couldn't have known what me and the team were," Dawn said. "Mihas is dead and your schoolgirls are humanized. You're done."

"Bugger off!" She didn't sound moved by Mihas's termination as much as by what she'd just witnessed Jonah doing to Nigel.

But why would Lilly have been surprised about the Mihas news when they probably had cameras to update them?

The remaining keeper stared at her, still fighting the binding Friend. Lilly was so young that Dawn felt as old and used as Claudius probably had, even though Dawn çouldn't have been too much older than the *custode*.

Her thigh was being pressurized so thoroughly by Kalin that she felt her pulse in it, spreading through the rest of her body like something infecting her. She tried not to think about her broken arm, hanging at her side, the screech of its pain.

As Jonah made his way over to Dawn, she felt another Friend carefully making herself into a sling to ease her arm's anguishing position.

"You were never prepared for an attack like ours," Dawn said to Lilly.

The girl shook her head. "We've *always* been prepared."

This one wouldn't admit defeat. "I know. Your kind protected the big master for over a century. But we couldn't allow him to rise."

Lilly stopped fighting the Friends. "You think the world is fine as it is? He will change it, just as he tried to make life better for many of his subjects when he was a prince."

Dawn had read the accounts of Vlad Tepes, national hero. Over on his side of the world, they still celebrated his historic attempts to keep his lands free of "the enemies of the cross of Christ." Ironically, he'd become pretty much one of those enemies when he'd made his deal with the devil.

"But good men don't take pleasure in death like he did." Dawn rubbed her neck with her healthy hand. The beauty marks were blazing on her skin. "No one should take that much pleasure."

By now, Jonah was next to her, his mask back over his nose and mouth so the blood wouldn't overcome him. But she saw that the silver was gone from his eyes. And they weren't even blue.

Costin?

Had he been the one who'd torn off Nigel's head?

From the shame and sadness in his gaze, she knew the answer was yes. The vampire hunger—or probably the hunger for freedom—had finally claimed him, and he'd taken what she'd just said to heart, too.

Good men don't take pleasure in death like he did.

The both of them, just as bad as Vlad.

They looked to the box—the unassuming, utilitarian coffin that had to be holding the sleeping dragon. Obviously, the creature wasn't about to wake up before his two-hundred-year rest was done. That was why he'd needed bodyguards.

"What should we do with her?" Dawn asked Costin, indicating Lilly.

"We cannot leave her alive."

Lilly thrashed at the Friends again, and something spindly and black fell from her belt, clinking to the floor—a weapon?

Costin began to walk toward the coffin. "Let's finish this."

With the help of Kalin and the other Friend, Dawn made

her way toward him, groaning with the effort. She was about to fall apart, she could've sworn it, and she didn't just mean her body.

"We'll get you there," said Mary-Margaret, coming from behind to help push Dawn forward.

As she looked at the coffin, it seemed like such a long journey that Dawn couldn't help but think that it'd never end, not even now, when they were just feet away.

She didn't want to imagine what would happen afterward, either, in real life with Costin.

Her earpiece crackled to static, and Kiko's rushed voice came on.

"Dawn—damn it . . . The girls already woke up. They're human, but they're . . ." He battled for breath, as if he was running or fighting. "They're freaking out and going for the exits, crying and shit. We're going after them—will do our best to make sure they don't lead anyone back down here before you're done!"

"Okay, Kik."

Maybe it was a positive thing that Kiko and Natalia wouldn't be here in the Underground from this point on. Maybe the dragon would hit Dawn and Costin hard, and she didn't want the others anywhere near that.

Costin had heard the transmission, and he rested his hand in the small of her back while leading her the rest of the way to the coffin. As they passed Lilly, he stepped on whatever had fallen from her belt, and the *custode* moaned, as if she'd been a part of the item that had been ground into the floor.

"No," Lilly said, like this was her own dark chant—something that might keep Dawn and Costin away from the dragon. "No . . . no . . ."

When they came to the foot of the altar, where the vibrations were so strong that Dawn felt like she was caught in a live wire, Costin stopped, lowering his gaze, concentrating.

His Awareness, Dawn thought. *He's bringing it out for what could be the final time. . . .*

Without warning, the coffin exploded, sending wood and soil everywhere. A drill-on-teeth cry grated while green eyes came alive, peering through the debris as it fell.

The Friends seemed to heave a massive breath, and they retreated, taking Lilly with them, but Costin held steady, glaring through the shrapnel as it clattered around him and Dawn, some of the wood smacking them as she raised her good arm to ward it off.

Awake . . . This close to the coffin, Costin's Awareness had woken up the dragon. . . .

She realized that Costin was already connecting to the eyes of whatever had come out of that coffin, attacking as best as he could, but from the way he started rocking back and forth, Dawn knew he was already at a disadvantage.

As the last of the debris clapped to the ground, she saw through the parting dust the vague shape of a stocky, naked long-haired man changing into something . . . else.

Then, as the air fully cleared, she saw just what he was.

Rising, swaying, stretching out from its deep sleep, a creature hovered, and it shuddered Dawn's flesh, like scales were rippling over every inch of *her*, just as the dragon literally grew scales, itself, in a red, iridescent wave.

She should've lashed out with every remaining bit of her mind powers, but she was too enthralled with what the creature was becoming.

Its consciousness expanded in its gaze as the vampire locked onto Costin, completing its change, revealing a hulking dragon's—or more accurately, *serpent's*—head sitting on top of a slithery body with arms that extended into stiletto-like claws. With its long tongue wiggling past thick fangs, it looked like it was testing the air, still coming to the waking realization of where it was and when it was.

Dawn couldn't move. Scared . . . never been this fucking scared in all her life . . .

The dragon paused, then snaked its tongue toward Costin, as if the loosed Awareness irritated it.

The Friend who was slinging Dawn's arm disengaged from the injury just in time to push Costin out of the way of that tongue, and the motion woke Dawn right the hell up.

It was going after him.

Key, she thought. I'm *key.*

I'm supposed to do something.

The darkness in her surged into every fiber of her body like never before, almost like the anger wanted to get to the dragon and join it. Almost like she was waking up with the monster.

Costin's swaying had become surreal, his body rooted to one place as it circled, like how one of those punching bags with sand on the bottom moves after it's been pushed.

Do something before it really wakes up. . . .

Just like earlier, when Dawn had distanced herself from her body while fighting Lilly, she withdrew from herself. Then, with a drugged kind of wonder, she watched as Dawn Madison let loose with all the power she had, her body flinching with the burst of her projected rancor. She saw the force of her fury impaling itself into the dragon's flesh, tearing it open, exposing its innards.

Behind Dawn, Lilly screeched.

Dawn barely heard it. Instead, she was locked to how the dragon's blood and vital organs spilled out. Then it was as if teeth had fixed on the creature's heart and was ripping that out, too. Blood spurted, covering one side of Dawn's body, but not Costin's, as her mind held the dragon's heart in midair.

The organ rotated there, as if she wanted the dragon to see it as the creature wavered, sleepily realizing that it had been gutted.

Then, chunks began to fall out of the hovering heart, and Dawn realized that she was mentally dismantling it.

The dragon bellowed, looking down at himself, then back up at her.

Then he smiled with those dragon teeth before collapsing.

At the thud of his body, Dawn jammed back into herself, gasping at the memory of that smile. Costin grabbed one of Lilly's deserted swords plus the flamethrower, then leaped forward to chop away at his creator's head then burn him to a crisp, all with such quickness that it happened in what seemed to be a strike of crimson lightning.

When the first lick from the flamethrower consumed the dragon, Dawn stumbled backward from the fire—sheets and sheets of fire as the dragon burned.

Armageddon, she thought. And it was here in her tiny corner of the world.

As the Friends pushed her farther backward, Dawn felt the blood weighing on her skin, almost like in Kiko's prophecy. She was covered in a vampire's red, but only on one side, opposite her beauty marks. She was victorious. And she was . . .

Dawn tripped as the Friends pushed her harder to leave. She felt like the dragon's blood was acidly tunneling into her, far worse than any beauty mark, eating its way inside, down to her very bones.

The dragon's body exploded, and the entire room became a roll of thunder and orange, and as Costin grabbed her arm so they could both escape, he fell down.

Just like that, losing all power, convulsing there at her feet, his eyes blue as he leveled a horrified look at her.

Jonah was back?

And what the hell was wrong with him?

The Friends pushed against both him and Dawn, urging them to flee, and with Dawn's good arm, she picked up Jonah to help him as a rumble of fire bit at their heels and the spirits jarred them to a higher speed.

Flame breathed through the tunnels, chasing them out of

the Underground while destroying it at the same time. Then, as Dawn and Jonah pushed toward some exit, the fire became a living/dead thing, spitting out Dawn and Jonah and the Friends as they tumbled over the outside grass, the flames waggling out of the exit like tongues, then sucking back in.

Then . . .

It was quiet.

So quiet.

Dawn collapsed onto her back on the heath grass under the moon, gasping for breath, her body a length of stabbing rips and breaks, her skin and everything underneath it prickling with its own fire on the side of her body where the dragon's blood had covered her. She saw Jonah as immovable as the new night, eyes closed, but she didn't find Lilly.

Kalin's voice came from the spot where she was still pressing down on Dawn's leg. *"You okay?"*

"I don't know." Then she remembered the dragon. "I think I'm okay. Everything's good, right? Isn't it?"

Kalin just held to Dawn, and she was real quiet, too, just like the cold air around them.

But Dawn was getting used to others judging her in the aftermath of every fight because of the lines she'd crossed. It amazed her that Kalin would be one of them, even if this was a line Dawn herself didn't understand.

She'd made a mess of the dragon. Of course, the creature hadn't been fully awake, but she'd really done a number on him. Bloodlust had made it possible.

And, at the end, he'd smiled, just as if he'd appreciated her enthusiastic kill.

Shoving the final image of him aside, Dawn shut off her headlight, groaning at her injuries, dragging herself toward the place where Jonah lay prone on the grass.

Mary-Margaret made like a sling on Dawn's arm again and said, *"Lilly's gone. When the fire exploded, we lost control of her, and she either got caught by the flames or found a way out. From all reports, she knew every trap-door."*

Another Friend skidded over. *"It looks done down there. We'll go back in soon to make sure, but we got it, y'all. We cleaned them out! Yee-haw!"*

As the stupefaction started to wear off of Dawn, her skin really acted up on the side of her face where the dragon's blood had splashed. In its throbbing singe under her skin, she felt the bite of the dragon's smile as it'd died. No matter how hard she tried, she wasn't going to forget it.

The immediacy of seeing that Costin was okay overcame her. When she got to him, he opened his eyes.

Even in the moonlight, she could see they weren't quite the same Jonah electric blue as before.

"Jonah?" she asked.

He glanced at her, and the blankness in his gaze hit her hard.

He was looking at the burning side of her face, and she put her hand there.

"Blood." His tone seemed . . . changed. "You're covered with his blood."

He was talking about Kiko's prophecy, and he was getting even more confused as he sat up, testing his limbs with shaking hands.

The Friends gathered around, watching.

"What's wrong?" Dawn asked. "Jonah . . ."

His devastated expression made Dawn grasp his arm, and his body tone didn't feel as hard as usual. A jolt of adrenaline rocked her, and she touched his face. It wasn't as cool.

A thought wormed into her mind: Vampire blood weakens from generation to generation, and the dragon's blood had been more powerful than any master vampire's or progeny's. Its death would inflict more damage than when Benedikte or Claudius or Mihas had died, wouldn't it? Its termination could turn all of its line human again. . . .

Had Costin known this and he just hadn't wanted to get her hopes up if he was wrong? Had she been so bent on saving him that she hadn't thought beyond the obvious to *this*?

"My body," Jonah said.

He'd only been a vampire for about a year, so he would've looked the same.

But if he wasn't vamp, wouldn't that mean his body had stopped being undead? Wouldn't that mean . . . ?

"Costin," she said. *"What about Costin?"*

"He's not here." Jonah touched his chest, his voice choked. "He's gone."

TWENTY-TWO

Once a Keeper

Lilly slowly opened her eyes to find that she was in a bed, tucked under stiff white sheets, the walls round her just as sterile, too. She stared at the ceiling, not knowing where she was or how she'd got here until the particles of her mind sifted and settled into grains of memory.

Fire. Screams.

Many screams, many of them her own.

When she tried to sit up, she found she couldn't, due to bandages swathing flesh that felt raw under the gauze. Bandages that made her feel as trapped as a mummy. Even her face was encapsulated except for her eyes, nose, and mouth.

Her mind took a minute to catch up to a heart that'd begun to hack out a painful rhythm. Now she saw blades, blazing green eyes, a tuner crushed under a boot, Nigel's headless form falling to the ground . . .

Then it was all washed out by a wipe of fire.

Mortification welled in Lilly's chest as it all clamored

back to her—the Underground, destroyed, burning her just before she'd used a trapdoor to escape. And the dragon . . .

A flow of dread crushed her to the mattress. The hunters—Dawn and the mean vampire—had slain the dragon, who was supposed to be so safe under Lilly's watch.

Biting back a furious, helpless sob, Lilly wrestled the image of Dawn taking down the master after he'd been awakened from his sleep by the mean vampire. The creature had to have been a blood brother, but he hadn't fit the descriptions of the others on file, and he hadn't been detected by any Meratoliage through their black-art crystal gazing.

Then again, none of her family had known about what she had done with Claudia, either.

A shadow seemed to cover one side of the bed, and Lilly focused on the stern face of her father. Her mother's designer perfume signaled that she had come to stand on the other side of the mattress, and Lilly twisted her bandaged neck to look at her, too.

A safe house, she thought. Her parents had brought her to a secure location.

Then, one by one, family elders surrounded her. Meratoliages: rejected *custode*s with bad hearts, plus a small group of breeders, all of their faces like those of a gathered jury's.

But Lilly saw their stiffness for what it truly was— loathing.

Her father, in his clipped voice, said, "You were found, crawling in the grasses near an explosion just outside of Highgate and the Underground ruins. One of us got there before the public arrived."

Ruins.

Her intellect still wasn't quite accepting that the dragon was no more. Surely he must be functional. He was their god, their hope.

Mouth dry, she tried to ask if perhaps their liege had escaped, but her thick tongue produced words much different than she'd intended.

"The mean vampire crushed my tuner by walking right over it," was what she dumbly said. Her lungs felt shredded, leaving her voice smoke torn.

The stoic woman with the gray bun—Lilly's mum—revealed her disdain with only a sentence. "Whoever it was crushed much more than that."

Her father's voice wobbled with sorrow. "Nigel was . . ."

Mum speared a harsh glance at her breeding partner. It was only after activation that Lilly realized her parents were siblings and not really a true couple who had once wished to produce children out of love. Then again, they had never acted as if they even liked each other and it had merely been Lilly's fanciful notions that had built the other dream.

"Who is this 'mean vampire'?" Mum asked Lilly. "Who desecrated the dragon?"

With much difficulty, Lilly told them of the hunters—Dawn, in particular, always Dawn at the front of Lilly's mind—and by the time she finished her abbreviated version, she needed water so badly that she was gagging for it. One of the Meratoliage breeders slipped an ice chip into Lilly's mouth, but it was as if the sleekly styled, sandy-haired woman with slanted lime-hued eyes was only being kind due to wishing to hear more of Lilly's story, not because she cared for Lilly herself.

Amber, Lilly thought. She recognized her cousin as the doctor who had pronounced her sterile years ago.

"This was certainly the attack of a blood brother," Amber said. "But if we saw him in the crystals, he didn't resemble any description we have of the brothers. He ran a careful operation, it seems."

Had the other Meratoliages known about the mean vampire, they would have only expected their *custode*s to stop the threat. Lilly had tried.

Lilly had failed.

Her father asked, "Why would he vanquish his own creator?"

Her mum ignored him. "It leaves me to wonder what has become of the other brothers now that the dragon has perished. Is there anything left of them?"

"What does it matter?" her father asked. "There's nothing left of *us*."

At this comment, one of the breeders at the end of the bed turned away, as if affected by the dragon's demolition. However, the rest stayed immobile, their reaction to losing their lord clearly caged in anger.

"We did our best," Lilly whispered, wishing they could feel just how beaten she was, too. If only the dragon had got merely a few more moments to awaken and come to his full powers. . . .

Tears gathered in her eyes, and when one slipped out to catch in her facial bandage, she wanted to slash the moisture away with a hand.

Her father made a derisive sound. "Clearly, your best was paltry. How did these hunters even find the Underground?"

"Claudia." And, really, because of Lilly herself. In her attempts to fortify the community, she had somehow opened it up, hadn't she? Misstepped. *Over*stepped. Mihas, who'd been too flaccid from years of decadence, had let them all down on his end, and the attackers had been so much stronger than even he.

She closed her eyes as another truth weighed down on her. Had Mihas and his charisma led Lilly astray, just as with Claudia and the schoolgirls? And, here, she'd thought she'd been above them all.

Her father sniffed. "How did Claudia contribute to this?"

Although Lilly craved more ice, she told them everything, except of her own part, where she had used Della to run out the co-master.

"On your and Nigel's shift," her mother said. "For shame, Lilly."

It was as if her daughter had disappointed her most of all. And perhaps she had. She was proof that a female *custode* had been an unwise choice for service.

"This would not have occurred with Charles or any other male still activated," her father said, and the other men sounded off in acquiescence.

Her cousin Amber silenced everyone. "Or perhaps a female was only there to witness everything's collapse after a century of male fuckups."

Hearing a prim, proper voice saying such words was rattling. Everyone round the bed adjusted their positions, then went back to being stiff-necked.

"In any case," her father said, reaching into his large coat pocket to fetch a black, spindly tuner, so much like her own crushed one, "we must close this out."

Lilly waited for him to offer her the instrument, to show her that they were presenting her with another opportunity to right every wrong, though she didn't know the reason they would arm her again with the dragon gone.

But then he slid the tuner under her bandages and clamped it to her temples.

"No," Lilly said, realizing this tuner wasn't a replacement at all. Realizing . . .

When her father, the rejected *custode*, activated the instrument, it cast her into a dark place far down into her mind. A place of haunted, echoing sounds and blackness that tore at her from every side.

The last thing Lilly heard were the words every *custode* feared.

"You're retired," he said before she disappeared altogether into a mental coffinlike, wooded darkness.

TWENTY-THREE

Farewell to Babylon

It was just before dawn on the streets of St. Albans, but the schoolgirls hardly paid mind to the rising sun.

They had finally stopped running and had taken up here, in the city near Queenshill, under a set of stairs at the train station's outside tracks after hours of screaming away from the Underground. Yet it wasn't far enough.

As Della shivered under those stairs, she thought of how her former master had well and truly deserted them this time. Wolfie had left them to these coarse human bodies . . . and appetites that hadn't seemed to adjust to their change back to humanity.

She was still so hungry. . . .

Della picked up one of the males whom she and the others had found on the fringes of the train station and dragged under the stairs. The boys had been drinking from vodka bottles and laughing until Della, Stacy, Noreen, and the few remaining recruits had arrived wearing only bits of blood-stained clothing. Some, such as Della, weren't even wearing a shirt. Their skin, which had never possessed the opportunity to fully heal from the UV attack, was burned, and with Stacy, Noreen, and Della's still-clumped hair, they seemed like wild things let loose.

The boys had backed away from the very sight, but the girls had caught them, even without vampire powers. Human teeth had nothing on the fangs that she and the others had lost, but they still had the cravings. They had known nothing else but nightcrawls and greedy feasting for too long to turn from them.

Really, this way of coping was *all* Della knew.

With the frenzied confusion of an animal, she bit into the boy's neck, remembering the attack on the Underground: the flashes of fire and UV, the raining silver, the death of Wolfie. The death of what she had once been . . .

The boy made a pitiful sound, and Della pressed her hand over his mouth. She gnawed at his skin, his flesh tasting of a dull, salty muskiness. It lacked the bang of satiation she had grown so used to, yet she sucked hard at him. Harder. Taking in his blood, gulp after gulp.

But it wasn't enough, and she spit the blood out, tears forming in her eyes as she realized feeding wasn't the same. Nothing was, and no matter how much blood she took in, nothing would be as she'd hoped it would when Wolfie had promised her such a wonderful future.

The other girls were also tearing off their prey's clothing, seeking flesh, blood. For a suspended instant, Della watched the worst of them: Stacy, who had been mercilessly returned to her real age, with wrinkles and wiry strands of gray hair marring her appearance. She had been a vampire for so many years that she seemed the most vicious about clinging to her pattern of existence. She also seemed the most teched of them all upon the return of their diminished souls.

Noreen and the recruits who had followed the last of the Queenshill girls were still fairly young, since this group had been turned into vampires only recently. Back in the Underground, just after the girls had started to unfreeze, Della had seen the older recruits grabbing the nearest sharp objects, unable to withstand the new terror stamped on their souls. She didn't know where the rest had gone to—if they had outmaneuvered the little man who had been attempting to round them up with his partner, or if the former vampires had fled to the explosion that had rocked a deeper section of the Underground.

But Della did know one matter for certain: none of them had *anyone* to turn to—no real families, no sane friends. She suspected that those who were here had only come along because, like Della, they were just now realizing how alone they truly were. It had merely taken them longer than most of the other former vampires who had already ended their humanized lives. Stacy was the notable exception, most likely because she had told Della of a distant cousin who might take her in.

Yet Della had seen the doubt growing in Stacy's gaze hour by hour.

Blood dried on Della's chin and round her mouth as her prey went still. She set him down on the pavement, the shadow of the stairs chopping his body into sections. An object crinkled out of one of his down jacket pockets. She squinted at it, because, compared to how she used to see and hear, she felt nearly blind and deaf now—a muted palette surrounding her, almost as if she were being suffocated by dullness.

When she scooped up the dropped item, she found upon close inspection that it was a plastic bag bulging with multihued pills.

Della stared at it for a moment, then tucked it into her fisted, bloodied hand.

Next to her, Noreen glanced up from where she was chewing on her victim's ear, and Della unintentionally backed away.

Humans who had their souls again? That was what they were now?

Just behind Noreen, Stacy paused in the act of stripping off the skin of her own victim while her old woman's body hunched in the near darkness. The recruits, as ill-bred and aimless as always, continued feasting on their shared prey.

Creatures of the in-between, Della thought, feeling herself sinking inside, just as if all of her was being pulled into a hole. And in that hole were so many things that were now coming to the surface: this hunger. The method in which she had murdered Violet.

Now, with a soul, she saw the vampire Della through a tint of horrifying twilight. Had *she* really committed such a crime?

As she glanced at her bloodied mates, she knew that she had, and she couldn't bear it.

"Murder," she said, though she hadn't meant to say anything.

Even the recruits hesitated at Della's comment.

Stacy and Noreen were retreating from their prey, moving away like wounded jackals. Della could see they understood better than the recruits, since Queenshill training had been so much more intense, introducing them to higher appetites that would create the officers Wolfie had required for his army.

Was this what was in store for all the little girls?

Was this how they would live from this point forward, with no true home to slink to after a hunt? Would the blood always taste like metal and would their bodies always be this slow and heavy?

She rested her free hand on her chest, where she felt her heart beating, but not with the same vivacity as before. No, there was only the echo of the sleeping city: the pause that occurs just before vehicles begin to roam the streets, the waiting limbo before the darkness is consumed by light.

All of it so pale now.

"I know you feel it, too," she said to Stacy and Noreen. The multiplied hurt in their souls, the darkness.

Stacy wiped at her mouth with her gnarled fingers, but blood still remained there. "It's been a long time since I was last human," she said in a frail old woman voice, "yet . . ." Her hand dropped to her side. "I don't remember ever feeling like this."

Noreen only nodded as a drop of blood from her chin fell to her victim, hitting his flannel shirt where a nest of shattered bottle glass lay. She'd used the shards to let blood from his skin, as she'd had no claws.

Della backed away from her own dead victim. Her stomach protested all the thick blood she'd consumed, and it pushed up her throat.

Something had altered in her, but it wasn't physical this time. Something that was dragging her down inside and not allowing her to go back to what a human should be. She didn't even have anyone to help her discover how to get back there, and the alienation only allowed the stain inside of her to spread. She wished someone could help her stop it, but there were only the others, just as wounded and lost as she.

With the hand that wasn't holding the bag, she gripped the first stair, using it to bolster her.

Stacy asked, "Where are you going?"

"Where is there to go?"

Noreen said, "Anywhere. We can still go anywhere."

But it didn't seem as if Noreen believed this. She sounded just as stranded as Della. *None* of them knew how to be anything but a soldier vampire.

One of the recruits spoke. "I miss Wolfie."

The three Queenshill girls rounded on her.

"Don't ever say that name," Stacy whispered. "Never again."

Yet it was too late—Della was already thinking of how he had abandoned them even before he had been put down by the hunters. She thought of how her parents had left her, long before her master had done so, and how the days that stretched ahead of her would contain so many more desertions.

She couldn't imagine enduring any more of them.

Turning away from the carnage, she wandered away from the station, into the lamp-lit streets that seemed to coat the buildings and pavements with an ill hue. Cut off from her higher sense of smell and hearing, she felt so very removed.

There were footsteps behind her, and she glanced over her shoulder to see the others following, directionless.

But where *was* she off to? Home to her parents?

They wouldn't want her.

Queenshill?

A misty dream of snuggling into her house bed then rising in time for classes smoothed over Della. But then she remembered how she had fed on Melinda, the classmate she'd always admired, and the blood seemed to run down into a pool that festered in the center of her.

There was no going back to anyone.

Della meandered up a hill, through an alley, which was darker, with its enclosed brick that scratched her as she brushed against it with her bare arm.

Nowhere to go . . .

She and the others walked out of the city, toward a stand of trees. Just beyond, train tracks slashed through grass while the sky slouched further to daylight. Belatedly, it occurred to Della that they hadn't cleaned up their feeding scene.

Careless. But it didn't seem to matter now.

When she came to the train tracks, she stopped, the cold air picking into her skin. She wasn't used to being chilled, and she shivered, belly deep. Then she bent so she might rest her free hand on the tracks. She waited there until she felt the quiver of an approaching train. Glancing into the distance, she identified the shape of it coming, but it was only a blur.

Moving away from the tracks, she walked, then halted just before the trees, where she found Stacy inspecting her own aged skin as if seeing it for the first time, now that the light was coming.

This *is where we're going,* Della thought at the tragedy of Stacy's failing body. They would become old, but before that, they'd be actual women, with all the qualities Wolfie had rejected from everyone but Mrs. Jones.

She opened her fist, where she'd been carrying the bag of pills. As the recruits sat in the grass, pulling it out by the roots and madly trying to scrub their bloodied skin clean with it, Della opened the bag.

Nowhere to go but here.

She enjoyed the first lift of hope she'd felt in a while, then took one pill. Two. More.

As she lay back on the grass, the blades pricked at her skin, her fingers, and she looked at a sky that was warming with color.

She smiled, already drowsy. But perhaps that was because of everything but the pills. She was so very ready to sleep.

Noreen said, "Wolfie never cared what became of us, did he? If he were still here now, he would only replace us with others. More Queenshill classes, more recruits to take up our spots."

Stacy had been watching Della with the pills, a sense of longing in her old, faded blue eyes. Della offered the bag to her, and she accepted it, taking her fill, too.

The train approached, and the recruits blankly watched as it streamed by. Stacy handed the bag to Noreen, who consumed the rest of the pills. Then she joined Della on the ground, linking hands with her and Stacy, friends until the end. This time, they wouldn't lose each other to Mrs. Jones.

Sunrise burgeoned, even as the sky grew fuzzier in Della's gaze. It reminded her of a pastel bunch of yarn unwinding from a spindle as she fell deeper and deeper into sleep. She thought she heard the recruits whining as they stood over Della and her friends, the three of them still holding hands.

Then the girls left Della, Stacy, and Noreen alone, running off, crying.

The final thing she remembered was the sensation of flying like a raven into the wide open sky, free and disembodied, before being swallowed by a black stain that hugged her in a floating, liquid peace that finally welcomed Della to the home she'd always tried so hard to find.

TWENTY-FOUR
The Soul-Searching

ADDLED by discomfort, Dawn cradled her sling-bound, cast-covered broken arm while wandering down a hall in the old headquarters, passing the paintings that had been refilled by the Friends hours ago. The spirits rested peacefully in sleep mode, the portraits reflecting beautiful women from various locations, from a fifties-inspired diner to a log cabin in the woods to a tepee.

It'd only been about fifteen minutes since Dawn had gotten back, having taken a cab from the hospital emergency department, where she'd told the docs and nurses that she'd been a victim of a hit-and-run on a deserted lane—hence the broken arm, the gouge in her thigh, and the various cuts all over her. No one from her hunting team had been there to see the med professionals be all "hmmm" about the gouge in Dawn's leg in particular; Dawn had insisted that Natalia and Kiko take Jonah straight to headquarters after they'd stopped chasing the humanized vamp girls and picked her and Jonah up in one of their modified Sedonas.

Of course, Dawn's ER car-accident lie hadn't explained the mass of red markings on her face, either. She hadn't been able to wipe off the splashes of dragon's blood that seethed from the side of her face opposite the beauty spots, but she'd told the staff it was only a birthmark.

Yet Dawn knew it had to be worse. Much worse. She just wasn't sure why right now.

After passing Mary-Margaret's Savannah sunset portrait, Dawn entered her dad's room, finding it empty. She didn't know why she'd even come here, because Eva had left a landline message telling the team that Frank was still resting from his sickness in the temporary headquarters. Based on Breisi's empty portrait, Dawn expected the Friend to be with him, especially since he'd probably needed comfort after being turned human again and getting the soul stain. She only hoped that Breisi had found a little time to recharge in her picture before she'd gone to Frank.

Dawn came to stand in front of Breisi's picture, which featured the lab in L.A. where she'd been so at home. What would her Friend think about the splashes of dragon blood on Dawn?

It charred below her skin, not so much on it. In fact, the blood seemed to be inching farther *into* Dawn, encroaching like a mini army.

But that had to be in her mind, which she was definitely losing now that Costin wasn't here.

She leaned against the wall, against her good arm. She'd taken some Tylenol, but the injury that had needed the most medicating had been Costin's disappearance, because he'd been gone so suddenly; she'd always thought that, when his mission was done, she'd have time to say whatever it was she'd never been able to say to him, before he got yanked off the earth and put into that "better place" he'd earned.

Even though she'd been trying to fend off the panic of not knowing where he was or how he was doing, Dawn found it hard to concentrate now. And she kept looking at Breisi's empty lab portrait, wishing for a sympathetic ear for probably the first time in her life.

When she heard someone come into the room, she perked up, hoping Breisi was back. But she turned to find Jonah, bandages marring the skin that had once been so smooth and vampire perfect after Jonah had become a vamp and his body had healed from the self-inflicted facial scars he used to have as a human the first time around.

Now, he had a slightly rosier human color back in his face, and he moved without the ease of a preternatural. He wasn't even dressed in the "I must look like a cool vampire" way he'd adapted, instead wearing a pair of faded jeans and a long-sleeved blue top under a cable-knit sweater. His hands were shoved into his pockets, his dark hair hiding his brow.

He was . . . just a guy.

"I could've picked you up at the hospital if you'd called," he said.

She couldn't get over the lack of ethereal glow about him. Relating to his normalness was . . . awkward.

"I used a cab." She hadn't wanted him to go far from Kiko, so she'd taken care of herself. She'd asked the psychic to watch over Jonah, based on his returned, tainted soul.

"I'm surprised you haven't launched a full-out search for Costin in every nook and cranny of London," Jonah said.

If she thought Costin might still be in the city, and not someplace far out of it, she might've been out there, injuries and all. The Friends were already doing their best to try, anyway, as they combed London for any clue of him.

"Where would I look for a Soul Traveler?" She wasn't sure if she meant to lighten the mood or really ask him, in case he had any ideas.

"I wish I knew." He paused, then said, "Kiko took Costin's old field of fire portrait out of storage and put it in your bedroom. He was hoping that Costin might've landed there, just like he used to when he would take rests from our body before we were a vampire."

The painting had been a way station for him during the agreed upon free time he used to give Jonah, back when Costin could move in and out of the body for short durations. But he had needed to root to humanity, so he couldn't stay away from Jonah for long.

"Maybe he'll find the portrait," Dawn said, but she was lying to herself. Costin was more than a Friend. He'd always been more, and he'd made a deal with The Whisper to be rewarded accordingly. A fire-filled painting wouldn't be his ultimate prize.

Jonah took his hands out of his pockets and folded his arms in front of his chest, where she guessed he felt the heaviness of a soul stain. It was telling that the former vamps who managed not to go nuts or commit suicide right away were the ones who seemed to have more to come back to, like Dawn with her need to make up for what she'd done to Costin, Eva with her longing for a second chance with Frank, and now Jonah with what Dawn suspected was the yearning to find Costin again. She'd bet that Frank's true love for Breisi was keeping him sustained, too.

They had each other. They had purpose. And she'd never known how important that was until now.

"Who wants to go outside, anyway?" Jonah asked, reverting back to the earlier topic as he stood there, looking awkward, too. "Did you hear any newscasts on the way back in the cab? Things are dicey out there."

"No, I didn't." She went to Frank's bed to sit on it, too tired to stand anymore.

"There're extra cops on the streets because of 'terrorist rumors.'"

"Rumors that could've stemmed from those reports

about the charmed humans the girl vamps used the other night?"

"That's probably a part of it. But Natalia also heard some chatter on a police scanner. There're girls in custody, and they're wearing torn, bloody clothes and babbling to the cops about fire and hunters."

Sounded like the Underground girls hadn't all disappeared into obscurity like Dawn had hoped. "Any talk of vampires from them?"

"Not yet. I wonder if they were trained to keep quiet about their own roles, and even in their craziness they're obeying."

"It'd be great if they *kept* quiet." Still, the team needed to think about getting the hell out of London before heat came from any authorities who might connect them to "terrorism." Detective Inspector Norton would probably do his part to shield them—Costin had trusted their ally to that extent—but who knew what might happen with other cops?

Yet she didn't want to go anywhere. What if Costin did return and he couldn't find them . . . ?

"Also," Jonah added, "there was the explosion near Highgate last night." He cleared his throat, an acknowledgment of the Underground victory. "It scared the people around the area, but the authorities haven't found a cause for it yet."

"Hopefully they won't because the Underground's gone."

As Dawn's dragon's blood marks seemed to flare even lower into her, she thought that, wiped out or not, nothing could erase the image of the dragon's final smile.

But she *made* herself forget. At least for as long as she could.

"The other big story of the day," Jonah said, "is a trio of suicides, plus some murders up in St. Albans."

"Girl vamps?" Dawn said.

"Yeah." He stared at the carpet. "A group of Friends reported that the vamps we met on the Queenshill campus, Della and Noreen, were two of them. Not sure who the third was, but they were laid out in the grass near some train tracks, just like they'd fallen asleep with these sweet smiles on their faces. Friends think it was due to over-doses."

Oh, God.

It was one thing to kill vampires, but another to hear about the suicides of humanized vamps. And young girls besides.

Dawn rubbed at her face. Della and Noreen. Especially Della. Even though Dawn didn't know how old the girl had really been, she had the feeling Della was really just a kid inside. Someone innocent who'd gotten caught up with these damned dragon vampires.

Had the girls taken their lives because they thought no one would care enough to stop them? Dawn remembered being a teenager, too, and a lot of times, she hadn't even needed a soul stain to hate the world around her. But with these girls, had it been impossible for them to live with all the bad things they'd done as vamps? Had the stains taken every last bit of hope and persuaded those kids that there hadn't been any way to face life with such darkness in them?

Dawn's marks thudded, as if trying to answer her. As if trying to say, "You could be Della, too, if you're not careful. . . ."

"I keep waiting for him to come back," Jonah said, pull-ing her out of her mourning. He was talking about Costin now. "He's out there somewhere, Dawn. He has to be, es-pecially if there are remaining blood brothers to kill. That was part of the deal with The Whisper."

If only she could be so optimistic. "We don't know ex-actly what The Whisper had in mind when he recruited Costin as a Soul Traveler, so we need to be prepared for the worst. Maybe he really is gone."

When she looked up at Jonah, she saw something in his eyes that she couldn't grasp. An openness that had escaped her, even with Costin. So she glanced away. After all the fights she'd gone through and all the psychotic-ass things she'd seen, she had no idea how to handle this gash inside of her—a wound that made her arm and leg seem like pinches in comparison.

"Why didn't The Whisper tell Costin it would happen so fast?" Jonah asked. "Maybe The Whisper wasn't sure what effect the dragon's death would have on his line, even though we knew their blood weakened generation after generation and we could've taken an educated guess that the dragon would have the biggest effect of them all."

"So you think the blood brothers are dead, too, and that's why Costin's not around? Do you think that the remaining ones turned human and they just destroyed themselves, like the lower vampires tended to do? Masters have been vampires longer than their progeny, so if they found themselves without the talents they'd had for centuries, alone and isolated, wouldn't they find a way to end it faster than anyone?" Then Dawn thought about how Benedikte had craved humanity back in L.A. "Unless they *wanted* to be human."

But *none* of this explained why Costin had just . . . disappeared. He'd been taken faster than the time required for any blood brothers to even realize they'd turned human. Costin's mission had seemed to end before any suicides could happen.

She tried to recall the last time she'd seen his topaz eyes, but she couldn't. All her moments with him just jumbled together, and she couldn't latch onto any one of them.

But something she could hang on to was the fact that it should've been *her* death that made Jonah's body human again and allowed Costin to escape the undead matter. In a way, she felt cheated out of that.

Sick. A tiny laugh jittered out of her, even though this

wasn't funny. Maybe the pain from her wounds was screwing up her system. Or maybe she really *was* sick. Sick because she'd sunk so damned low since just over a year ago, when she'd met Costin. Sick because he wasn't here anymore. Sick because everything seemed so abstract right now—an avant-garde painting under carnival lights.

"I guess," she said, trying to end the discussion, "all that's left of the dragon is our stains. Like a gift that keeps on giving from big daddy. *It* obviously doesn't disappear with a higher vampire's death, and that's why me and Eva had it after Benedikte died."

"That's why we have it now."

Hell, she had that and more, she thought as the dragon's blood kept burning.

But what exactly brought the soul stain out on the skin? Dawn hadn't been a vamp for very long and she'd had more problems with the stain than Eva. But did it have to do with the amount of time you were a vamp . . . or with the bitterness you had when you weren't? Eva had tried valiantly to erase her old life and become "Mia Scott"—she'd found new hobbies, a new home. She'd tried very hard to keep any anger or despair at a distance. Dawn had let emotion fly. Plus, unlike the other vamps, Eva might have avoided suicide by submerging her real self in another identity. But was that a sort of suicide in itself?

As for Dawn, she wondered if she'd been running from death by causing it. . . .

"At least Costin wouldn't have gotten a stain after the dragon died," she said, wanting to move on. "Right?"

"Right. I was the one who lost my soul when I became a vamp. He was only along for the ride because he couldn't get out of my altered body. He should be in his state of grace, wherever he is."

Jonah sat on Frank's bed next to her. It was strange, smelling his human skin—the earthiness of it. She missed the preternatural buzz of energy from his body.

He said, "Have you thought that maybe Costin was pulled away to take care of loose ends for the other Undergrounds? All of their lower vamps might've gone crazy before succumbing to the stain—if all of them even do—and he could've been assigned damage control. Maybe he's so busy he hasn't had a second to contact us. You know how it is when you're fighting vamps."

"That task could take a long time to deal with." But at least that'd mean he was out there.

She must've looked just as forcefully optimistic as Jonah or something, because he seemed pleased that she was going along with his theorizing.

But false hope wouldn't do either of them good in the long run. "Wouldn't it just be nice if that damned Whisper would give enough of a shit to drop us a line about it, either way?"

"Or to extend a bit of gratitude for saving the world?" Jonah added.

That got a self-aware smile from her. The good of the many outweighed the good of the few.

"If Costin would just come back," Jonah said, "I'd even give up my body again."

Surprised, she frowned at him.

"I know it sounds weird," he said, "seeing as all I did was complain about being stifled. But now it's like living in a really big house by myself. That was how I went through most of my life before Costin came into it, and I didn't like it then."

"Him being gone has made you a recluse again."

He nodded, and the exact problem with Jonah became real apparent.

The grass was always greener, whether it was about hosting a Soul Traveler or wanting what someone else possessed. If he did get Costin back, he wouldn't be happy for long.

"You think," she said, "that having Costin here again would find you the peace you need? To conquer the stain?"

"Yeah. I'd do anything for what I had."

Anything, she thought. She'd said the same a year ago, when Frank had been missing and Costin had asked her what she'd do to find him.

"Careful what you say, Jonah."

"Why—because I might get what I ask for?" Jonah smiled. "If only."

She saw something off in his gaze—a gleam of the Jonah who had used a razor on his face once when Costin had said he was looking for a different body to inhabit.

This was the real Jonah.

He shifted next to her on the bed, and she realized that they were alone, sitting on a mattress. It was the way he'd moved that had clued her in to it, as if their situation meant a lot more to him than it did to her. Then again, Jonah had set his sights on Dawn because Costin had her.

Was that the only way he'd ever experienced intimacy? Through a Soul Traveler who shared his body as well as through his borrower's relationship with another person?

Jonah touched Dawn's face, where the dragon red marks splotched her skin in what seemed right now to be permanent, hideous splashes.

She tried to angle away from him, because she'd seen the medical professionals' expressions when they'd inspected her skin at the emergency department. They'd tried to hide their curiosity, but Dawn still felt like she could've turned any one of them to stone with just a well-placed glare.

Jonah wasn't deterred. He kept his fingertips against the splashes.

"Stop it," Dawn said, and he took his hand away.

He kept sitting next to her, hardly chased off. She wished he wouldn't keep looking at her.

"Does it hurt?" he asked.

"On the surface, not really. Just a weird burning. I suppose that it felt so good attacking the dragon that I got the best beauty mark ever."

Not wanting this to go any further, she started to get up from the bed, but he grasped her good hand.

"Damn it, Dawn, you're really one for taking it all on you, aren't you? Blame, shame, responsibility."

She pulled away, but she saw that openness in him again—a willingness to share everything, including what he'd learned as Costin's host.

"Even going back to when you were a girl," he added, "you had to assume care of Frank. When you got older, you rebelled against taking any more of that kind of thing on, but when a bigger situation called for you, you stepped up and took care of it in the only way you knew how. But if you're going to find any kind of satisfaction with yourself, you've got to start letting go."

He sounded like Costin in one of his psychiatry moments. No wonder Jonah had been chosen as a host.

"Enough." She went for the door. "There's too much to do and—"

"If he *is* gone, Dawn," he said softly, "I'm not."

His naked statement waited there, just like a ghost hovering to be noticed and acknowledged.

She wasn't even quite sure he'd said it . . . or meant it. What was he thinking—that he'd step into the spot Costin had vacated if it came down to it?

Dawn didn't look back as she went through the door, limping as fast as her injuries allowed her to while navigating the rest of the hallway to the stairs. From there, she headed for the sitting room, where she heard Kiko and Natalia listening to a TV.

She tried not to think of Jonah still back in that room, sitting on the bed, smarting from the callous way she'd left him. But he'd said the wrong thing. He had no right, even if she despaired of Costin ever coming back. Jonah had told *her* to let go, and he needed to, also. Now that he was human, he could go out into the world and find some nice, unscary girl who didn't advertise her screwups so obviously. A girl with pretty skin and way fewer hang-ups who would give him a good reason to continue living.

Dawn got to the sitting room, and the hellhounds on the wall tapestries seemed to leer at her as she approached Kiko and Natalia, who were together on a rose-upholstered settee, tuned in to a BBC news station.

Or maybe it'd be more accurate to say that a slightly bandaged Natalia was diligently watching TV and taking notes while a more heavily Band-Aided Kiko was tapping his fingers on the settee, staring off into space.

Then his gaze zeroed in on Dawn as if she'd just—*pop!*—appeared. The first thing he looked at was the splotches of red on her face, and Dawn stopped herself from wincing.

It made her appreciate Jonah's acceptance just a little, even if he was suspect.

Kiko said, "There you are."

"What're you up to?"

"Oh, just thinking."

Natalia glanced at Dawn, blanching at the red marks and going back to the TV.

It was enough to drive Dawn out of the room. "I'm going to temp headquarters to see Frank. It's been a while since Eva checked in, and even though she said things are okay and he's just resting, I want to make sure."

Kiko gave her a salute, but she could tell his mind was still elsewhere.

After grabbing her cell phone and stuffing it into the pocket of a jacket she wore over just one side of her body, she took the same doorway off the foyer where the Friends had ushered the team the other night, just before whizzing them away to temporary headquarters. When Dawn descended to the tunnel, then got into one of the railed carts, she realized that her trip there wouldn't be as quick as it'd been when the Friends had pushed the team along. But the spirits who weren't looking for Costin outside needed to recharge from the Underground attack, and Dawn wasn't about to rouse any of them just to make her trip faster, so she accessed the electric motor and sailed along at a decent enough clip.

All the way there, she couldn't shake off thoughts of Della laid out on the grass, that sweet smile on her face. Were the girls at least happier now?

Dawn hoped to God they were.

When she arrived at temp HQ, the shelter seemed filled with dead air.

"Eva?" she called.

All she heard was the ricochet of her voice off the concrete on its way down the length of the shelter.

She passed the spot where she'd slain Claudius, taking care not to look at it too much, then came to Eva's room.

Which was empty.

She had a bad feeling about this.

When she opened Frank's door, she expected to find him huddled under his blankets in the dimness, just like before when she'd first discovered he was sick. But, this time, she was pretty sure she'd find a humanized Frank because of the dragon's death. She'd be lying if she didn't admit that she wondered if his change would signal a return back to the "old Frank"—the drunk who'd never had his shit together.

Then again, Breisi was with him, and she'd been a salvation to him.

Dawn saw him in his bed, and she went to it. "Hey, I'm sure you already know this, but the dragon's toast. That's why you're human again."

Under the wool, his breathing seemed to be labored, but she couldn't tell for certain with the lights off.

"Frank?"

When he turned away from the wall, he seemed to be caught in Dawn's pained haze . . . or in scary-movie slow motion, where the nightmare had second upon dreadful second to permeate your head.

She stared at him—a freak from a painting called "The Scream." A haunted being with a wide mouth, wide eyes in a skeleton of a face draped with wrinkled skin.

Dawn screamed, too, long and hard, and it didn't stop even when she smelled a wisp of jasmine from the floor, where something felt like a pool dragging at Dawn's boots.

Breisi?

Eva's voice came from behind them, in a corner.

"Congratulations on your victory," her mother said, just before Dawn turned around, another scream clogging her chest when she saw what Eva had become, too.

TWENTY-FIVE

THE WHITE LADY

Dawn only knew it was her mother because Eva was sitting there in a rickety chair dressed in a long white night-gown, one leg crossed over the other, her hands folded in her lap with a sense of silver screen chic that a real star never surrendered, even with a change of identity.

Then there was the rest of her.

Even in the hallway-lit room, Dawn could see Eva's snake-tangled blond hair, and her eyes. . . . God, it was her staring eyes that did it. She had the gaze of a wife who'd been locked away in an attic by her husband.

But Eva was also smiling, looking happier than Dawn had ever seen her.

It's my state of mind—pain, exhaustion, Dawn thought, closing her eyes, fumbling for something to hold on to for bal-ance. She found a table near the head of Frank's bed that took her weight. This *had* to be her nutso state of mind at work on her, because Eva was acting like everything was normal.

But when Dawn opened her eyes, Eva was the same

mess. Dawn didn't even know how much time had passed as she grappled to accept that what she saw in front of her was real.

Then she remembered Frank. After working her way around to actually talking, Dawn didn't overreact. Instead, she spoke quietly, as if a loud word would rile Eva out of her corner and hell would break loose.

"Mom, what happened here? Did Frank's vamp sickness get worse before he went human again?" *And what the hell happened to you?* she wanted to shout.

Eva sighed, as if this would be a real long story. "Frank will eventually be fine. I've made sure of it."

"He should be at a hospital." Dawn didn't care how many questions a doctor would ask. "Why didn't you take him there?"

"I tried my best to see that matters wouldn't go that far. I've been taking care of him, Dawn."

There was something about Eva's lullaby voice and constant smile that went beyond spooky. Went beyond basic shudders. This was a more primal fright that made the center of Dawn's bones go ice-cold.

Her mom continued. "He was healing, but then, out of nowhere, he seized up, then started altering, and I realized that something had to have happened in the Underground to affect him."

Dawn could explain the dragon's death later. "Right—Frank went human again, so that means he won't heal like he did when he was a vampire. This vamp sickness that he contracted obviously didn't work itself off when—"

Eva's smile disappeared as her voice sliced out. "He isn't sick." Then she uncrossed her legs, crossing them the other way, another pleasant smile counteracting her sharpness. "I simply took too much from him."

What?

Frank was wheezing in an attempt to breathe, and Dawn had to concentrate on him more than Eva.

"We're gonna get you to a hospital, Dad. Just hold on." She reached for the cell phone in her jacket, not sure if it'd get reception, but she had to try.

"Please don't," Eva said. "I told you, he doesn't need medical aid. I'll take care of him. He'll want me to now."

With one hand, Dawn flipped open her phone to the bright LED screen.

What happened next seemed like a flicker of time—here and gone before she could even react.

Eva rose from the chair, her nightgown a mass of white as she repeated "*no*" in a voice that smacked of charm, but wasn't quite the same as a vampire's. Then she touched the phone and went back to her seat, her hands folded in her lap again as if she hadn't moved.

Dawn stared at Eva as her consciousness caught up. *Just like déjà vu,* she thought. A blur of reality mixed with the surreal.

Thinking that she'd imagined the moment, Dawn accessed her phone, but it was dead, as if the battery had suddenly gone kaput.

Ice wiggled up her spine as she slowly put the phone away. She didn't like what she was thinking about her mom, who'd stowed herself away in her room for nights without anyone really paying attention to her. Dawn should've followed up after the wine bar, should've gotten her head out of saving the world and concentrated on what was right in front of her instead. Wasn't that what a good daughter would've done?

"Interesting," Eva said. "You went ahead and tried to phone out, anyway. It seems my charm only works on men. Or maybe just on the people who really do want to be charmed."

"Mom," Dawn said, even more softly now. "Just how have you been taking care of Frank?"

Her mother smoothed her hands over her white nightgown. "I'm not sure how to explain."

"Try."

Frank kept wheezing, as if he was attempting to tell Dawn everything in his own way. She rested a hand on his frail shoulder to make him stop wasting his energy. At her feet, Breisi was making the same efforts to communicate, and Dawn had the feeling that Eva had done something to Dawn's friend, too.

"I needed him," Eva said simply.

"Needed him for what?"

Her mother's smile grew, and Dawn realized that she and her mom were in two different worlds. Dawn just wished she knew where Eva's was.

The heft of a revolver in Dawn's jacket pocket seemed to pull her down. She didn't like that Eva was making her realize the weapon was there.

"Are you a vampire again?" Dawn's voice betrayed a wisp of approaching dread. Damn it. She put more force behind her question. "Is that what happened at that wine bar when you were alone, without anyone watching you?"

"Not a vampire," Eva said.

"Then *what*?"

"I. Don't. Know." The responses were bladed, but they had the cool grace of butterfly knives.

Frank's fingers wrapped weakly around Dawn's wrist. He was moving his pruned mouth, laboring to produce sounds, but nothing came out.

Dawn was reaching her wits' end. "Start talking, Eva."

Her mom didn't even blink, just kept smiling. Happy, bursting smiling that seemed so out of place with what she ended up saying. "You, out of everyone, should know this was bound to happen. I lasted as long as I could after everyone else in the L.A. Underground took their lives or ran away, never to be heard from again. They're probably all dead now, and that's how I've felt for this past year, too. Dead. The only thing that's kept me alive was how you tried to make us a family again."

Dawn gripped Frank's thinned fingers, as if that would help her to withstand what Eva was saying. If she'd known her mom would end up like this, she might've done something. She wasn't sure what, but look at them now. Look at what she'd brought on by not realizing Eva's stain would turn out to be just as bad as her own.

Her mother's hands were still in her lap, her bare feet peeking out from beneath her nightgown, her hair a bristled cloud around her face from the stray hairs sneaking out from the coils. "I couldn't go on, day after day, pretending things were okay with Frank living just a block away with Breisi. So I offered myself to him through my blood, and he rejected me. And I left, thinking there was no more left for me."

She'd gone to the wine bar.

"Were you bitten by the time I got to you?" Dawn asked, recalling the giddy difference in Eva—a bliss that really *had* gone past drunkenness, now that she knew better.

"I told you—I wasn't bitten."

Frank groaned on the bed, and Eva got out of her chair as if he'd sent her an invitation to come to him.

"If you don't mind," she said, motioning for Dawn to move aside. "I've recovered from taking care of him the last time, and I'm ready to do it again."

The only reason Dawn surrendered her place was that Frank was in trouble and Eva seemed to know a way of helping—at least until Dawn could get him out of here.

Breisi clung to her ankles, as if warning Dawn. Then, in the subdued light from the hall, Dawn watched as Eva used her nail to open a wound on her wrist and hold it over Frank's shriveled mouth.

He turned his head away as the blood dripped to him, leaking from the sides of his lips as he refused Eva once again.

Dawn went light-headed, the pain from her injuries still working its muddiness on her. "He's not a vampire anymore. Why would he want your blood?"

"Because of what I am. I think that my blood is the reason he survived going human again. He might not have
been strong enough to take the change without me. But
don't worry—he won't turn into anything nonhuman because he's drinking from me. My blood doesn't seem to
have any power beyond a higher nutrition. I'm only nursing him back to the way he used to be."

Her mom was mostly talking about bringing him back
to the days when he'd loved her.

"What I want to know," she said, moving toward Eva out
of an instinctive need to protect her dad, "is how the hell he
got this way."

Her mother lightly pushed Dawn away, as if she was
nothing but a pest. Dawn's ire churned, the dragon's
blood heating in her, but she was so tired, so injured that
there was only a pathetic spark that stung her. The spark
didn't even flare up the dragon's blood as much as it
made the marks pound, like a living thing that'd been
prodded.

Frank's tongue licked at Eva's blood, and he whim-
pered, as if he hated himself for knowing it would help
him.

Eva said, "There we go, baby," and gave him more. He
took in every bit, and there wasn't a damned thing Dawn
could do—not if this would make him better, like Eva
claimed. Dawn wouldn't deprive him of the only medicine
at hand.

"You tell me what went on in that wine bar," Dawn said.

Eva's smile beamed in the near darkness. "A man. And
he gave me just what I'd been hoping for."

Then she told Dawn of his enthralling eyes, his foreign
accent, his way of talking a woman into trusting him. When
she arrived at the part where she and the man had melded
their blood, skin to skin, deal to deal, Dawn took a sudden
step away from Eva.

Sweet Jesus.

Not again. This was a joke. Eva was trying to get attention. This was . . .

This was actually happening.

Dawn had read about things like this before—bargains with demons, advocates who took advantage of desperate, sad, or greedy humans—but she'd been so focused on vampires that she'd never imagined . . . never thought . . .

"He took your soul," Dawn said. Hadn't the team suspected that London was a gathering ground for the paranormal? Shouldn't she have been on watch for more than just vamps?

Lost, Dawn thought. Eva was never coming back, was she? She'd slipped right through the cracks of Dawn's life.

Why couldn't she have stopped this?

"Yes, he took my soul," Eva said. "And, in trade, he gave me a new chance with Frank."

Could've stopped this . . .

Frank had finished drinking, and Eva was pressing her fingers to her wrist. With a grimace, he rolled his head to the side, breathing more evenly, in spite of his clear dismay at having given in to her.

But why wouldn't he? He used to like Eva's bagged blood more than any other because it did something for him, and it seemed that this craving had continued into a different era. Dawn wondered if he would always need Eva in some way.

Her mom was watching her former husband as if they were married again. "I would've given up my soul a thousand times over for him."

"You mean you would've given it so Dad could be sick and dependent on you?"

When Eva merely gazed at him with warped affection Dawn had her answer.

"So this man in the wine bar . . ." Dawn said, still searching, still hoping there was a way out of this for all of them. If she just tried again. . . . "It sounds like he was a representative, a lower demon who goes around collecting souls for whatever you want to call it . . . the devil . . . the dark side . . ."

"And if he was?" Eva said.

"That doesn't scare the ever-loving *shit* out of you?"

Dawn heard herself, recognizing that a woman who'd given up her soul to be a vampire one time probably wouldn't be afraid of much.

Eva calmly swiveled her gaze over, doubling the fear in Dawn's jumping pulse.

"I never really had my soul back," her mother said. "Not as it was before I gave it up the first time when I exchanged blood and became a vampire. I think all our souls returned with the need for us to destroy ourselves, didn't they? They've been raked through a place they weren't meant to be, whether it was stored in one of Benedikte's vials or wandering through the atmosphere not knowing where to go. It dirtied them. There was a price for us to keep on living after our humanity returned." Eva lavished her attention on Frank again. "To tell you the truth, a tainted soul wasn't all that valuable to me when I was asked to give it up this time."

"Don't say that." This woman on the bed . . . she couldn't be Eva . . . she hardly even looked like her.

Then Dawn thought of Della and the girls: how they'd been monsters, too, but had seemed so human in their last actions. Wasn't there hope for Eva in the end if Dawn could save her?

She bunched her good hand into a fist. She couldn't give up, especially not on her mother.

Eva tossed off another comment, but this one hit its target smack in the center of Dawn. "I was never going to be truly human again, and I accepted that. You should, too."

Dawn had been thinking it all along. But Eva saying it verified all her worst nightmares.

Never human again . . .

Eva touched Frank's shirt, and he cringed. Breisi went taut around Dawn's ankles. She seemed to be a little stronger, but she wasn't moving.

Was she saving herself for something . . . ?

"So you couldn't be a vampire," Dawn said, "and you settled for this. A creature I can't even really identify."

"I'm better than a vampire. I take what I need with a touch from anyone."

Breisi rubbed against Dawn's legs, as if trying to tell her something else, and Dawn took a guess at what it was.

As Eva had said, Frank wasn't sick. Eva had touched him. Obviously, she sucked energy from her victim— maybe even emotion, too—and Frank was her unfortunate obsession.

Eva didn't know it, but she *was* a vampire of sorts. A psychic one by way of a demon. And as Dawn coasted her gaze over her mother's crazed appearance, she realized that she didn't know how to fight this kind of danger.

"Is Frank the only one you've 'touched,' Eva?"

Her mom stroked down Frank's clothed chest. He'd shut his eyes, acting like if he couldn't see it, it didn't exist. She was getting awfully close to his bare skin.

Dawn's hand hovered near the revolver in her pocket.

"There was my first experiment, the other night," Eva said. "I slipped out of headquarters because I was . . . hungry. I didn't even have a hint of what I was capable of until I moved past the Friends without being noticed—probably, I suspect, because I didn't want them to see me—and disabled your alarm with a touch."

The alarm at one of the back entrances? That'd been Eva?

She added, "And when I realized just what I was hungry for, I touched the boy, just like I'd touched the laser tracker and camera. But he . . ." Eva laid her palm flat on Frank's shirt-covered chest and said, "*He* fed me."

"How?"

"With his desire. With his appreciation."

"Where is he now?"

"In a grave."

"Mom," Dawn said, reeling.

Eva had killed someone, and she didn't seem to have any remorse. Even the L.A. vampires had been careful about bloodletting by taking willing victims.

Dawn couldn't look at Eva. But she had to hear the rest.

"Then," her mother said, "I touched Breisi when she came here to 'defend' Frank from me."

"You *sapped* Breisi?" Scenarios attacked Dawn: What would happen to a Friend if she lost all energy? Had Breisi reached that point? Was she just a sentient being that melted to the floor, unable to move but feeling everything anyway?

That had to be a certain circle of hell, and Dawn wasn't about to let Breisi settle there for the rest of her time on earth.

Then a quieter thought slid in on the tail end of all the others. She hadn't stopped to realize this before, but if Costin had really left, why hadn't the Friends gone with him? They had a deal: they were supposed to help him with his mission, and when they all finished, the spirits could seek eternal peaceful rest.

The notion actually gave Dawn a positive lift when she'd had nothing but hopelessness before.

At Dawn's feet, Breisi held on.

"You know she can't even get back to her portrait now," Dawn said. "Were you just going to leave her like this?"

"I didn't think much about it."

"You should have."

"I . . . don't believe I have it in me anymore."

She said it as if she were just discovering she had this power, too—the freedom to not care.

Dawn was speechless.

"You really don't understand, do you?" Eva asked. "You

think you can bring me back. But I like the way I am. Hour after hour, I've erased all the truths in me and I'm finally content. Can't you be happy for me?"

That was it. The end. Dawn didn't hear her mother anywhere in there, didn't really even see her in this white lady who didn't care about anything but her own wants and needs. This killer who'd touched a boy the other night and taken his life. She'd do the same to Frank when she finally realized that he'd never love her again.

There really was no going back.

Dawn got ready to grab the revolver. What else was there to do? Eva wasn't just acting soulless, she sounded that way, too, her tone as remote as the ten-mile distance in her gaze.

"There's no humanity left in you?" Dawn asked. "None?"

Eva seemed to think about it. "I'm not sure. Not yet."

"You'll decide later or something?"

"Dawn." Chiding. Disappointment. "Don't be petulant."

"This is beyond petulance."

"This is how you've always been, even as a one-month-old baby. So focused on yourself."

Ape-shit crazy—that's what Eva was. Yet, even through it all, Dawn sensed that some kind of truth was about to roll down on her. But hadn't she wanted to get to it for a while? She'd never quite believed all the excuses her mom had leaned on about her managers telling the young, naïve actress that she was helping her family by going Underground.

"Go for it," Dawn said, just daring her mom to be as inhuman as she seemed. Polite humanity had obviously kept Eva from revealing anything hurtful to Dawn, probably for good reason. "Tell me how you really feel, Eva."

She just offered an uncanny glance. "I took Benedikte's blood into me and gave my own to him because I *loved* the way it felt when I was worshipped, and I wanted that forever. You never looked at me the way the fans did, Dawn. Even as a baby, I could see you wouldn't love me like they would."

Breisi seemed to hug Dawn from where she was at her feet, but that only served to squeeze every last bit of rage from the bottom of Dawn's body up, making the dragon's blood stir even more, like it wanted to spring alive.

But she was too . . . done, especially after Costin's disappearance. She had nothing left, especially for this woman she realized she didn't know at all. She didn't even have enough anger to lash out.

"So that's how you've always felt, deep down," Dawn said. "You just have the balls to say it now."

"The truth hurts."

Eva turned back to Frank, whose face was averted, just as it'd been throughout Dawn's whole life.

"This isn't to say that I really didn't want you and Frank to be with me again," she added.

"Because it *completed* you?" Dawn chuffed. "Is that what you told yourself?"

"I do love you." Eva's eerie, smiley voice didn't entirely reflect it, but there was a hint that made Dawn think she wasn't lying. Dawn just couldn't compete with the love everyone else had given *to* Eva.

She limped toward a light switch and flipped it on, flooding the room with illumination. It was too easy for Eva to get through this in the near darkness. She wanted her mother to look at her while she rained these blows down.

Eva said, "You know I plan to leave, of course. With Frank."

Breisi jerked against Dawn, who agonized for her friend. It was then she sincerely realized that Breisi had been more a part of Dawn and Frank's family than Eva had ever been.

She'd had them all along, but what had she concentrated on instead? Eva. Always Eva.

With a sinking feeling, Dawn realized it was time to let go of her mother. "I can't let Frank leave," Dawn said.

On the bed, her father turned his face toward Dawn, his eyes brighter.

"Don't bother putting up a fight," Eva said. "I've been feeling that the man from the wine bar wants me to come to him. I think he was just waiting until I was ready."

"Then go, just not with Frank."

The second Dawn said it, she wanted to pull it back, even after everything. If her mom hadn't said that she did love her—even a little—this would've been so much easier.

Eva held a hand out to Dawn. "You can come with us."

Dawn had always wanted to hear that, but not in this way.

"Dawn, what else is left for you here?"

Breisi, she thought. Kiko. And the need for Dawn to find out, once and for all, where Costin really was before she gave up on him.

Eva meant nothing next to all of it, and Dawn felt a part of her die at that.

But she had a dilemma: if she stopped Eva from leaving with Frank, it would mean no more nourishing blood sustenance from Eva for her dad, and already, Dawn could see that her father looked a little improved because of what Eva had given him. Then again, letting him go *with* her . . .

No contest. Eva would just drain him of energy when he got better. The cycle would never stop.

"Eva," she said, "you need to leave now."

Her mother just kept her hand out, as if expecting Dawn to grab on to it. Dawn took out her revolver, letting it rest by her side.

Strangely, Eva laughed. Then, in another déjà vu moment, she got up, touched the gun, twisting it into a steel pretzel, and was back to sitting on the bed within the stutter of a heartbeat.

Dawn dropped her useless weapon to the floor. She didn't have anything else to fight with. She was too beaten down, her emotions limping through her like a dying pulse, and she couldn't conjure any anger beyond the tiny reminder of the dragon's blood, which felt like it was struggling to come alive in its own way.

Could she use that instead? Clean Eva's clock and keep her from ever hurting Frank and Breisi again?

The temptation made the splashes on her skin flare, heat traveling below her flesh, toward her soul stain, which seemed to expand, reaching out to the dragon.

As they almost touched, Dawn mentally separated them, ice jolting through her veins.

What the hell had just happened?

Shit. *Shitshitshit.*

As she calmed down, she kept herself frosty, beating her urges. The dragon's smile . . .

Was he inside of her?

Dawn had no time to think when Eva reached toward Frank. If she touched him, he'd suffer the loss of more energy—

Just before Eva made contact with Frank, Breisi came to life—she'd obviously been saving energy in case Eva attacked—and she darted from Dawn's feet to fly at the other woman, pushing her to the mattress.

Frank sat up, too, dragging his hand out from under the covers, where the flash of a blade glinted in the light.

He always carried a knife, but Eva obviously hadn't checked him. Had she stunned Frank so thoroughly before that she believed her former husband wouldn't be able to fight back now?

Maybe she even thought he wouldn't want to fight back. . . .

He arced the knife at Eva's chest, and as she gasped, the blade sank into her.

Frank fell back to the bed, wheezing, and Breisi slipped

to him. Dawn merely stood by, frozen in mind and body as blood spread over Eva's white nightgown.

She just lay there, her mouth twisted. Then her fingers crept up to touch her wound, as if she couldn't believe it.

"Frank?" she asked.

He was clawing the sheets as he took in more breaths, but then Dawn realized that he was actually reaching for Breisi.

Eva realized it, too, and she trained her blank gaze on the ceiling, her hand over her heart, near the bloodstain.

"Mom?" Dawn asked, still immobile, on the edge of going to Eva, even after everything.

Eva seemed to cower from the name "Mom," and Dawn stood rooted. This wasn't her mother anymore.

Eva had died a long time ago.

The white lady rose from the bed, her body stiff, almost as if she was on a board and being lifted to a stand, and Dawn went for the knife Frank had dropped, not knowing if it would work on Eva since she hadn't died yet from Frank's strike.

Then her jaw unhinged to a startling length, and she screamed with such great fury that Dawn fell to the floor.

She shielded herself from that scream, which seemed to hold all Eva's anger at being set aside. All her wounds bled into a sound that made hell seem as if it was right below them, opening up while the walls shook, the door swinging out into the hall.

Dawn pressed one ear to the side of the bed, her good hand over her other ear, blocking off the sound just like she'd had to do with Claudius. But Eva's scream lasted longer, and it was as deep as a gouge that would never heal.

The seemingly endless scream brought down chairs, cabinets, almost like they were trees falling, clearing the area. Then the keening quickly trickled to a gurgle, and Dawn looked up at her mom to find that Eva's face was a mask of almost human defeat and sadness.

She'd been stabbed near the heart by the only man she'd ever loved.

Then a blank Eva stiffly moved out of the room, sobbing, "But he promised me . . ." As she left Frank behind without another look, she almost seemed to float in that nightgown with the scarlet chest stain.

In the aftermath, Frank whispered Breisi's name, and they huddled together as best they could, as if they were afraid the white lady would come back. But if she did, Dawn was going to use the knife on her, getting her in the heart this time.

She'd had to let go of her mother, all but burying her in a box that she could store away, where it couldn't be opened again.

She crawled to the door, her own injuries protesting. But when she got there, there was no Eva.

Just as if there hadn't *ever* been an Eva for Dawn.

TWENTY-SIX

The Art of Playing
with Fire

Flames.

Dawn felt them in her body as the dragon slipped through her, just like Costin used to do when he'd been a Soul Traveler, merging with her, making her ache in places no one else could ever touch. But the dragon only left damage in its wake, its blood soaking her, creeping down toward the heaviness in her center. It was hot and boiling as it came closer, leaving charred scars in its wake.

Closer to the soul stain.

Closer.

As if it knew it was being tracked, it paused. Pounded. Throbbed. Then, rounding, it reared up, the pop of fangs in a mouth that smiled, just before it struck with those teeth—

Dawn startled and pressed her hand to her heart, which was beating so hard that she thought it would turn to steaming water and trickle out of her. She'd been halfway between sleep and consciousness, but the dream had shaken her to a wide-awake place where adrenaline blinded her until she looked around the room, grounding herself to the sheer curtains around the bed, the darkened window, the walls.

She finally leveled out her breathing. Two days since Costin had left and the dreams had started. Two days since Eva had gone MIA, too.

Dawn hung her legs off the bed, grabbing a bottle of water from the nightstand and drinking the remainder of its contents in a few gulps. Then she slipped to the floor, walking toward the side of the room, her wounded leg slightly better from all the healing gel she'd been rubbing on it.

When she got to Costin's field of fire portrait, which Kiko had propped against the wall, she peered into the flames, hoping beyond hope that Costin would magically appear.

Once, back in L.A., she'd found him resting in the painting. He hadn't revealed what he really was to her yet, and he was as mysterious as ever with a red cape covering his form, his face hidden by the long, dark hair he'd sported when he'd had a body, before it'd been destroyed and he'd moved on to an existence of borrowing the "vessels" of others.

But now, there was only the fire that had always flamed in the background.

She stared at it, her heartbeat gradually mellowing. Then she backed away from the portrait, frustrated that Costin hadn't come to it.

But what had she expected?

Knowing it would do no good to sit here staring at a picture, she went to the closet, fumbled into some dark jeans, boots, and a black sweater that had one sleeve cut off for her cast and sling. Then she went to Frank's room to continue the vigil she'd deserted when she'd almost collapsed from need of rest a few hours ago.

Once there, she grasped her father's hand as he slept in his bed. In human age, he was a candidate for Rogaine and a midlife crisis—he'd been a vampire for only a little over a year—but if a person saw him for the first time now, he'd look like he was in his nineties. His health hadn't improved since Eva had left, but that was because he didn't have any of her blood to drink. Yet, at least the dose she'd given him had seemed to clear his breathing and lend him a little gusto after the sustenance had infiltrated his body. Dawn was sure that Eva's blood feeding had been the only reason Frank had even pulled together enough energy to stab Eva in the first place.

When Dawn had told him that he needed to see a doctor, Frank had begged the team not to take him to one. He felt much better, he said, and if he could just keep drinking the supplement juice Breisi had previously invented for Dawn and Eva when they'd been blood donors, he was sure he'd improve on his own. He'd insisted that there'd be too many questions about his "amazing disease" at a hospital, and those might result in some kind of investigation that would put the team in the spotlight. Dawn had said that she didn't know what the big deal would be if they were fingered now for their vamp hunting.

Were there any more Undergrounds left to track down? Why did they even need secrecy anymore?

But she'd only been arguing on the basis of emotion, because there were still TV news reports that mentioned terrorist suspicions, which could lead to the team because of those charmed humans and the Highgate explosion. Even two days after the Underground's end, things weren't comfortable for the team out on the streets, and putting themselves in a featured role at the hospital probably wouldn't be the best move. Also, Frank had been adamant about sticking to his own program, and since Dawn knew half the battle for recovery would be psychological, she'd let him have his way. But only until the end of today. Past that, if he didn't show progress, she was hauling him in.

As he woke up, he smacked his lips, obviously thirsty.

Dawn reached for the glass of supplement juice on his nightstand, held up his head, then helped him drink.

Just like the old days. How many times had she nursed Frank back from a hangover when she was growing up? Little had she known that, someday, she'd be getting him through the mother of all bad times.

Breisi must've sensed Frank awakening because Dawn felt her brush by. The Friend had been resting in her portrait, still recharging, off and on. She'd needed the extra time in the painting because of the amount of energy Eva had sapped out of her. But even with that, she wasn't back to her full awesome Breisi-ness.

As the Friend hovered next to Dawn, not saying anything as she checked on Frank, the spirit's essence seemed thin.

"How is he?" Breisi asked, sounding old.

Frank answered in his own grandparent voice. "He's fine, Breez."

Dawn had never heard her dad's voice hold such a slant of resignation, but she couldn't say just what he'd resigned himself to.

Breisi leaned her essence against Dawn's shoulder. In spite of her being a spirit, the touch felt like a maternal show of comfort. It was enough to remind Dawn of what she'd never really gotten from Eva.

To her, Eva had gone back to being the mother who'd been murdered when Dawn was a baby. It was the only way Dawn could cope with the white lady, even though it wasn't the truth.

But sometimes the truth didn't work in real life. Sometimes the truth, in itself, was a lie.

Frank was looking at the network of beauty marks on the left side of her face and neck, then the red splashes on her right. Feeling like the freak she was, she got out of her chair. Now that Breisi was awake, Dawn would give them some alone time. Besides, she'd planned to do a lot of work, like poring over the story Costin had told her about The Whisper. She'd written down everything she recollected from the time he'd confessed his past to her, and she'd been going over it again and again, trying to find any detail that might've escaped her before—anything that'd give her a clue about where he was. She'd also been through his library, thinking that there had to be a hint somewhere in there.

Jonah had been shadowing her the whole time, helping with research, but neither of them had mentioned how he'd made a bid for her the other day. As for Kiko and Natalia, they'd been going through Costin's belongings, attempting touch reads. Also, the Friends had still been out and about, conducting their own search.

They were all sticking with the hope that Costin would be back, and sometimes Dawn believed this was the only thing keeping her going. If the Friends disappeared, then she would throw in the towel, because that would be a sure sign that he was out of earthly bounds.

But they were still here, and that was good enough.

As she left Frank's room, she sent one last glance to her dad, his hair blowing at Breisi's light touch. Then, while limping down the hall on her way to the library, Dawn ran into Kiko, who seemed to have been looking for her.

He grabbed her hand and started pulling her along, past the Friend portraits. "Don't kill me, but I've got a plan."

A plan? That was a great thing. A plan was what they needed.

"Why would I kill you for that?" she asked.

When he sent her a sheepish grin, she knew she wasn't going to like this plan.

"I've been thinking about how to present this to you," he said, "because your permission is important."

"For what?"

"I've got something set up in a sitting room. Indulge me until we get there, okay?"

He helped her down the stairs, minding her recovering leg. A gimp and a freak. She was a real package.

"Thing is," he added, "you gotta promise not to kill me when we get there."

"No guarantees."

He didn't know just how true that was. She hadn't told anyone but Breisi and Frank about the dragon dreams or about what she felt creeping through her body. It was a good idea for someone to be privy to the information, though, and Dawn trusted Breisi to inform the Friends so they could keep an eye on Dawn. In the event something did happen to her or in case her fears about the dragon's blood still living in her weren't just her imagination. No use worrying the rest of the team about it. Not yet.

Kiko brought her to the sitting room with the hellhound tapestries, where he and Natalia seemed to be hanging out a lot lately. She was waiting there, reclining on the rose-upholstered settee, her curly dark hair gathered in that barrette at her nape. If Dawn hadn't seen the psychic looking like such a black-garbed spy queen the other night when they'd gone Underground, she would've sworn that Natalia never got out of those tweed skirts of hers.

In front of Natalia on the mahogany table, a Ouija board waited.

Dawn groaned. Always with the Ouija.

"Hear me out, if you please," Natalia said, her accent just as smooth as Costin's used to be. Somehow, their Wallachian and Romanian vibes made Dawn think they were far wiser than she was. Probably true, too.

Dawn said, "Have you guys been trying to contact Costin through the board? Because if the answer's yes, I *will* kill you."

"No, no," Kiko said, taking a seat next to Natalia. Two of a kind—Tweedledee and Tweedle-Innocent. "We waited until we brought you in on this. I told you—we want your permission before we start anything up."

"Bring me in on what exactly? On . . ." Dawn was about to say, "On pulling Costin out of his paradise so we can chat with him?" But wasn't that like admitting he was really gone? Wasn't that the last thing she was prepared for if it was somehow true and the Friends were still around because of a cosmic fluke?

Kiko's voice softened. "Dawn, what exactly are you afraid we'll find?"

"I . . . don't know." But she did. Aside from not finding Costin at all, she was afraid she'd get a final answer from him; that he'd tell her that, wherever he was, he far preferred it to being here, just like Eva had pretty much done.

"Listen," Kiko said, "if you're uncomfortable with the Ouija, we can do this another way that I myself feel more in control of. I can try channeling, since that's how Costin always operated. He liked to assume bodies, and I'd give him the chance to talk through mine."

Dawn knew without a doubt that Kiko and Natalia had only put the Ouija board on the table to make this option seem all the better. *Acting!*

Shysters.

"Kiko, channeling's dangerous," she said. "Besides, I've never seen you do it before."

"I've studied it and dabbled before I came on the team, but Nat and I consulted Josephine Spencer over in Clerkenwell recently. She's considered an expert, and she guided me through a dry run with other spirits. That's what we've been doing the last couple of days, but we didn't want to spring it on you until we were sure it would work."

Natalia had her hand on his arm. "He's good at it, Dawn. A natural."

"And Costin would never hurt me," Kiko added.

"What if another spirit interferes?" Dawn asked.

"Then I know how to cast it out if I want," Kiko said. "Natalia would interfere if she felt things were getting out of hand, too."

"What if Costin doesn't come?" Dawn asked.

Kiko gave her a smile. "What if we don't try and it would've worked? The Friends are still around, remember? Odds are good that Costin's available, and you know it."

"Did you ever think," Natalia said, "that perhaps Costin was thrown out of Jonah's body by the force of the dragon, and he's disoriented? He might be trying to find his way back here, even now."

This wasn't fair. They were tossing too much at her, and it all sounded so logical.

"Are you saying he has amnesia?" Dawn asked, making sure they heard her doubt.

Natalia said, "Josephine Spencer suggested something along those lines."

"We didn't tell her specifics about our Underground hunts though," Kiko was quick to say. "Just so you know."

Dawn heard someone enter the room. It was Jonah, and from the scent of jasmine surrounding him, a safe guess would reveal that Kalin was here, too.

The spirit only confirmed it when she bumped into Dawn, like a body check on the street from someone who wanted to start shit. Now that the Underground hunt was over, the Friend was back to being a pain, and it should've made Dawn feel right at home. But it didn't.

Natalia and Kiko thanked Kalin for fetching Jonah, then caught him up on their idea. He got a light in his eyes. The hue didn't match the old vampire blue, but excitement made it close.

"I vote yes," Jonah said. "Dawn, why would you even have to mull it over?"

Razor Blade Jonah. His desire to bring Costin to him again hadn't abated one bit.

"He wouldn't be resuming his place in your body, Jonah," she said. "Kiko's inviting him into *his* vessel temporarily. You know that, right?"

It was like she'd roundhouse kicked him in the chest,

betraying some kind of agreement between them that she hadn't really been aware of.

Good God—did he think she was all for still having their ménage à trois or whatever you wanted to call it? Did he think Costin would still want to reside in his body and that Jonah could stay close to Dawn that way?

She didn't want to flatter herself, but when Jonah had told her that he was still here even if Costin wasn't, it'd unsettled her.

Kiko had already hopped down from the settee, going over to dim the chandelier light while Natalia put away the Ouija. They were taking Dawn's inability to say yes *as* a yes, and she was strangely grateful for that. She'd never doubted that she would give her approval for a channeling; it just would've taken a while to get there.

"Kalin," Kiko said, "it'd probably be easier for me to sense another spirit if you weren't in here. Can you scram?"

With a drawn-out sigh, the Friend left.

Psychic #1 lit a candle in the middle of a table that already had four chairs around it. Interesting to note that the candle had been planted there, too, as if they'd fully expected Dawn to give in right away.

Totally set up.

Kiko waved everyone over. "I'm no fairground hack, so I don't use no fancy stuff. This won't be any kind of big show."

"Just do what you need to do," Dawn said, sitting next to Natalia. She couldn't believe they were going to try this now. Wasn't there anything more to prepare before they got into it? Like, maybe, her psyche?

But even though she was dragging her feet, her heartbeat was hopping.

Kiko went for the seat on the other side of Dawn, near her dragon marks. "I want to be linked with you. I think Costin would be most drawn to where you are."

He climbed into the chair, his legs tucked under him to

add height. Jonah assumed a spot across the table, his dark hair covering one of his eyes as his gaze swept over Dawn, then away. He was still bruised by her comment about Costin taking up Kiko's body and not his.

Dawn considered apologizing, but not now. Bringing up the subject with him would open a whole can of worms no one needed. Jonah would get over it. Everyone got over her.

Psychic #1 put his hands on the table, urging them all to do the same. Dawn took her arm out of its sling, bearing the ache and knowing it was a bad idea, but she needed to hear Costin again. To know he was fine.

Natalia gently took Dawn's fingertips, and they all formed a circle.

"Never break the chain," Kiko said. "No matter what happens, stay with me, okay?"

He sounded reassuring, and Dawn found herself willing to follow him into this, especially since she knew he hadn't partaken in any Friend lulling since she'd gotten on his ass about it the last time. Still, her heart seemed to bubble in quick bursts, her veins popping with blood.

What if this didn't work?

She wouldn't think about it. Instead, she tried to clear her mind, to think of where Costin might be.

"Eyes closed now," Kiko said. "Listen to me, but think of him, too. Really *think*."

Dawn did as he asked, hearing everyone breathe around her as their rhythms fell into a linked pattern.

Quiet. Just the creaks of the building. Just the huff of the candle flame as it burned.

After Kiko meditated for a while, he finally spoke, his voice merging with the hush of the room.

"Costin?" he whispered. "We've been looking for you . . ."

He hadn't truly summoned him yet, and Dawn wondered if this was just a warm-up of some sort—Kiko's own way of getting into it. Across the table, she thought she heard Jonah's breathing outpacing the rest of theirs, as if he had invested more in Costin's return than any of them.

"Costin . . ." Kiko said. "Costin . . ."

She heard the burning candlewick struggle under a wind and cracked open her gaze to see the flame angled, flickering, casting shadows on the faces of those around her. She tightened her hold on Kiko's hand, but he didn't react.

"Costin," he said even more softly.

The candle flame contorted, and she saw it reflected in Jonah's eyes as he opened them, a look of wondrous expectation on his face.

Then Kiko stiffened, crushing Dawn's fingers.

She whipped her gaze over to him to find that his neck was bent, and he was breathing harder. Then he started to shake his head, but in a disjointed way that made her think his neck was growing or that something was trying to twist it off.

His hand began slipping from hers, but she held on to it.

Don't break the chain—

She couldn't wait anymore. "Costin?" she asked. Then with more urgency. *"Costin?"*

Kiko's head shot up, and Dawn squeezed his fingers, but not out of reassurance. Out of . . .

Oh, God.

As he opened his eyes and peered at the candle, she could tell that there was another entity in there and, for some reason, it didn't strike her as being Costin.

Natalia spoke. "Costin?"

Whoever was in Kiko answered, and it was in the psychic's voice . . . except not really. It was too serene, too . . .

Dawn wanted to describe it as "sonorous," like an otherworldly tune being played on a familiar instrument.

"I am not Costin," he said. "But I *am* visiting so I might stop any one of his team from completing the unthinkable and formally inviting him to come to you."

Dawn wanted to pull away, but she held on to Natalia's and Kiko's hands for all she was worth, her pulse on overdrive.

Natalia asked, "Then who are you?" She wasn't chasing this intruder away yet.

Not-Kiko smiled blankly. "You would know me as The Whisper."

TWENTY-SEVEN

THE REPLACEMENT

THE first thing Dawn thought was, *He's lying. The Whisper hasn't been around Costin for centuries.*

Then again, wasn't this a perfect time for him to show up again, with things in such disarray?

Dawn told Natalia, "Don't chase this one off."

The new girl nodded.

Kiko—or Whisper Kiko—had relaxed in his chair, as if whoever was in his body had made itself cozy. He still held on to Dawn's and Jonah's hands, though, and when she gauged Jonah across the table, she saw that his cheeks were flushed.

Again, the memory of prevamp Jonah, with his face slashed by a razor he'd used to manipulate Costin into staying in his body, descended on her.

Kiko's channeled voice sighed. "Ah, such a relief to root once again. I have not been in a human body for . . . I cannot even say."

His tone had changed, but then Dawn remembered

when Costin had allowed her into his mind to see his birth
as a Soul Traveler. She'd witnessed how The Whisper had
greeted Costin in the borrowed body of an old sage who'd
been tossed in the same dungeon and labeled a "madman."

This sure sounded like the guy Dawn had heard. . . .

"If you *are* The Whisper," she said, "what did you do
with Costin?"

Whisper Kiko turned to look at her so deliberately that
her skin chilled. And his eyes . . .

They were a bottomless gray: glassy, like deep mirrors
that'd been covered by black shrouds until someone had
been fool enough to expose them.

"Dawn," he said, as if he'd been anticipating meeting
her.

The chills folded into prickles over her.

He smiled again, the tips of Kiko's mouth barely turning
up. She'd never seen her friend with this kind of ominous
civility in him before.

"Questions, questions . . ." he said. "I tend to forget how
many you people have until I am required to mingle with
you. I am here for my own reasons, not yours, and if a
question leads to an answer in the process, then there it is."

Dawn started to talk again, but Whisper Kiko stopped
her.

"What games you play. You were on the edge of summoning Costin, and you have no idea of what you almost
did to him."

As The Whisper kept watching Dawn, she had a feeling
she knew why else he was here. He saw the red splashes on
her face, and he had to know what they were, what these
new marks were doing in her.

Was he also here to take care of that because Costin
couldn't?

"When the dragon was slain," The Whisper said, "*I* was
not even certain that all his vampire line would turn human
with his passing. He was a creature unlike any in existence.

So, after Jonah's body freed Costin, your 'boss' was delivered to me, where I had been waiting to receive him."

Dawn flicked her gaze away from The Whisper long enough to measure her companions' reactions. Natalia was studying Kiko, clearly taking notes on the stencil pad of her brain. Jonah was fascinated.

"Where did you receive him?" he asked.

"How shall I explain this element?" Whisper Kiko pursed his lips in reflection. Then he said, "I would call it a resort, in your terms. Very well outfitted with comforts that have kept Costin occupied while he lingers. I have been rather busy of late—this is the reason he has been on his own so long—so I made certain he had an upgrade."

Dawn's fears sped up.

"I don't understand," she said. "He told me that, after the dragon and blood brothers were taken care of, his soul would be whole, and it would be all his. He'd go to a permanent, better place and not the hell he would've been sent to if he'd failed—the perdition he'd expected from exchanging his soul for vampirism in the first place."

"And his whole soul *is* his." The Whisper sounded like he had all the patience in the world. "It is only that he has not traveled on. Not as of yet. And this is the reason his Friends have not journeyed to their ultimate resting place, either."

Heart . . . beating even faster now . . .

Jonah leaned forward. "Why hasn't he gone anywhere?"

Whisper Kiko fixed his attention on the former host. "In earthly language, you would say that he has been reluctant to go into the light."

This was all too lofty to absorb. But here it all was now, staring her in the face.

Costin . . . staying back from the light . . .

Natalia finally spoke, the representative of reason. "Who precisely *are* you to have such powers?"

"There is only one being here who needs to know." The

Whisper laid his gaze on Dawn again. "And it is housed in you. I was preparing myself to come and announce myself to your passenger, Dawn, before all of you gathered to summon Costin. You only saw to it that my arrival was scheduled earlier. Now, I should like to see how much has stayed with you."

No one moved, probably because they were figuring out the secret Dawn had been keeping from them. The dragon.

Thank God The Whisper was here to see just how far the "passenger" had gone into her.

"I'm glad you're going to come in and let it know you're there," she said, not knowing if she'd feel better or worse after The Whisper made his introduction to the dragon's blood. But relief finally relaxed her shoulders, as if something had been partially removed from them.

The Whisper would get the dragon out of her. He could do that, right?

With Kiko's hand, he gripped Dawn tighter, and a wave of airy energy flowed through her fingers, her arm, down her side, halting just short of where she felt the dragon's blood beating, as if it was lifting its head to see what approached. It was like the serpent and The Whisper were assessing each other—one burning, one cool.

As The Whisper "introduced" itself, a flash took over Dawn's vision, containing images almost like the ones Costin had given to her on the day of his confession in L.A., when he'd revealed who *he* was.

But this was more intense, and she rocked with the force.

A field of white, then lightning among the clouds, then a sound—a voice?—that registered only on the tip of her nerve endings until it became individual sighs that brought her back to the present as The Whisper's energy began to retreat.

At the same time, the dragon's heat in her flailed around, as if it was in shock at what it'd just seen. With every one of its thrashings, she flinched, but The Whisper's energy remained in her, soothing, breezy, and within seconds her mind eased to a calm.

The voice of God, she thought, hoping he'd hear. *Was that what the last sound was?*

No, no, dear, he said inside her. His own voice seemed to rotate, like the turning of endless time. *That was only me you heard, announcing myself.*

Are you an angel? she asked.

Such limitations to a definition. Let us use the word "enforcer" instead. Earth is my purview, and I have watched over it since its inception. I have, in times of need, balanced it until a day of judgment removes my responsibility. Until then, if I am needed, I travel in willing bodies. Contacting you humans in this way is far less traumatic for your sensibilities.

Balance, she thought, finally understanding this small part of it as The Whisper gathered its energies and then pulled out of her, leaving her cells feeling like they were sucking back together.

At his departure, the dragon's blood seemed to shrink, too, but it didn't entirely pull away from where it'd been headed—to her soul stain.

Dawn's adrenaline pumped. The blood was still in her. The Whisper hadn't banished it.

Why? Was it too strong?

As her vision put itself back into focus, she saw that Natalia and Jonah hadn't moved a muscle since the last time she'd seen them, and she wondered if only a fraction of a second had passed. She tried to recall what The Whisper had told her when he was inside of her, but she couldn't remember exactly what he'd said—only that he had told her something, and it'd left an impression of power.

He'd erased an explanation from her, the bastard.

Was this his fail-safe? she thought. After introducing himself to the dragon, had he taken answers away so no one outside of her would know them? Was that how his kind operated?

Part of her couldn't blame him, because how else would he be able to move around the world in secret? But she still wanted some of those answers back, just like anyone would. Didn't everyone want to know what really ran things, even though there were a million different theories that mostly depended on faith?

Maybe there was no one answer, but she used what she vaguely remembered from his visit inside of her to try to find it, anyway.

"You and Costin were both Travelers, but you aren't like him at all, are you?"

The Whisper's gray eyes reflected balance—not dark, not light. "I only loaned him a few of my skills for ease of accomplishing his mission."

The others were following the conversation with frowns, because they hadn't had The Whisper inside, and they seemed even more puzzled than she was.

"You used Costin to balance out what the dragon had planned," Dawn said.

"Certain areas do require . . . adjustment. And I am afraid that the dragon was one of those requirements." Whisper Kiko lifted an eyebrow. "There is no good without evil, and there are those who wander among you, seeking to sway one to the other. They know despair or ambition or blind greed when they sense it. They are drawn to it, and it is an entry point into the world for them."

"Eva," Dawn said, knowing he wasn't only talking about the dragon.

The Whisper nodded. "All it takes is the trading of a soul for power. In the dragon's case, he was always hungry for blood, and he received the ability to have it, both figuratively and literally. To feed off of it in the extreme. Thus, through giving up his soul, a vampire was created from his lusts; a vampire built to satisfy. He was one of a kind, though other vampires do exist in various other forms. But the dragon dealt with the very devil himself, whereas the rest strayed into the sights of lesser beings. Eva would be among those who greeted a lower creature."

"She met a demon?" Dawn didn't care so much about The Whisper's issues now. And maybe he'd planned it that way.

"That name will do for your purposes." Whisper Kiko held her hand tighter. "But you must know that I cannot directly interfere with the contract she made. There is no undoing matters so they might return to the way they were. It is all I can do to balance via indirect persuasion."

The ridiculous side of Dawn shouted, *Then balance her! And balance my dad back to the way he was, too!*

But she knew that there was always a price. You couldn't right the world without one. Costin had paid his own admission into wherever he was going.

"So you just don't get your hands dirty," Dawn said. Maybe, in a way, The Whisper had to preserve his state of grace, like the Friends. Maybe that was the only way he could exist as what he was.

"I can tell," he said, as if misdirecting her further—and maybe he was an expert at doing it to anyone who got too close to really knowing what he was—"that you are worried about your father, who is only suffering due to Eva's new contract." He lowered his gray gaze at her. "Keep in mind that there are always offers to be made, as I made with Costin."

Jonah interrupted. "No, Dawn. Don't."

Whisper Kiko was staring at her, as if expecting her to pursue the idea. And what if she did? Was there something Dawn could do to save Frank?

She considered The Whisper and if he was coming from a good place. He'd given Costin the chance to right his wrongs, so he couldn't be all bad. He'd wanted to tip the scales back to evenness for the world. . . .

Jonah sounded off again. "Frank's fine with who he is—he's got Breisi with him, and that's all he wants. She's enough to lighten his soul stain, so don't you dare think that anything you could do would change him for the better, Dawn."

His emotion was bared on his face: Jonah was telling the truth. He was looking out for her, reminding her of the price.

And he was right. It was just hard for her to accept it when Frank seemed like a mockery of who he used to be.

She shook her head, and she could tell The Whisper knew a reluctant refusal when he saw one. And he also seemed content that he had gotten her off of questioning him about what he was and on to more urgent things.

"Then what about Costin?" Dawn asked. "Is he lingering in that resort of yours because he has to come back and take care of the remaining blood brothers?"

"No need." Whisper Kiko shrugged. "When the remaining master vampires turned human again, they were nothing more than string and dust, barely held together, primed for disintegration. I was not certain this would be the case, but centuries of wear on a body that no longer had extraordinary powers did its duty. Consequently, when Costin found himself rejoined with his soul for good, he held back from claiming his final reward. You see, he has been watching you, Dawn, just as I have been after the dragon's death."

The comment clanged in her head, the side of her chest, where the burn of the dragon's blood waited.

Now, Kiko's prophecy took on its full meaning: She was "key," all right. The dragon's key to moving on, even past his bodily termination.

The burn of the blood, above and below, throbbed, as if it'd been resurrected by Dawn's realization. The room seemed to tip and tumble.

"It seems," The Whisper said, "due to the strength that

Costin always saw in you, the dragon has had difficulty in getting to your soul, where he would settle and grow in the darkness it absorbed, even during the short time you were a vampire. But the duration of your vampirism did not have as much to do with the force of your soul stain as your emotion. Specifically, in your case, anger. That is what has fed your darkness."

She already figured that. "I didn't give the dragon permission to come into me."

"The dark marks on the other side of your body seem to have been invitation enough—signs that you were open to the darkness. And, surely enough, you did absorb the blood."

Natalia and Jonah looked just as stunned as Dawn, and it almost seemed like they expected her to turn into the dragon right here and now. But Dawn was still Dawn, except she had this . . . thing . . . in her. A prophecy come true, but in a way she'd never expected.

"Costin could not have predicted," The Whisper said, "that his soul would still be telling him that his work is not done here."

"But it is—he did technically kill the dragon."

"And he did fulfill his contract. You are correct."

Dawn still wasn't getting it. Her mind was stuck on one point. "Is he going to come back and slay me then?"

It wasn't a joke. If he did return, would Dawn just spread her arms and allow herself to be terminated?

"Think, Dawn. Does Costin *need* to slay you?" The Whisper asked.

Cryptic as ever.

"Why can't *you* just get the dragon out of me?" she asked.

"I could not end its contract the first time, and I cannot do so now. It is not my purview."

She was getting sick of that word.

"I see," she said. "Costin's done, and you're looking for

another person to step in and fight the dragon for round two."

"Not precisely. Dawn, you can expel it yourself, without any deals."

What?

Should she get a knife and start cutting?

"Dawn," The Whisper said, "once you accept that this is a choice for you, you will see that all is not lost."

Okay then—she could control this like she'd controlled the postvampire darkness in her? Yeah, that'd work out.

He added, "Costin took what I gave him and used it properly. He *could* have become as terrible as the dragon, yet he did not."

A quiver wracked Dawn—one that trembled up from the bottom of her and threatened to do the worst thing she could think of. Make her cry. Sob at the unfairness of this. She'd never asked for power, and even with what she'd already been given with the psychokinesis that'd grown and grown in her, she wasn't sure she could ever use it in the right way.

All she knew was that, with Costin around, she'd had a conscience. He'd *been* her conscience. And without him here, she might fall into some kind of void.

She asked, "Why isn't Costin here to tell me this himself?"

"Yes," Jonah said. "Bring him back. I offer my body again—he can have it."

The Whisper seemed to pity Jonah. "You must understand that Costin is so near his peace. He has been caught between that and making certain Dawn is secured. Yet she has kept the monster at bay, and the dragon has been as good as buried. As Dawn mentioned, Costin *did* slay it, after all, and he technically completed his contract with me. He is deserving of his reward, and for you to call on him now is to distance him further from fulfillment. His soul cries to go to that light you humans speak of so fondly, and it would pain him to be pulled away from it."

Jonah said, "Don't you think it's paining him now to see what's happening to Dawn?"

"Jonah," she said, harshly chiding him, even as she was thinking that if she could manage the dragon and find a way to banish it in the end, all on her own, she'd do it. She wouldn't pull Costin out, even if she wanted him to come back. She'd kept him alive once and learned that it'd been partly out of selfishness. Twice was unthinkable. This was eternity they were talking about and, no matter how much it killed her, she wouldn't deny him that.

Right?

"I can do this on my own," Dawn said. She sounded so tough, but she was disintegrating inside. "Costin can't be called back."

But could she do this? Without him?

"Very well," The Whisper said.

"I just won't kill anymore," she said fervently. "I won't *want* to do it, and I'll stop with the mind puppeting. That'll mean the dragon won't be attracted to any darkness. I can keep him out of my soul stain for as long as it takes."

But, even now, she could feel that dragon burn regrouping in her. What would happen if, one day, she strayed from her determination and it got where it wanted to go?

She realized there was a better way to make sure the dragon never came out—a way that would make Costin go to that light and keep them all safe at the same time.

With all the guts she had in her, she turned to Natalia. No other person at this table would put their emotions aside, suck it up, and do what needed to be done.

"Get a machete and a flamethrower," she said, her voice so far removed that she didn't even recognize it as hers. But it was.

It had to be her who initiated the only option left.

Jonah was half out of his seat, still holding hands with

the new girl and Kiko, refusing to break the chain. "Natalia, if you do, you won't ever be able to hold a weapon again."

Natalia glared at him. "Oh, so you can fight the dragon if it should come out, can you?"

They'd taught her well. She was a real hunter.

"Costin *can* take care of this," Jonah said, appealing straight to Dawn. "He wouldn't even have to slay you. He has his ways—The Whisper gave him the means to deal with it." Jonah shot Whisper Kiko a jaded look. "In his own indirect way."

Dawn spoke to Natalia again. "I'm asking you." Then she swallowed, the lump in her throat growing. "Hunter to hunter."

Natalia didn't do anything; she only looked into Dawn's eyes, as if not knowing which way to go.

But Dawn knew what the new girl had to be seeing in her: the night Dawn had worked over Claudius. The dark marks she'd gotten every time she'd stepped over the line.

Natalia rose from her chair, but before she could break the hand chain that would result in chasing The Whisper from Kiko, Jonah did what none of them had any right to do.

"Costin, come back! We need you here, now!"

A formal summons from one of the team—exactly what The Whisper had come to warn them about.

The Whisper sighed, unable to do anything more.

Dawn's first instinct was to attack Jonah, but even thinking about it caused the dragon's blood to rear up inside her, like this was the opportunity it'd been waiting for. Terror forced her to stay in her chair as she gripped Kiko's limp hand, unwilling to give herself over to the blood.

Do it, half of her urged, anyway.

But Natalia took over where Dawn couldn't.

She sprang at Jonah, unlinking the hand chain that held

them all together, liberating The Whisper as Kiko slumped out of his chair and to the floor.

On her way to Jonah, the new girl upset the table, then crashed against him as he caught her and got her into a headlock. She swung at Jonah with her arms, and he kept restraining her.

"Stop it!" Dawn was out of her chair now, inserting her good arm between them.

"I know you'll hate me for this," Jonah said, his voice rough with his efforts. "But Costin's business isn't done. Not with *any* of us. If he was still down here, he would've insisted on being summoned, even if he 'technically' slayed the dragon. That wouldn't have been good enough for him."

"*I* could've kept the dragon away," Dawn said, still controlling that anger. The bad blood stomped inside her, like it was trying to kick down a door.

She had to keep it behind the barrier.

"It wouldn't have turned out well, Dawn," Jonah said, "and you know it."

"You did it because you can't live without him." She tried to push him away from Natalia. "You can't stand the thought of him being whole up there without you."

"Can *you*?"

Dawn ground her teeth together. But it wasn't because of physical pain.

She finally got him off of Natalia, but instead of facing the new girl, Jonah turned to Dawn.

"*Can* you?" he repeated.

"Yes, I can stand it," Dawn said, her tone level. The dragon's blood slunk back to its place, as if waiting for another time that it knew would come, because anger always did with Dawn, even if she'd avoided it this once. "I can be happy with knowing he was finally released from the tragedy that's been his life for centuries. I *wanted* that for him—peace and quiet."

It was the first time she meant it, and it felt right. Not good, but right.

During the impasse, Natalia had gone over to Kiko and was catching him up on Costin and The Whisper. But now it didn't seem like he remembered much of it, based on his confused questions.

Then the new girl shook up the room. "If Costin was summoned, where is he?"

Dawn forgot Jonah, looking around instead, trying to see if Costin was sweeping the room with his invisible, yanked-out-of-limbo essence.

Then she remembered the portrait in their bedroom. The field of fire where Costin used to rest when he'd give Jonah out-of-body free time back in L.A.

She ran toward the stairs the best she could, forgetting her bad leg and grunting at the aftershocks in her broken arm.

TWENTY-EIGHT

†HE DRAGON WAITS

THE rest of the team came with her up the stairs.

Please be there, she thought. She didn't know where the hell else Costin would've gone if he hadn't resumed Jonah's body yet.

She busted into her room, heading straight for the portrait, which had been only fire when she'd last seen it.

But that was then.

Now, there was a figure, and it was positioned differently than it'd been when the painting had been filled with his essence in L.A.

For the first time, she could see his true face.

Dawn got to her knees, touching the texture of the portrait. His long, wavy hair streamed down his back and away from him, exposing the pensive, downturned tips on a wide mouth. The slant of cheekbones under tanned skin. The topaz of eyes that held all the hopeful sorrow of a man who'd sacrificed everything—including his nearly completed journey to a final rest.

"I'm so sorry," she said. "I could've done it without you . . ."

Behind her, Jonah was laughing, but in a way that someone dancing on the splinter between disbelief and joy laughed. Then the room filled with jasmine, as if the Friends had all been roused at once. They cried out mournfully, muffled by their wind-tunnel voices.

Costin's figure seemed to move in the portrait, then . . .

Then his topaz eyes focused on her.

She sucked in a breath, just as he disappeared, leaving her with only a view of the fire field.

The Friends wailed, voicing Dawn's own feelings, but then she sensed him next to her, just as she had been able to feel his invisible force in L.A.—a shivering presence that tied up her veins.

When he spoke, The Voice filtered through her with its deep, dark assonance, and Dawn sobbed once, covering her mouth with her free hand, taken over by the old feelings plus the new ones—the love that had somehow developed along the way.

"The air," he said, as if he'd never experienced it before. He'd been in Jonah's body a long time, then far out of it. "I remember it now. It is not quite like it was just a moment ago. . . ."

Back at that resort, so close to paradise.

"Costin," Jonah said. "I'm here. You can come into me."

"I know." Still, Costin hovered. "You brought me back because you missed having me with you."

"Because of Dawn, too."

Jonah's words were heartfelt, but she still wanted to choke him.

"Yes," Costin said. "You called me back for that reason, as well. As usual, you tried to make good in the most misguided method possible, Jonah, but I understand." He moaned slightly, as if the reality of being away from the light was pulling at him.

"You don't have to hurt," Jonah said. "Come into me. Root. It'll make you feel better."

"You would offer your body to me so I might move among humanity unnoticed again, though it means for you to be pushed down into that vessel when I am present?"

"You know I would. I know a body makes you feel more human, and that's what you've always wanted."

Costin floated around Dawn, and her hair moved with him, just like he was trailing a hand against her. She leaned her head back, needing to feel him.

"Once a recluse, always a recluse," he said to Jonah. "But you do know that I would leave your body whenever I wish. Before, I was forced to root to humanity because The Whisper needed to make certain I would fulfill my vow. That would not be the case now."

Dawn looked around. Was he actually planning on re-claiming Jonah as a host?

If he did, was he doing it for her sake? She was used to him in this body. Even with seeing his true persona in the portrait, he seemed like a stranger when he wasn't in Jonah. But didn't he know that she would do whatever it took to get used to another one? Or that she'd be fine with a spirit, just like Frank was with Breisi?

But maybe this had nothing to do with her: Maybe he and Jonah were linked because of what they'd gone through together as a vampire. Maybe Costin had found a type of camaraderie with his host—something he'd only had with his blood brothers, once upon a time.

Costin floated up to Dawn; it was obvious that he intended to ask permission to enter her mind so he could make this decision with her. Yet neither of them had allowed themselves to be so open with each other for a while—they'd been too shut off from each other . . .

But now she was only too happy to open up.

His voice eased into her head, and it felt like a soft, cleansing baptism.

She shivered, welcoming him back.

What would you think if I assumed a different body? he asked, his voice spinning through her thoughts.

It'd be your choice, Dawn said, meaning it.

Jonah would hurt himself if I left. There is more than that though. He has always done his best for me. He has loved me in his own way, more than any other host. At leaving him, I realize that he has become . . . a home. He stayed in Dawn. *Just as you have.*

She couldn't help a barrage of sadness. *You shouldn't be here. You should've never been called back. Can't you return? You should, Costin, you—*

Dawn. He swept around her mind, and she went weak, even as she stayed strong. *I could not move on. Don't you know that?*

He had to be talking about his responsibilities with the dragon. *You feel like you need to close out every loose end.*

No. I could never stray far from you.

She didn't grasp that at first. Her? Unspecial, angry Dawn Madison?

Do you think I would leave you, especially at your darkest time? His essence was a caress that eased her darkness to a lighter shade. *I am not Eva. I am not the others.*

Her shoulders racked with another sob, but he lifted her up from the inside out, easing her sadness. Yet the tears still came. Happy ones.

The dragon died and I was spirited away before I could ever show you just how much you mean, he said.

If I would've known his death would take you—

I did not wish to present the idea and raise your hopes.

Dawn nodded; she'd thought so.

Imagine, he added, *if the dragon had expired and I was still trapped in Jonah when you had the idea that I might be released. Your guilt would have surpassed even what you already carried with you.*

I could've handled it. She bent her head. *Please, just*

*promise that you're always going to be open from now on.
I'll be that way, too.*

I vow it.

It was as if her head and heart had been cleared, opened so that eternity stretched over her, in her.

But was that how long he would really stay? Even with his reward waiting for him up there, somewhere?

He enveloped every doubt, wrapping around them like a warm, soft blanket. *I am back with you until death. I cannot go toward any paradise without you—I would suffer a million pains after being pulled away from the light so that I might feel your illumination.*

She put her hand over her heart, just as he slipped out of her mind, leaving a flow of that warmth behind. He was willing to go this far for her. No one ever had, and she hadn't believed that anyone ever would.

She repeated it to herself again. He'd come back for *her.*

His physical-world voice captivated the room with its low, full vibration. "Friends."

The spirits wavered, knowing this was it for them.

"Though I am here, you are released from your vow to me. You have served beyond anything I ever hoped for and deserve more than the little piece of home you have in your portraits."

They stayed.

"I cannot force you to go," he said, "but there is such calm where I was, even in limbo. There is happiness that you have never experienced before, and I would be so relieved to know that you have found such an eternity."

"But the dragon . . ." one of them said. Kalin, who was camped out near Jonah.

"If you wish to see the dragon tempered, I shall give you that, certainly. Then we will see to your going . . ."

He hovered before Dawn, vibrating. She felt every bit of him on her skin.

"Time for me to finish business," he said.

"Can you?" Dawn asked.

He only floated there, humming like the all-consuming vibration of a massive bell after being struck.

He was The Voice, and he'd taken on masters, taken on the world.

And, with no more of a warning, he dove into Dawn's body, not just her head. Past her skin, filling every pore with his electric charge, he flushed through her. But this time, she felt the pain he'd carried back with him from limbo—the hurt of being away from his final paradise.

With a rush, she infused him with all the love she'd kept back, and he paused, as if surprised. He floated in her, suspended, absorbing it, and she knew that he was accepting something he'd never been able to before: her ability to help and even save him.

She joined with him, twining, and they drew strength from each other, pulling, pushing, expanding to something that would be impossible to beat.

Go get him, she thought.

She pushed off, releasing him, and he zoomed ahead toward the dragon's blood.

She felt herself physically sinking to the floor at the intensity of the speed inside of her, at the surge of him finding the dragon's blood then blasting into it, its mass exploding into thousands of tiny globs that hit the walls of her body.

But then she felt the blood immediately coming back together, as if the dragon was getting composed for this final showdown.

They circled each other inside of her, stretching and burning the portion of her body where the dragon's blood had been loitering. Then, with a tear, they both surged forward, crashing against each other and making Dawn buck up from the floor.

She closed her eyes, pushing aside her anger at being invaded by the dragon and concentrating on everything good about Costin coming back.

As they tore at each other, her vision began to fade: slams and explosions that bruised her like internalized punches. Twisting, throttling, bangs that hurtled through her, until the dragon blood burned on its journey to being pushed back, back toward the inner walls of her being . . .

With a flare, she felt the skin on the right side of her body heat up, just as the Underground had licked out in flames when it had expelled Dawn and Jonah the other night.

Then Costin burst out of her, and she opened her eyes, hearing his essence rush away as it headed straight for Jonah, as if out of habit. At the impact, the host stumbled backward, his eyes going topaz as he reached for one of the bedposts to keep him standing.

Costin didn't need to root anymore, Dawn thought, but maybe it just felt good to do it inside Jonah after a throw down.

When he straightened, he smiled Costin's smile while Natalia and Kiko simply looked on.

Dawn's heart flipped. Her skin on the dragon splash side hurt like a bitch, as if knife tips were digging into it, but she couldn't feel the dragon inside anymore.

It was away from her soul stain.

She smiled, more tears slipping down her cheeks. Costin had done it.

They had done it.

When Jonah spoke, it was Costin's tone that came out, exhausted. But Jonah would be sheltering him, lending his own strength to bring him back to rights.

"What I have done might not be enough," Costin said to Dawn. "I might have to push it back again if the blood should encroach."

"Then that's what we'll do."

It was more than she could've ever asked for—to have him here, free and willing to be inside her again. To have the dragon on the retreat.

Kiko and Natalia came to help her up from the floor just as the Friends gathered around Costin. It was time for him to say good-bye—to tell each one of them what they'd meant, and she would leave them alone for that. But first, she, Kiko, and Natalia also thanked the women, and Dawn wished she could give them more than just words.

They brushed against her with their jasmine, liking Dawn's sentiments just fine as they were. Then she finally left the room with the human members of the team.

She glanced back at Costin, who was looking at her, too, a smile still on his face.

Together, she thought. *They could do this together.*

Kiko linked his hand through Dawn's good arm, showing he'd also be there for her, as he held Natalia's hand on his other side. The three of them walked down the hall while the Friends' pictures began filling up, one by one, then disintegrating to blank spots on the walls, as if the portraits had never been there at all.

Then the three went to Frank's room, where he still lay in bed and Breisi clung to the man she loved, refusing to leave like her fellow spirits were doing.

Her portrait remained on the wall as Dawn sat in the chair at her father's side, Frank placing his hand on hers to show that he wasn't going anywhere, either.

TWENTY-NINE

FOUND

Months Later

Eva sat in front of the large oval mirror in a Roman hotel suite, tucking a strand of her light hair into a diamond pin that swept the rest of the curls into a loose bun. The luminous bulbs around the mirror made her pale skin glow and her brown eyes shine now that she had grown comfortable with her new existence.

She touched her fingers to her cheek, dwelling on the face that wouldn't age beyond what she saw now—a woman of classical middle-aged beauty.

And her man had promised she would stay this way.

Trailing her hand down her throat, she reached for a delicate crystal bottle of Chanel No. 5, using the stopper to dab the fragrance on her wrists, behind her ears, in the cove of her throat. Then she smoothed a bit of lotion on the arms and shoulders left bare by her strapless white evening gown.

When she heard the suite door opening, she paused, rested her hands on the vanity table.

He was here.

In the mirror, she saw him appear in back of her, where he stood by the door in his black tuxedo, his dark, straight hair slicked down to the level of his chin, his slightly tilted eyes flashing like honeyed glass, his smile debonair and a bit naughty. He was still her man from the wine bar, still her enticer.

"I've brought you a treat," the man said in his creamy accent—a touch of Hong Kong on the surface, though Eva knew he actually came from a place much farther away. Months ago, she had found him waiting for her in the London streets, where she had been wandering in her nightgown. He'd kissed her softly, murmuring, "I see you've learned that I'm the only one who will guide you to true love." From that moment on, she hadn't remembered what had happened before—only that there'd been a stain of blood near a healing wound by her heart. Then he'd given her only his first name and nothing else.

As Eva smiled at him in the mirror, the man named Kane sauntered closer, coming to her shoulder, where he rested his hand. She sighed, his touch an aphrodisiac.

"Enjoy the local delights while you may," he said, bending to kiss the sweet spot that connected her neck and shoulder. Then he murmured against her. "Soon, I'll be bringing you home, after I find what I expect to in this city."

She didn't correct him by saying "who" he expected to find instead of "what." She knew he was pursuing another white lady or even a man, but Eva wasn't jealous. He had brought her on so many travels since delivering her from London. They had been following a certain trail—a "hunch"—that had led them to Rome. Soon they'd be on their way to the States, where he said she would be among more like her, just as she'd been in the Underground.

But she was a little confused about that. "Underground." The word sounded like something Eva thought she remembered but didn't. And, every day, it faded a little more from her, just like other names that drifted through the debris of her memories, like "Frank" and "Dawn."

Eva only knew that she was happier not knowing what the words meant; this was her gift from Kane. Forgetting the pain, her conscience as white as the dresses he bought for her.

He had given her what she needed.

He took her by the hand and led her to the common area of the suite, with its rich velvet upholstered furniture, Cristal champagne waiting on ice, and old music playing from the digital music TV channel.

"I Only Have Eyes for You." That was the song, and she thought she should know it—that it had something to do with the name "Frank." Maybe the name had liked this music.

But then, as Kane brought her to the settee, where a young man in backpacking gear sat with his eyes glazed due to the stupor Kane had leveled on him, Eva forgot "Frank."

"There he is, my queen," Kane said. "I promised you would be loved as you used to be—and it wasn't necessarily by Frank."

"Thank you." She touched the boy's face, making him jump in his seat from the shock of her contact.

He gaped at her, wide-eyed, and Eva released her dazzling smile on him. His gaze softened as he saw everything he wanted in her, the softness in his eyes soon turning to a harder desire.

Yes, he already loved her, and she leaned forward, pressing her mouth to his, sucking electric life and adoration into her.

Leaving even more of the past behind as she went forward into her happily ever after.

THIRTY

The Eternal

A CLEAR, endless morning sky opened over Dawn as she lay on the sand of a beach. The big blue canvas, plus the murmur of waves, almost made her believe that she was somewhere timeless, just like a painting Costin had once taken her into when they'd initially met—a fantasy locale where he'd seduced her, come into her, made her a part of his world during those first days with him.

"Where are you?" It was Costin's voice. *The* Voice—deep, midnight low, except not as dark now. Not anymore.

"I'm in Del Mar," she said, closing her eyes against the sky. The blue survived on the backs of her lids. "On a beach, with you."

"I meant to ask where your mind was."

He laughed, and it was good to hear. He'd been doing it a lot more. She supposed that, since his emancipation, he could finally give in to that side of himself—a part that Jonah had maybe even taught him a few things about since welcoming his Traveler back. The host had been respectful and helpful to Costin in many ways, and in turn, Costin always left Jonah with enough free time to keep him content. It was interesting, though, that Jonah had used that free time away from Dawn.

She didn't know how long that would last, and sometimes, she admitted that she wouldn't mind seeing him come out to hang around a little. In a weird way, she missed him. But maybe he'd taken her rejection of him harder than she'd thought.

Then again, maybe he'd learned to enjoy what he had and he wasn't going to pull any stunts that would encourage Costin to leave him—and that included making more bids for Dawn's affection. He'd experienced life without Costin, and when Jonah had balanced that against life *with* him, he'd sacrificed his autonomy.

Still, Dawn wondered if he might ever get lonely, especially since, back in London, he'd told Kalin to go on her way since there wasn't a future for them. The spirit hadn't liked that at all, throwing a real fuss until Costin had intervened, asking if she'd like to reside in her portrait for, say, half a year, and come out again to see if Jonah had reconsidered. Even if she was a dickens, she'd been a good, true Friend, so she'd deserved the offer.

She'd accepted, and the portrait was in a study in their house. Jonah never visited that room, as far as Dawn knew. She only hoped that this didn't mean he'd be investing too much emotion in *her* through Costin's own attentions. Maybe he was even doing that while he lived through Costin again.

But so far? It was all good.

Dawn rolled over, toward where Costin's voice had come from, sand sticking to the back of her long, ocean-damp hair and her wet suit. When she opened her eyes, he was there, in Jonah's body, sitting on a real beach with her, just like he'd done every morning since she and Costin had settled into a cliff-perched home that overlooked the Pacific Ocean. After she'd gotten the cast off her arm, they'd started waking up before sunrise so she could teach him what she remembered about surfing, an activity he'd never, ever thought to do during his extended lifetime.

It was just a part of what he called "rehab" for them both, but she knew that it mostly applied to her. She'd needed to find peace to counter the anger that had marked her with the constellation of beauty spots, plus the dragon splashes, that still decorated her skin. The waves did a lot of soothing.

So did Costin.

She rested her hand on his leg, which was covered by his own sand-glittered wet suit. His dark hair was damp, too, carelessly disheveled in a very Jonah-like style, although his host was resting deep inside their body right now and he wasn't dominant. Behind him, two surfboards stuck out of the sand near a sheltering, concave curve in the rock wall.

For a minute, she stayed touching him like that, the surf coming and going in the background, the smell of brine in the air. She'd gotten used to touching, to opening up.

Nothing like a near-apocalyptic scenario to bring that out in a person.

"I know what you are thinking," Costin said.

"No, you don't." Usually, he called her out on her habit of returning to the memories: of Della and how she'd made Dawn realize that she still had a life and she could do great things with it. Of Eva, who was dead to Dawn.

She couldn't get through a day without reverting back to those old thoughts; she wasn't that good at rehab yet. But she was trying to change. Trying hard, because Costin had come back for her, and he deserved her best.

"Then what is going through your mind?" he asked.

"I was just listening to the waves. Not thinking of much, really. But now that you mention it . . ."

Costin placed his hand over hers, and she reveled in the flesh-to-flesh warmth. Human skin with its smooth roughness and scars.

"Every once in a while," she said, "they all cross my mind. Especially Eva."

He slid his thumb over hers, and a tickle of awareness—of finally taking in his love—traveled through her chest.

She added, "Kiko keeps saying he'll go after her for me, if I ever want him to."

Spurred on by the validation he'd received from channeling The Whisper, Kiko was setting up shop nearby in Solana Beach with Natalia in the hopes of getting a business running someday. He and the new girl planned to do PI work, but they'd be using their psychic talents, first and foremost. Natalia, who was working on becoming an American citizen, insisted that they'd be focusing on cold cases and supposedly missing persons whose voices she heard, but Kiko was up for some more paranormal adventure besides. Right now, they were doing all kinds of training with spirit guides as well as taking traditional PI courses.

Since Kik and Natalia had decided to stick together, he hadn't gone back to his meds, and there was no lulling available to him, either, since almost all of the Friends were gone. Natalia had made a promise to Dawn that she would watch over him, and Dawn had left it to the new girl, thinking that there was even something more than a friendship in the cards for Psychics #1 and #2.

"Will you take Kiko up on his offer?" Costin asked.

As he traced the tender area between her thumb and forefinger, Dawn shifted closer, her head near his thigh.

"You know better than that."

"You say as much. Yet, within you, there will always be the girl who lost Eva more than once. There will always be a longing." He pressed his palm against hers, their fingers entwining. "But I have faith that, one day, you will awaken

to find that Eva is with you somewhat less in your topmost
thoughts. Then, another day, there will be only a single
memory that comes to you, and it will not be as painful.
Soon after, she will truly be gone."

Dawn nodded, her face rubbing against his wet suit. She
could feel his muscle beneath it. A man. Her man.

"I've let her go," she said. "I really have."

"But you have not accepted the concept that you cannot
save *everyone*, even if you think you are beyond Eva. In
that lies a sleeping anger. You must let it *all* go, Dawn."

"I will." Maybe she'd get there with more time behind
her, because it was all still so recent, her failures still healing under the balm of her successes.

Getting to an elbow, she brought the back of Costin's
hand to her cheek. She connected with his gaze, topaz and
calming.

Everything was there, in him.

Then she saw movement down the beach: an old man
sitting in a folding chair under a red umbrella.

Her heart contracted. Frank. He lived in a cottage on
Dawn and Costin's property, and he liked to wake up early
and watch their surf sessions. Now, he was still keeping
tabs on other surfers as they bobbed in the green gray water
and caught the waves.

His body had improved slightly these past few months—
enough to sustain an argument for Dawn to get off his back
about going to a doctor—but he still slumped in his chair,
wearing sunglasses, a Chargers ball cap, and loose, faded
black sweats that his limbs didn't quite fill. Even though
Dawn couldn't see Breisi, she knew that the Friend was
draped over his shoulders, her own movements diminished,
too.

Dawn bit her lower lip, trying not to lose it, just like on
most days with the two of them. Neither him nor Breisi had
ever really recovered from Eva's attacks, but they were
damned intent on sticking together until the end of Frank's

days. In spite of the rest of the Friends going to their just rewards, Breisi had said no place was better than with Frank, so she had put off leaving him until they were both ready.

Dawn let go of Costin's hand and looked at the ocean, hoping that focusing on it would chase away the wet heat in her gaze. And the more she looked, the more she thought about how the water seemed to go on forever, just like Breisi and Frank would, wherever they ended up.

Just like she and Costin would, too.

They didn't say anything for a while, and her tears backed off. Soon, the sun strengthened its shine, and the marks on her face started beating. Costin came into her each morning before they surfed to make sure the dragon's blood didn't infiltrate her again. When she went outside, she used a bit of makeup to tone down the red, but she'd resigned herself to her appearance. Like she'd told the emergency room personnel in London, the blood was a birthmark. And, hell, the beauty marks could've been a wild-girl tattoo that resembled a cheetah's spots. They were no less than the scars she used to carry from her stunt work before everything had become all too real.

She glanced up at Costin and knew the look on his face—the desire in his eyes—and she opened her mind to him, ready for the intimacy, welcoming it. And although they had decided to stay away from vampires and other paranormal adventures as much as they could, he took Dawn by both hands now and maneuvered them both back into the cove, behind their surfboards.

When they got there, Costin abandoned Jonah's body, leaving his host with blue eyes. As Jonah breathed in, experiencing the fresh air, he stretched.

Dawn cleared her throat, and he grinned at her. She cleared her throat more emphatically.

He gave her a glance that said, "Don't worry—I'm getting out of your hair," then left.

She watched him amble out of the cove, past the surfboards and down the beach, probably to Frank and Breisi, but then Costin's essence swept into Dawn with a crash that mimicked the force of a nearby wave, making her forget about everything else.

Dawn's fingers dug at the sand, letting him in, no holds barred. This was how they connected, not body to body with Jonah there, just soul to soul.

Like a full circle, he whisked around her, stroking her deep inside, making her sigh at the giddy pleasure of having him here, always, a part of her that she'd never known she *could* have.

As he swirled, caressing her until even the outside of her body responded—her skin goose bumping, her breasts peaking to hard, sensitive nubs against the bathing top under her wet suit, her clit aching and swollen—Dawn took every bit of him in.

He brought her all together, every side of her, lightening the darkness without banishing it altogether, mixing her and working her with gentle force, wrapping himself in her until she pulled together with taut ecstasy, winding up, straining to let go. He primed her to be the best of what she could be, and her vision blurred with the heights of this complete arousal.

Pressing against every tender spot, he made her arch, groan, and just when she didn't think she could stand any more, she plunged down deep into her own consciousness, as if he'd dived within her and taken her with him into a bottomless pool in the center of her, hot and liquid. The drops splashed against every part of her, spinning and drilling, forming the heat of a hundred more pools that spread through her, stretching as far as the ocean that was murmuring in her ears again. . . .

As she came down, he was still with her, inside, and she embraced him there, clenching him in.

"The Whisper did promise me a better place when I finished my quest," Costin said, resting in her with a carnal hum.

Dawn wrapped her arms over her stomach, as if she'd never let him go, even though he'd be returning to Jonah's body soon.

"We're both in a much better place," she said.

As the waves continued outside, Costin spread through her inside, taking up the rhythm of eternal whispers.